I0632786

The Love-Story of Aliette Brunton

©2020 Spire Books
Historic Romance Book #3

The Love-Story of Aliette Brunton is a work of fiction. Names, characters, businesses, organizations, places, events and incidents are either the products of the author's imagination or are used fictitiously. Any resemblance to actual persons, living or dead, events, locales or institutions is entirely coincidental.

All rights reserved. Printed in the United States of America. No part of this book may be used or reproduced in any manner without written permission except for brief quotations for review purposes only.

Hardcover ISBN 13: 978-1-5154-4342-1
Trade Paperback ISBN 13: 978-1-5154-4343-8

The Love-Story of Aliette Brunton

by Gilbert Frankau

IN ALL LOVE AND A GREAT REVERENCE
THIS STORY OF A WOMAN'S COURAGE

But woman's gamble (there's only one;
And it takes some pluck to play,
When the rules are broke ere the game's begun;
When, lose or win, you must pay!)
Is a double wager on human kind,
A limitless risk—and she goes it blind.

For she stakes, at love, on a single throw,
Pride, Honor, Scruples, and Fears,
And dreams no lover can hope to know,
And the gold of the after-years.
(And all for a man; and there's no man lives
Who is worth the odds that a woman gives.)
—From "The Judgment of Valhalla."

Preamble

1

In our heart of hearts—which we in England take almost as much pains to hide from ourselves as from our fellow-creatures—most of us realize that life without love is a weariness, a conflict bereft of hope, a struggle for no victory. Yet Love, the Real Thing—whether it be love of a god or love of our fellow-creatures, the love of a man for his mate, of a mother for her son, of a friend for his friend or a girl for her chosen—is not the law of the majority. Because Love, the Real Thing—as all real things—demands infinite self-sacrifice: and infinite self-sacrifice is too divine a code for the average imperfect human being, who must needs make himself other codes or perish.

This, therefore, Aliette's love-story, deals of necessity with the self-sacrifices endured not only by Aliette but by many of those who came within the orbit of her personality.

Rightly to understand the people of this tale and the motives which swayed them, it is vital that you should comprehend, at the very outset, how essentially English they all were; how essentially old-fashioned, in the best sense of that much misused word; and how difficult it was, even for Aliette, to learn that Love, the Real Thing, had come into their lives, making blind havoc of every unwritten rule and every written law to which they owed allegiance.

For all these people, Bruntons, Fullerfords, Wilberforces, and Cavendishes, were ordinary orderly English folk; trained in that school of thought which prizes sheer character above mere intellect, which teaches self-restraint and self-respect and self-reliance, and believes—as an ultimate issue—in "playing the game."

It is no bad code, this old-fashioned English code of "playing the game." Humanity owes it much, will owe it even more. But, like all forms of discipline, it is apt to weigh heavily on individuals; and heaviest on those who, believing in the code, must needs make choice between playing the game according to the rules of love or playing the game according to the rules of average imperfect human beings.

The Love-Story of Aliette Brunton

That Aliette Brunton and Ronald Cavendish played their game according to the dictates of love and their own consciences, remains the sole excuse—if excuse be needed—for the happiness to which, at long last, they both won.

2

Of the various English families here concerned, the Fullerfords of Clyst Fullerford are at once the oldest and the least distinguished—according to modern standards of "distinction." Yeomen by original birth, yeomen at heart they have remained; content, in an age of ostentation, to serve their country quietly, and retire—at the end of service—into the lush obscurity of the Devon countryside, there maintaining modest state and modest revenues until such time as a Church of England God is pleased to summon them elsewhere.

Aliette's father, Andrew, born in the very early sixties, followed the Fullerford tradition of service, and became puisne judge of an obscure colonial law-court before retiring. His marriage, at the age of twenty-four, to Marie Sheldon, caused—owing to Marie's abandonment of the rigid Sheldon Catholicism for the scarcely less rigid Protestantism of the Fullerfords—no small sensation.

This marriage, founded on a self-sacrifice of which only Aliette's mother knew the full burden, yielded two sons, both of whom give their lives for their country early in 1915, and three daughters: Eva, eldest of the family, who married Captain Harold Martin of the Devonshire Regiment in 1910, and became "colonel's lady"—a position she filled most admirably; Aliette; and Mollie, youngest of the five.

It was not until her second daughter's birth in 1892 that the Sheldons fully pardoned Marie Fullerford's infidelity to their religion—Aliette, named after a remote French ancestress, becoming as it were the symbol of family reunion, and inheriting, on the death of Grandmama Sheldon, a little block of consolidated stock in further token of forgiveness. Shortly after which inheritance, in December, 1912, she married—for reasons which will be apparent in our story—Hector Brunton, barrister of the Middle Temple, and no small gun in the legal world; while Mollie, then a long-legged flapper of tomboy proclivities, reluctantly returned from Wycombe Abbey School to "assist mother in looking after things."

Mollie "looked after things" until the boys were killed. Then she joined the nursing service. To that service her body still bears witness in the shape of three white scars—souvenirs of a bombed hospital.

3

Although, socially speaking, there is little if any difference between the Fullerfords and the Bruntons, the latter family shine considerably the more effulgent in the public eye. One finds them in newspaper paragraphs; one sees them at court, at the opera, at the Ritz. In fact, wheresoever the ostentatious world of the nineteen-twenties foregathers, the Bruntons forgather with it; not because they themselves are ostentatious, but because, being of their period, they must needs follow the tide—as Rear-Admiral Billy, in that bluff manner which fifteen years' absence from the sea-service has scarcely impaired, is the first to admit.

"Damn vulgar commercial age, but we can't put the clock back, worse luck," says Rear-Admiral Billy Brunton to his brother, Sir Simeon Brunton, K.C.V.O., recently retired with ambassadorial rank from the diplomatic service. To which Sir Simeon, after three glasses of port, has been known to retort with a suave: "It hasn't done us so badly."

And this is a fact! For the Bruntons, originally sea-folk, and as poor as most of the senior service, have developed an uncanny instinct for marrying money.

Rear-Admiral Billy, head of the clan and now rising seventy-five, yielded to the instinct before the age of thirty; bringing home as bride, from his first cruise to Australia, a distinguished daughter of the Melbourne squatocracy, by whom he had two sons, Hector and Adrian; and from whom, on her death in 1906, he received sufficient money to make his declining years perfectly comfortable—though in a very modest fashion when compared with his younger brother Simeon, whose first wife was a Sturgis, of Sturgis,

Campion & Sturgis, the high-speed steel manufacturers, and whose second, an Anglo-Indian, still very much alive at the time our story opens, inherited a largish slice of shares in her father's main enterprise, "The Raneegunge Jute and Cotton Mills, Ltd."

"Still"—once again employing the language of Rear-Admiral Billy—"Simeon's feeding a pretty long string of unmated fillies in his stables; and I've only got a brace of colts who seem tolerably capable of foraging for themselves in mine."

The "colts," Hector, born in '77, and Adrian two years later, certainly foraged for themselves with considerable assiduity. Adrian entered the church; and developed the Brunton instinct to such purpose that he endowed himself with a bishop's daughter and a Mayfair congregation at the early age of thirty-five—though it must be put to his credit that he abandoned his Hill Street surplice for a chaplain's khaki tunic in the Holy Land, and did not return to his bishop's daughter until early in 1919, by which time she had maneuvered for him the comfortable vicarage at High Moor, a prosperous Oxfordshire living, whose exact center is Admiral Billy's Moor Park.

Meanwhile Aliette's husband—having persuaded himself that he was indispensable to his country—became a king's counselor, dividing his days between the common law courts, where emoluments were fat if advertisement lean, and the criminal courts, wherein, as prosecuting counsel for the crown, he on occasions glittered exceedingly.

A large and a successful family—they look—these Bruntons, when you make their massed acquaintance in three pages of "Who's Who." But Julia Cavendish, *née* Wixton, used to have a page to herself!

4

You will find mention of the "four sisters Wixton," of their "charming" mother and their "distinguished" father in most mid-Victorian memoirs. Tennyson wrote a poem to the baby Clementina. Robert Browning is rumored to have stopped May's perambulator on more than one occasion in

Kensington Gardens. Alice had an affair, very nebulous and of her period, with one of the less celebrated Preraphaelite painters.

But on the demise of Josiah Wixton (his wife and book-publishing business survived him a bare three years), all but one of his daughters disappear from artistic history. May married a tea-broker named Robinson, and was left a childless but affluent widow in 1908. Alice vanished with John Edwards of the Indian civil service into the Punjab—finally returning with a livery husband and one daughter, Lucy, to settle down among the retired Anglo-Indians of Cheltenham. Clementina allied herself—no less pompous phrase is adequate—with Sir John Bentham of the Bank of England.

Remained, therefore, to carry on the literary tradition, only the eldest of the Wixtons, who married Maurice Cavendish, the Oxford don, presented him with a son, Ronald, and became "Julia Cavendish, the novelist."

It is a curious commentary on the ingratitude of our educated classes that the Rutland Cavendishes, who are at least as distinguished scholastically as the Bruntons in the social world, have to rely for their public fame almost entirely on Julia.

"Because in Julia Cavendish," as wrote her one-time friend, "Dot" Fancourt, "we have a really great Victorian. She stands for everything that is best of that bygone school: for a technique, now, alas! despised. Her novels are not perfect; they lack, perhaps, that warm touch of humanity which one finds in Charles Dickens, in William Makepeace Thackeray. But at least they are the novels of a true educated Englishwoman, reflections of a fine, faithful spirit. Even apart from her skill as a story-teller, Julia Cavendish, with her great belief in the traditional decencies, with her reverence for the teachings of the Protestant Church, for discipline and the subjugation of self to the common weal, towers like a rock above the wish-wash flood of cheap sex and cheaper psychoanalysis which obsess most young writers of this self-conscious Georgian epoch."

And with that, to our story!

Chapter I

1

Miracle, by St. Peter out of Three-to-a-Flush, a thoroughbred chestnut not quite good enough for steeple-chasing but considerably too good for that very quiet hunt, the Mid-Oxfordshire, was just out of his box, and pretty fresh. Looking over the flint wall which separated the well-kept gardens from the newly-swilled tiling of the stable-courtyard at Moor Park, the horse's questing eyes could just see, between clipped yew-trees, the red-brick façade of the modest Georgian house, its windows glinting in the March sunlight. Miracle knew that a footpath led straight across the gardens from the front door of the house to the white gate in the wall of his stable-courtyard; and suddenly, hearing a footfall on the path, he whinnied.

"All right, you," soothed Miracle's groom, a little lame man with tattooed forearms and a wry smile. The white gate clicked open, revealing Aliette.

Hector Brunton's wife had never accustomed herself to riding astride. Her small figure, in its short black habit and loose-fitting coat, looked modern enough. She wore the conventional bowler hat, white stock, and patent-leather riding-boots. Yet there was something old-fashioned about her, despite the fashionable get-up; something, to use an old-fashioned word, distinguished.

She closed the gate, and came slowly across the courtyard. Her yellow-gloved hands carried a thonged hunting-crop and a leather sandwich-case.

"You might fasten this on for me, Jenkins," said Aliette. The voice, low yet with each tone perfectly clear, held a hint of diffident shyness, alluring in so poised a creature.

While Jenkins busied himself with the sandwich-case and girthed up, Aliette held Miracle's head, gentling his nose with deft fingers, and explaining—half to herself and half to the horse—why she had brought no sugar for him.

"No sugar for gee-gees these days, Miracle. Not at the admiral's. Billy's mean about his sugar. Pity you don't drink port, Miracle dear. There's plenty of port."

She laughed at that; and it was as though you saw a woman transformed. Her face, smooth in repose, almost colorless save for the scarlet lips and the big wallflower-brown eyes under the dark lashes, broke into a hundred dimples. There were dimples at the corners of her mouth, in the cream of her oval cheeks, on the crinkled upper-lip under the small fine nose; even—if you looked carefully enough—behind the close-set ears.

Miracle began fidgeting; and laughter went out of the face, leaving it smooth, purposeful.

"Those girths are too tight, Jenkins."

"I don't think so, mum."

"Loosen them one hole, please. They can be tightened at the meet." Now Aliette spoke with the quiet certainty of one who understands both serving-men and horses; and with that same certainty—her orders obeyed—bent down to insert a finger between clipped skin and taut webbing. As the head under the hat-rim stooped to its task, her coiled hair showed vividest brown, almost the color of flames in sunlight, against the cream of her neck.

Miracle stood quietly enough while his mistress gathered up the reins; put her unspurred left into Jenkins's hand; mounted; arranged her apron; and thrust foot home into the stirrup. Then, for the sheer love of hunting that was in him, he tossed at the snaffle, hogged his back, and whisked round toward the big arched gateway which gave on to the highroad.

"Steady, old chap," soothed Aliette. She looked too light a rider for that raking horse; but her little hands settled him down easily enough. "I'm in plenty of time, aren't I, Jenkins?"

"Yes, mum." The groom pulled a silver watch from his moleskin waistcoat. "It hasn't gone nine yet, mum."

As she rode quietly on to the highroad Aliette saw, either side of her under the archway, Rear-Admiral Billy's stables—empty save for the admiral's black cob, a luggage pony, and a huge charger-like animal which, on rare occasions, carried her husband. Horses are even more expensive to keep than children nowadays!

2

The little woman and the big thoroughbred danced left-handed down the highroad; passed Admiral Billy's unpretentious lodge, half-hidden by yew-hedges, clipped with nautical precision to turrets of dark-green velvet; skirted Moor Pond; and took the bridle-path for Upper Moorsby.

It was a great morning of earliest March. The ground under hoof still sparkled here and there with surface frost; but there was no "bone" in it. Warmth softened the tang of the air. Above the bare tops of the trees between which they trotted, Aliette saw a thin cloudless sky. In the clearings, crisscrossed with uncarted larch-poles, primroses sparkled softly. Almost it seemed as though a purple bloom already showed on the young birches.

She pulled to a walk, thinking as she rode. Her thoughts came slowly, precisely: Aliette was not the type of woman who liked rushing her fences, either mentally or on horseback.

"Spring," she mused; "another spring! And hunting nearly over. Then there'll be nothing but tennis till next winter. Except 'the season.' How I dislike 'the season'! It wouldn't be so bad if one had children. One could watch them riding in the park."

A little ripple of dissatisfaction submerged her mind. She leaned forward and patted Miracle's arched neck. The clipped skin quivered in response.

"What's the use of making one's self unhappy?" thought Aliette. "All that's done with. Best forget."

She trotted on, rising squarely from the Mayhew saddle, hands like velvet on Miracle's bridle-reins. The path rose through fragrant woodlands; met the roadway. Now, at walk between leafless chestnuts, thought troubled her once more.

This must be the third springtime since her discovery of Hector's infidelity. She re-lived the scene: he, big and blustering, in the paneled dining-room at Lancaster Gate: herself quiet, controlled, but furious to the core. She heard herself saying to him: "You misunderstand me, Hector. It isn't a question of

12

jealousy. It's a question of loyalty, and—cleanliness." That last word hurt the man. She had meant it to hurt.

Three years! It seemed a long time. Since then—despite occasional entreaty—she had withdrawn herself. She was too fastidious, perhaps. Suddenly, she wished herself less fastidious. Her childlessness cried out in her, "Condone!" But she knew she could never condone. The time for that had gone by. Other infidelities, she knew, had followed the first. Hector was not the man to restrain his natural impulses. His very entreaties proved him more libertine than husband.

And Aliette rode on, through Upper Moorsby, red-cottaged behind tumble-down palings, disused cycle-shop at one end, shut church at the other; past Moorsby Place, ring-fenced and inhospitable; across the common toward High Moor.

There was love of the countryside in her heart as she rode, love of horse and love of hound, love for the quick scurry of hoofs on turf, for the white scuttle of rabbits to bramble. But there was no love for any man. That love she had never known. Marriage—as she still imagined marriage—meant affection: mutual regard, mutual interests, children. Especially children! If only she could have had children!

Putting thought away from her, Aliette let Miracle have his head, and cantered on between the gorse and the brambles.

Cantering, her heart sang to her. "Fox-hunting! Fox-hunting! Fox-hunting!" Padded Miracle's hoofs. She watched their shadow lolloping the brambles; watched the track ahead. And suddenly, at the bend of the track, she grew aware of a horse coming fast behind her. Miracle gathered himself for a gallop. Checking him, she heard a man's voice:

"I say, I'm most awfully sorry; but can you tell me if I'm right for the kennels?"

Man and beast, a great raw-boned, rat-tailed gray with a huge fiddle head and enormous withers, which she knew belonged to Ross Titterton, the horse-breaker at Key Hatch, hove fighting alongside. As though by mutual consent, they eased to a bumpy walk.

"Yes. This is quite right," said Aliette.

Examining the man, she saw a serious, clean-shaven face, eyes of pale clear blue, a broad forehead, a lean jowl, full lips, the nose prominent and almost pure Greek in shape, the chin determined, and the hair a curious goldy-gray as though bleached by the tropics.

"Thanks so much."

She judged him just over six feet and just under forty. He looked a horseman in his high black boots, dark cord breeches, pepper-and-salt cutaway coat, and buckskin gloves.

"I hope I didn't startle your horse. This brute of Ross's pulls like a steam-engine," he apologized with an almost imperceptible drawl.

"I know." Aliette smiled. "Mr. Titterton tried to sell him to us last year."

"Oh, I can't afford to keep horses," confessed the man. "This is only a loan. Ross was sergeant-major of our yeomanry crowd in Palestine. He offered me a ride once—and I've taken him at his word. You don't mind my jogging along with you like this, do you?"

"Of course not. We turn off to the right here."

They rode down, chatting with the easy camaraderie of fox-hunting folk, into sight of a village. It lay just below them, on a spur of the common—pointed church-spire, gray vicarage crouching at foot, among a blob of slate-roofed smoke-plumed cottages. Beyond it, the ground unrolled to a brown and green checker-board of square hedged fields, lozenged here and there with pale woodlands.

"That's High Moor Church," announced Aliette, pointing her whip at the spire.

"High Moor!" The man cogitated. "Isn't a fellow named Brunton the rector?"

"Yes. You speak as if you knew him."

"Only slightly. I see a good deal of his brother. The K.C., you know. I'm at the bar."

"Oh!" Aliette hesitated a moment. "I'm his wife."

"Whose! The parson's?"

14

"No. The K.C.'s."

Both laughed, feeling the conventional ice broken.

"My name's Cavendish, Mrs. Brunton. Ronald Cavendish. You probably know my mother—most people do."

"Julia Cavendish, the novelist. Of course I know of her; but we've never met. What a wonderful woman she must be!"

"She is." Ronnie's serious face lit. Usually shy with women, he felt quaintly at ease with this one. She seemed so sure of herself. And how she rode! That horse must take some steering. He wanted, suddenly, to see her across country; to send his gray pelting after her chestnut. Of her peculiar beauty, except as a horsewoman, he was not yet conscious.

But Aliette, even in those first moments of their meeting, knew herself stirred, ever so subtly, to interest. Julia Cavendish's son! Didn't she remember something, something rather decent about Julia Cavendish's son?

It flashed into her memory just as they made the lich-gate of High Moor Church. "Conspicuous gallantry . . . rallied his squadron under fire . . . great personal risk."

3

The sight of the Rev. Adrian disturbed further musing. He tittuped out of the rectory drive as they came by—a little clean-shaven creature, jovially wrinkled, his short legs in their canvas gaiters gripping the flanks of a cock-throppled bay mare with a bobbed tail and a roving eye. The Rev. Adrian on Thumbs Up contrived, somehow, to look far more like a keeper than the proverbial hunting parson.

"Morning, Aliette," he greeted. Then, before she could introduce Ronnie, "I say, didn't you and I meet at Jaffa?"

"We did." Ronnie laughed. "Delightful spot."

Explanations over, they rode three abreast past the slate-roofed cottages, the Rev. Adrian acknowledging with perfunctory bridle-hand the salutes of his parishioners; and veered left along a metaled road between high telegraph-poles.

"Are you stopping at Titterton's?" asked the parson, eying Ronnie's gray.

"No. He couldn't manage me a room. I'm putting up at the pub in Key Hatch just for the week-end."

"Do they do you well at the Bull?"

"Not badly."

They jogged on, Adrian and Ronnie chatting. Aliette rather silent. An open car, whose occupant waved greeting, purred past. Miracle shied, bumping the gray.

"Dash that fellow Moss! Why can't he ride to the meet like a Christian?" muttered the parson.

Ahead of them, on the straight white of the road, they could see various other horsemen and horsewomen, a slow-moving dogcart, and two or three figures a-wheel. They overhauled and passed a flaxen-haired young farmer, very red of face and waistcoat, on an unclipped four-year-old; they added to their cavalcade a surly-eyed woman with weatherbeaten features who straddled a ewe-necked black, and answered to the inappropriate name of "Lady Helen." They came upon the dogcart, and Aliette reined alongside for a chat. The parson and Lady Helen jogged on.

"Mr. Cavendish—Mrs. O'Riordan," introduced Aliette.

The lady in the dogcart appeared to fill it, dwarfing the man at her side. She was a vast, voluptuous blond, full-nosed and full-lipped, slightly too well tweeded for the country. Her blue eyes, as they surveyed Aliette and Ronnie, held that peculiar twinkle common to all over-sexed women; they seemed to be pondering the problem, "Has Aliette at last found a lover?"

Mrs. O'Riordan herself, after a hectic but—with one exception—camouflaged career, had recently settled down to her second (and, she believed, final) adventure in matrimony. The "exception," a semi-literary, semi-theatrical Irish land-owner who drove the dogcart, had caused her considerable trouble to capture; trouble which involved an elopement, a year of uncertainty, a brace of arranged divorces, various columns of undesirable publicity in the Sunday papers, and the loss of several influential acquaintances. During these troubles Aliette, an old school-friend, had championed Mary O'Riordan's cause; and earned, by so doing, if not gratitude at least a very tolerable counterfeit thereof.

Ronnie's horse, bucking violently at a passing cyclist, interrupted conversation. The riders trotted on.

"Nice man," commented Mary O'Riordan.

"Good-looking woman, Aliette," remarked her husband.

Mary O'Riordan eyed her new male possession jealously. He was very attractive to the sex, this dark-haired, lantern-jowled Irishman she had captured from his first wife. It displeased her to hear him admire other women—especially women like Aliette, whose poised slimness set her own hoydenish bulk at such disadvantage.

<h2 style="text-align:center">4</h2>

It is a fifty-year-old custom of the Mid-Oxfordshire Hunt—the pack, started by old Squire Petersfield of Great Petersfield just before Waterloo, has changed hands many times but never failed its subscribers of their two days a week, with one "bye" monthly—that the first meet in March should be at the Kennels, an unpretentious building of sandstone and concrete which shelters under the black slope of Petersfield Woods.

Already, half a mile away, Ronnie could see two blobs of pink, and hounds—a runnel of moving white—pouring out of the gate their kennelman held open. Hounds and pink disappeared from view as Aliette led off the road up a sandy track between high blackthorns, and kicked Miracle into a canter.

Following, Ronnie's pulses tingled. He hunted so rarely; but always, hunting, this zest got into his blood. Only to-day, somehow, the zest seemed heightened. It was as though the cantering figure ahead typified the game. He felt drawn to her, drawn after her round the bends of the track, drawn instinctively, drawn irresistibly.

All the last four miles of highroad they had been meeting people. Now, just for a moment, they seemed utterly alone. And he knew, abruptly, that he wanted to be alone with this woman; that he desired her companionship.

The Love-Story of Aliette Brunton

They came to a locked gate. He dismounted, put his back against it, and lifted it off the hinges for her. She smiled down at him, "Thank you, Mr. Cavendish." He noticed, for the first time, how laughter dimpled the cream of her cheeks. They could hear other people coming up the track.

The gray waltzed to Ronnie's remounting. Aliette watched him swing to saddle, appraising—as she imagined—only his horsemanship. But now, in her too, zest stirred, a strange new zest not entirely attributable to the chase.

Three other riders trotted through the gateway, dispelling illusion. "This way," said the wife of Hector Brunton, K.C.

They ambled, side by side, diagonally across rabbit-bitten pasture; ambled, single-file, through a gap in the hedge-rows; struck an uphill bridle-path; and arrived, almost last, at the meet.

On the flat strip of grass behind the kennels—the direct road to them zigzags steeply down through Petersfield Woods—Will Oakley, the huntsman, his crab-apple face a trifle less saturnine than usual under its cap-peak, was just getting ready to throw off. Fifteen couple of fairly level hounds desisted from their rolling and watched him eagerly.

Colonel Sanders, the M.F.H., a heavy old-fashioned soldier, white-mustached, in a heavy old-fashioned hunting-kit (his special low-crowned bell-toppers were the despair of a certain aristocratic hatter in St. James's Street) had just finished his inevitable pow-wow with the kennelman. Ross Titterton (the whippety ex-sergeant-major came early, bent on a little profitable horse-copery) stood, bridle over arm, by Sir Siegfried Moss, an immaculate scarlet-coated, black-mustached young politician who rode, by horse-show standards, magnificently.

The Rev. Adrian, no thruster, was finishing an early cigar to be followed by an early nip from his silver flask. Lady Helen had engaged the whipper-in in a reluctant monosyllabic conversation—Jock Herbert was a shy, moon-faced young man from the North—on the eternal question of scent. The remainder of the field, about sixty in all, stood in equine groups of threes and fours a little away from hounds.

Mrs. O'Riordan's dogcart, Sir Siegfried's car and second horseman ("Must hunt in one's own constituency occasionally, even if it is a provincial pack," pronounced that very astute young politician), three flappers and a brace of young men on push-bikes, Mrs. Colonel Sanders and a trio of hard-bitten daughters afoot, a farm hand or two, and the socialist doctor of Key Hatch (who was on a walking-tour with his knapsacked wife and had come quite by accident on this "parasitic sport-crazy gathering of the capitalist class") completes the picture.

The M.F.H. greeted Mrs. Brunton, whom he secretly thought an adjectival nice little woman, adjectivally too pretty for that dimmed husband of hers, and gave orders to throw off.

Low ripple of black, white, and tan between high bobs of black and scarlet, pack, whip, and huntsman circled the dark of Petersfield Woods and headed down-hill in the March sunlight. Bay, black, and brown against green turf, followed the field. Very last, fighting-mad for a gallop, boring sideways along the slope, came the fiddle-headed gray. And "Confound the brute!" muttered Ronald Cavendish, seeing, over one shoulder, a slim black figure on a big chestnut; a slim black figure which seemed suddenly more important than the business of the chase.

But Aliette, watching hounds ahead, had utterly forgotten that one strange flash of premonition.

5

"Not much luck so far, Mrs. Brunton."

They had been at it nearly two blank hours; trotting from covert to tenantless covert; waiting vainly at covert-side for the "welcome whimper" of hound to scent, for the full music which follows the whimper, for the twang of the huntsman's horn and the "view-halloo" of fox's departure.

"We ought to find here," said Aliette.

Ronnie's gray, at last mastered to good manners, stood quietly beside her chestnut at the west corner of Parson's Copse. To the left of them a ditch and an elder-hedge screened the wood. All along the ditch and the elder-hedge other horsemen and horsewomen were waiting. Through the hedge they caught glimpses of browned bracken, of dun tree-boles, of a green ride here and a clump of dead bramble there. In front, the mole-heaved turf crested in shadow to a clouding sky. To the right and below them Parson's Hill sloped to an open valley country: first a strip of ill-fenced waste-land, a white road; then hedged grass-fields, young wheat, brown plows, a gleam of water; beyond, a church-tower, squat among poplars; further still, rising turf and twin hills dark with gorse.

Now, from the other side of the wood, they heard Will Oakley's voice: "Leu in, Ranger! Leu in." A whip cracked. They caught the soft twang of a horn.

Life stirred in the wood: a wary pigeon rose blue through branches; bracken rustled as a bunny sprinted to hole; a blackbird popped out of the hedge, popped in again. They were wise to hounds moving in covert; saw white sterns waving through brown bracken; heard a whimper, another whimper, the horn again. Dubiously, a hound gave tongue; then a second hound. The horses under them twitched excitement. Something red and furtive whisked across the ride. They heard Oakley's echoing voice: "Yooi push him up, push him up"; heard a touch of his horn; caught the flicker of his scarlet among tree-boles.

And suddenly, the pack crashed to deep-toned melody. The copse rang to it. The horses under them began to dance. The whole copse was a crash of hound-music, now drawing away, now nearing them.

"Fox all right this time," said Ronald Cavendish; and even as he spoke, Aliette, watching the rise in front, saw a low shadow streak across the shadows and disappear.

Then, simultaneously, Jock Herbert bellowed from the south corner of the wood: "Tally-ho! Gone away, gone away, gone away"; a hound or two in full cry leaped down out of covert fifty yards ahead; the colonel's voice roared, "Keep back, gentlemen, keep back," behind them; fourteen couple of crazy hounds streamed down after one; and Will Oakley's roan came thundering up the ride, crashed through the hedge, over the ditch, and up the crest after a pack you could have covered under the "pocket-handkerchief," without which no reporter considers his account of a run complete.

Gilbert Frankau

The rest was a mad scurry of eight hoofs to skyline, glimpse of a low fence, flown without thought, of the hounds pouring down-hill, of Will Oakley, horn still in hand, tally-hoing them on.

*

"Now where, in the name of all that's holy," mused the Rev. Adrian, "will that fox make for?" Most of the field were already away: he could see them galloping alongside the wood, topping the fence at crest-line. To the Rev. Adrian's eyes it looked as though they were leaping into eternity.

Himself and a few wise ones, Ross Titterton included, had waited; and so waiting, they saw that the fox must have circled for the valley.

Hounds, going far faster than the parson approved, crossed the white road below him. He put his cock-throppled nag to a cautious canter, and bumped downwards across the wasteland. Ross Titterton passed him at a furious gallop; Lady Helen gave him a lead through a gap in the dilapidated fencing. He could see hounds beyond the road: the master and Will Oakley were well up; close behind him rode his brother's wife, Jock Herbert, and that "young Cavendish" whom he remembered at Jaffa.

*

So far, Aliette and Ronnie had scarcely spoken. The dog-fox had gone away too suddenly, the ground beyond that first flown fence had been too full of rabbit-holes, for anything except concentration on the immediate job. But even in that first moment they had been aware of comradeship. Their thoughts, if either could have uttered them, would have been: "I'm glad we were together—just in that place, just at that moment."

Now, as they swept side by side across the twenty-acre grass—gray pulling like mad; chestnut scarcely extended; wind of their going in their faces; field behind and hounds in full cry ahead—the man spoke:

"We got away well."

"Rather." Aliette, drawing in front, smiled at him over her left shoulder. He let the gray have his head. Hounds topped their hedge, flashed on. They saw Will Oakley's roan fly over; saw the master's scarlet back and bell-topper lift disappear; and cleared the stake-and-bound side by side.

21

More grass. They grew aware of other riders behind them: Sir Siegfried, very pleased with himself; Ross Titterton, riding jealous to be up; Lady Helen.

The next fence was blackthorn, thick as night, not a gap in it. The hounds, spreading out, scrambled through. Will Oakley's horse balanced himself like a good hunter; jumped; and took it clean. Jock Herbert followed him over. The colonel, hat crammed to pate, galloped at it; blundered through somehow.

Sir Siegfried, on his bay, shot past Ronnie. Aliette, easing Miracle for his leap, saw the self-satisfied smile wiped from the politician's face as he took off; felt Miracle rise under her; landed safe on plow; turned her head to glimpse a big gray horse in mid-air; and, turning, heard the thud of a fall as Sir Siegfried's four-hundred-guinea bay pecked, slid, and rolled over sideways, wrenched to disaster by clumsy hands.

"Good toss, that," laughed Ronald Cavendish as they cantered slow over the heavy plow. "Who is he?"

"The member for Mid-Oxfordshire." Aliette, too, laughed: it had been a great little burst from covert, and the heart in her—the heart that loved hounds and horses—still beat to it.

"Good fox," said Ronnie.

"Isn't he!" said Aliette.

He was! By now four good fields separated its brushed quarry from the loud pack that labored—sterns and heads level—across sliced loam.

"Devil take the stuff!" muttered Colonel Sanders, watching hounds draw away from him. And "Thank God for a gate!" muttered Colonel Sanders as he made for it.

Huntsman and whip, too, were making for that gate. Aliette and Ronnie followed their lead, the gray plunging across the holding furrows like a ship in a storm. Looking back, they saw the pink politician struggling with his horse, half a dozen black-coats safely landed, Lady Helen barging in their wake.

A bumpkin in corduroys at the open gate shouted the master to "mind they wheatfields." The colonel damned his impertinence, and rode on after Will Oakley. Aliette and Ronnie shot single file down the trodden path between pricking corn, and flew the stile at end of it.

The pack, overrunning scent, had thrown up half-way across the next wheatfield. Casting themselves to pick up the line, hounds—noses to ground, sterns high—hunted on their own. Huntsman, whip and master, motionless on their horses, glad of the breather, sat watching. Suddenly Ranger feathered with eager stem, whimpered, and gave tongue. They were off again—Ranger in front, Audacious at Ranger's flank, a quiet smile on Will Oakley's face as he cantered after them.

"Pretty work," said Ronald Cavendish. He and Aliette still led the field; but the moment's check had given Ross Titterton and half a dozen others their chance. They came now, full split after gray and chestnut, across the young wheat. Among them, though the wheat was his own, galloped the red-faced, red-waistcoated farmer—and the Rev. Adrian, whose eye for country had compensated for his dislike of jumping.

Something inside Aliette, some curious instinct, vague and incomprehensible, seemed to resent those crowding horsemen. She was aware, dimly, that she would rather be alone, alone with the man who rode at her side. She wanted hounds to mend their pace, to run mute on a breast-high scent, clean away from the field. She wanted to feel Miracle extended under her, to hear the gray thudding after.

But now the hounds hunted slowly, puzzling out their line across a sheep-fouled pasture. As Miracle sailed a low fence, Aliette saw Key Hatch Church, squatting among poplars a mile to their right; a plowman, hat off by halted team, pointing the line; some foot-followers in a lane on the left; and in front, six fields away, the sudden gleam of water.

Then the pace mended. The pack raced in full cry to Parson's Brook; plunged in, plunged through; and checked dead on the far side. Will Oakley, putting spurs to his horse, got over. Jock Herbert just managed it. Pulling up this side the brook, Aliette and the rest of the first flighters watched the huntsman as he cast hounds forward.

The Love-Story of Aliette Brunton

"There's a ford half a mile down," spluttered the Rev. Adrian; and made for it, followed by Lady Helen, Sir Siegfried, his hat dented, his pink plow-plastered, who had at last managed to catch up, the red-waistcoated farmer, and half a dozen others.

Ronnie glanced at Aliette. He had no idea if his horse would face water or not. The brook, broadish under rotting banks, looked formidable; and it was almost like taking it in cold blood—this waiting for hounds to pick up the scent again. All the same, he knew that if Miracle went over he would get the gray across if he had to swim for it.

"Better make for the ford, Mrs. Brunton," called the colonel. He and Ross Titterton galloped off.

They were alone again: two ordinary orderly English people, a little dumb in each other's presence, both moved by very extraordinary thoughts, thoughts to which they were quite incapable of giving exact expression.

Aliette's red lips had pursed to stubborn determination. "I hate funking things," thought Aliette. To her, subconsciously, it was as though the water typified something more than a mere obstacle encountered in the day's hunting. She knew Miracle could jump it. Neither she nor Miracle would "funk things." Then why the thought? "Because," some voice in her gave clear answer, "*he* might."

"It isn't as bad as it looks," said the voice of the man at her side. "I'll give you a lead over."

And at that the voice in her began laughing. She felt unaccountably comforted. "Why should I mind?" she thought.

Beyond the brook, at the big bullfinch on the far side of the meadow, a hound feathered. "Yoi-doit, then. Yoi-doit," came Will Oakley's voice. The hound gave tongue, owning to the line; Aliette saw Ronnie take his gray short by the head, ram his spurs home, and ride straight at the water.

Miracle raced after the gray, catching up with every stride. Side by side, they galloped the fifty yards to the brook, rose at it, glimpsed it deep under them, flew it, landed.

Landing, she knew him safely over. Racing on, she heard the thud of his horse-hoofs behind. Her heart thrilled to the horse-hoofs; it seemed, suddenly, as though some string had snapped in her heart. The pack in front was utterly mad: she heard a burst of hound-music from beyond the bullfinch, knew that they were running a breast-high scent, running clean away from her. She gave Miracle his head, shielded her eyes with her crop-arm, crashed through the hedge, heard the gray crash through behind her.

Now she saw the hounds again, a close ripple of black, white, and tan, eight hundred yards away across post-and-railed common land. Miracle went after them, drawing up stride by stride, steeplechasing his fences. But the man on the gray would not be denied. A rail smashed behind her. He was following, following. He mustn't catch up with her—must never catch up with her.

The ground rose. Not very far ahead she saw a dark-red dot making for the gorse-clad hills. She heard Will Oakley's "Halloo! Halloo!" as he capped hounds on. They ran nearly mute now, sterns straight, hackles up. The fox vanished from view as they raced up-hill; reappeared again.

But Aliette was no longer aware of the chase. She could barely realize that hounds were running into their fox, that the two pink coats twenty yards ahead of her were whip and huntsman. All her conscious mind was at her left shoulder, listening, listening to the horse-hoofs behind. Could it be that she herself was the quarry of those thudding hoofs, quarry of the man who drove those thudding hoof-beats onward? He mustn't catch up with her! He must never catch up with her! And yet could it be that some instinct in her, some instinct earth-old and primeval, wanted to be caught?

That same instinct had been at work in the man on the fiddle-headed horse, the man who rode with his hands low and his teeth clenched, sitting down to his job as though he would go through Oxfordshire and out the other side in pursuit of Aliette. He had been aware of it, dimly, as they waited by the brook; aware of it, furiously, as he jumped. But now, instinct was blurred by the actual chase. He had come out for a "good gallop"; he was having his gallop. His feet were jammed home to the hunting-heel, his hat rammed to his head. His eye took in and loved the whole scene: the sky clouding blue-gray above them, the shadows skimming green turf below, the speeding pink of the hunt-coats behind the speeding black, white, and tan of the pack, the flame of gorse on the crest-line ahead.

Yet always, as he galloped, the man knew an urge stronger than the mere urge of the chase; knew that there was some dim reason why he had waited at Parson's Brook on a strange horse instead of going full split for the ford; why he must ride on—on and on—ride as he had never ridden before—ride the gray's shoes off, rather than lose touch with that black-habited figure in front. God! How well she went! How magnificently she went!

Will Oakley was not worrying about either of them. For once in their lives the Mid-Oxfordshire hounds were going like the Belvoir or the Cottesmore. Their fox was sinking before them. Will Oakley knew, as his roan topped the green bank which runs like an earthwork round the foot of Gorse Hill, that he would view "the varmint" close; viewed him.

No need, now, to lift hounds from scent: they, too, saw that draggled down-brushed shape, making its last effort; and crashed to fiercest music. Will Oakley hallooed them on, and Jock Herbert. "Yooi to him, Ranger," they hallooed, "Yooi to him, Audacious." Reynard swerved snarling from Ranger's teeth; Audacious snapped, missed; Victory rolled him over; massed pack were on him, mad for blood, as Will Oakley flung himself to ground.

Aliette, pulling up by instinct, saw the huntsman's scarlet ringed with leaping hounds; heard his joyful "Tear him and eat him, tear him and eat him"; and came back to sanity as the gray galloped up, halted, and stood with steaming flanks and steaming nostrils while his rider slid from saddle.

6

"By Jove, Mrs. Brunton, that was perfectly great!"

"Thanks to your lead over Parson's Brook."

They stood by their sweating horses, two perfectly normal people, rather pleased with their prowess, quite childishly delighted with the brush which Will Oakley held out to her.

"'T isn't often we gives you a run like that, ma'm," said the huntsman; and his saturnine face might have been a boy's, as he produced a piece of whipcord from his breeches pocket and began fastening the brush to Aliette's saddle-ring.

Various belated riders, the wily parson, the panting colonel, and the chagrined politician among them, came up and began congratulating. Sandwich-boxes were produced, flasks, cigarettes. Sir Siegfried looked at his watch; and started in to consider what degree of exaggeration might be warranted in subsequent reports of their day. It was nearly half-past two o'clock—call it three. They had begun to draw Parson's Wood at about one—make it half-past twelve. It is to be feared that the hour's run, by the time it was reported to Sir Siegfried's connubial fireside, had suffered considerable extension.

But neither Aliette nor Ronnie, as they walked their horses side by side into Key Hatch village (Gorse Hill is twelve miles from kennels, and the colonel, well satisfied with his kill, had ordered the pack home), spoke of the run.

Indeed, they hardly spoke at all. And when she said good-by to him at the open posting-doorways of the Bull, neither remembered to ask the other where or whether they should meet again. Which forgetfulness, thought Aliette as she turned Miracle's head for home, was the strangest part of a strangely joyous day.

But Ronald Cavendish, watching her mounted figure disappear down the village street, thought only of their ride together.

Chapter II

1

"You can't possibly want to brush it any more, Caroline." Aliette's maid, a square-hipped, square-shouldered, square-faced woman who had been in service with the Fullerford family ever since Judge Fullerford came back from Trinidad, laid the ivory-backed hair-brushes on the dressing-table, and began to twine the vivid coils round the small head.

There is neither gas nor electric light at Moor Park. In the slanted oval of the old-fashioned mirror, Aliette could only see, either side of her rather serious face, two primrose points of candle-flame. The long low bedroom behind her—furnished in mid-Victorian mahogany, Morris-papered with tiny roses on an exiguous trellis—was almost in darkness, darkness against which the primrose candle-glow showed Aliette's full beauty.

You saw her now—bathed after hunting, peacock-blue kimono round her dimpled shoulders—as a creature of supreme health. Her arms were smooth, lustrous; her wrists rounded; her hands small, a little broad in the palm—resolute strong hands for all their smallness. Her neck was smooth, full, lustrous as her arms; her bosoms low and firm; her feet fine; her legs, under their black silk stockings, slim-ankled and smooth-muscled—almost classic in their perfection.

Caroline Staley's mistress hardly moved while Caroline Staley completed the simple hair-dressing. Her deliberate mind was busy with the past day. She relived it—moment by moment,—loving it. The primeval instinct which had momentarily and subconsciously troubled her was asleep again, lulled to civilized quiescence by the air and the exercise. She remembered her pursuer in the field only as a pleasant companionable figure against the background of March sunlight and English countryside. Nevertheless, she found herself wishing, vaguely, that he were coming to dinner that night.

It would be a dullish dinner. Her husband had arrived by the afternoon train, bringing the usual bagful of legal papers to assimilate over the week-end, and her sister Mollie. Mollie and Hector always got on well with each other. She had found them taking tea together when she arrived home;

28

and left them alone after a brief greeting. The Rev. Adrian was to be there, with his bishop's daughter. "Billy" would want to know all about the day's run. "Dear Billy!"

Hector Brunton's wife inspected her maid's handiwork, and rose to be frocked. Mollie came in without knocking; lit another candle or so, and helped with a hook or two.

"Nice frock," decided Mollie Fullerford, surveying Aliette's black lace and silver tissue. Her voice resembled Aliette's; but there resemblance ended. The girl stood half a head taller than the woman. She had violet eyes, a broadish brow, and dark, almost black hair, bobbed during convalescence. Her coloring was white in comparison with Aliette's cream; but two patches of natural bloom glowed in her cheeks. She wore a panniered dress of blue and mauve shot taffeta, wide over the hips, tight round the ankles, short-sleeved, neck cut high to conceal one of her wound-scars. Her arms, hands, and feet, well-shaped as her sister's, looked more powerful. Altogether rather a hefty, healthy, happy young creature—the sort of creature a decent hefty young man would single out at a dance.

"No nicer than yours," retorted Aliette, slipping her rings on her fingers, and adjusting the short single string of pearls round her throat.

A knuckle rapped the door-panels; a loudish voice asked: "May I come in, dear?"

"Yes. I'm just ready."

Hector entered—a big, over-big man, the glazed shirt-front already bulging out of his black waistcoat. The K.C., shorn of legal wig and trappings, did not look very dignified; nevertheless, he gave an impression of force. The sandy hair was scant on his wide mottled forehead; his eyes were a cold gray; his nose tended to the bulbous. The clean-shaven lips appeared thin and a trifle cruel; his jowl was heavy—almost the jowl of a mastiff. He had the hands of a gentleman, the feet of a clodhopper.

"Is it time for dinner?" asked the wife. The husband drew from his waistcoat pocket a heavy gold watch; consulted the hands of it; and admitted the accuracy of her suggestion.

"Then we'd better be going down," decided Aliette.

2

The dining-room at Moor Park possesses, or is possessed by, the largest suite of mid-Victorian mahogany ever fashioned. The sideboard, gleaming always with massive silver, occupies the entire east end of the apartment, barely leaving room for a white-paneled Adams door. Either side of the marble mantelpiece stand two colossal serving-tables. Gigantic horsehair-seated armchairs, ranged between the long red-curtained windows, spill a brood of slightly less gigantic offspring round the mastodontic board.

The mulligatawny and the cod with oyster-sauce had already been served by the two cap-and-aproned wenches, whom the rear-admiral declared to be "a damned sight better than any heavy-handed son of a gun who smoked a fellow's cigars, drank his port, and did as little work as the old bumboat-woman of Portsmouth."

Rear-Admiral Billy was enjoying himself. His jovial eyes, a little red-rimmed with age under the heavy brown thatch of his hair, kept glancing round at "his two colts and their fillies" (one is, alas! forced to modify a good many of the admiral's pet expressions) and at that "jolly little piece in the No. 5 rig," Aliette's sister. His trim beard, grayed only at the extremities, kept wagging accompaniment to Aliette's account of the run; the course of which his hairy-backed hands were trying to trace, in bread and salt, on the table-cloth.

"'Spose you funked as usual, Adrian," rumbled the old man across the enormous table. "God knows what I've ever done to deserve a son in the church."

The Rev. Adrian, in clerical evening dress, only laughed at his father's criticism; but the Rev. Adrian's Margery fired up in defense of her spouse.

"Adrian's seen more active service than most men of his cloth," began the little aquiline, dark-haired, dark-eyed, dark-skinned, and darkly determined woman, who dressed (when natural circumstances permitted her—as they did not at the moment) with the severe precision of unadorned royalty.

Aliette continued her low-voiced description of the day's run; Hector tried explaining to an attentive Mollie the exact difference between a disbarred barrister and a solicitor who has been struck off the rolls; the cap-and-aproned wenches set an enormous joint of mutton before the host, who always insisted on carving with his own hands; and dinner proceeded.

To Hector Brunton's wife the dullish meal was less unpleasant than her anticipation of it. She liked her father-in-law—though his occasional coarseness always jarred her sensitive mind. She appreciated her sister's week-end visit; and anticipated with some pleasure the family talk which would precede their going to bed. But above all, she liked being away from the constraining intimacy of her home with Hector.

Recently Hector had been growing more and more difficult to deny. She caught him looking at her now, sideways across the vast white of the table-cloth. Vaguely she felt sorry for him. His cold eyes almost held an appeal. "Look round," they seemed to be saying, "it isn't so bad; really it isn't so bad, this little family party. Can't we make it up, you and I?"

"Poor Hector!" she thought. "He's a very simple person. He doesn't understand"; and checked thought, not abruptly, but with the same quiet firmness she had applied to Miracle that morning.

For Aliette never posed, even to herself. She was the very antithesis of the usual misunderstood married woman; so far, the mere thought of a compensating lover had never entered her head. All that happened afterward—and sometimes, looking back, it seems to her as though it all began from that chance remark of Adrian's—happened of its own volition. At the moment Adrian spoke she was just an ordinary woman, who had married an ordinary man in the expectation of a home and children, found him out in various infidelities, and decided—after due thought—that she could no longer pay his physical price for the dwindling possibility of motherhood.

"We had young Cavendish out with us to-day," said the parson. "Julia Cavendish's son. You know him, I suppose, Hector?"

"Yes. Clever fellow. No orator, but very sound on his law. He's doing junior to me in the Ellerson case. Rather an interesting case—"

"He and Aliette gave us all a lead."

31

"Rides well, does he?"

"Rather. A fine horseman. Handsome looking chap, too." The parson glanced at his sister-in-law, not maliciously, yet with a certain puzzlement. Listening with half an ear to her description of the run, he had wondered why she made no mention of the stranger. "Didn't you think so, Aliette?" he went on.

"I can't say I noticed his looks. He certainly rides well." The wallflower-brown eyes betrayed no startle, the pale, cream-tinged cheeks did not blush. Nevertheless, deep down in the inmost recesses of her nature, Aliette felt herself startle, not guiltily, but in wonderment at her inexplicable omission. What possible reason could there be for not mentioning the man?

Adrian continued to discuss Ronnie, and Ronnie's mother, and Maurice Cavendish, whom he had encountered years since at Oxford.

"His son's rather like him; but of course he's got the Wixton chin," said Adrian.

All the time Adrian talked, Aliette was asking herself questions. Why hadn't she even mentioned the man's name? Why? Why? Why? Harking back to her conversation, she seemed to have made the omission deliberately.

She tried to laugh herself out of the absurd mood; to join in the conversation. Deliberate? Ridiculous! She just hadn't thought about him. And yet, subconsciously, the man's face rose up before her, serious and strangely vivid against the glow of the table-candles. She could almost hear his voice, "I'll give you a lead over, Mrs. Brunton."

3

"Do you know, Alie, I've sometimes thought that you and Hector don't get on very well together."

Mollie, in dressing-gown and bedroom slippers, sat on the edge of her sister's bed. Margery Brunton, inclining to the aggressive about her forthcoming infant, departed early; and the two Fullerfords had been talking for nearly an hour, quite unsentimentally, about frocks, parents, books, a theater or so.

"What makes you say that?" Aliette, shoulder-deep in bedclothes, looked up from her pillow.

"Oh, I don't know." The girl blushed; and there fell a moment's awkward silence, during which it flashed through Aliette's sleepy mind that perhaps Hector had been confiding their matrimonial differences to his sister-in-law. But she dismissed the thought: Hector's reticence, even about small matters, was proverbial in the family. Besides, the reason for Mollie's question was sufficiently obvious.

"We get on as well as most married people, I expect," protested Hector Brunton's wife.

"I'm afraid I'm a terrible sentimentalist," went on Mollie. "Sometimes," she blushed again, "I think I'm even worse than that. I've never met a man I liked well enough to marry. Though, of course, I've let two or three men make love to me. It's rather nice to feel that a man's fond of you." She hesitated, and broke off—Aliette being hardly the kind of sister to whom one confided one's love-affairs.

"Most women are awful rotters," said the girl, after a long pause. Aliette restrained the retort at her lips; and Mollie's naïve revelations continued. "Most men aren't. They've got a higher sense of honor than we have. I found that out while I was nursing. Reading the women's letters to fellows who'd been gas-blinded. There was one, I remember, who wanted a divorce. She wrote: 'I'm afraid I haven't been playing the game while you've been away.' And she didn't seem a bit ashamed of herself."

"Did you read him the letter?" interrupted Aliette.

"No. But I wrote to the woman; and she wrote back, thanking me. *Thanking me!*" Mollie's voice rose. "She'd decided that 'after all, and especially as he was so bad, it would be better not to tell him. Would I burn her silly letter?' I think that's beastly." Her violet eyes kindled. "I'm not a prig. I don't believe divorce is wrong. But I do consider it dirty, when a woman or a man do—that sort of thing."

Aliette's face, smooth on its pillows between braided coils, gave no hint of the thoughts in her mind. Vaguely she resented an unmarried girl, or, in fact, any woman discussing "that sort of thing"; but her resentment, she knew, would only make the younger generation laugh. The younger generation of girls, as represented by Mollie, did not believe in squeamishness. Perhaps—Aliette seemed to remember that Julia Cavendish had touched on the subject in her last novel—the younger generation were no less virtuous because they faced facts instead of hiding their heads, ostrich-like, in the sands of innocence.

"I don't see," Mollie's decided voice closed the conversation, "why being in love should prevent one from playing the game."

She rose, gathered her dressing-gown round her, asked if she should blow out the candle, did so, and made for the door.

"By the way," said the figure silhouetted against the glow of the corridor-lamp, "I suppose there's a service at Key Hatch to-morrow afternoon. If there is, let's go. It's such a ripping little church; and I can't bear being preached to by Adrian."

"If you like, dear," replied an unguarded Aliette. But when the door closed and she lay alone in darkness, her mind reverted to its problem, to that peculiar omission of Ronald Cavendish's name.

4

Morning broke to gusts of rain. Hector locked himself in the library; the admiral inspected his greenhouses; Mollie refused to get up; and Aliette wrote letters.

Somehow, the letters took a long while to write. She found herself, pen in raised hand, dreaming. In her day-dreams happiness and dissatisfaction mingled incoherently, as the voices of two people heard through a wall. She could not catch the words of the voices, only the tones of them: one low-laughing, the other querulous. For the first time since girlhood—and even in girlhood she had been deliberate—deliberate thought abandoned her. She felt content that her mind should drift idly through an idle day. Only when Mollie—appearing brogued and tweeded for luncheon—reminded her of the agreed church-going, did her brain resume its normal function.

Gilbert Frankau

"In all probability I shall see Ronald Cavendish"—the thought came startlingly as Aliette watched Hector at work on the inevitable roast beef and Yorkshire pudding of the admiral's Sabbath. "I hope I shall see Ronald Cavendish"—so distinct were the words that they might have been actually spoken.

"It's clearing up," announced her father-in-law. "You'll have a jolly walk. Ought to start about half-past three. Better have some tea at the Bull. Service is at half-past five."

"I don't think I'll go," said Aliette. "I've got rather a headache."

"Do your headache good," rumbled the admiral.

She pulled herself together. Why shouldn't she go to Key Hatch; why shouldn't she meet Ronald Cavendish? Not, of course, that she really wanted to meet Ronald Cavendish. . . .

5

"I wonder why on earth I invented that headache," thought Aliette, as she and Mollie tramped down the drive. Hector had returned to work in the library; he waved them au revoir from the desk by the window.

A fantasy came to her: "I shall never see Hector again." She said to herself: "I hope he hasn't gone back to town." She said to herself: "Aliette, don't be an absolute idiot."

For, after all, could anything be more idiotic than that a woman of nearly thirty—and that woman Mrs. Brunton, Mrs. Hector Brunton, wife of Hector Brunton, K.C.—should feel like—like a schoolgirl going to meet her first choir-boy?

And yet, instinctively, Aliette knew herself somehow caught, somehow entangled. No escape from that knowledge! Ridiculous or not, this stranger she was going to meet—of course they would meet him; he couldn't have gone back to town—interested her. Interested her enormously. She saw him again in the eyes of her mind, his serious face, his blue eyes, his hair—such curious hair, goldy-gray as though bleached by the tropics,—all the while she swung, listening to Mollie's chatter, along the familiar lanes.

35

The Love-Story of Aliette Brunton

A low sun, emerging from between gold-edged clouds, shone on them walking. The hedges dripped cool sparkles. Cow-parsley pushed its feathery green through the tangled grass of the ditches. They topped the rise by Moor Farm, and saw Key Hatch below them. It lay in a cup of the valley, gray and brown and slate-blue through leafless branches against the concave jade of pasture-land. Half a mile on, midway between them and the village, two figures strolled up-hill.

Social sense, banishing idiotic fantasies, reasserted itself in Hector Brunton's wife; and, five minutes later, the four figures met.

"How do you do, Mrs. Brunton?"

"How do you do, Mr. Cavendish?"

Ronnie introduced his friend; Aliette introduced them both to Mollie.

The friend, James Wilberforce, carried his five feet eleven well. He had broad shoulders and a rather clever face, aquiline of nose, brown-eyed, high cheek-boned, full-lipped under a "toothbrushed" mustache. His mustache and his hair only just escaped being carroty. His voice carried a faint suggestion of superciliousness.

"An overworked solicitor," he told them with a humorous twinkle of his brown eyes, "taking a day off in the country." He was "charmed" to meet Mrs. Brunton. He had had the pleasure of knowing her husband for some years. "A great man."

Mollie liked the way he spoke. She thought him much more agreeable than Mr. Cavendish, who appeared to her rather a sobersides—almost ill at ease, in fact.

"We were just having a stroll before tea," announced Wilberforce, after about five minutes of uninspired conversation.

"And we are going to have tea at the Bull before church," retorted the girl. "So we'd better all have tea together." She marched Wilberforce off down the hill.

Her sister and Cavendish followed slowly. Now that they had actually met, Aliette felt thoroughly ashamed of the mental fuss she had made about him. He was a perfectly ordinary man, who happened to have given her a lead over

Parson's Brook. Rather a nice man, of course. She liked the way he wore his clothes, his assumption that she did not require him to chatter. He walked—she noticed in the gathering twilight—almost as well as he rode, easily from the hips.

"You've let your pipe out," she told him.

He stopped to rekindle it; and she saw that his hand trembled ever so slightly in the glow of the match. "Nervy," she thought. She did not divine that the long scholarly fingers trembled because the man had scarcely slept for overmuch thinking of the woman at his side; that he had been saying to himself, ever since he espied her on the brow of the hill, "Don't be a fool. Don't be a *damn fool*. She's Hector Brunton's wife."

That afternoon her sheer physical beauty thrilled him like fine poetry. He had no idea how she was dressed. Her clothes seemed part of her—deep wallflower brown, the color of her eyes. He wanted to acknowledge her beauty, to say: "You're wonderful; too wonderful for any man's sight." Actually, he opined that they had had a jolly run, and hoped he'd get another day with the Mid-Oxfordshire some time or other.

On horseback he could thrust with the best of them, this long, loose-limbed young man with the serious face above the Wixton chin; but he was no thruster after women. Too much the poet for that—one of those many dumb poets who have no desire to flaunt their emotions in cold print.

The four came down the hill, Mollie and Wilberforce still leading, round a whitewashed farmhouse, along a strip of wet road whereon a few bowler-hatted chawbacons strolled arm-in-arm with their red-cheeked, silent Dollies, under leafless elm branches, into the main—and only—street of Key Hatch.

England's Sabbath brooded obviously over stone cottages, picturesquely inefficient, flower-pots blocking their tiny windows, doors closed. Already, here and there behind the flower-pots, an extravagant light twinkled. Half-way down the street, its bow-windows inhospitably blinded, stood the Bull, relic of posting-days, whose rusty signboard had so far failed to attract the motorist. At street-end, dark against the cold cloud-banks of declining day, loomed the square tower of Key Hatch Church.

Mollie and Wilberforce waited at the side door of the inn till the others joined them.

"You won't mind having tea in my sitting-room. I'm afraid there isn't a fire anywhere else," said Cavendish; and led his three guests down a narrow corridor—rigid fish in glass cases and an iron hatstand its only decorations—into a parlor where firelight danced invitingly.

Wilberforce lit the lamp, revealing a five-legged tea-table set for two, a hard sofa, three antimacassared chairs, a stuffed barn-owl between Britannia-ware candlesticks on the mantelpiece, and the usual litter of photographs in sea-shell frames without which no English inn considers itself furnished.

Cavendish jerked the bell-tassel; Mrs. Wiggins, a pleasant-featured young woman already attired for church-going, bustled in with the brown teapot; nearly courtesied to Aliette; bustled out again, and reappeared with the extra utensils.

"You'll pour out for us, won't you, Mrs. Brunton?" asked the host.

"If you like." Aliette spoke in her usual deliberate way. But now, for the first time, she felt self-conscious. Was her hat on straight? Had she remembered to powder her nose before starting?

Pouring tea, handing cups, busied with the most ordinary social duties, there swept over her mind the most extraordinary fantasies. And quite suddenly she wanted to take off her hat!

"But this is ridiculous," she said to herself. "I can't take off my hat." Nevertheless she wanted to. She must! This was *his* room. His cap lay on the sofa, his pipe on the mantelpiece. Therefore . . . She realized with amazement that her hands were already raised to her head.

"Alie, you haven't given me any sugar." Her sister's irritated voice dispelled the moment's illusion. One hand dropped to her lap, the other to the sugar-tongs.

"Sorry, dear." She recognized the shyness in her own words, and covered shyness with a conventional laugh, "I'm getting forgetful in my old age."

Discussing ages with their bread and butter, they made the original discovery that a woman is as old as she looks, et cetera. Over hunks of Mrs. Wiggins's home-made cake, Ronald admitted to thirty-six, Wilberforce to forty.

"You don't look forty," decided Mollie: and at that moment, just as she was thinking she had never listened to a more artificial conversation, Aliette trapped her host's blue eyes in a glance no woman could possibly mistake.

In a way the glance, so momentary, so quickly veiled that only her heart assured her that she had actually seen it, resembled the glance she had trapped in her husband's eyes over dinner. And yet it was utterly different. It held reverence, a resigned hopelessness, a devotional quality of which Hector's cold gray pupils could never be capable.

Now, with amazement, she knew herself panicked. Panicked, not because of the look in his eyes, but because she realized that, in another second, her own would have responded to them. She was not "shocked" at his daring; her inaccessible beauty had not passed through seven years of married life in London without various similar experiences. But she was "shocked" at her own impulse. Heretofore such glances, even the words which on occasion accompanied them, had left her completely indifferent, utterly uncaring, positively contemptuous. This—did not leave her indifferent. This—this mattered. . . .

Subconsciously, she who never swore began swearing at herself. "You're a fool, Aliette. A damn fool." Doubt nagged her. "You made a mistake. You only imagined that glance." The code nagged her. "Even if you didn't imagine it, he had no right—"

And all the time her outward self, the socially-trained Aliette, was behaving as though nothing unusual had occurred, filling teacups, nibbling cake, talking this or that triviality. No, she was not an ardent church-goer. Yes, her brother-in-law preached splendidly. But she objected to seeing him in the pulpit. Why? She didn't quite know why; it seemed too intimate, somehow or other. Like being introduced to the Deity as a relation by marriage.

Mollie and Wilberforce laughed at that. Their laughter disturbed Aliette. She and Cavendish sat stupidly silent till church-bells began.

"You'd better come with us. It will do you both good," said Mollie to the solicitor.

"I haven't been inside a church since I left the army," declared Wilberforce.

"All the more reason to come with us," smiled Mollie, who liked this big auburn man, had liked him more and more ever since he was first introduced.

And to church, casually, those four went.

6

As she knelt by the stone pillar on the thin hard hassock, it seemed to Hector Brunton's wife that she had forgotten how to pray, that her eyes were being drawn sideways through her fingers. Only by concentrating could she achieve a moment's devotion. Settling herself back in the pew, she was vividly aware of Cavendish's proximity.

By no means a fanatic, Aliette nevertheless accepted her father's Protestantism. Religion formed part of the code, of those indubitable laws on which one based existence. But on this particular evening Protestantism seemed a farce. She could not imagine any god taking pleasure in the gas-lit ceremonial, in the vacuous-eyed congregation, in the artificial intonations of the parson or the hymn-numbers on the board. All these seemed hugely distant from any concept of worship. Somehow, she caught herself yearning for a richer ceremonial, for a warmer faith. Somehow, she seemed to remember—dimly out of childhood—her grandmother's voice:

"My dear, we've decided to forgive. But, O Marie! aren't you lonely? Don't you feel as though God had gone out of your life?"

And her mother's voice seemed to answer: "Mother, can't you understand? It's the same God. He hasn't gone out of my life just because I worship Him differently. He couldn't abandon any woman who sacrificed herself for love's sake."

The two voices faded into the past.

But now Aliette realized struggle in her soul. It was as though her soul stood at bay, at bay with some terrible decision; as though her soul were being swept toward some contest whose ending, whether victory or defeat, only God could foresee. Once again she felt panic. Yet how should there be panic here in Key Hatch Church?

Already they were singing the last hymn. This man, this man beside her was called Cavendish. Ronald Cavendish! She could see his eyes, now dropped to the hymn-book, now raised again. She could see his ungloved hands on the pew-rail. She could hear his voice.

And abruptly, panic passed; abruptly, she felt the very spirit of her a-thrill, a-thrill as though to fine music.

7

Hector Brunton's wife and Julia Cavendish's son said good-by to each other in the cottage-twinkling darkness at the foot of Key Hatch hill, shaking hands coolly, impersonally—merest acquaintances. Indeed, Aliette's "Good night, Mr. Cavendish" sounded a hundred times less cordial than Mollie's "I hope we shall meet again, Mr. Wilberforce."

And yet forty-eight hours later Aliette bolted.

She bolted, neither with Cavendish nor from Cavendish. She merely bolted to Devonshire.

To herself she succeeded in pretending that she was running away from Hector, from the inevitable recurrence of his amorousness; to Hector, that—hunting being almost over—Mollie's return to Clyst Fullerford furnished an excellent opportunity for her to pay the annual visit to her home.

Hector grumbled, but gave in; and the two sisters traveled back together, Mollie chattering all the way down, Aliette silently speculating whether "home" would cure the mental and spiritual unease of which she now felt acutely conscious.

But the unease persisted. Either "home" had changed its attitude toward her, or else she had changed her attitude toward "home." The little wayside station with its one porter and its six milk-cans, the up-hill drive in the twilight, the first sight of the pilastered lodge, meant less than ever before. Her heart did not warm to anticipation at thought of the lit drawing-room,

41

of her mother's hair white in the lamp-glow. Even when her father welcomed her in the antlered hall, she felt like a visitor.

They seemed to her so old, so settled, so remote from the actuality of life, these two: Andrew (Aliette was of that age when children think of parents by their Christian names) with his veined hands, his tired eyes and patient mouth, his slow voice and stooping shoulders; Marie, thin, pleasantly querulous, all traces of beauty save the eyes, wallflower-brown as her daughter's own, dead in the lined face.

The very house, long and low, browned by time, its mullioned windows dim with staring down the vale, seemed uncaring of her presence. Even her own room, the room always kept for Aliette, the white furniture bought for Aliette when she came back from boarding-school in France, could not give her the peace she sought. These things, and the things in the gardens, the pink-hearted primulas and the sheathed daffodils, seemed insentient of trouble, of the trouble in her mind.

It had not been thus when she returned after marriage. Then the place had smiled its wanderer welcome. Now it was the wanderer who smiled; wanly; conscious of chill response; conscious—daily and hourly more conscious—of an issue she must face unaided.

People, people she had known since cradle-days, came and went, busied as ever with the same pleasant trivial country round, keeping much to themselves, a little resentful of the war-rich who were creeping into Devonshire, ousting war-poor county-folk, transforming old places, building themselves new.

"Dear Aliette," said the people she had known since cradle-days, "you're looking younger than ever."

"Dear people," she used to answer, "how nice of you to say so." For outwardly she remained the same calm Fullerford who had married a Brunton. Nobody, not even Mollie, guessed the emotions that obsessed her. To them she was Hector Brunton's wife; not a girl of twenty-seven, dreaming herself in love, in love for the first time.

Outwardly, she remained so calm. Her eyes were unruffled pools; her voice a mannered suavity. Even the Martins failed to irritate her.

And Eva Martin would have irritated most sisters. The dignity of "colonel's lady" sat heavily on Eva's narrow shoulders. She resembled Mollie in vivacity, Aliette in complexion; but her eyes were their own cold blue, her hair its own fading gold, and her lips, which smiled often, but never in affection, two thin lines of anemic red across her undimpled cheeks.

Mrs. Martin and Mrs. Martin's husband—a tall, gaunt soldier-man, uncompromising in speech, direct of dark eye, whom Aliette and Mollie would have liked well enough had he not been Eva's—spent a full ten days. They brought their children with them; and left them behind when they departed: two well-drilled little girls, who gave no trouble to anybody—and no enjoyment.

*

So, for Aliette, Devon March warmed toward Devon April, bringing neither peace of mind nor solution of the issue; only the certainty that she who thought herself invulnerable had succumbed within thirty-six hours of making his acquaintance to the temporary attractions of a man.

"For, of course," she used to muse, "it was only temporary; a moment's infatuation; the sort of thing I've always heard about and never believed in. Curious, that I should still think so much about it! Am I still thinking about it—or about him? I am being funny. What's the matter with me? Love at first sight? The coup de foudre? But that's ludicrous; simply ludicrous. The sooner I get back to London and leave off brooding, the better."

Nevertheless, as she ordered Caroline Staley to pack, Hector Brunton's wife realized herself desperately grateful that her husband—as announced by telegram—had been "called out of town."

Such wires, coinciding with vacation-times, usually signified that he had grown weary of entreating her fastidiousness!

Chapter III

1

If you, being a stranger to this London of ours, inquire after Temple Bar, your inquiry will be fruitless.

Temple Bar was removed about forty years since; but if you traverse the Strand, and, leaving the jostle of the Strand behind you, venture on—past Mr. Gladstone's statue and the two churches which part the streaming traffic as rocks part the waters of a river—you will become suddenly aware of two pointed wings and a grotesque dragon-shaped head showing black between high buildings against a narrow slip of sky.

This is the "Griffin." He stands where Temple Bar stood. Above him tower the clock and gray pinnacles of the law courts. Westward, he looks toward the seethe of near Aldwych, and far Trafalgar Square. Behind him clang the news-presses of Fleet Street. At his right wing and his left you will find the advocates of our law; "barristers," as we call them.

They are not quite of the every-day world, these barristers. Their minds, even their bodies, seem to move more precisely. The past influences them rather than the present. Sentimentality influences them hardly at all. At home—even now very few of them live at the wings of the Griffin—these men may be lovers, husbands, friends. Here they are advocates of a code, a selected body, inheritors of a six-hundred-year-old tradition. Very pleasant fellows on the whole: not at all inhuman; only—as befits their calling—a little aloof.

It may perhaps help our stranger to understand this aloofness if, turning southward from the Griffin down the clefts of Inner or Middle Temple Lane, he will explore some of the "courts" where these barristers of ours have their "chambers"—Hare Court, Pump Court, Fountain Court, Miter Court, and the rest.

Here, not a newsboy's shout from Fleet Street, our exploring stranger will find a veritable sanctum of time-defying quiet—red-brick and gray-stone houses, paved or graveled walks, fountains, courtyards, trees, gardens, cloisters, colonnades, and quadrangles; the whole set, as though it were a

Gilbert Frankau

symbol of tradition controlling progress, midway between the moneyed "City" and the governing "West End."

But the quiet of the Temple—Gray's Inn and Clifford's Inn lie north of the Griffin and beyond our story—is an illusive quiet; the quiet of good manners concealing busyness. If you watch the faces of the men who walk those graveled courtyards, you will see them as obsessed by thought as the faces of any merchant in the moneyed City. If you climb the uncarpeted stairs of those Georgian houses, and read the names painted in block letters on the doors, you will find many whom the clanging presses of Fleet Street have made familiar—and many, many more to whom even the fame of Fleet Street has never come.

*

So far, Ronald Cavendish, who shared his chambers in Pump Court with three other barristers and Benjamin Bunce, their communal clerk—a little melancholy individual with a face like parchment, the clothes of a waiter off duty, and watery blue eyes which perpetually craved recognition—belonged to the latter category. "But the Ellerson case," thought Benjamin, "might easily bring 'us' into prominence."

It meant a good deal that "we," who had lost five years at the bar through "our" going to the war, should be briefed by Wilberforce, Wilberforce & Cartwright, that very solid firm of Society solicitors, as junior to the great Brunton. "We," backed by our friendship with young Mr. Wilberforce, "our" mother's name, and an undoubted grip of common law problems, were certainly going to get on—an excellent circumstance for Bunce.

"Ellerson v. Ellerson to-day, sir. King's Bench Seven. Mr. Justice Mallory's court. I have put the papers on your desk." The little man spoke as though "we" were so busy as to need reminding; and withdrew into the anteroom.

Ronald Cavendish threw an amused "Thanks, Bunce," after the retreating figure; and applied himself to study. Ellerson (Lady Hermione) v. Ellerson (Lord Arthur) presented features of intense legal interest. Could a wife, actually but not yet judicially separated from her husband, sue him for libel? If successful, could she obtain damages? There were precedents, of

45

course—Hill v. Hill and another, Rowland v. Rowland. To say nothing of the celebrated Clitheroe decision!

Long ago the junior, acting on Brunton's instructions, had looked up those precedents. Now another possible one crossed his mind. He rose from the ink-stained table; searched among the bookshelves; found a volume; and stood thumbing it. The precedent was useless: Brunton, as usual, had drawn the covert like a pack of beagles—leaving not even a rabbit unscented.

Brunton! Thinking of his "leader," professional instincts blurted in the barrister's brain. The low, dingy, paneled room, the shaft of sunlight on the worn carpet, the green of trees at his window, seemed to vanish from view. He was on horseback again—fox-hunting—with Brunton's wife.

"March," he thought. "And now it's May. Why can't I forget?"

But he couldn't forget. The woman's face, flawless, almost colorless, the vivid wallflower-brown of her eyes and hair, had haunted him for nearly three months. He was "in love" with her. At least, he supposed he must be "in love."

He had been "in love" before; with a girl in Hampshire (long ago, that—he could scarcely remember her name—Prudence); with the usual undesirable; with his cousin, Lucy Edwards, when he went to the front. Remembering such milk-and-water affairs, it seemed impossible that this new emotion could be love.

Was it perhaps passion! He began, standing there in the sunlight, to consider passion—as dispassionately as Aliette herself might have tried to consider it. (In deliberation of thought, they resembled each other, these two.) Although by no means an ascetic, he hated the abstract idea of passion, finding it rather indecent—like the letters not meant for public eyes which, defying the vigilance of solicitors, occasionally found their way into that stereotyped farce, the divorce court.

And yet this emotion could hardly be other than passion.

The blue eyes under the broad brow grew very serious. Inwardly Ronald Cavendish, despite his outward poise—the result of training—had remained extraordinarily young. "Passion," he thought; "how beastly." And for another man's wife! That made it impossible. That was why the emotion must be fought.

He had been fighting it ever since they parted. But the emotion would not be conquered. At times it became an ache, a sheer physical ache.

At such times—and one of them, he knew, was on him now—Ronnie conceived an amazing distrust of his own self-control; an amazing gladness that they had not met in London: although he had seen her, at a distance, more than once, walking across Hyde Park, a Great Dane dog at her heels. They looked, to his imagination, the tiniest mite forlorn—a little lonely woman (he always thought of her as little) with a big lonely hound. Invariably, the sight of her dispelled mere passion, melting it to a strange tenderness, akin to the tenderness he felt toward his mother.

"Mr. James Wilberforce on the telephone, sir," announced Benjamin Bunce; and shattered introspection. Ronnie went outside to the communal telephone.

"Hello, Ronnie." The solicitor's voice sounded irascible over the wire.

"Hello, Jimmy; what's the trouble?"

"The Ellerson case. Lady H. has got the wind up. She's with the pater now; wants to go and sit in court till the case comes on; wants a conference with Brunton; wants anything and everything. Of course we can't get hold of H. B. Can we bring her over to you?"

"Bring her along, by all means," said the barrister.

2

The offices of Wilberforce, Wilberforce & Cartwright, which occupy three floors of a modern red-brick building at the foot of Norfolk Street, fifty yards from the Thames Embankment and the Temple station of the Underground, are rabbit-warrened by white-wood partitions and frosted glass doors into a maze of conflicting passages.

On the top floor are the bookkeeping rooms, whence issue—still in stately clerical handwritings—those red-taped folioed bills ("To long and special interview when we informed you that we had taken counsel's opinion and he was of the opinion that . . .") which are never disputed though often delayed in payment by an aristocratic clientéle.

Below these, the Cartwrights—an old-fashioned firm of City solicitors and commissioners for oaths, with a practice one third commercial (Mr. Jacob Cartwright), one third admiralty (Mr. Hezekiah Cartwright), and one third criminal (Mr. John Cartwright), who amalgamated with the Wilberforces in 1918—hold undisputed sway.

On the ground floor, guarded by a bemedaled commissionaire, sit Sir Peter Wilberforce and his son, surrounded by their secretaries, their telephone-exchange, their notice-boards, and their waiting-rooms.

Jimmy Wilberforce finished his conversation on the private telephone; left the box; gave a casual glance at two obviously seafaring gentlemen who were importuning Sergeant Murphy to "hurry up Mr. Hezekiah"; and went back to his father's office—a scrupulously tidy apartment, black gold-lettered deed-boxes lining one of its walls, the rest pictureless and painted palest écru in contrast with the mahogany furniture and the tobacco-brown carpet on which Lady Hermione Ellerson's ermine muff now sprawled like a huge white cat.

Jimmy's father—a white-haired, white-mustached old gentleman, gold-eye-glassed, black-coated, a little bald of forehead but still ruddy of cheek—sat in his favorite attitude, one fine hand on the chair-arm, the other grasping an ivory paper-knife, at the leather-topped desk by the big bright window. By his side drooped his client.

"Well?" queried Sir Peter Wilberforce.

Jimmy turned to Lady Hermione. "I am afraid I can't get hold of Brunton for you. But Cavendish can see us if we go over at once."

"Oh, that is kind of Mr. Cavendish!" purred Lady Hermione.

3

"Lady Hermione Ellerson, Sir Peter Wilberforce, Mr. James Wilberforce," announced Benjamin Bunce.

Ronald, rising to receive his client, was met with an outstretched hand and

48

a torrent of words.

"Oh, Mr. Cavendish, you will help us, won't you? It's like this, you see. Last night while I was playing bridge at the club, Mr. Vereker—he's a barrister, you know—told me that I ought to settle. Of course, as Sir Peter says, he is in a kind of way a friend of my husband's—"

The tall willowy creature—she had dark hair, dark eyes, long nervous hands, and a long pearl necklace which bobbed nervously on her flat young bosom—rattled away till Wilberforce senior stopped her. Then she drooped to the offered chair, and sat interjecting staccato comments while the three men did their best to reassure her.

"And still I think I'd rather settle," she ejaculated, after half an hour's conference.

"My dear Lady Ellerson"—old Peter Wilberforce employed his softest purr—"of course I'll settle if you want me to. But I do ask you to consider the effect on your reputation. And besides, we have an excellent case. A really excellent case. Your husband's own admission, in the interrogatories, that he had discussed the question of divorcing you with other people besides his father. The fact that he never did institute proceedings for a divorce, that he never had the slightest grounds for instituting such proceedings—"

"Still, Mr. Vereker said—"

"Can't we forget Mr. Vereker? Mr. Cavendish has assured you that legally—"

"Oh, I hate the law!" burst out Lady Hermione. "I wish that Arthur—" She began to cry, in a ladylike lace-handkerchief way that made her extraordinarily alluring; and Ronnie, who had only been giving his sober opinion on the professional subtleties involved, without considering the human aspect, felt suddenly sorry for her. Women, in matrimonial cases, nearly always got the worst of it.

Besides, he knew the Ellersons socially, knew a little of their history—war-marriage, quarrels about money, separation, and now this curious case in which she was suing her husband for libel and slander. It seemed a pity that they did not arrange a divorce and have done with it.

The telephone rang. Benjamin Bunce came in to say that Sir Peter's office wanted him, that Mr. Justice Mallory was already summing up the preceding case, and that Ellerson v. Ellerson would come on immediately after the adjournment. The conference broke up.

4

"I'm afraid she won't fight it out," pronounced Wilberforce, snatching a hasty meal, at Ronnie's invitation, in the somber paneled splendor of Inner Temple Hall.

All up and down the long monastic tables, under the stained-glass windows and dignified pictures, other barristers and their guests were lunching, their low talk hardly reaching their neighbors' ears.

"Unless Brunton makes her," went on the solicitor.

They discussed their client with some frankness for another ten minutes, consulted watches, and moved themselves to a second monastic apartment for coffee and cigarettes.

"Talking of H. B.," said Wilberforce, "reminds me that I had a letter from his wife's sister the other day. She's staying with the Bruntons at Lancaster Gate, and wants me to call on her."

"Really?"

"You'd better come too. There's nothing like a bit of social work for getting briefs. Besides, little Mrs. Brunton's charming. We'll go next Sunday afternoon."

"Sorry, I'm going to play golf." Ronnie spoke calmly, his serious face giving no hint of the emotions which his friend's suggestion had set stirring. "What made Miss Fullerford write to you?"

"Oh, we've been corresponding for some time. I promised to help her about—a legal matter." Wilberforce nearly blushed. "She's a nice girl, isn't she?

"I'm getting on for forty, you know," he went on, getting no reply. "And they'll make the pater a baronet one of these days. About time I got married, don't you think, old man!" Then he consulted his watch again; and hurried off to Norfolk Street.

Ronnie, having paid for their coffee, sauntered out through the colonnades to his chambers, and back through Inner Temple Lane toward the law courts. Sauntering, brief under arm, he thought of his friend.

So Jimmy intended proposing to Mollie Fullerford. She would accept him, of course. Jimmy was a splendid match. Reticent devil—he hadn't even mentioned the girl since their return from Key Hatch. Jimmy would be Aliette's brother-in-law. Aliette! He had no right to think of her as "Aliette." Jimmy to marry Aliette's sister—that would mean the end of their friendship. How women complicated one's life! Why should he end his friendship with Jimmy, his best pal, just because . . .

"Because of what?" asked the schoolmaster Cavendish in Ronnie's mind.

"Because you're in love with his future sister-in-law," answered the imaginative Wixton.

5

Passing up the broad steps into the law courts, Ronnie was aware of unusual commotion. Society, mainly represented by the "Ritz crowd," had decided to patronize the Ellerson case. Lady Cynthia Barberus and her friend Miss Elizabeth Cattistock were posing to massed batteries of press cameras. An aristocratic poetess with bobbed hair had draped herself by the railings. Two actresses, so fashionable that they only needed to act when off the stage, drove up with Lord Letchingbury, the latest patron of the unpaying drama, in a Rolls-Royce limousine, causing mild excitement among a crowd of collected loafers. The constable, saluting Ronnie, positively beamed approval.

Ronnie, returning the salute a trifle grimly (like many of his kind, the publicity side of the law always irritated him), entered the archway and turned left-handed into the robing-rooms.

Here all was quiet again. Hugh Spillcroft, a rising young specialist in commercial cases, spoke to him as he arranged the white bands round his collar, tucked in the tapes and drew on his black "stuff" robe before adjusting the light gray, horsehair wig.

"Going to win?"

The Love-Story of Aliette Brunton

"Settled out of court, I should say."

"Not if H. B. can help it," snapped Henry Smith-Assher, am enormous Pickwickian fellow with a bull-neck and a bull-face. "That chap never misses a chance of self-advertisement."

Two or three other men chimed in. Brunton, it appeared, was paying the usual penalty of the successful—unpopularity. Ronnie put on his wig, and passed out, a dignified legal figure, into the great hall of the courts.

This place, so vast and bare that the largest cloud of witnesses would leave it uncrowded, so high and dim that even at noon its vaulted roof seems lost in a brown haze, exercised a peculiar fascination over Julia Cavendish's only son. The Wixton in him saw it as the gigantic anteroom of traditional justice, a symbol whose hugeness hushed even scoffers to an awed silence.

For he loved his profession, this diffident, difficult young man; and, loving it, held its code, despite all the imperfections he was first to acknowledge, very high.

But this afternoon, somehow or other, the inhumanity of the place depressed him. Outside, there was sunshine, traffic, life, even love; here, only gloom and rules. As he strode diagonally across the flagstones up the tortuous staircase to "king's bench division," he met Thurston, the divorce specialist.

"Hello, Cavendish," greeted Thurston; "you've got the spicy case to-day."

Lady Hermione was standing by the embrasure of the corridor-window, talking to Sir Peter. Already a little crowd had foregathered round the glass-paneled oak doors of the court-room. She smiled at Ronnie over their heads. He smiled back at her reassuringly; caught Sir Peter's conference-forbidding eye; and pushed his way through the swing-doors and the red curtain into court.

The square, high apartment, paneled in dark oak as a church—judge's daïs, jury-box, clerk's table, and pulpit-like witness-box dominating its raked pews (above which the spectators' and judge's galleries already rustled anticipatory silks and feathers),—was still half-empty. Ronnie insinuated his long body into the junior's pew, which is behind that reserved for king's counsel, and began turning over his brief. Turning it, he could not help thinking of his "leader"—of Brunton—Brunton whose "war service" had not cost him five years' loss of briefs—Brunton, who had fame, and fat fees, and a house in Lancaster Gate . . . and Aliette for wife. The court began to fill. Twelve "special" jurymen, equally fed up with a bad lunch and the disappointment at not having been dismissed after the last case, clattered into their box. The clerk and the reporters took their places. Barristers, some with applications to present before the opening of Ellerson v. Ellerson, some mere spectators, pushed their way along the front pews. In the back pews crowded various witnesses, solicitors' clerks, and a favored few among the public who had bluffed or bribed their way in.

Lord Arthur arrived with his solicitor. They stood talking for some moments, and finally sat down. Ronnie, looking up from his brief, could see their two heads, still conferring, below him to his left. The opposing K.C., Sir Martin Duckworth, a smooth-faced, smooth-voiced politician, arrived in a very new silk gown, and asked audibly of his junior if he'd seen the plaintiff. The plaintiff and Sir Peter sidled to their places in front of the clerk's table, turning courteous backs on the defendant. Last of all, five seconds before the opening, Brunton rushed in.

Aliette's husband, looking dignified enough in full legal trappings, nodded at Ronnie; and leaned over to greet his client just as the bewigged clerk announced "Silence"; and Mr. Justice Mallory, a benevolent-looking old image—scarlet baldrick across his wide-sleeved gown, winking spectacles across his creased forehead—appeared through the curtain at the back of his daïs; was risen to by the court; and took his seat.

Various barristers rose up; presented various applications; and sat down again to hear "Ellerson v. Ellerson" or withdrew—according to the degree of busyness they had attained.

For Ellerson v. Ellerson, as "opened" a moment later by Hector Brunton, was more than a *cause célèbre*: it might, if fought to a decision, go down to legal history as a "test" case, a precedent established for all time. Wherefore the barristers—such as could—stayed.

But the twelve men in the jury-box were not barristers. "His lordship," Brunton told them, "will direct you on the legal questions involved. All I ask you to consider is this. If I prove, as I shall prove to you by the mouths of competent witnesses, that this unhappy, this innocent lady, my client, has been slandered, and vilely slandered—for, mark my words, there is no slander so vile as a slander on a woman's virtue—by the man at whose hands she has the right most to expect protection—by her husband: if I prove to you that, through this slander, she has suffered damage, intellectual damage, social damage, damage to her health and to her reputation: then, gentlemen, I hope you will demonstrate by your verdict that, in England at any rate, a wife is not her husband's property, his chattel to do with as he will, but a free citizeness, as much entitled to be protected from the slanders of her husband as from those of any other man or woman in this country."

Brunton boomed on—his appeal all to sentiment. The judge drowsed. Ronnie, nonchalant behind his leader, could not help envying the even flow of his oratory. "If only I could speak like that," thought Ronnie vaguely.

But suddenly, as the K.C. neared his peroration, Ronnie's nonchalance vanished. "Marriage," boomed Brunton, "is not slavery. A man, just because he happens to marry a woman, does not own her."

"But he does," thought the junior; "in law he does own her. In law this man owns Aliette."

And suddenly the broad black-silked back, the bulging neck under the horsehair curls, the loud confident voice, and every gesture of the gentlemanly hands grew hateful. He, Ronald Cavendish, the man and not the lawyer in him, resented all these; and resented them all the more furiously because he hated himself for the resentment.

At last Brunton sat down.

"Opened high enough, didn't he?" whispered Jimmy Wilberforce, who had insinuated himself to the side of Ronnie's pew. "Wonder what he'll make of her in the witness-box."

But now, before Brunton could call his witnesses, Sir Martin Duckworth rose to address his lordship.

No case, submitted Sir Martin, had been made out for the jury. A husband—in law—could not slander his wife; nor a wife her husband. In law they were both one. Therefore, even if his learned friend succeeded in obtaining a verdict, he could not succeed on the question of damages. That had been laid down in . . . The politician produced authorities, calf-bound volumes book-marked with strips of paper. He began quoting them in his singsong sleepy voice. Lady Cynthia yawned audibly.

Brunton turned to Cavendish, as a sportsman to his loader; and, as a well-trained loader, Cavendish supplied the legal weapons—books. The flash of hatred against Brunton was forgotten in his eagerness to win.

The judge began arguing with the politician. "He, the judge, understood that the parties in this case were not actually living together. Did not that, in Sir Martin's opinion, make any difference?" In Sir Martin's opinion, it did not. Brunton chipped in. The lawyers in court stiffened to interest. Miss Elizabeth Cattistock blew an irritated nose.

The wrangle between bench and bar persisted: only Ronnie, who took no part in it, saw Lady Hermione's black hat turn slowly from right to left. It seemed to Ronnie's imagination that the invisible eyes under the hat-brim were making some call to Lord Arthur. Then he saw Lord Arthur's head turn, almost imperceptibly, from left to right; saw Lord Arthur's eyes light with understanding, soften to that invisible appeal. "She'll never go into the box," thought Ronnie. "She'll go back to her husband." And despite his eagerness to win, he felt glad—glad that humanity should triumph over the law.

But Brunton was not bothering about the humanities, Brunton protested that Sir Martin had not made good his argument. Brunton pressed his lordship to allow the case to go to the jury.

His lordship thought it quite possible there might be a case to go to the jury. Nevertheless, his lordship felt it his duty to impress on both parties the painfulness, the unnecessary painfulness, of such a case as this. Would not the distinguished counsel on both sides consult with their clients? Surely there must be some way by which—Mr. Justice Mallory coughed judicially—a compromise, if necessary a financial compromise, could be effected.

"Interfering old fool," whispered Brunton to his junior.

Ensued a further orgy of whispering: Lord Arthur, his solicitor and Sir Martin on one side: Brunton, Lady Hermione and Sir Peter on the other. Behind him, Ronnie heard Lady Cynthia's muffled staccato, "I say, she isn't going to settle, is she?" and Miss Elizabeth Cattistock's "If she does, I win my bet."

Now the K.C.'s withdrew from their clients; drew together, still whispering; drew away from each other; whispered with their clients again; and returned to conference.

"I'm afraid it's a wash-out, Cavendish," the leader managed to convey behind his hand as Sir Martin Duckworth rose to address the court.

His lordship and the jury, announced Sir Martin, would not—he was delighted to say—be further troubled with this—er—very painful case. His client had agreed to terms, the financial aspect of which—with his lordship's permission—Sir Martin did not think it necessary to disclose.

Did he understand, interrupted Mr. Justice Malory, that the action would be withdrawn?

Brunton took up the cue. "My client," boomed Brunton, "has consented to withdraw her action; not that she feels her case in any way weakened, but because—acting on your Lordship's advice, and, if I may be allowed to say so, on my own—she has, at the very earnest solicitation of her husband, decided," the K.C.'s voice dropped to its point, "to return to him."

Lady Cynthia's audible "Well, I'm damned!" a little rustle of mannerly applause, and a beam from Mr. Justice Mallory marked the ending of Ellerson v. Ellerson—a happy ending, as it seemed to Lady Hermione's junior counsel.

6

But Hector Brunton thought otherwise. Recently it had seemed to him as though Aliette might relent. Ever since her return from Devonshire he had been conscious of some subtle, incomprehensible change in her. Therefore it piqued his pride to find her, on his return from court, not even vaguely interested in the newspaper reports of his speech—more especially as that speech was quoted almost verbatim under the heading: "K.C. says woman is not man's property."

"We ought to have fought the thing out," he told her. "That's what I said to Cavendish."

Aliette's face did not betray her, but her heart—the heart which had almost persuaded itself of cure—dropped two telltale beats.

"Clever chap, young Cavendish," went on the K.C. "I'd like to have him to dinner one evening."

With a thoughtful "Why not take him to the club, Hector?" the K.C.'s wife went upstairs to dress.

Chapter IV

1

Julia Cavendish was always at home on Saturday afternoons. You used to meet nearly all social sorts and conditions of men and women in that exquisitely tended Bruton Street house: literary folk, financial folk, embassy folk, Anglican priests, politicians, schoolmasters with their wives, young soldiers with their fiancées, old soldiers with their grievances, the "Ritz crowd" (which thinks itself Society), and real Society (which does not need to think about itself at all), intellectual aristocrats and democratic intellectuals—the whole curious "London" which an eclectic woman of means can, if she be so minded, gather about herself by the time she reaches sixty.

But the house itself betrayed, to a trained observer, the fact that Ronnie's mother really preferred things to people. Not necessarily expensive things—only occasionally could she afford a real "piece": but pleasant things; beautiful things that became, as it were, part of one's life; things one could feel about the house as though they were people, but people without too many claims on one.

Despite which, No. 67a was neither over-large nor over-crowded with possessions. Old prints had space on its panels, old furniture on its floors. Jade idols, Toby mugs, Dresden, Chelsea, and Japanese figures did not jostle one another on its mantelpieces or in its cabinets. Spanish velvets and Venetian brocades forbore to pose as "specimens," but were curtains, cushions, or chair-covers as use demanded. Georgian silver employed itself in a hospitable capacity; Satsuma vases held flowers; Bokhara rugs covered the parquet, not the walls.

"I'm a practical old woman," said Julia; and she looked it now, as she lay reading on the sofa in the square bow-windowed drawing-room.

A rather stern face was Julia Cavendish's: the Wixton chin dimpled but very determined; the eyes, under their tortoise-shell spectacles, bluer, harder than the eyes of her son. The wrinkles in the scarcely powdered cheeks and at the high temples, as well as the graying of the light brown hair, not all her own, betrayed her age. But the hands which held the novel still appeared the

58

hands of a young woman; nor had the years robbed her of her figure. Her dress—a black tea-gown, real lace at bosom and wrist—was so unfashionable as to be almost smart. Black silk stockings and black satin shoes—she had elegant feet—complete the picture.

A bell rang below. Julia laid her novel on a little lacquered stand by the sofa; took off her spectacles; and sat up to the maid's announcement of "Mr. Fancourt."

Dot Fancourt, a sentimental, unhappy old man with over-red cheeks, sunken eyes and beetling gray brows, his weak mouth hidden by a walrus mustache, extended both dry hands in effusive salutation.

"My dear, how are you?"

"In the best of health, as usual." Julia Cavendish released her fingers from the dry hands. "Tell me what Fleet Street thinks about the Ellerson case."

The editor of "The Contemplatory Magazine" began to gossip; and she listened to him. The pair had been friends for thirty years, the man's weakness of character finding comfort in the woman's strength. "Poor Dot!" thought Julia. His last illness, and the inevitable last sentimental complication, had aged him. Probably he would go next of the Victorians. That would leave only Harrison, Gosse, Hardy, and . . .

"Mr. Paul Flower, madam," announced the maid.

There entered a pale, hairless sexagenarian who resembled nothing so much as a very large white slug. He greeted them both sluggishly; and began to discuss, with an almost Biblical frankness, the psychology of Lady Hermione Ellerson—whom he had never met.

"A passionate limpet," he pronounced her, pulverizing that imaginary mollusc between thumb and forefinger. "The clinging type. I remember when I was a young man in Paris—"

Paul Flower's conversation, unfortunately, will no more bear the ordeal of cold print than Rear-Admiral Billy's. He continued holding forth on the subject of his Parisian youth till interrupted by tea, and Lucien Olphert—a bald-headed, under-sized creature whose real life was as mild as his historical novels were heroic. Various other novelists—Jack Coole, Robert Backwell, and John Binney with Mrs. Binney—dropped in. Literary "shop," inanest of all "shops" to an outsider, was in full blast when the maid ushered in Lady Simeon Brunton.

The ex-ambassadress swept across Julia's drawing-room like a well-bred monsoon. Her Paquin confection—frailest gossamer black with gold underskirt—rustled condescension. The ospreys in her Lewis hat waved approving patronage to art and letters.

"You see that I took you at your word, Mrs. Cavendish."

The hostess, who had been introduced to Lady Simeon (and promptly forgotten her) at a Foreign Office reception some weeks previously, said the appropriate word and made the appropriate presentations.

"But this isn't a mere social call." explained the new-comer. "This is a call with a purpose."

She accepted some tea; and subsided on to the sofa. Paul Flower judged her a Philistine (i.e., a woman who did not regard Paul Flower as the last living exponent of English literature), but decided her attractive. He approved her age, about forty-five; her eyes, which were darkly vivacious; her figure, which was inclined to the abundant; her hair and complexion, which were both soigné, the one matching her eyes and the other her pearls.

Jack Coole, the two Binneys, and Robert Backwell, his prominent teeth parted in a valedictory grin, departed. Flower, Fancourt, and Olphert continued to talk shop.

"A call with a purpose sounds very serious," prompted Julia.

Sir Simeon's wife smiled diplomatically. "The fact is, dear Mrs. Cavendish, that I want you to dine with us. Next Thursday. You will, won't you? Although it is such a short invitation. We shall be quite a small party—not more than twenty at the outside. And will you bring your son?"

"My son—" Julia, whose inclination was to decline—for some time now, late nights had wearied her—became visibly more gracious.

"Yes. My cousin Hermione—poor dear, what a time she's been going through—and all this publicity—so distressing for everybody—says he was simply charming to her during the case. So wise! So calm! So helpful! You must be very proud of your son, Mrs. Cavendish."

Not for nothing had the heiress of The Raneegunge Jute and Cotton Mills married an ambassador!

"Ronnie's coming to dinner this evening," said Ronnie's mother. "If he's free on Thursday we shall both be delighted. May I telephone you?"

2

Ronnie, who had been watching the polo at Ranelagh, arrived ten minutes late for dinner.

He came unannounced into the drawing-room; kissed his mother; complimented her on her clothes (she had changed into a dinner-gown in his honor); and inquired about the afternoon.

"Dullish," pronounced Julia—and broached the Brunton invitation.

"The Bruntons!" He seemed a little taken aback at the name. "I don't think I care to go."

"Nonsense. Of course you must go. A barrister's career is mainly social."

She prolonged the argument over dinner; she mentioned the Brunton "influence," the Ellerson case: till eventually—somewhat against his better judgment—she persuaded him to go.

A very different Julia this from the hostess of the afternoon! Always a little constrained, a little too dignified in company; with her son, she hid affection under a mask of brusquerie almost dictatorial. In boyhood Ronnie had been frightened by the mask; even at thirty-six he was only just beginning to realize the affection it concealed.

Only since his return from the war had full knowledge of this affection come to him. He saw her now—sipping her coffee in the print-hung, walnut-furnished dining-room—as a lonely old woman dependent on his love. And the sight hurt, because his heart was already aware of the possibility that one day there might be another woman, a younger woman, in his life.

"I wish you'd let me make you a decent allowance," she said abruptly. "You ought to be about everywhere. You ought to stand for Parliament. Even if you don't get in, it's an advertisement."

"I thought you hated publicity, mater."

"So I do—for myself." She cogitated. "I could manage another eight hundred a year."

"And deprive yourself of—"

"Of nothing. I don't want any money. I'm too old to know how to spend it. You'll have it all when I'm dead," she added.

"Mater!"—he was the softer in many ways—"I wish you wouldn't talk like that."

"Why not? Death's a fact. I've no patience with people who won't face facts. Life isn't a kinema show."

Coffee finished, they removed themselves to Julia's work-room—a square box of an apartment, book-lined, an Empire desk in its exact center under the illuminated top-light. Julia sat down at the desk; opened a drawer; and took out her check-book.

"Eight hundred a year," she said, writing. "That's two hundred a quarter. I'd better cross the check."

"Don't be absurd, mater." Ronnie frowned.

"But I want you to have it."

"What for?"

"Oh, clothes. You ought to dress better. Club subscriptions. Entertaining. Cigars. I don't know what men spend their money on. Women, mostly, I suppose."

Blotting the check, she would have given anything in the world to say: "Ronnie, darling, do take it. I can't slobber like other women. But I love you—you're everything I have in the world. Please, please Ronnie, don't refuse this. It's not money—it's just a token—a token of my love for you."

Actually, she said: "If your father hadn't been such a fool about money matters, he'd have left you his estate. He knew that I could always make all I wanted."

Ronnie frowned again. "You know perfectly well that I won't take it."

"Not even to oblige me? I—I want you to take it. It may cheer you up. You've been looking depressed lately."

"Have I?"

They had played this comedy of the allowance more than once since his father's death; but never before had he seen her so insistent.

"Yes." She stretched out the check to him, knowing her offer already rebuffed. In a way, she was proud of his independence. All the same, it hurt. One ought to be able to do more for one's child.

"I'm not depressed. And I'm not hard up. Really."

He smiled at her across the desk—one of those rare smiles which reminded her of the boy she had tried to tip at Winchester. She seemed to hear his boyish voice, "The pater gave me a fiver when he was down last. I don't need any more. Honestly, mater."

"You're quite sure?"

"Quite." He watched her tear up the check; noticed a sheaf of proofs on her desk; and questioned her about them. "Another short story!"

"No. It's an article on 'Easy Divorce' for next month's 'Contemplatory.' These are the duplicate proofs."

"You're opposing it?"

"Of course."

"On moral grounds?"

"Not entirely. Listen!" She put on her spectacles, and read him the opening paragraphs. "The woman of to-day is asking that divorce and remarriage should be made easier. Why? Because the woman of to-day refuses to face the simple fact that primarily she is her husband's helpmate. Personally I am a Churchwoman; and therefore find it impossible to believe the remarriage of divorced people justified. I am willing to admit that, in a limited number of cases, divorce itself may be expedient. But I feel that to make divorce easier would be a direct encouragement of immorality. We have to face facts. Woman is not, never has been, and never will be capable of resisting the sentimental impulse."

"You're a real Puritan at heart, aren't you, mater?" he interrupted.

She put down the proofs, vaguely distressed that he should prefer her conversation to her written word. For work, to Julia Cavendish, counted more than anything in life—except this lean, clean, sober-minded son of hers.

"It isn't a very good article, I'm afraid. Dot was in too much of a hurry for it. I never could write quickly."

These last months she had discovered herself writing even less quickly than usual. Once or twice, even, she had been forced to break off in the middle of the morning by a strange fatigue—a pain in her back. She had meant to consult a doctor; meant to ask Ronnie's advice. But she hated fussing about herself, hated fussing Ronnie. And besides, Ronnie was depressed—in some trouble or other. She could feel that trouble instinctively.

"You're sure nothing's worrying you?" she asked him as they said good night.

"Quite sure. Sleep well, mater."

He kissed her, and went.

"No," he thought, striding home to the rooms in Jermyn Street which she had insisted on furnishing for him. "No! Nothing's wording me. In point of sheer fact, I've never been so bucked in my life."

And he was "bucked," ludicrously so; "bucked" because he had yielded to his mother's persuasions; ludicrously so because, just for the moment, he had altogether forgotten Hector Brunton's existence.

Only when he awoke next morning did Ronald Cavendish remember that Aliette was a married woman—and the possibility that, after all, she might not be one of the guests at her uncle-in-law's dinner-party.

3

The ambassadorial branch of the Brunton family occupies a palace of a house in that palatial avenue, Kensington Palace Gardens.

Driving thither with his mother in the electric brougham with which she compromised between the horseflesh of the Victorian past and the petrol of the democratic present, Ronnie knew himself feverishly excited. All the suppressed emotions of three months leaped to new anticipation as they rolled away from Bruton Street, through Berkeley Square into the park.

It was still daylight. Happy lower-middle-class folk crowded the seats under

64

the trees, the grass beyond. Here and there, lovers, splendidly indifferent to the public eye, embraced one another with the frankness of post-wartime. Subconsciously, the sight of these couples affected the serious young man in the silk hat and stiff shirt of formal party-going. Almost he envied them.

"The season has been the fiasco one expected," commented his mother. "Decent people have no money to spend—the other sort don't know how to spend it. I wish you'd order yourself a new dress-suit, Ronnie. And those waistcoat buttons are very old-fashioned. I must get you some new ones."

"Rather a contradictory sentence," he commented.

"Nothing of the kind. It's a man's duty to be well-groomed." She sighed—it had been a tiring day, and she hated dinner-parties. "I often wish you'd stayed on in the army."

"Why?"

"I think you were happier; and the army, in peace-time, is so healthy."

"You do worry about me, don't you?"

"Of course. That's what mothers are for."

The remark, coming from her, sounded curiously pathetic. For the moment, Ronnie forgot his anticipations. He put a shy hand on his mother's arm.

"Cheer up, mater," he said, seeing her, once again, as a lonely old woman—the intellect, the public fame of her, merest surface-stuff.

By now, they were through Hyde Park, and into Kensington Gardens. She removed her arm; made her usual acrid comment on the Albert Memorial; and the pair of them subsided into contemplation.

Contemplating, Ronald Cavendish realized for the first time exactly how far he had already drifted toward violation of his mother's code. He imagined himself saying to Julia, "Mater, I'm in love with Aliette Brunton."

But he could not imagine Julia's reply. The old fear of her came back, chilling him.

And yet, code or no code, mother or no mother, he had to admit himself in love, passionately in love with Aliette Brunton. Even the possibility of meeting her thrilled his whole being. Looking back now, he saw that not for one hour since their ride together had she been entirely out of his thoughts.

Their electric circled out of the gardens, climbed Palace Green, and swung left between high lights, on to gravel, under an awning. A footman opened the brougham-door. Ronnie, jumping out, helped his mother to alight. "Thanks, dear. Tell him to be back by eleven," she said.

Obeying, Ronnie was conscious that he stood in the glare of impatient headlights. Behind and above the glare, through the plate-glass front of the approaching cabriolet, he saw two faces: one heavy-jowled above its starched collar, the other—Aliette's.

4

"That looked like young Cavendish. If it was, and you get an opportunity, don't forget about asking him to dine with us," said Hector Brunton.

Aliette did not answer; but her gloved hands, as she alighted from her husband's car, trembled ever so slightly. She had seen him. He had seen her. And the wound, the wound in her heart, was not cured. She could feel it throbbing, throbbing with sheer joy. "I'm glad I wore this dress," she thought.

Her chinchilla cloak, ermine at neck and wrists, covered a gown of soft grays and softer mauves, silver-girdled. Pearls gleamed at her lustrous throat, in the tiny ears under her vivid hair. Crossing the black-and-white tessellated hall to the ambassadorial cloak-room, she looked a very picture of dignified composure.

But the composure was mainly superficial. Her heart throbbed and throbbed. She forgot Hector, remembered only Ronnie. This stately old lady, just being divested of her mandarin opera-cloak, must be his mother. She resembled him, about the chin, about the eyes.

"What a charming woman!" thought Julia Cavendish. "I wonder if she's Hector Brunton's wife. I wish I could find a wife like that for Ronnie."

"I'm afraid we're the last," smiled the elder woman, eying the formidable collection of furs.

"I'm afraid so too," smiled back the younger. She took off her own cloak;

gave one swift glance at the mirror, and was ready.

"Practical, too. Makes no fuss about herself," thought Julia Cavendish, as they reëntered the hall together.

Aliette could not think. The meeting, unanticipated, had taken her off her guard. Delight, apprehension, sheer eagerness, and sheer diffidence made her utterly the girl. It seemed as though, at the instant, something tremendous must occur.

But nothing tremendous occurred! Or if it did, their social sense saw them through it. Ronnie was talking to Hector in the hall. He shook hands with Aliette. He introduced her to his mother. He introduced Hector to his mother. The four of them went up the wide stairs together. Aliette heard them announced, "Mr. and Mrs. Hector Brunton. Mrs. Julia Cavendish. Mr. Ronald Cavendish."

How silly she had been about him. How calm he was! How calm they both were! Naturally! He hardly knew her. They hardly knew one another.

Hector Brunton's wife realized suddenly that her left glove had split in the clenched palm, that she had forgotten to take off her gloves before entering the drawing-room.

"My dear child, how are you? En beauté, as always. A credit to the family." She found herself, among a mob of people, shaking hands with Simeon.

5

The craftswoman in Julia Cavendish, the literary memory and sense of "copy" which make her books such exact social pictures, functioned quite independently from the rest of her personality. No one, watching her as she talked international politics with her host, would have guessed that, behind the calm, dignified face, the novelist's brain was busy. Kodak-like, that brain registered its impressions, rolling them away for development at leisure.

First impression: an oblong room—paneled—Venetian bracket-lights—brocaded French windows either end—low scarlet flowers on a long gold-decked table, narrowing as you looked down it—many faces either side, two faces at each end—hum of subdued conversation—servants' white-gloved hands and dark-coated arms proffering bottles, plates, dishes.

The camera in the brain clicks, rolls away the picture.

Second impression: Sir Simeon, sixty-eight, a little man, white-haired, blue-eyed, mustache floppy, charming, not very efficient, presumably the weaker matrimonial vessel—his wife ought never to wear pink—Sir Simeon's three daughters, obviously by his first marriage, two with wedding-rings, thirty-eight, thirty-six, nonentities—their partners ditto—an ugly one, younger, rather interesting.

"My sympathies are entirely with the Jugo-Slavs, Sir Simeon. Italy is not entitled to a yard of territory more than we guaranteed her by the Treaty of London," says Julia Cavendish, society-woman.

The camera continues its work.

Third impression: the secretary of the Spanish embassy would look exactly like a bull-fighter if he wore the national costume instead of civilized evening-dress—General Fellowes has aged since the War Office inquiry—a fine type—the big woman he has taken in to dinner would look like a cantaloup melon if you cut her in two—the pretty girl flirting with the young soldier (Guards?) must be her daughter.

"Aren't you rather hard on our allies, Mrs. Cavendish?" chips in Hector Brunton.

"I have no patience with d'Annunzio."

"But at least you will admit that he is a patriot," protests Sir Simeon.

"No bombastic person is really patriotic. Patriotism is a dumb virtue."

"But is patriotism a virtue?" asks the K.C.

"Almost the greatest."

Julia's mental camera snaps again.

Impression of Hector Brunton: a would-be cave-man—not as strong as he imagines himself—putty in the hands of a sexful woman—rather a difficult problem for a fastidious wife—obstinate—capable of cruelty.

At which precise moment, the mother ousted the craftswoman from Julia's brain. She began to wonder if Ronnie were enjoying himself. If only he weren't so shy with women! Women made men's careers. He had taken down that charming Mrs. Brunton. She looked down the table and caught his eyes across the scarlet flowers. He smiled at her. He must be enjoying himself. She had done right, then, to make him accept the invitation.

"I gather you prefer patriotism to the League of Nations," remarked her host.

"Your League of Nations," answered Julia, "is merely the sentimental impulse translated into terms of international diplomacy. Every one wants it to work—every one realizes it unworkable."

Answering, she thought that she had rarely seen Ronnie look so happy.

But not even the mother in Julia Cavendish knew the cause of Ronnie's happiness; she was as blind to her son's infatuation as Hector Brunton to his wife's. She could not divine that the pair of them had passed beyond mere happiness into a little illusive world of their own making.

For the moment, Aliette and Ronnie dwelt in a rose-bubble of enchantment. A frail bubble! Yet it cut them off, as surely as though it had been opaque crystal, from their fellow-guests. Physical passion found no place in that rose-bubble. Their bodies, the bodies which made pretense of eating and drinking, which uttered the most absurdly conventional sentiments, dwelt outside of its magic; while within, their minds, their natures, their very souls, held secret commune—as two friends so set in friendship that words have become unnecessary. Yet actually, magic apart, they were merely a man and a woman, each lonely, each too healthy for that loneliness which is the prerogative of the sick and the abnormal.

They had been lonely; now they were no longer lonely. They had been obsessed with visions of each other; now they no longer saw visions. They saw each other; and their souls were satisfied.

But of all that their souls knew, their lips spoke no word.

"I've often thought about that run we had," said the man. "One doesn't get a gallop like that every day of one's life. Did you have many other good days?"

"I didn't go out again last season," said the woman.

"Really? How was that?"

"Oh, I went down to Devonshire with my sister."

"You didn't take Miracle?"

"No." It pleased her that he remembered Miracle's name. "By the way, I'm quite angry with you, Mr. Cavendish. Mr. Wilberforce told us on Sunday that you preferred golf to our society."

"Jimmy's a mischief-maker. Why isn't your sister here to-night, Mrs. Brunton?" Man-like, he wondered—now—why he had refused to call on her.

"Mollie's at a dance. I believe Mr. Wilberforce will be there too."

"Jimmy's a great dancer." Did she know, he speculated, about Jimmy and her sister? Probably. Women—according to Ronnie—always told one another that sort of thing.

"And you?" she asked.

"Oh, I'm like the Tenth. I don't dance."

Aliette dimpled to laughter at the old jest. It mattered so little what he said to her with his lips. His eyes gave her the answer to the one question; the only question she had ever asked herself in vain. His eyes said: "Yes. This is Love. This is the Real Thing." She wondered if his brain knew the message of his eyes. She marveled at herself for not having sooner known the message of her heart. "I'm in love with him," she thought. "I've been in love with him ever since that Sunday at Key Hatch." All the gray unease of the past months, of the past years, diffused to amber sunshine.

The Spanish secretary, sitting on her right, chimed in to their conversation. "You do not dance, Cavendish. That is strange. I thought all English people danced."

The rose-bubble of enchantment was broken. Talk grew general. Dinner drew to its end.

6

"You look a little tired, Mrs. Cavendish. Can't I get you some more coffee? A cigarette, perhaps?"

"Thank you so much. I think I would like a cigarette."

Aliette and Julia sat together in a palm-screened corner of the vast Louis Quinze drawing-room. The men were still downstairs. The younger woman rose; and fetched a silver cigarette-box, matches.

Julia lit her cigarette. She felt very old, very weary, quite unlike herself. The pain nagged at her back.

"I'm afraid I'm not a very gay companion for a beautiful young woman. You mustn't mind my paying you compliments." Aliette had raised a protesting hand at the word "beautiful." "When I was your age, compliments were in vogue. Nowadays they're out of fashion—like good manners."

"Surely good manners are never out of fashion," said Aliette. "Only—like fashions—they change."

Lady Simeon veered toward them, but diverted her course. They talked on, drawn to each other by a kindred obsession—Ronnie.

"I'd love to ask her what she thought of him," mused Julia Cavendish. "I simply daren't mention her son," mused Aliette Brunton.

Thus the man found them when he came upstairs. They made an exquisite picture, there, under the green—his mother, dignified, strong (not wishing to let him guess her weariness, she had pulled herself together at his approach), the halo of intellectual achievement setting her apart from every other woman in the room; and the vivid, exquisite, but equally dignified creature at his mother's side.

"You don't often smoke, mater." He felt consoled that these two should be together. For the last twenty minutes the sight of Hector Brunton—holding forth, loud-voiced, over a cigar—had made him feel a little guilty.

"Mrs. Brunton insisted. Come and sit down, Ronnie. Unless"—servants with card-tables made a belated appearance—"you want to play bridge."

"I'd just as soon talk."

They made place for him. He and his mother began to discuss their fellow-guests, critically, but without malice. Listening, Aliette felt like an interloper. Even if she had been unmarried, how could she interpose her love—for it was love, she knew that now, knew it irremediably—between these two? Her mind reacted from happiness to depression.

He said to her, "You're looking very thoughtful."

She answered absent-mindedly, "Am I?"

He said: "Yes. Don't you want to play? They're making up tables."

She said: "No. I'd rather sit here and watch."

Sir Simeon drifted up to them, bringing the young Guardee and the pretty girl he had taken down to dinner. The pair were still flirting, butterfly-like. Their host had insisted on introducing them to Julia. They suffered the introduction, and flitted away. "Who *is* Julia Cavendish?" asked the boy. "Silly! She writes poetry," answered the girl. "Oh, I say, ought I to have read it?"

"Of course you ought. I wish we were going to dance, don't you?"

"Rather."

The cantaloup lady rolled up to Sir Simeon, and dragged him away to show her his pictures. Julia relapsed into mono-syllables. It must be nearly half-past ten. Thank goodness! She could just manage another thirty minutes. Meanwhile Ronnie could continue talking to this pretty woman. Perhaps he would stay on. That would be best. She wanted to go home alone. In the morning she could telephone Dot for the name of his doctor.

And so, once again, the rose-bubble of enchantment formed itself about those two lovers. But now both were conscious of the bubble's frailty.

And the man thought: "This cannot endure. I cannot endure this. To-night must be the last time we meet." He saw her husband, pompous, considering the call of a hand. He knew that he abhorred Brunton for the possession of this exquisite woman. He loathed himself for abhorring Brunton.

The woman, too, saw her husband. But she could only feel sorrow for him. Poor Hector, who would have been satisfied with so little of her; who had never known how much she had to give. And now—now no man would ever know. Unless—Her fastidiousness revolted abruptly from introspection. She felt glad of Julia's:

"I think the brougham should be here by now, Ronnie. Do you mind finding out? And don't worry to see me home. I'm sure Mrs. Brunton will never forgive me if I drag you away."

"Don't be absurd, mater. Of course I sha'n't let you go home by yourself." Ronnie rose, and made his way across the room.

"You'll persuade him to stop? I—I'd rather go home alone," said Julia.

"Because you're tired. Because you don't want him to see it." The words escaped Aliette before she could control them. She covered herself quickly. "I'm sure that must be the reason. I'm sure, if I had a son, I should never want him to think that I was tired."

"You have children then—girls? You couldn't have known otherwise." The novelist in Julia was asleep; she could see no other reason why this "charming creature" should have divined her mentality.

"No. I have no children, worse luck!"

Ronnie came back to say that the brougham waited.

"You mustn't come with me, Ronnie." Julia got to her feet.

"Mater, I insist."

"Persuade him to stay, Mrs. Brunton."

Subconsciously, Aliette knew the incident momentous. His blue eyes were looking down into hers. Behind them she read indecision. He wanted to see his mother home: he wanted to stay with her. She could keep him at her side. Only, if she did keep him—and it would take the littlest look, the littlest gesture,—then she would be interloper indeed.

Consciously now, she made her first sacrifice.

"I think a son's first duty is to his mother," smiled Aliette Brunton.

Chapter V

1

Ten days went by.

For Aliette, the trivial round of London continued.

She attended a terrific *tamasha* of a wedding—all frocks and roses—at St. George's, Hanover Square; she dined at the Carlton with Hector and a sumptuous client from the money-making North; she walked the park with Ponto, her harlequin Dane, who, as though he understood his mistress was troubled, kept close at heel while she footed it, and thrust a consolatory nose into her lap whenever she sat down; she played lawn-tennis at Queen's; she did her household duties at Lancaster Gate, fighting and defeating a miniature revolution among the female staff. But her emotions she could neither fight nor defeat.

These emotions were all strange, sweet, disturbing. For the first time in her life a man obscured the entire mental horizon. Constantly she thought of Ronnie—imagining him her confidant, her friend, her lover.

Her mind took a whole week to formulate that last definite word; and even then the word seemed inadequate.

Except for Mary O'Riordan and Mollie, Aliette possessed no intimates of her own sex. Common gossip, however, credited various women of her acquaintance with "lovers": some permanent, accepted as institutions by every one except the husband; some transitory of the season; most merest "tame-cats," fetch-and-carry men. Hector's wife wanted none of these. She wanted Ronnie—not an occasional Ronnie, not a clandestine Ronnie, neither a merely physical nor a merely platonic Ronnie: but Ronnie himself—all of Ronnie—Ronnie for her very own.

Comprehension of this fact—it came to her with peculiar clarity one late afternoon at a crowded tea-fight in Mary O'Riordan's house off Park Lane—brought the woman up short by the head.

She realized herself wholly in love—dangerously, perilously, passionately in love. And the realization frightened her. It meant the abandoning of her own fixed point of view. It meant, actually, if not by intention, sin. At least it ought to mean "sin"—only somehow she could no longer regard it in that light. If she had not thought of Mary as sinful, why should she apply a different standard to her own case?

If this immense new tenderness in her, this accentuation of all her femininity, was "sin"—then nature's self must be sinful. If, by religion, she belonged body and soul to Hector, forever and ever amen; if, in the sight of God, his infidelities counted for nothing; if his occasional desire to possess her (only the night before she had been subtly aware of that desire's recrudescence) constituted a lifelong claim—then religion, as she had so far understood religion, must be a mere code designed in the interest of husbands, and God Himself a mere male.

2

Meanwhile, to Ronnie's mind, the problem presented itself differently.

Having no formal religion, the aspect of "sin" did not trouble him. He came, as he imagined in those ten days, to regard the entire question from a legal point of view. He wanted a woman who belonged to somebody else; by no manner of means could he possess that woman unless the law set her free. Her freedom being outside the sphere of practical politics, one's duty was self-control, forgetfulness.

On the question of self-control there could be no compromise; but to forget Aliette was a tough job. Mere passion—since their last meeting—represented only the tiniest fraction of his feelings. Already she had given him an entirely new outlook—the lover's outlook: so that he caught himself regarding the faces of his fellows, faces in his club, at the courts, in the streets, on tubes and in omnibuses, solely from his own obsessed point of view. What secret, what *emotional* secret, concealed itself behind those unemotional English faces? What sentimental impulse goaded them about town?

"The sentimental impulse" was his mother's favorite phrase. She had used it no less than five times in her article for the "Contemplatory"—which article, astutely boomed by Fancourt, had very nearly created a first-class "stunt."

One paragraph of his mother's seemed peculiarly applicable to the barrister's problem.

"If," wrote Julia Cavendish, "the Sentimental Impulse—for I will never consent to regard the unlawful attraction between a married woman and a man other than her husband as love, the very essence of which is obedience and self-denial—once comes to be considered a palliation for adultery, then the entire foundations of family life will be in jeopardy."

Six months ago Ronnie would have been the first to uphold such a doctrine. Now he could only find the flaw in it. The gospel according to Julia Cavendish—argued her son's mind—amounted to this: If a married woman loves her husband, she merely does her duty. If she doesn't love him, she must do her duty just the same. Obedience, to a man; and denial, of one's own inclinations, constitute the whole duty of woman. In other words: A husband can do no wrong.

And at that precise point in his meditations Ronald Cavendish remembered certain rumors—heard and forgotten three years since, on his one leave from the East—about Hector Brunton and a certain red-headed lady of the stage.

All the same, even admitting certain modifications—a wife's right to fidelity, for instance,—did not his mother's code form the only possible basis of society? What reasoning human could substitute the sentimental impulse for the existing marriage laws? "Free love" would only mean free license for the unbalanced, the over-sexed, the abnormal, the womanizer, and the nymphomaniac. Matrimonial bolshevism, in fact!

"Matrimonial Bolshevism," he remembered, was to have been the title of his mother's next article; but for the moment she had been forced to give up work. Sir Heron Baynet, the specialist called in by Dot Fancourt's puzzled doctor, had implored her—so she told Ronnie—to rest.

"I've got to take care of myself," she said. "Sir Heron says I'm not exactly ill, but that I'm disposed to illness."

Actually, Sir Heron's words had been far more disturbing; but Julia, who had never consulted a medicine-man in her life, resented the little man's seriousness, and pooh-poohed most of his advice.

"Don't worry about me," she went on. "Except for being a little tired, I feel like a two-year-old."

Ronnie, obsessed with his own troubles, accepted her version of the interview; and went off to play tennis. Despite all the hair-splitting and all the self-analysis, despite all the resolves never to see Aliette again, and all the attempts to bluff himself lawyer against himself man, the sentimental impulse persisted. And hard physical exercise, he thought, might help to cure that impulse!

Chapter VI

1

"If Aliette hadn't given up the game to do war-work, and if I hadn't got cut over by that bomb, we might have done some good together in the club doubles," said Mollie Fullerford.

"Well, you're both of you too hot for me," protested Wilberforce.

He balanced a cup of tea on his white-flanneled leg, and surveyed his companion admiringly. They were sitting in the sloped veranda of the clubhouse at Queen's. Below them, on the oval of green turf between the red West Kensington houses, a dozen marked courts hummed with the ping of ball against racket-face, with the swish of running skirts and the voices of the players scoring—"love fifteen,"

"fifteen all," "fifteen thirty."

"Oh, well played!" ejaculated the girl. Aliette, practising with Mrs. Needham on No. 2 court, had just banged a forehand drive down the side-line. "She's getting it back. Don't you think so, Jimmy?"

Mollie spoke the last word with some hesitation; they had only just got to the point of calling each other by their Christian names.

"Rather," agreed her companion, whose interest in Brunton's wife was of the vaguest, but who knew that he must at least simulate it—because, to Mollie, Aliette represented a good deal more than the average sister.

James Wilberforce did not possess a very emotional personality. He was not at all the sort of person to be swept off his feet by any woman. Marriage being "indicated," alike by parental desires, personal tastes, and a growing income, he had cast about for a possible mate; found her by accident; and was now "making the running" in the approved manner.

So far, the "running" had been rapid enough. Nevertheless, Sir Peter Wilberforce's son and heir already understood that this calm young creature of the broad forehead and the violet eyes would not yield herself without a struggle. "Takes life rather seriously, does Mollie," he thought; and liked her none the less for that.

"Does Mr. Cavendish play?" she asked casually. "If so, you ought to bring him one afternoon."

"He used to. But since he took to golf, 'patters' has lost its attraction."

"Rotten game, golf," said Mollie. "Takes too long. I believe in getting one's exercise over quickly."

They discussed the point for a second or two; and then veered, like most people in their position, to the personal. Aliette, looking up at them as she changed courts, knew a quick flash of envy. For those two, love would run its legitimate course; whereas for her— She put thought away, and concentrated on the game.

"Two five, I lead," announced Mrs. Needham—a hard-featured, soft-hearted woman with a mop of unruly black hair, an eye like a hawk, and the hands of a mechanic. "Why don't you give up that overhand service?"

"It'll come back in time."

Aliette went to her own base-line, and took two balls from the boy. Mrs. Needham crouched in her favorite position on the other side of the net. Aliette tossed up a ball, swung up her racket, served.

The service, railroading down the center-chalk, defeated Mrs. Needham. The server crossed to the left-hand court; stood to serve—and saw Ronnie.

For a fraction of a second they looked at each other through the high side-netting. He plucked off his soft hat, and stood watching. Aliette served; faulted; faulted again.

"Fifteen all," announced Mrs. Needham.

And suddenly, Aliette's game came back to her. Once more her first service struck chalk from the center-line. But this time Mrs. Needham got back a swingeing shot. Aliette ran—back-handed—flew to the net, killed the return.

"Thirty fifteen," she announced.

She knew, as she crossed, that Ronnie was still watching; that she must not look at him; that if she looked at him she would double-fault again; that she mustn't double-fault; that she must win.

But now Mrs. Needham was all out for the set. Aliette's service came back like white lightning down the side-line. She struck—ran for the net—guessed Mrs. Needham's lob-stroke—got back to it—slammed it across the court—got to the net again—won her point after a tremendous rally.

"Forty fifteen," announced Aliette; and abruptly, preparing to serve, she knew that Ronnie was no longer watching. Concentration failed her: the game didn't seem to matter: the sooner she lost the game, the sooner she would be able to talk with him.

2

"Why, there is Mr. Cavendish," said Mollie Fullerford. "And that's Hugh Spillcroft with him. I haven't seen Hugh for years."

She ran down the steps; and Wilberforce followed—a little jealously. The four stood chatting.

"Yes," said Ronnie. "Spillcroft had insisted on his playing 'patters.' Spillcroft had promised to lend him a racket."

"Cavendish used to play a pretty fair game at the House," interjected Hugh—a clean-shaven monocled young man, who looked, once divested of wig and gown, a bit of a blood.

To Ronald the ensuing conversation was almost meaningless. He took part in it automatically. He didn't want to talk with these people; he wanted to watch that white embodiment of graceful strength, Aliette. He could hear her voice, "Forty thirty," followed by the swish of two balls along netting, and Mrs. Needham's "Deuce." She had lost two points since he turned away.

The unexpected sight of her had paralyzed his self-control. He forgot all the resolutions, all the ratiocinations of the last ten days. He clean forgot Hector Brunton. His inward vision reveled in memories of her beauty. How glorious she looked—on horseback, a-walking, in evening dress, even on a tennis-court. Curious, that last! "Patters" women nearly always looked disheveled—those of them who could play.

Aliette—her set thrown away—and Mrs. Needham joined the four of them.

"How do you do, Mr. Cavendish?"

"How do you do, Mrs. Brunton?"

They clasped hands.

"I had to go all out that last game," said Mrs. Needham.

Neither she nor Ronnie realized that Aliette had lost deliberately. Aliette seemed so calm, so radiantly self-possessed. The vivid coils of her hair shone smooth in the sunlight; her eyes, as they looked into Ronnie's, were unruffled pools of dignity.

Yet inwardly Hector's wife shook like a ship in storm. The tempest of feeling—released, as it were, by the touch of his fingers—swept her through and through. To stand there, talking rubbish, undiluted "tennis" rubbish, became sheer torment. Her heart ached for his to recognize it.

"Oh, but I'm a fool all right," said the new voice in her heart; the voice she had been trying to stifle ever since March. "I've lost my head for good this time. I wish I could run away from him. I wish he'd go and change. What's the use of meeting him? Like this—with all these people. Why aren't we ever alone? I wish he'd go."

But Ronald Cavendish could not tear himself away. He, too, stood there, "like a perfect idiot," as he phrased it to his mind, saying anything that came into his head; anything that would keep him for another minute, and yet another minute, within the charmed circle of her society.

"Mixed doubles seem distinctly indicated," broke in Spillcroft's voice. "Come along, Cavendish, you and I had better change."

"But I shall be absolutely rotten," protested Ronnie, as he allowed himself to be led off.

Mrs. Needham found another opponent, leaving the two sisters alone with Wilberforce, who offered Aliette some tea. She accepted, and accompanied them back to their table; where, after a few minutes, Cavendish and Spillcroft joined them.

Sipping her tea, listening with half an ear to the conversations all round her, Aliette Brunton was, for the first time, aware of social danger. She felt a furious desire to talk with Ronnie, to look at him. But to-day no frailest rose-bubble of enchantment isolated them from their kind. To-day all the other instincts warned that she must avert her eyes, avert her voice. Nobody—not even Mollie—must guess their secret. Somehow she no longer doubted it their secret. Her very fears gave her the certainty of him. She stole a look, sideways under long lashes, into his blue eyes; and knew—knew that he loved her.

Yes, he loved her. Not as Hector imagined love, solely in the possessive. But in all ways; with passion, with tenderness with as much regard for her as for himself.

Fleetingly, she marveled that this thing should have happened to her; to both of them. How had it happened? Why? What did the why or the how of the thing matter? Sufficed—for the ecstatic moment—the knowledge that they loved one another.

But the man did not know. Certain of himself, he held no certainty of her. Even his self-certainty seemed evanescent in her presence. Surely he had not dared to let himself adore this radiant, perfect creature! Surely, even daring to adore, he would never dare tell her of his adoration! She was like the goddesses, utterly removed from the touch of a man, utterly aloof from him. Then, fleetingly, he knew her no goddess, but a wife—Hector Brunton's wife. And all the scruples of his code made the knowledge bitter in his mouth.

"Cavendish hasn't got a word to say for himself," thought Mollie. "Jimmy's ever so much better-looking—though Jimmy's tennis is rotten. I sha'n't let Jimmy play in this set." And she insisted, following the high-handed method of the modern young, on playing with Spillcroft against Cavendish and her sister.

Ronnie's patters proved somewhat less out of practice than he had imagined.

"Thank you, partner," smiled Aliette, after the last stroke of the third, and decisive, set. "Your volleying saved, the day."

"Oh, I didn't have much to do with it," he smiled back.

Since the beginning of the match, except for the necessities of the strokes, they had hardly spoken to one another. But, for each, the forty minutes of partnership, the mutual will to win, the clean struggle on clean grass, the open air and the exercise had been one long delight.

Scruples, uncertainties, consciousness of danger, consciousness of fear—these and all the inevitable soul-searchings of a love such as theirs took

Gilbert Frankau

wings and departed from them. Surrendering their bodies and their minds to one another for the winning of a game; concentrating on the vagaries of a white ball, a net, and a few square feet of turf; they forgot their immediate selves, forgot that they were "Mr. Cavendish" and "Mrs. Brunton"—two poor human beings poised at the edge of emotional disaster, separated by law, by the church, by "honor," united only by the "sentimental impulse," and became, for the forgetful moment, one mind and one body.

But now, once more, they were twain. Now forgetfulness was over. Now emotion poured back full-tide, submerging both their minds and their bodies.

James Wilberforce lounged down from the clubhouse; drew Mollie away from her partner, and began whispering. Mollie called across the court:

"I say, Alie, Mr. Wilberforce wants to drive me back in his car. You won't mind coming home by yourself, will you? I don't think I ought to play any more."

"No, dear, I sha'n't mind," called back Aliette; and her eyes as she watched the two figures making towards the waiting cars; as she heard the chug of Wilberforce's engine, and saw his two-seater swing through the gates up the road toward Baron's Court, betrayed the truth of the remark. But when she turned once more to the flanneled man at her side, those eyes had regained their composure.

"Can't we find a fourth?" remarked Aliette.

"We'll get Mrs. Needham to make up," said Spillcroft. "She and I'll take you two on."

And so, for one last crowded hour, those two played together—brains and bodies attuned to the delight of working in unison.

The very cleanness of the game took all sense of guilt and all guilt of sense from them. They might have been boy and girl, young husband and younger wife, lovers whose love was sanctioned of the law—he and she, sinews taut, eyes keen, all the health and all the youth of them concentrated on rhythmic pastime.

The Love-Story of Aliette Brunton

3

"You'e got your car, I suppose?"

"No. My—my husband's taken it out of town."

The rhythmic pastime was over. Nervously now they faced one another on the empty court. Spillcroft had rushed away to change, Mrs. Needham to the tube. From their kind, they could expect neither help nor hindrance.

Already the shadows of the red houses lengthened toward them across green turf; already the bustle of the tennis-ground was hushed. Sparrow twittered on the silence. In the radiance of that summer evening the brown hair, the brown eyes of Aliette kindled to wallflower color against the rose-flushed cream of her skin. The sight of her beauty, so virginal in its white simplicity of attire, so alone with him in that emptiness of green, struck Ronnie speechless. He stood enthralled—the magic of her harping sheer music against the hush in his brain.

"I—I think I ought to be going home," said Aliette.

She, too, heard that sheer music which is love. Once more, tempest-wise, emotion swept her through and through: sweeping away inhibition; sweeping away all false fastidiousness; cleansing her soul of all instincts save the instinct for loving, for being loved. In that one magical, self-revealing moment, she was conscious solely of joy.

"I—mayn't I drive you—" stammered Ronnie. He hardly knew what he said. All the suppressed vehemences, all the pent-up longings of the past months craved utterance at his lips. Fear and love keyed him to any daring. He had had such happiness of her that afternoon. It made him fearful lest happiness should utterly escape.

"Thank you very much—" Once more she was aware of danger. Yet she could not bring herself to say him "No."

He left her without another word. Her own heart, the very world, seemed to have ceased pulsing as she awaited his return. She stood alone, woman eternal, hearing very faintly across hushed spaces the beat of music, the birth-cry of children.

Ten minutes later—looking, to other eyes, the most ordinary, most orderly of citizens—Ronnie came back. But that sense of utter solitude was still on

84

Aliette. She could only smile her thanks as he led her to the waiting taxi, handed her in, and closed the door.

She did not wish that he should speak with her. She was afraid lest even his voice should irrupt upon this exquisite solitude wherein her soul hung poised. And yet how good to know him beside her as London spun past them in the twilight.

Was this London, the London she had so hated, this wonder-town through which they sped together? Was this Aliette? This, Ronnie?

And suddenly, vividly, she desired to hear his voice. Solitude no longer sufficed her. She had been so long solitary—solitary in unhappiness. Now, in her new happiness, she craved companionship, the sound of a voice, the touch of a hand. Why did he not dare speak with her?

Descending as from great heights, her soul knew him afraid lest, speaking, he should destroy that rose-bubble of enchantment in which they had their being; afraid, too, because he still thought of her as another's. Yet she was no other's: she was his, his only. And he—hers.

How fast they sped through this miracle of London. Already, the trees of its park were fleeting by.

Oh, why wouldn't Ronnie speak with her? Had he no word to say? In a moment, in such a little moment, it would be too late.

Yet it was fine of him not to speak, fine that he should so steel himself against her. His eyes were like sharp steel; his lips one tense line above the determination of his chin. He had clenched his hand—his right hand. Aliette could see it—close—so close to her own hand.

Then the car swerved, almost throwing them together; and Ronnie's self-control snapped, as a violin-string snaps, to the touch of her.

Their hands met. She knew that he was raising her hand to his lips; she felt the brush of his lips warm against her fingers; she heard his lips whisper: "Aliette—Aliette—don't hate me for loving you."

4

Hector Brunton's wife entered her husband's house like a girl in a dream.

Chapter VII

1

When Aliette looks back on the three days that followed her lover's first avowal, she can only see herself moving in a strange, rapt exhilaration from room to room of Hector's great house in Lancaster Gate.

Hector, she realized thankfully, would be away till Monday evening: the other inmates of the house—Mollie, Caroline Staley, Lennard the butler, and his female satellites—seemed as though they had been screen-folk, flat phantoms, alive only to the eye.

Vaguely, among those phantoms, she can remember Jimmy Wilberforce, very correct in his evening-clothes, sitting between her and Mollie in the big cream-paneled dining-room.

Dinner over—Aliette remembers—she invented some pretext to leave the pair unchaperoned, and withdrew to the balcony.

It was good to be alone, alone with one's dreams—dreams that made even Bayswater Road beautiful. The road seemed a pathway of radiance. High silver edged it either side; between, the hasting car lights streamed their fans of luminous crystal. Here and there among the trees beyond, her eyes caught the orange flicker of matches, the red of kindled cigarettes.

"Under those trees," she thought, "Ronnie whispered, 'Aliette, don't hate me for loving you.'"

As though she could ever hate him!

A little breeze, blowing cool across London, ruffled her hair. Patting a scarcely displaced curl, she thought: "He kissed these fingers of mine. Another time he will kiss me on the lips. My lips shall answer his kisses."

And all those three days and nights, thought went no further. For the moment it sufficed to know one's self adored and adoring, to dream the impossible, to vision oneself untrammeled as Mollie, a virgin in bridal white standing meek-eyed before one's chosen.

2

But Hyde Park, of a crowded Sunday morning, is no place for dreams:

86

rather is it an epitome of actual London. Here, all along with brown men, yellow men, black men, swathed Arabs, Poles, Czecho-Slovakians, Turks, Spaniards, 5 per cent. Americans, and even (such is the bland insouciance of London) a Bolshevik or so, foregather representatives of all the thousand castes between peer and proletarian which people Democropolis.

Not that these castes commingle! Each, as though disciplined, has its assembly-place. Aliette and Mollie, for instance, taking the diagonal path from Victoria Gate, would no more have let themselves intrude upon the communistic sanctum near Marble Arch, than the fulminating prophets of social equality and unlimited class-warfare would have dared invade the stretch of turf and gravel by the Achilles statue which custom reserves for "church-parade."

"We really ought to have gone to church first," said Mollie.

"Ought we?" answered an absent-minded sister.

Aliette's thoughts were very far from church. That morning, alone in the bow-windowed library among the heavy pictures and the heavier books, she had tried to be her old self again, to reason out the whole issue involved by Ronnie's declaration. But her reasoning had been all confused, baffled, and confounded of the emotions.

One fact only, as she now saw, had emerged star-clear from her hour of introspection: the fact that she loved Ronnie. And she had no right to love Ronnie! She was a married woman. Socially, and in the eyes of the law, she belonged to Hector.

Walking, she tried to delude herself. Perhaps the love was all on her side; perhaps her dreams would endure, bringing no reality.

But even the momentary delusion did not endure. Peremptorily her heart assured her of Ronnie's devotion, of its permanence. Irrevocably she knew that, sooner or later, the whole issue would have to be faced.

The two sisters walked on, silent in the sunshine, till they came to the assembly-place of their caste. There, still silent, they sat them down under the trees.

All about them, some seated, some strolling, were other well-groomed people. Beyond the low-railed turf, a compact, orderly crowd sauntered four deep along the sidewalk. Beyond them, occasional cars, occasional carriages drew up to disgorge fresh arrivals.

"Morning!" said a man's voice. Aliette, who had been entertaining a stranger's Pekingese with the tip of her unfurled parasol, looked up; and saw James Wilberforce.

James Wilberforce asked if he might sit with them, and took the answer for granted. "Fine day for cutting church," he grinned, as he arranged his hefty bulk, his striped trousers, his top-hat (which shone with a positive mating splendor), his "partridge" cane, and his buckskin gloves in the appropriate poses. "Been here long?"

"No," Mollie answered. "We've only just come."

"Seen anything of Cavendish?"

"Not so far, Jimmy."

"Expect he and his mater'll be along pretty soon. I'm lunching with them at Bruton Street."

"Are you?"

And suddenly Aliette panicked. "I wish I could bolt," thought Aliette. "I ought to bolt. He mustn't catch me here, in public, undecided. I wish I hadn't come. I might have known he'd be here. Oh, why didn't I reason things out to a finish this morning?"

*

Nor was Aliette Brunton the only one to panic! Ronald Cavendish, walking with his mother from Down Street to Hyde Park Corner, felt equally unsure of himself. He, too, after three days of rapt exhilaration, after three nights during which the one predominant thought had been, "She yielded her hand, she loves me," had tried to face the issue deliberately.

But deliberation seemed utterly to have deserted him. Consecutive thought was impossible. Between him and thought shimmered the radiant face of Aliette, the wide, unstartled, tender eyes of Aliette, the yielding fingers of Aliette as he raised them to his lips.

They turned out of Piccadilly into the park.

Gilbert Frankau

"A weak sermon," said his mother.

"I'm afraid I didn't listen very carefully."

"So I perceived." Julia, covertly examining her son, saw that he looked pale, agitated. His dress, stereotyped enough in conception, betrayed a certain carelessness: the tie had been hastily knotted, a button was missing from one of the gloves. She felt, rather than knew, that he resented her company.

Mother intuition alone made Julia conscious of that resentment. But psychology, the long training of an astute mind, led her instinctively to the root of it. "Some woman or other," she decided. "Nothing else could make him resent *me*." And she remembered, with an acute pang of jealousy, his affair with her sister's child, Lucy Edwards. Had it not been for her, Ronnie would have married Lucy. She could not regret having prevented the match—marriages between first cousins, whatever the church might say about them, ought not to be encouraged. Nevertheless, if Ronnie had married Lucy, he would at least have married a known quantity. Whereas now, for all Julia knew, he might have fallen in love with a divorcé.

For undoubtedly love must be the cause of his mental trouble. No other emotion had ever made him resentful of her company. Moreover, why should he be troubled if the girl were eligible?

"I think we'll cross now," she said, trying not to feel hurt. "It may be cooler under the trees."

He gave her his arm across the road; and as they threaded their way, still arm in arm, through the saunterers, Julia Cavendish, bowing to various acquaintances, forgot her hurt in sheer maternal pride—a pride which had not diminished by the time that James Wilberforce came over to detain them from strolling.

*

Watching those three make their way through the sunlit crowd, Hector Brunton's wife felt the social sense desert her.

This creature, dressed so like its fellows that its fellows scarcely turned to regard it, was her man, her Ronnie. He, and he alone among the crowd, could move her to emotion. She could feel the limbs under her silk frock trembling to his approach. And suddenly, desperately, she hated the crowd; seeing it a living barrier between them. If only Ronnie could take her up, there and then, in his arms; if only he could carry her away, away from all these futile people. All the people about her grew blurred, unreal. She could see clearly only one face, the serious blue-eyed face of her man.

"How do you do?" said the voice of Julia Cavendish. And a moment afterwards, as she and Ronnie shook hands, reality and social sense alike came back to the mind of Aliette Brunton.

She found herself sitting pleasantly in the park, surrounded by pleasant people. She knew a great many of these people: but best of all she knew the man beside her. "Poor Ronnie!" she thought. "He doesn't know what to say for himself. He feels awkward. It is rather an awkward moment. I'd better make conversation." And she began to make conversation in her calmest, most charming social manner, with Ronnie's mother, inquiring about her health.

"Oh, but I'm really quite well," protested Julia. "A little overworked, perhaps. At least, so the doctors say. Personally I haven't much faith in doctors. But I'm taking their advice, and knocking off for a month or so."

"Does that mean that we aren't to expect a novel this autumn?"

"I'm afraid so." The authoress laughed to herself. It was so like "the public" to imagine that novels were written in a few months, between May and July, for publication in the autumn.

But abruptly, even while she was still laughing to herself, Ronnie's mother grew aware of trouble. Her mind sensed drama: a drama actually in progress; here; close beside her. This "charming woman," this Mrs. Brunton, radiated, despite her charm, an aura of tension, of the acutest mental tension. Meanwhile Ronnie had hardly opened his mouth since they sat down. For the next ten minutes Julia Cavendish also "made conversation."

"Almost time we were getting a move on; it's past one o'clock," interrupted James Wilberforce—and precipitated crisis.

For that this was crisis, a definite thought-crisis, each of the participants in it—Julia, Aliette, Ronnie—recognized as they rose to their feet. Behind their conventionally smiling faces seethed minds so violently perturbed that to each it seemed impossible for thought to remain unbetrayed.

"This is the woman," thought Julia Cavendish. "This is the woman whom Ronnie loves. Somehow I must save him from her. Somehow I must save them both. Otherwise it means ruin, absolute ruin. Disgrace!"

But no thought of ruin troubled the lovers.

"I can't let him go like this," thought the woman. "I can't lose him. I must speak. I must say, 'Ronnie, Ronnie, I don't hate you for loving me.'"

And the man thought: "I wonder if she is hating me. I wonder why she's so reserved, so aloof. I must find out. I must have a word with her. Just one word—alone."

And he had his word, the barest whisper as their hands clasped: "May I telephone you to-night?"

Only the tiniest pressure of Aliette's gloved fingers gave consent.

3

"It was the mater who insisted on my having a telephone," thought Ronnie. "The mater who furnished this room for me."

He looked round the room—at the Chippendale settee, the bookcases, the eighteenth-century engravings on the beige wall-paper. Looking, his heart misgave him.

The mater! He owed her so much in life. And now—now he was contemplating, more than contemplating, making definite, absolutely definite, a decision of which she could never approve, which might even cost him her love.

The mater! Ever since that moment of crisis in Hyde Park—through luncheon, through the rainy afternoon which followed luncheon, over the dinner she had insisted on his sharing—Ronnie had been watching her face, speculating about her, wondering what she would say if she knew. Now suddenly it seemed to him that she did know.

He tried to put the idea out of mind. But fragments of their conversation—fragments which memory could only imagine to have been hints—kept recurring to him. She had spoken—and this was rare with her—about his father; about a recent matrimonial shipwreck; about her article in the "Contemplatory." And not once, after Wilberforce left them, had she mentioned—Aliette!

The Chippendale clock on the mantelpiece gave a preliminary wheeze, and began chiming ten o'clock. At the sound, misgivings vanished. She—not his mother, but Aliette, Aliette, the very thought of whose name made the pulses hammer in his head—must no longer be kept waiting.

For a moment the shining black of the telephone fascinated Ronnie's eyes; for a moment, as one meditating a great decision, he stood stock-still. Then impulsively he lifted the receiver from its hook.

To his imaginative mind, the telephone became instrument of their fate. Waiting for the call, he saw, as one mesmerized, all their past, all the possibilities of their future; forgetting, in that mesmeric instant, his mother, the law, Brunton, everything in the world except the vivid of Aliette's hair, her deep brown eyes, the poised exquisite slenderness of her.

And an instant later he heard her voice. It came to him, very clear, very deliberate, across the wires:

"Is that you?"

"Yes."

"You're very late."

"I'm sorry. I didn't get away from Bruton Street till nearly ten. Are you alone?" Ronnie hated himself for that question: it sounded almost furtive. But Aliette's answer was the very spirit of frankness.

"Yes. I'm quite alone. In the library. Mollie's gone to bed. Why do you ask?"

"Because—there's something I want to say to you—Aliette." He paused a second, mastered by emotion; then again he said: "Aliette?"

"Yes—Ronnie."

"You're not angry with me—about Thursday?"

"No." It seemed to him that he could almost see her lips move. "No. I'm not angry—with you: only with myself."

"You know—" He hesitated. "You know that I love you."

"Yes, I know that." A little laugh. "It doesn't make things any easier for me, does it?"

"I want to see you again. Soon. May I?"

For a long time, the wire gave no answer. At last, very faintly, as though she were thinking rather than speaking, Aliette whispered: "This isn't playing the game."

"I know that. I've tried—" He could not bring himself to finish the sentence.

"Oughtn't we to go on—trying?"

"No." Now the man could actually vision her. It was as though she were in the room. Passion—banishing hesitancy—had its way with him. "Aliette! I can't go on living if I don't see you again. I've got to see you. Soon. To-morrow. You will meet me, to-morrow, won't you! I can't bear the thought of another three days without you."

Hesitancy returned, banishing passion. "I've offended her," he thought. "She's rung off." But after an interminable silence, Aliette answered:

"Where do you want me to meet you?" Then, faint again, and very shy: "I've got—we've got—such a lot of things to say to one another. Hadn't we—hadn't I—hadn't it better be in your rooms? I could come to you to-morrow afternoon. At about five o'clock. Would that do?"

"Aliette—dear—"

Before Ronnie could collect his wits for a further reply, he heard a whispered "Good night," and the click of a replaced receiver.

Chapter VIII

1

To a certain type of mind, the woman who goes to a man's rooms is already labeled. It seems therefore necessary to explain that Aliette—when she suggested going to Ronnie's—acted on no passionate impulse, but as the result of a whole afternoon's deliberation. It was, she felt, vital that they should have speech together; and equally vital that their speech should not be disturbed. Wherefore—fastidiousness revolting alike from a clandestine appointment in Hyde Park or at her husband's house—she chose the courageous alternative.

Now, however, as she strolled quietly down Bond Street at half-past four of a sunlit Monday afternoon, Aliette did not altogether succeed in bridling the fears with which both sex and training strove to stampede her mentality.

She had to say to herself: "How absurd I am! These are the nineteen-twenties; not the eighteen-sixties. Even discovered, I run no risk of scandal." Yet scandal, she knew subconsciously, was the least of the risks she ran in going to Ronnie.

Nevertheless, go she must: even if—worst risk of all—he had misunderstood her motive. The issue between them could not be shirked any longer. Rather a desperate issue it seemed as, at the corner of Conduit Street, Aliette ran into Hector's father!

Rear-Admiral Billy, having arrived at his club two hours since, was taking his first "cruise round." The old man looked the complete Victorian in his white spats, his "Ascot" tie, his braided morning-coat and weekday topper. But his "sponge-bag" trousers were Georgian enough.

"Well met, my dear." he greeted her. "Your old father-in-law's dying for a pretty woman to pour out his tea."

She let him rumble on; accepted his compliments about her hat, her lace frock, her parasol; but refused his offer of a taxi to Ranelagh.

"I'm so sorry, Billy. But I'm going—I'm going to tea with some one else."

"That be blowed for a tale," laughed the admiral. "You're coming with me. If Ranelagh's too far, we'll make it Rumpelmayer's."

He took her arm; and she began to panic. Billy, in his "on the spree" mood, could be very persistent. A few yards on, however, they met Hermione Ellerson. She too, declared the sailor, "must have a dish of tea with an old man."

Aliette seized on the opportunity with a quick:

"Be a dear, Hermione. Take Billy to Rumpelmayer's for me."

"You'll give me strawberries and cream—whatever they cost?" pouted the ex-plaintiff in Ellerson v. Ellerson.

"Give you anything you want," rumbled Rear-Admiral Billy. "Alie's going to meet her best boy; so we'll leave her out of the party."

Aliette, on the pretext of shopping, managed an immediate riddance of the pair. Watching them walk off together, she felt rather guilty. Yet the guilt held a certain spice of pleasure, of pride. She was on a dangerous errand, taking risks. She was going—in risk's despite—to Ronnie.

Her heart began to throb in anticipation of Ronnie. Passing a mirrored window, she glanced at her reflection, and saw herself well turned-out, en beauté. The sight gave her keenest satisfaction. She walked on, no longer fearful but excited—violently, tremulously excited—till she came to Piccadilly; and turned right-handed toward St. James's Street. But the clock of St. James's Palace told her that it still lacked more than a quarter of an hour to their rendezvous.

She turned back again; stood a full minute in admiration of Rowland Ward's trophies; debated with herself whether she should drop into Fortnum & Mason's or dawdle at the book-counter in Hatchard's; decided against both schemes; lingered to examine the Harrison Fisher drawings in the display-window of "Nash's Magazine"; examined the diamond watch at her wrist; and nearly bolted down the Little Arcade into the narrow Londonishness of Jermyn Street.

Here again she felt the need for courage; felt as though the whole place—the church under the tree, and the public-house at the corner, the shops and the restaurants—held spies. The street, after broad Piccadilly, seemed furtive, sunless, a street of danger. She wanted to avert her head from the passers-by.

The Love-Story of Aliette Brunton

By the time Hector Brunton's self-possessed wife reached the dark-green Adams door of 127b Jermyn Street, she was as nervous as any other woman in the same equivocal position.

But Ronnie's name-plate, the sedateness of the house, and above all the trim gentleman—obviously a retired butler—who answered her tremulous ringing, did more than a little to restore her confidence.

"Mr. Cavendish? Mr. Cavendish is at home, madam. He is expecting guests." (Aliette could have blessed Moses Moffatt for that final "s.") "Allow me to show you the way up, madam."

She followed the restorer of confidence up two dark flights of well-carpeted stairs; and found herself on a half-landing. The white door on the half-landing was just ajar.

"Whom shall I announce, madam?" asked the trim gentleman.

Aliette hesitated the fraction of a second before replying: "Mrs. Brunton, Mrs. Hector Brunton."

Moses Moffatt opened the white door, and they passed into the hall of Ronnie's flat. Automatically Aliette noticed—and admired—the black grandfather's clock, the one engraving, the beige wall-paper. Then her cicerone knocked on polished mahogany; and a voice, Ronnie's voice, called, "Come in."

Moses Moffatt opened the second door; announced the visitor in his best style; and withdrew. They heard the click of his final exit as they faced one another—she still in the doorway, he at the tea-table by the fireplace.

For a moment, social poise deserted them both; for a moment they could only stare—brown eyes into blue, blue eyes into brown. Then, her sense of humor conquering shyness, Aliette said: "You were expecting me, weren't you?"

"It seems too good to be true." Ronnie moved across the room towards her; took the hand she proffered; and raised it to his lips. At that, she felt shy again. Confidence deserted her. If he failed in this first test; if, by one word, he betrayed misunderstanding; then, indeed, she would have irretrievably demeaned herself. But Ronnie released her hand after that one kiss; and said, very simply: "I oughtn't to have let you come."

Relieved, and a little touched at his words, Aliette let him take her bag and parasol.

"I didn't mean you to have tea for me," she said, pulling off her gloves. "Shall I pour out?"

"I'll have to boil the kettle first," he stammered, fumbling in his pocket for matches. "You'll sit here, won't you! I—I've so often imagined you sitting here and pouring out tea for me—Aliette."

"Have you—Ronnie?" Laughter dimpled her cheeks. She let him lead her to the settee by the tea-table; and sat watching his struggle with the refractory wick. "Why don't you have an electric one? They're so much easier."

"Are they?" How shy he seemed!

"Rather!" She imagined herself infinitely the more at ease. "I like this room."

"I'm so glad. It isn't my taste, you know."

"Really?" As if she hadn't guessed whose taste had chosen that beige paper, those écru velvet curtains with their flimsy lace brise-bise, the Aubusson carpet, and the plain silver tea-service on the Chippendale tray!

He did not pursue the subject; and for that reticence her heart went out in thankfulness to him. Yet, at best, his reticence could only be a temporary respite: before she left this room which his mother had furnished for him, the whole issue must be discussed. And the issue—as Aliette well knew—depended, more than on any one else, on Julia Cavendish.

Yes! The whole issue, not only as it affected themselves, but as it might affect others, must be threshed out before she left him. Only—only—this respite was very sweet. Why couldn't life be just one long tea-time! She felt so unutterably happy. A sense, almost a sensuousness, of well-being pervaded her. She wanted no more than this: to be with Ronnie; to hear his voice; to watch his lips, his eyes, his hands as they poured from silver kettle to silver pot; to answer, quietly, impersonally, his quiet impersonal questions.

She thought how boyish he looked; how unlike Hector he was in his courtesy, his delicacy. Till suddenly, watching him across the table, she grew conscious of tension in him, of passion. And on that, this business of pouring out his tea, of accepting his cakes, turned to sorriest of farces. She wanted him beside her, close to her; she wanted to hear him whisper, "Aliette, I love you"; she wanted to whisper back, "And I love you, Ronnie. I've loved you ever since that first day."

All else she had meant to say seemed positively futile.

Meanwhile, to Ronnie, it seemed incredible that he should find the courage to tell her his thoughts; incredible that this vivid, radiant creature, alone with him in the intimacy of his own dwelling-place, should be willing to listen to them. Then, without warning, thought broke to words.

"All the same, I oughtn't to have let you come."

"Why not? I—I wanted to."

"Because—" The fire in his eyes blinded her. She heard, as through the maze of sleep, steady tick-tick-tick of the clock on the mantelpiece, sizzle of the kettle-flame, the hoot and drone of traffic from the street below. She heard, as a sleeper awakened, the throb of her own heart. She felt tears, tears of sheer joy, close to her eyes.

"Because?" she whispered back.

"Because I love you. Because I can't trust myself with you. Because you're"—he was on his feet now—"because you're not mine. And I want you to be mine."

"Ronnie! Ronnie!" Still mazed, she stretched out a hand to him. He seized her hand; and pressed it to his lips, to his eyes.

"Aliette—my dearest—sweetest—I'm behaving like a cad to you. I—"

Speech died at his lips; he stood before her, tense, tongue-tied—her hand held, like a shield against her beauty, before his eyes. She knew passion kindling in her, kindling them both to madness; knew the flames of desire a-leap between them; knew the overpowering impulse to immolate herself in the flames of desire.

"My dear," he whispered, "my dear."

Then, as in a dream, she divined that the flames leaped no more, that he had mastered passion, that he had fallen to his knees, that he was covering her hand with kisses. "Forgive me," she heard, "forgive me. I'm not that sort of cad. I didn't think, just because you came to my rooms—"

"Don't, don't." Her free hand fondled his hair. "You mustn't kneel to me. Please, please—"

He rose, her hand still in his; and she drew him down beside her.

"Ronnie—" She would have looked into his eyes, but his eyes avoided her. "Ronnie, I don't want you to think, either now or ever, that it's caddish of you to—to love me. I—I need your love. I need your love more than I can ever tell you." His hand trembled at her words. "I'm very lonely, and I'm afraid—I'm afraid that I'm very weak. You're the only person in the world who can help—"

"Then—" His eyes turned to hers, and she saw hope light in them. "Then, you do love me."

"Yes. I love you." She laughed—a little strained laugh that was almost a caress. "I oughtn't to say that, I suppose."

"Oh, my dear"—now he had prisoned both her hands—"why shouldn't you say it? No—no harm shall ever come to you from me."

"I know that." Her voice grew almost inaudible. "Otherwise—I shouldn't be here."

"No harm shall ever come to you from me," he repeated—and fell silent.

They sat for a while, hand in hand, taking quiet comfort from one another, each knowing what must next be said, each fearful of being first to speak. At last, releasing her hands, Aliette braced herself to the ordeal.

"About"—fastidiousness almost overwhelmed her—"about my—my husband. You understand, don't you, that he—that he isn't my husband any more—that otherwise I would never have come to you—that, that it's been all over between him and me—for, for ever so long."

"Yes, dear. I—I understand." Very slowly, he drew her toward him. His eyes no longer blinded her; looking deep into the blue of them, she saw only a great comprehension, a great reverence. "I should have understood—even without your telling me." Very slowly, she yielded to the pull of his hands;

yielded him her lips. Very clearly she knew herself—as they swayed to one another in that first kiss—his woman.

Again, it was a while before either spoke. Then Ronnie said, speaking as simply as any boy:

"I wish I knew what was the right thing to be done. I can't give you up. Not now! Tell me, if you were free—would you marry me?"

"You know that I would." She, too, spoke simply of the things in her heart. "But I'm not free. We're neither of us free."

"You mean that—that I'll have to give you up?"

Again she braced herself. "I—I'm afraid so."

"Why?"

"Because of—" She could not yet bring herself to mention his mother. "Because of your career."

"My career!" He laughed, holding her in his arms. "As if my career had anything to do with it. I'm only a poor devil of a barrister, living on the charitable briefs of Jimmy Wilberforce. It's you, your reputation that counts, not mine."

"I can't let my love bring you harm." She withdrew from him—her eyes still suffused with happiness; her lips still quivering from his caress.

"Never mind me. It's you we have to consider. In law you're—you're still your husband's. Unless he lets you divorce him."

"He'd never do that."

"Why not? It's lawful. It's done every day."

"Even if he would—I couldn't. It wouldn't be playing the game."

"Aliette"—stubbornly, Ronnie rose to his feet,—"I—I want you so much that nothing else seems to matter. But I can't—I won't ask you to—to do the other thing. You talk about playing the game. What's the alternative? If you divorce your—your husband, he won't suffer. Nobody cares what a man does. But the other thing—the other thing's all wrong—"

His words chilled her to fear. But she knew that she must master fear—even as he had mastered passion.

"Are you—are you so sure?" said Aliette. "Can love, real love, ever be wrong?"

He turned on her bluntly, almost rudely. "Yes, the whole thing's wrong. It's wrong of me to let you come here. Wrong of me to love you." Then, his reserve breaking down: "I've tried to reason this thing out till I've grown nearly mad with it. I've always loved my profession; always thought that a lawyer's first duty was to obey the law. But now, loving you, the law doesn't seem to count. Only you count. You and your happiness. It's only you I'm thinking of, not my—my rotten career."

Once again he fell on his knees to her, protesting, incoherent; once again he took her in his arms; and kissed her, very tenderly, on her eyes, on her half-closed lips. His kisses weakened her.

"Ronnie," she whispered. "My Ronnie, I love you so."

Her whisper kindled him again to passion.

"Aliette," he said hoarsely, "Aliette, I can't give you up. I can't live without you."

For a moment she yielded herself; for a moment her lips, her hands, her whole body clung to their happiness; for a moment all her fears, all her self-torturings were stifled. Then she broke from him; and her eyes grew resolute.

"Ronnie, there's some one whom neither of us has considered—your mother."

"The old cannot stand between the young and their happiness." His eyes, too, were resolute. "We're still young, you and I. We've all our lives to live. And besides"—he weakened,—"the mater likes you."

"She'd hate me if I didn't make you give me up."

"You don't know her, dear."

"I do." It seemed to Aliette as though her lover were indeed only a boy. "I know her a thousand times better than you ever will. Mostly because I'm a woman; and a little, perhaps, because I love her son. She would hate me. And—and she'd be right."

"Nobody could hate you," he broke in. "Nobody who knew the fineness of you."

The Love-Story of Aliette Brunton

"I'm not fine." She put away the joy of his words. "I'm just a very ordinary person. There's nothing fine in me—except perhaps my love for you. And, for your sake, I mustn't let that love blind me to the truth. Can't you see what my freedom—however I won it—would mean to your mother?"

She waited for him to answer; but he sat obstinately silent—his hands clasped about his knees, his eyes on her face. She went on:

"Your mother doesn't believe in divorce. It's against her principles, her religion."

"But surely, if he lets you divorce him—"

"I could never do that. Not now. It would be just—just hypocrisy. And we can't hurt your mother. We mustn't. I don't care about myself. If I thought it were for your happiness, I'd run away with you to-night. But I'm afraid for your career. And I do care, terribly, about making hersuffer. Think of the fight she's put up, all her life, against this very thing; and then, try to think what it will mean to her, to both of you, if you, her son, her only son—"

He interrupted violently.

"She would have no right, no earthly right to interfere."

"Oh, don't, don't speak like that about her." There were tears, tears of real sorrow, in Aliette's eyes. "I can't bear it. I—I can't bear to think of coming between you. It isn't fair. She's loved you all her life. You're everything in the world to her. And then—then—oh! can't you understand—"

He strove to kiss away the tears; but her hands covered her face from his kisses. He knew himself all one weakness at thought of this hurt in Aliette. And weakening, it seemed to him as though Julia Cavendish were here in the room with them; as though he said to her: "Mater, this is my one chance of happiness. I can't let even you take it from me."

The vision passed; and he knew himself strong again. His hands parted Aliette's fingers; he kissed her on the closed eyelids, on the wet cheeks. She clung to him, tearful still. Her lips murmured:

"Life is so difficult—so terribly difficult."

He said to her: "We mustn't make it more difficult. We love each other. We must be true to love. Nothing else matters. As long as you are mine—"

"I am yours. Only yours. You don't doubt me?"

At that the last of Ronnie's scruples vanished. Fiercely, crudely, he strained her to him. "Aliette, Aliette, my own darling, don't ask me to give you up. I can't give you up! I couldn't endure life without you. Come to me! We needn't do anything mean, anything underhand. It's for your happiness—for my happiness—"

"Ronnie—Ronnie—"

Her lips were fire on his cheeks. The perfume of her was a fire in his mind. Her arms were chains, chains of fire about his body. He crushed her to him; crushed her mouth under his lips. Her whole body ached for him, ached to surrender itself. A sharp pang as of hatred went through her body: she hated him for the thing he would not do; hated herself for the longings in her body.

"You hurt me, you hurt me." With a sharp cry she broke herself loose from him. "I thought I was so strong. And I'm weak—clay in your hands."

She stood up, trembling; feeling herself all disheveled, abased.

The flame under the kettle had gone out. The tea had gone cold in their half-empty cups. The street below still hooted and droned with traffic. The clock still ticked from the mantelpiece.

"I ought to be going," she said, eying the clock.

"Yes." He, too, had risen: he, too, was trembling. "You ought to be going. It's nearly half-past six. But you'll come to me again. You'll come again—Aliette."

He found her gloves, her bag and parasol. Taking them, she knew that her hands had lost their coolness; little pearls of emotion moistened either palm. Her face, seen in the mirror over the mantelpiece, looked strangely flushed—different. For the flash of a second, her fastidiousness was in revulsion.

"You'll come again—soon?" he repeated.

"I don't know." Revulsion passed; but her hands, straightening her hat, shook as though in self-disdain. "Somehow, it doesn't seem fair—on either of us."

"But you must." His voice thrilled. "You must. We can't leave things like this—undecided."

Self-possessed once more, she faced him. "Don't try to hurry me, Ronnie. We've talked too much this afternoon. My brain's weary. I can't decide anything. I thought that, being with you, things would be easier. They're not. They're more difficult. You must give me time—"

"Then"—his voice saddened—"I haven't been any help to you?"

A laugh rose in her throat, dimpling it. "I'm afraid we're neither of us very wise; but"—she offered him her ungloved hand—"it's been very sweet, being with you. That's why—you haven't helped me very much."

Silently, hating that she must go, he released her fingers. She was all a wonder to his eyes, all a riddle to his brain. He wanted to say: "But you mustn't go. You're mine, mine. I don't care a damn for your husband, for my career, for my mother, for the law. Stay with me. Stay with me to-night."

Actually, he forebore even to kiss her good-by!

3

Aliette had been gone an hour. . . .

Moses Moffatt came in. Moses Moffatt cleared away the tea-things. Moses Moffatt asked: "Will you be dining at home, sir?" Some one answered, "No!" Moses Moffatt went out.

Aliette had been gone two whole hours. The some one became Ronald Cavendish.

He found that he must have been smoking cigarettes—one cigarette after the other. Ash and paper smoldered on the silver tray at his side. The room stank of tobacco. But tobacco could not drive away that other perfume—the perfume of Aliette's womanhood.

She had been in this very room! The essence of her still pervaded every nook of it. His imagination conjured up the image of her: Aliette dimpling to laughter: Aliette's brown eyes, now bright with joy, now dimmed with tears: the vivid of Aliette's hair: the little gestures of Aliette's hands. All these he saw, and possessed again in memory.

Again she lay in his arms. Again she let him kiss the tears from her eyes. Again she yielded him her hands, her hair. But she had yielded him more than these; she had yielded him her very thoughts: she had said, "I'm very weak; you're the only person who can help me."

Remembering those words, he grew ashamed. He must not think for himself: he must think for her. She had said that she would marry him if she were free. But there was only one way to freedom—unless Brunton let her divorce him. And that alternative she had refused to contemplate.

No! There was only one path to her freedom, to their happiness—the path of scandal. Dared he demand that sacrifice from her?

After all, why not? The scandal would be short-lived—the happiness enduring. She was Brunton's merely in name. She had no children. Legally, they might have to put themselves in the wrong; but morally they would be justified. Between them and happiness stood only the shibboleths.

Nevertheless, the shibboleths mattered. Shibboleths were the basis of all society.

Certain people, too—people like his mother,—hated divorce, believed it wicked. His mother still clung to the old faith. His mother would say: "God joined Aliette and Hector in holy matrimony. You have no right to sunder God's joining."

As though humanity were any deity's stud-farm!

Chapter IX

1

By that strange perversity which is peculiar to loving womanhood, Aliette's first thoughts—as the taxi rattled her away from Jermyn Street—were for her husband.

For the second time in three years her mood relented. "Poor Hector!" she thought. "He'll be home when I get back. It isn't much of a home for him—ours."

Yet, even relenting, she knew that she could never forgive. The physical Hector was dead, killed by her knowledge of his infidelities—as dead to her as the physical Ronnie was alive.

Then she forgot Hector, remembered only Ronnie. Her memory thrilled to his caresses. She began to yearn for him with a bodily yearning so acute that—had he been beside her in the taxi—she would have thrown her arms round his neck.

Her mind whirled. This way. That way. She, Aliette Brunton, who had always thought "that sort of thing" the prerogative of shop-girls and chorus-ladies, was yearning, physically, for a man. It was all wrong. She should never have gone to his rooms. They must part. She would never be parted from him. He ought never to have made love to her. She would have died if he had not made love to her!

She tried to blame herself for her weakness; she tried to think: "I made no struggle. I yielded everything. I virtually threw myself at his head. I should have been strong. I should have denied him my hands, my lips." But her heart refused to be blamed; her heart said: "He loves you. You love him. Nothing else matters."

The taxi swung into Bayswater Road; and instinctively Aliette opened her vanity-bag. Glancing at her face in the mirrored lid, she remembered Hector again. Hector mustn't see her as Ronnie had seen her. Hector mustn't find out!

Once more, she felt abased. Once more her fastidiousness revolted—this time from concealment. The commonplace impulse—to confess—appeared, disappeared. What was there to confess? Nothing!

Nevertheless, paying her driver, mounting the pillared door-step, ringing as she let herself into the square tessellated hall, Aliette felt guilty. In thought, if not in act, she was little better than the husband whom Lennard, appearing from his lower regions, announced to be in the library.

Caroline Staley joined Lennard in the hall. Aliette handed her gloves, her bag and parasol to the maid; asked Lennard the time; heard it was a quarter past seven; hesitated the fraction of a second; and pushed open the library door.

Hector sat in his big leather armchair by the bow-window—the "Evening Standard" on his knees, and a glass of whisky and water at his elbow. His gray eyes lit pleasurably at sight of her. As he came across the room with a smiled "My dear, how well you're looking," Aliette realized with the shock of a sudden revelation the cruelty latent in those thin lips.

(She was looking well, thought Hector; her very best. This evening, that subtle incomprehensible process, process alike mental and physical, which he had divined at work in her for so long, seemed to have attained its completion. Her very complexion showed it.)

"Am I?" she answered.

He gave her the cheek-kiss of connubial compromise; and she schooled herself not to shudder. "This is the price I must pay," she thought, "for those other kisses."

The front-door bell rang; and, a minute afterwards, Mollie rustled in.

"Hello, Hector," said Mollie. "So you've got back."

The girl's eyes were all luminous, subtly afire with happiness. Kissing Aliette, she whispered, "I must talk to you."

To Brunton, watching the sisters go arm in arm through the door, came a sharp pang of sex-consciousness. As Aliette, so Mollie: from each there radiated that same incomprehensible aura of physical and mental completion. The aura excited Brunton, stimulated him, roused his imagination almost to mania. All the way home in the car—and usually the car distracted him—he had been thinking of his wife, goading his mind with the mirage of the past. Now the prongs of the goad penetrated through the mind to the very flesh.

He poured himself another drink, and stood for a long while in contemplation of a photograph on his desk; a photograph of Aliette, taken just before they became engaged. He remembered how then, as always, her fastidiousness had lured him; how then, as now, he had ached to conquer her fastidiousness, to make her desires one with his own. And always, from the very outset to this very day, he had failed. Against the refinement in her, even when she yielded, his will to sex-mastery beat in vain; till finally there came the break.

The break, as Hector saw it, had been of her making. The things he most desired of her, the unfastidious intimacies, she either could not or would not endure. Those intimacies she had driven him elsewhere to seek. And he had sought them for three years; sought them, he now realized, without assuaging his desire.

Dressing for dinner, he heard—from the room she had barred against him—his wife's voice. His wife and her sister were talking, talking. The incomprehensible talk maddened Hector, even as the incomprehensible physical aura of them had maddened him. Surely—surely it was high time to put an end to this—this nonsensical chastity.

2

Her sister's dressing-hour confidences seemed to Aliette the final complication. Mollie had met James Wilberforce, by accident, in Bond Street. Although too late for tea, he had insisted on her eating an ice at Rumpelmayer's. At Rumpelmayer's they ran into the admiral and Hermione. The admiral had spoken of his meeting with Alie.

"Where did you have tea?" asked the girl.

"Never mind about my tea," retorted her sister. "Tell me *your* news."

Whereupon Mollie, not in the least hesitantly, told it. Jimmy had asked her to marry him! That is to say, he had spoken about marriage in such a way as to leave no doubt about his intention to propose. That was one of the admirable things about Jimmy. He never beat around the bush. She, of course, had "choked him off." Jimmy must be taught that these things couldn't be fixed up over an ice in a tea-shop.

"Still," concluded the modern young, "I'm very fond of James. The chances are that I shall marry him in the autumn."

"And James Wilberforce," thought Aliette, as she went down to dinner, "is just the person whose wife's family must be *sans reproche!*"

Dinner completed her mental *bouleversement*. Hector she divined even before they sat down—was in a difficult mood. Hector insisted on champagne, insisted on their sharing it. He grew boisterous on the first glass. "They would have a cheery evening," said Hector. "They would get the car round after dinner, and drive to Roehampton." But on Aliette's suggesting that he and Mollie should go alone, he dropped both the scheme and his pose of boisterousness. Catching the look in his eyes, she began to be frightened.

Only twice before—once after her first discovery of his infidelities, and once a year later—had Aliette seen that particular look in Hector's eyes. It betokened contest. Not the casual entreaties of recent months, but contest—contest almost physical! Formerly, though resenting the indignity of such a contest, she had never dreaded it. But to-night—to-night was different.

When Lennard brought in the port, Hector refused to be left alone. They stayed with him while he drank two glasses; and again, watching him, Aliette's mood relented. The look in his eyes had grown soft, almost pleading. "Poor old Hector," she thought; "so many women could have given him all that he requires from a wife. Only I—I can't. I'm Ronnie's—Ronnie's."

Once more her mind whirled. This way. That way. Guilt, fear, love, uncertainty drove the wheels of her mind.

Yet both mind and body possessed one certainty: that the physical Hector had died three years since.

3

It was late, nearly midnight; but Mollie still sat strumming on the piano in the big balconied drawing-room.

The Love-Story of Aliette Brunton

Ever since dinner began the girl had been conscious of domestic tension. She could see, over the shining instrument, that neither husband nor wife listened to the music. They sat, either side the fireplace, avoiding speech, avoiding each other's eyes.

Occasionally, when he thought himself unobserved, Hector would glance at Alie. Mollie knew, of course, that Alie didn't get on very well with Hector. On more than one of her visits to them there had been such periods of tension. But this—to the girl's intuition—seemed far more serious, far nearer definite crisis than anything before. Somehow the situation frightened her; somehow she felt averse to leaving Alie alone with Hector. All the same, one couldn't go on playing ragtimes till dawn.

Mollie fired a final rafale on the bass keys, and closed the piano.

"I'm going to bed," she announced. "You too, Alie?"

"Not just yet." Aliette kissed her sister good night. During the last two hours her relenting mood had almost evaporated under the fire of Hector's covert glances. Her mind no longer whirled. She knew now—definitely—that contest between them was unavoidable; and, though she still dreaded it, her courage refused to postpone the ordeal.

The door closed behind Mollie; and, after a moment's hesitancy, Hector leaned forward from his chair. Aliette saw that there were pearls of sweat on his forehead. His hands gripped the blue grapes of the cretonne chair-cover as though he would squeeze them dry.

"I'm glad she's gone to bed," he said hoarsely.

"Are you? Why?"

"Because it's time that you and I had things out with one another."

"What things?" Her voice sounded a little shy, but she no longer averted her eyes. They met his—brown cold and resolute, against gray kindling to passion.

"Everything. Aliette," he began to plead with her, "we can't go on like this for ever."

"Why not?"

"Because the whole position's intolerable. Either you're my wife, or you're

110

not. I—I can't stand this sort of life."

"What sort of life?"

"You know perfectly well what I mean. Aliette," he pleaded again, "can't we make a fresh start—to-night?"

She felt her whole heart turning icy to him as she answered: "We threshed that matter out a very long time ago. I can see no use in referring to it again."

"Possibly you can't." Hector rose. Her very aloofness urged him, despite better judgment, to immediate mastery. "But you're not the only one to be considered. As your husband, I have certain rights."

"If you have, I shouldn't advise you to try and enforce them."

The words sounded calm enough; but there was no calm in Aliette's heart. Suddenly she grew conscious that the sense of rectitude which had sustained her for three years sustained her no longer. In thought she had descended to her husband's level. Her cheeks flushed.

"Why shouldn't I enforce them?" The flush did not escape his eye. Perhaps, after all, she was no different from other women, from the women who liked one to be forceful. He made a movement towards her. "Why shouldn't I enforce them?" he repeated.

"Because you have no rights." Even his blurred judgment knew better than to touch her. "Because you forfeited them—three years ago."

"That old affair," he muttered sullenly; and drew away from where she sat. Then, excusing himself, "Reneé's in Australia. She's been in Australia two years. I paid her passage—"

Proudly, coldly, Aliette answered him back: "I hope you do not discuss your wife with your mistresses in the same way that you discuss your mistresses with your wife."

The cold pride weakened him. "You're very harsh. I made a mistake—three years ago. I admitted it at the time. I admit it once more. I've made—other mistakes. But that's all over. You're a woman, a well-bred woman. You can't understand these things."

Three days since she would not have understood; now, understanding a little, she relented again.

"Hector—I'm very sorry. But it's—it's impossible."

He came toward her again; bent down, and tried to take her hand. She drew it away from him. The overwhelming physical hunger of his eyes worried her. His feet, on the white rug, showed suddenly enormous, grotesque—grotesque as his affection.

"Why is it impossible?"

She thought how often she had asked herself that same question; knew that—in Ronnie's arms—she had at last found the answer; knew that she must lie. And she hated lying. Yet more than lying she hated the knowledge that her body, which had lain in Ronnie's arms, should be cause of that overwhelming hunger in Hector's eyes.

She said quietly, "Must we go over all this old ground again?" And since he did not answer: "It does no good. I don't want to hurt you more than I can help. Won't you just leave things as they are? Won't you believe me when I tell you that it's just—impossible?"

His legal mind, suddenly active, caught at the pleading note in her voice; fastened on it. "You're very solicitous, apparently, about my feelings?"

For a second, wondering if he could suspect, she grew fearful. Then, putting away fear, she rose and faced him. The flush had gone from her cheeks; her eyes—aloof, impersonal—told him the utter hopelessness of his cause. And with that knowledge came suspicion—a suspicion formless as the first shadow-haze of storm in a brazen sky.

"I don't wish to hurt you," she reiterated. "But the thing you ask is out of the question; and will always be out of the question. Even the discussion of it offends me."

He took a step towards her; but she did not recoil.

"Aliette—do you realize the meaning of what you've just said?"

"Perfectly." Her eyes met his, beat them down.

"And what do you expect me to do under the circumstances?" Again suspicion came to him; and with suspicion, anger at his own impotence. "You're not a child. You know perfectly well what happens to a man whose wife refuses to live with him. I've never pretended to be a saint: I've left that

Gilbert Frankau

to you."

"Hector!" Temper clenched her fingers. Her whole fastidiousness revolted against the man, against the topic he would not relinquish.

"I'm sorry if you're shocked"—all his cruelty wanted to shock her, to see her fastidiousness in degradation—"but I'm trying to tell you the truth—just for a change. If you persist in your saintliness, there's only one course open to me. Another Reneé! A man can't live without a woman. It isn't fair to his nature. It isn't healthy."

"Healthy!" she burst out.

"Yes. Healthy. Does that upset you?"

Her eyes blazed as she answered: "How dare you talk to me like that? How dare you? Healthy! I suppose that was your idea when you married me. You took me—medicinally."

"Aliette!" Her fury cowed the cruelty in him. "I married you because I loved you. I love you still."

"Love!" Her cheeks kindled. Caution was ripped loose from her as a sail is ripped loose by the wind. The shreds of it flapped against her mind, infuriating her. That this man who might have been father of her children should cloak his lusts with that divine word, seemed the ultimate defilement. "Love!" Her breasts heaved. "Don't talk to me of love. Talk of your rights, of your health, if you like; but spare me the degradation of what it pleases you to call your love."

At that, definitely, the lawyer in Brunton suspected. Black thoughts drove and drove, thunder-cloud-like, across the sky of his mind; and through the rifts in those thunder-clouds his mind saw two visions—his wife, infernally desirable, infernally distant from the reach of his desires, and a woman to be probed, a hostile witness for cross-examination.

"You speak as though you were an authority on the subject," he sneered; and, as she deigned no answer, "a saintly authority."

"You're insolent." The last shred of her caution parted. "Insolent."

"Perhaps"—his voice dropped two full tones—"I have the right to be insolent."

113

"Explain yourself, please."

He came so close to her that she could see every pore in the skin of his face. "I should hardly have thought an explanation necessary. I said, 'Perhaps I have the right to be insolent.' It is for you to explain why"—his lips worked—"you regard 'what I am pleased to call my love for you' as a degradation."

"And if I refuse to explain?"

"There is only one conclusion to be drawn."

"And that is?" she dared him.

Abruptly, Brunton the lawyer became Brunton the husband. He no longer wanted to cross-examine; he wanted to possess—to possess this woman. Why should he not possess her? She was as much his as the furniture in his home, the books in his chambers. By law and by religion, she owed him her body. He had always been chivalrous to her; he had always tried to fall in with her whimsies, to be kind. She had never been kind. All she had tried to do was to hurt him.

"And that conclusion is?" she flung at him.

God! How much she could hurt him. God! How he wished to spare himself. He wanted her so; his whole body ached for her little hands, for her lips, for the touch of her hair. Why should she thus goad him? Even if—even if she had cared—virtuous women did care sometimes, platonically of course—for somebody else, he could forgive her.

He did not want, even, to forgive. He only wanted to know nothing. He only wanted her to be kind to him, to let him love her—in his own way. Without all this—all this fuss.

But her eyes refused him kindness; her lips demanded their answer. She maddened him with her rigid lips, with her blank unfriendly scrutiny.

"Your conclusion, please, Hector?"

"Since you insist," the words seemed torn from the man's throat, "the conclusion I draw is that—you're in love with somebody else."

He had expected indignation, furious abuse, furious denial; anything but the deadly calmness with which she answered: "And supposing there were somebody else? What right would you have to object?"

Aliette saw Hector recoil as though she had struck him; saw rage, incredulity, fear, apprehension, chase in scarlet chaos across his face. His thin lips writhed—as though in torment. But she could feel no pity for his torment. In her eyes, he was the beast, the defiling beast: defeated, he yet stood, shifty on those great feet of his, between her and happiness, between her and her chance of motherhood, between her and—Ronnie.

"Well," she shot at him, "what right would you have to object?"

"I should have the right," he stammered, "the right that any husband possesses. But you're not serious. For God's sake, tell me you're not serious. I haven't been such a bad husband to you. I haven't deserved this—"

Suddenly she remembered Ronnie's words: "Unless he lets you divorce him. Why not? It's done every day." Suddenly she remembered Hector's own words, the speech he had insisted she should read after the Ellerson case.

"You're not serious," he challenged.

"I'm perfectly serious. Please answer my question. And before you answer it, let me remind you of something you said in public not more than a fortnight ago. You said: 'A woman on marriage does not become her husband's property.' I want to know if you still abide by that question."

"And I"—rage mastered the apprehension in him—"I want to know, definitely, if there is anybody else."

Her lips pursed to silence. She could almost see Ronnie—and her silence was all for him. For herself she had no fear, only the violent instinct to be free, to be free at any cost, from Hector Brunton.

"Answer me!" He almost shouted at her.

Quietly, she answered, "There is nobody else—in the way you mean."

"Will you swear?"

"You have my word. If that's not enough for you—"

The unfinished sentence tortured him. He saw himself alive, tormented; her as a statue of fate, unmoving, cold by his cold fireside. If only she would make some movement—not stand there like a statue: her lips rigid, her hands taut, every line of her body tense under the frozen draperies.

"I don't doubt your word," he said sullenly.

"Then answer my question. Do you regard me as your property or not? If I asked you for my freedom, would you give it to me?"

"You mean—let you divorce me?"

For a moment, aware of hypocrisy, Aliette hesitated. Then she said, "Yes."

"On what grounds?"

"Your infidelities."

"My infidelities!" He laughed, his legal mind seeing the whole strength of his position. "You have no proof of them. And even if you had, infidelity by itself is no ground for divorce. Besides"—his cruelty could not forbear the blow—"you've condoned them."

"Condoned them! I?"

"Yes. You. By not leaving my house. By continuing to live with me."

"That's untrue. I've never lived with you, since—since I found out."

"You'll never make the world believe that."

"What do I care about the world?"

"Aliette"—for the last time he forced himself to plead with her,—"think of my position, our position. Even if it were legally possible, you wouldn't ask me—"

He continued to plead till he felt utterly worn out, utterly beaten; till it seemed to him that he had been arguing with her—arguing uselessly—for hours. And all the time he argued, one thought nagged at him: "There is somebody else. There must be somebody else. I must find out who he is."

"Then you refuse," she was saying. "You refuse me my freedom. You go back on your own words."

She, too, felt worn out. She could not even hate the man, because she had no right to hate him. At least—Mollie's words about James Wilberforce came into her weary mind—Hector had not beaten around the bush. He had been straight-forward enough; whereas she—she was not being straight-forward, was not playing the game. But the instinct to be free did not abate its violence.

"Very well"—the cross-examiner in Brunton urged him to the playing of his last card,—"I won't go back on my words. I'll admit the justice of everything you've said. You shall have your freedom." Her eyes lit; and his suspicion became certainty. "I'll arrange everything. There need be very little scandal; only the usual fake—a suit for restitution of your conjugal rights. You'll get an order of the court, an order for me to return to you. You needn't worry, I sha'n't comply with it. After that—"

He broke off, watching her. Her face had softened, renewed its coloring. Yet she was nervous. She fidgeted ever so slightly, first on one white-shod foot, than on the other.

"But before I consent, there's one condition I must make; one question I must ask you." His voice grew stern, became the voice of the K.C. "Before I take any steps in this matter, I must have your assurance, your definite assurance, that you are not asking for your freedom with a view—with a view"—he hesitated—"to marrying any one else."

The blood ebbed from Aliette's cheeks: it seemed to her that her heart had stopped beating. This was the test! One downright lie—and she might win to freedom. That issue she saw clearly. But she saw another issue—the issue between herself and Ronnie. Even though Ronnie himself had suggested that she should divorce Hector, his suggestion—she knew—had implied telling Hector the truth. Surely Ronnie would be the first to reject freedom won at such a price.

And, "I've got to play the game," cried the soul of Aliette; "otherwise, even my love for Ronnie becomes a degradation." Yet, still, instinct cried in her for freedom.

The decisive seconds lengthened; lengthened; stretched, taut as piano-wire, into the eternities. The scene imprinted itself, sharper than sharpest snapshot, on unfading memory. Always, burnt into memory, would remain Hector, his sandy hair awry, his thin lips parted under the bulbous nose, his jowl set; would remain herself, torture-pale on the rack of indetermination; would remain the light white room, blazing with electrics, the stripes of its wall-paper upright as prison bars. No freedom from that prison—save at the price of truth!

But at last, truth spoke.

"I cannot give you that assurance, Hector," said Hector's wife.

About her, the snapshotted scene trembled, shivered and broke to whirling fragments. She was conscious of Hector's hands, itching to take her by the throat, of Hector's feet, of the red fury in Hector's eyes. His hands itched to strike her. If he struck, she would strike back—madly, through those whirling fragments.

But Brunton could not strike; he could not even speak. The insanity of balked desire dumbed his mouth as it numbed his limbs. Nature, fighting like a wild beast, wrenched at the cage of his self-control. He could hear nature wrenching ape-like at his ribs, howling to him: "Kill! Kill both! Kill both the man and the woman!" The blood-lust and the sex-lust were knives in his loins.

"You!" he stammered. "You, you—" Then his hands ceased their itching, and the red in his eyes flickered out, smoldering to gray.

*

She heard his great feet go creaking across the room, creaking through the doorway, creaking up the staircase. She heard the slam of an upstairs door. She heard herself whisper to the wide-eyed distraught woman who peered out from the mirror over the mantelpiece: "That leaves only one way—only one way to freedom."

Chapter X

1

The "grand passion" (it is unfortunate that no single word in the English language exactly pictures that emotional process) was a little beyond Caroline Staley's philosophy.

Yet within twelve hours of Aliette's interview with Hector, even Caroline Staley realized that "Miss Aliette was about through with that husband of hers." Lennard and the rest of the staff—though Caroline refused to gossip—were also aware, basement-wise, of the connubial position. In fact, at Lancaster Gate, only Mollie remained in ignorance.

For, at the moment, Mollie Fullerford was far too absorbed to bother herself overlong about either sister or brother-in-law; a sublime selfishness held her aloof from both.

The girl's mind was concentrated on Jimmy. It had become a point of honor with her not to think of anybody except Jimmy. Jimmy—for his own sake—must be neither "fascinated" nor "put off." He must be given his exact measure of attraction as of repulsion, his exact chance of finding out her faults as well as her virtues. Then, when he had definitely fallen in or out of love with the real her—she would decide exactly how much she could love the real him. "Marriage," the girl said to herself, "is a pretty serious business. Jimmy and I mustn't make any mistake about it."

Mollie Fullerford, you see, was of the modern young, who are trying, vainly, to avoid the troubles of their romantic and unreasoning elders—such troubles, for instance, as Hector's.

Hector, reticent always, confided his troubles to nobody. He spent the first twelve hours after the quarrel in kicking himself for a fool and a savage who had nearly thrashed his wife; the next twelve in cursing himself for a fool and a softy who ought to have thrashed his wife—and the rest of the week fighting against the impulse to apologize.

Meanwhile he was a stranger in his own house; excluded, as surely as though he had been a servant under notice, from domestic conversation. His wife had taken to breakfasting in bed (the rattle of the tray infuriated him every morning), and refused to get up till he had left the house: he, retorting in the only way open to him, dined at his clubs. On the one occasion when they did meet, her manners were beyond criticism—and her unattainable beauty a positive bar to any plans for sex-consolation.

As a matter of psychological fact, both husband and wife were in a momentary state of complete sex-revulsion. Hector, thwarted of his one desire, seeing Aliette unobtainable as the only woman in the world; and Aliette—love's dream obscured by thought of love's material consequences—regarding herself, for the nonce, as the mere quarry of two males, a quarry anxious only to escape both pursuers.

Twice, at least, Aliette's thoughts renounced womanhood completely. The physical Hector, the Hector of the writhing lips, she hated; but when her yearning for the physical Ronnie grew so desperately acute that she had to rush out of the library lest she should telephone to him; when every post which brought no letter seemed the last bodily hurt she could endure: then, looking back on her lost virginity of temperament, she could be amazingly sorry for, amazingly grateful to the abstemious Hector of the last three years.

Yet all the time, she knew subconsciously that she loved Ronnie; that, without him, life was one mazed loneliness.

Aliette, like Hector, kept her own counsel. Mary O'Riordan, to whom—as in duty bound—she confided a hint of her distress, pumped her for full confession, but pumped in vain. Only Ponto, the huge harlequin Dane with the magpie coat and the princely manners, shared her mazed loneliness. She used to fetch the dog, every after-lunch-time, from the garage in Westbourne Street where he had his abode; and wander with him by the hour together through Hyde Park and Kensington Gardens. Ponto, unlike her other pursuers, desired nothing but an occasional caress. He would pad and pad after her, close to heel, disdainful of all distractions, his eyes on the hem of her skirt, his stern slapping only the mildest disapproval of an occasional fly. And when she sat her down to meditate, the beast—as though conscious of the fret in his mistress—would content affection with the rare up-thrust of an enormous consolatory paw.

Vaguely during that week Ponto's mistress conceived the scheme of sending to Moor Park for Miracle, of condescending to ride in the Row. Dumb animals, of a sudden, seemed so much wiser, so much kinder than men. But to ride in the Row would make one conspicuous, and instinct warned her that the less conspicuous she made herself during the season, the easier things might be—in the event of a social crash.

2

One other woman in London—during the days which followed Aliette's definite break with Hector—was meditating the probabilities of a social crash.

"Julia," said Dot Fancourt, dropping in to lunch on Friday, "you're not looking so well. You ought to see Baynet again. You've nothing on your mind, have you?"

"My dear Dot," retorted the novelist, smiling, "I'm quite well, and I have nothing on what you are pleased to call my mind—except the vulgarity of your methods in booming my divorce article."

But after Dot had gone back to his office, Julia Cavendish's face lost its smile.

Surveyed in cool retrospect, her momentary thought-panic in Hyde Park appeared a mere firework of the literary imagination. Nevertheless, ever since Sunday, when she had tried, over dinner, to let him inkle her knowledge, to warn him, she had been reproaching herself about Ronnie. Other mothers—her own sister Clementina among them—did not apparently find it at all difficult to discuss sex matters with their sons. Yet she, the celebrated psychologist, had found it impossible.

"If only I could have been open with him," she thought, "if only I could have said: 'I'm afraid that you've fallen in love with that charming Mrs. Brunton. You won't let it go too far—will you? Women's heads are so easily turned.'"

She would not, of course, have said more than that. Ronnie was so sensible, so straight and clean, that he would have needed no further warning. Ronnie—her Ronnie—did not in the least resemble the heroes of her

121

novels, the passionate men with cleft chins who occasionally counted the world well lost for love. Ronnie was the very spit of his father, the Oxford don.

Still even dons were human. And Ronnie, unwarned, might have lost his head.

As for the woman—women, according to Julia Cavendish, could always fall prey to the sentimental impulse. If only a man were sufficiently ardent the entire sex yielded to him. Why should this Mrs. Brunton be the exception? Ronnie—her Ronnie—must be terribly attractive. Therefore—

And quite suddenly, Julia panicked again. Her literary imagination saw the worst; Aliette in Ronnie's arms, Ronnie in the divorce court. Her heart went cold at the imaginary prospect. The mother, the religious woman, and the Victorian in her were alike appalled.

Jealousy spread a yellow jaundice film over her intellect. Seen through that film, the "charming Mrs. Brunton" became a harpy, an over-dressed, over-scented, over-manicured harpy, her unguented claws sharp for an innocent boy.

Whereupon Julia Cavendish—turning, as most literary people in a crisis, to her pen—began the composition of a letter which should convey, tactfully, of course, the picture of the harpy to the mind of the boy. But the letter, completed, read so much more like a piece of fiction than a statement of fact, that she tore it up; and contented herself with the usual note ordering him to dinner on Saturday.

3

The note itself contained nothing to alarm Ronnie; and yet, dressing to obey its commands in his severe mannish bedroom, he felt nervous about the coming interview. For five days now he had been on edge; sleepless, unable to concentrate thought.

Every night he had expected that Aliette would telephone; every morning, every evening, he had expected a letter from her. It never dawned on his mind that she should be equally on edge, equally expectant. Since she had admitted her love, asking only that he should not hurry her, chivalry forbade the obvious course which his impatient manhood dictated—attack. Chivalry, too, urged him not to make any final move before weighing the uttermost consequences.

For himself, he had already weighed them; and they weighed light enough. But for her, even though a man and a woman decided their love justified before God and the law, remained always their justification before their fellow-creatures. Under any circumstances, the consequences would include a divorce. And even the farcical divorce of the period carried—for a woman in Aliette's position—its stigma. Ronnie remembered the Carrington case. Suppose Brunton cut up rough; perjured himself in court as Carrington had done—purely for spite. In an undefended divorce case, the man and woman cited could not defend themselves against a perjurer without risking their freedom.

And then, then—there was Julia to consider.

The mind of the clean-shaven man who let himself out of the dark-green door of 127b Jermyn Street, and strode rapidly across Piccadilly, may be compared to the hair-trigger of a cocked pistol.

4

"Your mother is already in the dining-room, Mr. Ronald," said the uniformed parlormaid, who had valeted him while he was still at Winchester.

"Thank you, Kate." Ronnie handed the woman his hat and strode in.

Julia stood by the be-ferned fireplace, inspecting a newly-acquired print, only that afternoon hung. Kissing him, she called his attention to the treasure.

"It's 'The Match-Seller'—a proof before letters. Only two more to find, and my collection of 'The Cries of London' will be complete."

They talked prints, engravings and china throughout dinner. Julia, acting on Sir Heron Baynet's advice, ate sparingly, and drank nothing stronger than Evian water; but for her son she had ordered a miniature feast—all the particular foods of his particular boyhood—and the last bottle of his father's

Chambertin.

Usually, when she prepared such a feast, Ronnie would compliment her on her memory, her forethought; but to-night he seemed scarcely aware of what he ate. She had to coax him: "Turbot, dear, your favorite fish," or, "I remembered the *sauce Béarnaise*, you see."

Coaxed, he complimented her; but without enthusiasm—so that, hurt, she said to herself: "He's giving me only half his mind. He's thinking of that woman. I'm certain he'd rather be dining her at Claridge's"—(Julia's heroes often "dined" their discreetly illicit passions at the more expensive caravanserais)—"than sitting here with his old mother."

Meanwhile he said to himself, "She's taken so much trouble over this little dinner. I ought to be more grateful. Dash it, I am grateful! Good Lord, it's nearly nine o'clock! The last post will be in soon. Perhaps there'll be a letter. Perhaps Aliette will telephone to-night. I must get away by ten."

Resultantly, by the time Kate brought coffee and cigarettes, the moment for confidences was as unpropitious as any Julia Cavendish could possibly have chosen.

"Ronnie," she, began, as soon as they were alone, "I hope you won't be angry at what I'm going to say."

The opening, so entirely foreign to her usual abruptness, made Ronnie—on the instant—suspicious. The Wixton imagination in him said: "Danger! She's found out. She knows something about Aliette. She may know about Aliette's having been to your rooms." And immediately the magisterial Cavendish in him decided: "I shall refuse to be drawn. It's not her business. Even if she does know, she ought to have waited till I thought fit to broach the subject."

Nevertheless, the ghost of the schoolboy who had liked *sauce Béarnaise* and been vaguely frightened of his mother was in a funk. The ghost of the schoolboy, looking at his mother's determined chin, did not see the unhappiness behind his mother's blue eyes.

After a second's hesitation, the magisterial Cavendish laughed.

"It depends on what you are going to say, mater."

124

"It isn't much." Julia braced herself to the unpleasant task. "Perhaps it isn't anything at all. But I feel that you're keeping something from me. Something rather—important. Something that's making you unhappy. Can't you confide in me? I might be able to help. We've never had any secrets from each other, you and I."

Kate, coming in to clear the table, was shooed away with a calm "We haven't quite finished our coffee. I'll ring when I want you."

"We oughtn't to have secrets from one another," went on Julia diffidently.

Her son, stiff-lipped, uncompromising, made no answer; and she continued, a little afraid:

"You told me about Lucy. Can't you tell me about this—love affair?"

The tone irritated him.

"My dear mater, what love affair?"

"Flirtation, then?" Fleetingly, her suspicions lulled by his presence, she thought how ridiculous it was of him to be so stubborn. Dot Fancourt, Paul Flower, and many other of the literary among her acquaintances rather liked talking about their flirtations. Then his very stubbornness perturbed her.

"Ronnie," she said, "be open with me. You *are* in love?"

"What if I am?" He had never lied to her, and had no intention of doing so now. Apparently she did not know about Aliette's having been to Jermyn Street; otherwise—reticence with him not being one of her characteristics—she would have said so. Obviously, though, she suspected quite enough!

"What if I am?" he repeated.

"You mean—it's not my business?" she faltered.

"Yes. I do mean that. I don't want to be unkind, or unfair. But you must see that I can't discuss—that sort of thing with you."

"Why not?" Thoroughly alarmed now, she tried to hide alarm with a smile. "Lots of people do confide in me. I—you know I wouldn't betray your confidence."

"Is that quite the point?"

Julia Cavendish deigned to plead: "I've been so worried, Ronnie. I feel, somehow, that you're in trouble. I feel I understand why. And I only want you to let me help you."

His mood softened. "Poor old mater," he thought. But her next words dispelled softness; irritated him again.

"You see," she said, "you're still so young. Only a boy really. You don't know the world as I know it. You mustn't reject my advice."

"I'm thirty-six," he parried.

"And I'm over sixty."

"You don't look it, mater."

She felt herself being edged away from her topic. She saw a vision of Aliette Brunton—standing palpably between herself and her son. Vague jealousy clouded her love, her kindness.

"You don't deny the correctness of my statement," she shot at him. "You admit that you are in love?"

"Suppose I admit that much—" His lean face flushed.

"Then the least you can do is to tell me with whom. You say you don't want to be unkind or unfair. Is it fair, or kind, to let me"—Julia hesitated over the word—"suspect things?"

He said bluntly, "There is nothing to suspect."

She said with equal bluntness, "Then why am I not to be told?"

Ronnie's temper rose. He, too, saw a vision of Aliette, palpably demanding his protection.

"Because there's nothing to tell."

"Ronnie, that's not the truth." The words burst from her. "You've never lied to me before. Why can't you tell me the truth now? Ever since Sunday, I've known—"

"Known what?"

Her heart dropped a beat at his obvious anger. It was as though she already knew the worst. Love and jealousy, strangely commingling in her ego, ousted—for one flash of a second—all other emotions. So that it might have been an adoring wife rather than a religious mother who answered.

"That you and Mrs. Brunton were in love with each other."

"So she knew all the time," thought Ronnie. His first feeling was relief. At least the mater knew nothing of what had happened since Sunday. Only her uncanny intuition had led her to the truth. Then fear—no longer fear for himself, but fear for Aliette—keyed his legal brain to defense.

"You have no right to make that statement. Where's your proof, your evidence?"

She looked him full in the face; noted the blood at his temples, the working nostrils, the angry sparks in his light blue eyes. The effort to stand up against his obstinacy wrenched her in pieces. Her knees, her very stomach trembled. The known room, the beloved things, seemed suddenly worthless. She felt self-reproachfully that she had loved things too much, her son too little. She could have cried, then and there—she who had never let the tears to her eyes.

"Ronnie," she pleaded, "why must you be so hard, so hostile? Mothers don't need 'evidence.' At least, I don't. Not where you are concerned. You said just now that this—this affair was none of my business. Isn't it a mother's business to protect her child, to save him? Would it have been fair for me not to have spoken? It isn't as if you couldn't trust me—"

She broke off; and fear faded from the mind of her son. He was no longer even angry. Once again he saw in Julia the "lonely old woman," dependent solely on his affection; saw her—very radiant down the years—fetching him, still a child, from his "Dame's School" in Welbeck Street; saw her visiting him at Winchester, at the Varsity. Always, she had been the confidante, the rather stern confidante, of his troubles. Surely, surely when she knew the fineness of Aliette, when she knew how Aliette had refused to let him hurt her, she would help him, help both of them?

"Of course I trust you. It isn't that. And if—if we'd decided anything definitely, I'd tell you about it. But, as things are, I can't tell you anything. You see that, don't you?"

"No. I don't," said Julia sternly—the mother, the religious woman and the traditionalist in her alike roused to bay by the sudden frankness. "It seems to me that, having admitted so much, you owe me the rest."

"But it wouldn't be fair—"

"I can't see why. Unless—unless there's something you—you're both afraid of my knowing."

"Mater!" All the chivalry in him, revolting at the slur on Aliette, urged full confession. "You've spoken with her. You can't possibly imagine that she's the sort of woman who—"

Indignation dumbed him; and in his moment of dumbness the mother realized her mistake, realized him in that hair-trigger state of emotion when the slightest touch will loose the explosion; realized that he and Aliette were on the verge of disaster, that Aliette was the wife of a king's counselor, that she, Julia, must cut out her tongue rather than say the word which would decide her son to wreck his career. But realization came too late.

"You don't imagine that she—that we would do anything underhand," burst out the boy in Ronnie.

"Of course not, dear." Almost Julia had it in her to hate the woman's virtue. To love in secret was certainly a sin before God; but to commit open adultery was a sin before both God and what remained of English Society.

"And, mater," he bent forward boyishly, across the table, "I love her; we love each other."

"Another man's wife?"

"Only in name." His teeth clenched. "Only in law."

She wanted to say, "You believe that?"; but instinct restrained her. She grew frightened at the passion in Ronnie's eyes. He talked on—vehemently. "I can't live without her. I won't. Why should I? What's a divorce nowadays? Who cares? Except a few snuffy old priests. And half of them don't know their own minds."

"Ronnie!" She conjured up every atom of force in her to wrestle with his vehemence. "What's happened to you? divorce means scandal. It means sin. But I won't talk about the religious part. One either believes or one doesn't. I only beg of you, I implore you, to think of your career—"

"Who cares about my career—"

"I do."

"My career won't suffer—"

"It will. You'll be disbarred. Brunton's a power. You'll have him for enemy instead of for friend. You'll make a thousand enemies. The snuffy old priests, as you call them, aren't the only ones who care about divorce. Half the houses I visit will be closed to you."

"For six months."

"No. For good. And you'll never be able to go into politics."

"Politics!" scornfully.

"People will cut you."

"Let them." Opposition, clarifying his mind, keyed him to fight. "Let them! What do I care? We sha'n't have done anything wrong."

"It's always wrong to set ourselves up against the world."

"That's sheer cowardice. And it isn't true, either. What about Jesus Christ?"

"That's sheer blasphemy."

One of the dinner-table candles guttered and went out. To Julia, it seemed like an omen. She saw her son's career gutter out in that curling smoke; saw him entrapped by the powers of darkness, prey to the personal devil. Now no one except God, her own particular secular god, could help. She prayed voicelessly to that particular secular god for words to save the entrapped soul of her boy.

"Ronnie! You've always been so good, the best of sons. You've never given me a moment's anxiety—never—since the day you were born. Until now! And you've always trusted me. Won't you trust me in this? Won't you believe me when I tell you that the thing you contemplate is a sin?"

Quietly, he answered, "If God is love, how can love be a sin?"

The phrase shot a tiny sliver of doubt through the armor of Julia Cavendish's belief, pricking her unwisdom to retort:

"Love! Love isn't passion. Love is service. If you loved her, really and truly loved her, you'd save this woman from herself. And if she loved you, really and truly loved you, she'd be the last person in the world—"

He wanted to argue: "You don't understand. You're too prejudiced to understand." Instead, comprehending abruptly how far his confidences had outrun actuality, he blustered:

"We won't discuss her motives, please. Or mine. Neither of us is a child—as you seem to think. We're quite capable of deciding things for ourselves. When we do—"

"She hasn't consented then?" Julia grasped at the life-buoy.

"No."

Another doubt entered like a dart into the mother's mind. Suppose Sir Heron's warnings came true? Then soon there might be nobody to care for Ronnie. Suppose, suppose this woman really did care—as she, Julia, cared? A woman in Mrs. Brunton's position would hardly risk divorce for abéguin.

Nervously she played with her favorite ring—a diamond-set miniature of her son in earliest boyhood. Nervously she said: "You won't do things in a hurry. Promise me that."

"I can't promise anything," He blustered again, feeling that she was trying to fetter his independence. "I'd rather not discuss the subject any more."

The bluster, so foreign to him, irritated her dignity.

"Very well. It shall be as you wish. We'll say no more about this matter. It's been very painful to me, and I can only hope it won't be still more painful—to both of us—before it's over."

His irritated dignity answered hers. "Why to both of us? It's entirely my affair."

"Not entirely. I've tried to keep myself out of this question; but, as your mother, I have certain claims. And you know, or at least you ought to know, my feelings on the subject of divorce. I ask you to believe that I'm trying to sympathize with you, to see your point of view. But I can't. To me, any union, however legalized, between you and Hector Brunton's wife, means deadly sin. You call this passion of yours love. I don't. I call it by an uglier name." His eyes kindled. "That angers you. I'm sorry. But I'm speaking the truth, as I see it. If you and she decide to commit this deadly sin, don't come to me for forgiveness."

Julia rose, weary with words, to her feet. "Shall we go upstairs to the drawing-room? Kate will be waiting to clear the table."

"Not for a moment." Ronnie, too, rose. "What do you mean, exactly, when you say, 'Don't come to me for forgiveness'?"

"What do I mean?" Sheer physical fatigue unnerved Julia's mind. Jealousy, the mad mother jealousy for the mate which her brain had been holding in leash all evening, broke its bonds; so that she saw her only son, the baby she had cherished from his cradle, lost to her in another woman's arms. White arms—young and smooth and sinful! "What do I mean? Only this—that you must choose between your mother and your—mistress."

Even as that last word escaped the barrier of her teeth, Julia Cavendish knew the mistake irretrievable. Her dignity flickered out like a match in a storm. She wanted to throw herself on his mercy, to beg his pardon with bended knees. But the word, the unpardonable insult of a word, was out. Slowly, she saw his mind grip its full significance. Then his face paled to harsh granite; and his eyes, for once in their lives, grew sterner than her own.

"I *have* chosen," said Ronald Cavendish.

Chapter XI

1

"Aliette dear: You asked me not to hurry you. I've tried to be patient; but life without you has become impossible. I can't see what duty either of us owes to anybody except each other. It isn't as though you had children. It isn't as though you were really married. At worst, we only risk a little scandal. I wouldn't ask you even to risk that, unless I felt confident that I could make you happy. I can make you happy. Won't you come to me? We needn't do anything mean. We can play the game. Ronald."

*

It was nearly one o'clock on Sunday morning. The torn sheets of at least twenty letters in Ronnie's tiny legal handwriting littered his sitting-room grate. He reread the last of them; and thinking how utterly it failed to express his yearning, added as postscript, "I love you." Then he addressed his envelope; folded the single sheet; thrust it in; and gummed down the flap. The fragments in the fireplace he gathered up very carefully, and kindled to ashes.

As yet no sorrow for his quarrel with Julia had entered into her son's heart. He could see her only as an obstacle between himself and happiness. Of her last word, he could not bring himself to think sanely. That she, his own mother, the one person on whose help he ought to have been able to rely, should be the first to cast a stone at the woman he loved, seemed to him—in his bitterness—to make her his chiefest enemy; no longer "the mater," no longer "the lonely old lady," but "Julia Cavendish," publicly and in private the upholder of an effete religion, the champion of fust-ridden prudery.

No longer could he sympathize with that religious prudery. Passion, not the physical desires of a Brunton, but the grand passion, the passion of the poets, blinded him—for the nonce—to every point of view except his own. He and Aliette loved each other. To the torture, then, with whosoever loved other gods!

Passing, on his way downstairs, the door of the bachelor-flat beneath him, Ronnie heard, very low but quite distinct, a woman's laughter. "And that sort of thing," he thought angrily, "is what one is allowed to do. Moses Moffatt winks at it. The world winks at it. Meanwhile the women who won't stoop to concealment foot the world's social bill."

But the woman's laughter still echoed in his ears as he slid his letter into the mouth of the pillar-box.

2

Caroline Staley brought Ronnie's letter, the only one of Monday's post, on Aliette's breakfast-tray. The handwriting of the envelope was strange; but instinct warned her from whom it came. Her heart fluttered—breathlessly—under the satin bath-robe as she said, "I'll ring when I'm ready to dress, Caroline."

But once alone, Aliette did not dare touch the envelope. Casting thought back, she knew that she had loved Ronnie from first sight. Suppose—suppose he had written to make an end?

The breakfast on the tabled tray cooled and cooled. Through the curtained alcove came sound of a housemaid emptying her bath, polishing at the taps. Aliette heard nothing, saw nothing. The cheerful yellow-and-white of her bedchamber had gone dark about her, as though a cloud obscured the sun outside.

At last she took the envelope in her hands. But her hands trembled. And suddenly she saw her own face.

Her face, seen in the triptych mirror of the dressing-table, looked old, haggard. "I *am* old." she thought. "Nearly thirty. Too old for Ronnie. He ought to have some girl, some quite young girl, for bride."

Then, still trembling, her hands slit the envelope; and hungrily, she began to read.

Reading, joy flooded her face. He wanted her to come to him. He needed her! The mazed loneliness of the last week was a vanished nightmare. She would never be lonely any more. Love had come into her life, into their lives, making them one life. At his postscript, the scarlet of her lips crinkled to a smile.

No longer was the room dark about her. Sunlight flashed back into it, flashed square shafts of gold on the rugs at her feet. A warmth, a rare warmth compound of blood and sunshine, pervaded her body. She saw herself, in the mirror, young again, fit to be his mate.

"I love you." She repeated the words under her breath. "I love you." Rereading the letter, her eyes sparkled. Life was good—good.

But gradually the sparkle in her eyes dimmed; joy went out of her face. "Julia Cavendish," she thought, "Julia Cavendish!" And again, "But life's hard—hard."

Nevertheless life had to be faced.

She faced it, there and then, sitting tense and quiet in the sunlit room. Ronnie was a man. To him, love once confessed must seem a bond, an irrevocable troth. Ought she to take him at his word? Ought she not to strive once again—as they had both so long and so uselessly striven—to forget? Yet could she ever forget? Forgetting, would she not be false to the best in her? To the best in both of them?

Suppose—suppose she ran away with Ronnie? What would be the consequences? A divorce! She could face that, as Mary O'Riordan had faced it. Mary, other friends, would stand by her. If only Ronnie's mother were less the Puritan.

"I must go to Ronnie," she thought. "I must ask him if he has spoken with his mother."

Yes! She must go to Ronnie. No other's counsel could avail her now. No third party could help. They, and they alone, would bear the burden if—if she decided to run away with him. And yet—and yet other people would be affected by their action—his mother, her own family, Mollie.

Impulsively she decided to send for Mollie, to sound her. She rang the bell for Caroline, but Caroline told her that "Miss Mollie" had gone out.

"Will I dress you now, madam?" asked the maid. "The master's been gone nearly an hour." It seemed impossible to find any excuse for remaining longer alone.

Dressing, the unsolved problem still haunted her mind. But already one aspect of the problem had solved itself—the aspect of Ronnie. Ronnie's word was not to be doubted. He loved her, he needed her—as she him. For themselves, they must no more funk the issue of Hector divorcing her than they had funked Parson's Brook. "Parson's Brook," thought Aliette. "Was it an omen?"

And at that, ominously, her imagination concentrated on the other aspect of the problem, on the public aspect; till it seemed as though a whole host of people, his mother, her own parents, Mollie, James Wilberforce, and her husband among them, were actually visible in the bedchamber; till it seemed as though Aliette could actually feel the eyes of the host on her, appraising the curves of her figure, the vivid masses of her hair.

Fastidiously she tried to avoid the eyes; but the eyes would not be gainsaid; they turned to her breast, seeking out Ronnie's letter, his love-letter, which she had hidden there. The eyes were not yet hostile, only appraising; but behind them—imagination knew—lurked souls ready to kindle into hostility. "They're waiting," thought Aliette, "waiting to know my decision. Yet the decision is mine—mine only." Imagination petered out, leaving her mind a blank.

Caroline asked a question; and she answered it automatically, "Yes; the green hat, please."

Her maid brought the hat—and, in a second as it seemed, she was standing before the long cheval-glass, completely dressed, completely ready to—leave Hector's house.

Looking back, Aliette now realizes that moment to have been the definitive crossing of her Rubicon. Subconsciously, in that one particular instant of time, her decision crystallized. She, who had always hated "funking things," would not funk love. Love was either worth the leap, or worth nothing. If nothing, then life's self was not worth while. And the risk was the leaper's, only the leaper's. Considering others, she had forgotten to consider herself.

She looked at that self in the long mirror.

Surely those brown eyes, burning deep into their own semblance, were never fashioned for long perplexity; surely, they had been given her so that she might visualize truth. Surely, those scarlet lips were not made for lying; nor those slim feet for running away.

And suddenly, subconsciously, Aliette knew that all her life hitherto she had been lying to her own soul, running away from truth. Life, woman's life at its highest, meant mating. Without matehood, motherhood's self must be a failure. And she, she was neither mate nor mother. Remaining with Hector, her very bodily beauty would wither—wither unmated, sterile. For, to Hector—even if she yielded to Hector—and how, loving Ronnie, could she yield herself to Hector?—she would never be more than legal concubine. No matehood there, only degradation. Better to kill one's self, better to smash the sacred vessel in pieces, than allow it to be profaned—as profaned it must be—by any man's touch save Ronnie's.

"And surely," said some dim voice in that soul which was Aliette, "surely this is nature's verity: To each one of us, unhindered, our mate- and mother-hood! Surely, in nature's eyes, our parents are but dry and empty vessels, milkless gourds rattling on a dead tree."

*

Her letter, sent "express" to Jermyn Street, read: "If you are quite, quite sure of your own feelings, I will come to you to-morrow afternoon. Whatever we decide best to do, must be done openly. I love you—perhaps that is why I have been so afraid. I am not afraid any more. Aliette."

3

This time, ringing the bell at 127b Jermyn Street, Hector Brunton's wife was no more nervous than on the day she put Miracle at Parson's Brook. In that last flash of understanding, it seemed as though even the Mollie aspect of the problem were solved. Let Mollie, too, learn nature's verity; learn that if Wilberforce's love-flame blew out at a breath of scandal, she would do better to warm herself at some healthier fire.

The twenty-four hours which followed her decision had gone by like a single minute, marked only by Ronnie's second letter, by those eight sheets of tenderness, of passion, of high resolve and deep desire, which Aliette held close to her heart as she followed Moses Moffatt up the quiet stairs.

Ronnie met them in the tiny hall. The conventional smile assumed for Moffatt's benefit was still on his lips as he relieved her of bag and parasol, as he led her into the sitting-room. But so soon as the sitting-room door closed, his arms went round her; and their lips met in a long kiss. There was no passion in that kiss, only an overwhelming tenderness; yet, yielding to it, letting herself sink into his arms, Aliette knew that the die was cast, that she belonged to him, he to her, so long as life lasted. And freeing herself, quaintly, irresistibly, the impulse to laughter overwhelmed her mind.

"I'm going to take my hat off," laughed Aliette. "You won't object, will you? Do you know, I wanted to take my hat off, that first afternoon—at the Bull?"

He watched, dumb, while she ungloved her pale hands, while she lifted them to her hat-pins. The curve of her raised arms fascinated his eyes. Still laughing, she removed the hat; and stretched it out to him.

"You don't recognize this, I suppose?"

"No."

"Nor the dress? It's rather a funny dress for town—don't you think, man? Do you like being called 'man'? I decided that should be my name for you on my way here."

But he could not remember either the hat or the dress. "I like them both," he said, "they're wallflower-brown—the same color as your eyes."

"It's a winter dress—a country dress," she prompted. "So hot—that I'll have to take my coat off."

Recollection stirred in him. His mind went back to the winter. He saw two figures, his and hers, strolling down-hill in the low March sunlight.

"It's the dress you wore at Key Hatch."

"Man, you're getting quite clever. Now tell me why I put it on this afternoon."

Standing before him, her coat over one arm, the vivid of her hair uncovered, the brown silk of her blouse revealing the full throat, she seemed like a young girl; more an affianced bride than a woman who intended running away from her husband.

He took the coat from her, and their hands met. He raised her fingers to his lips; and again she dimpled to laughter.

"Tell me," said Aliette, "or I sha'n't give you any tea, why I put on this dress. Women, even when they're in love, don't wear their winter tweeds in the middle of the season."

Instead, he kissed her—still tenderly.

"How should I know, Aliette? This afternoon you're all a mystery to me. Tell me, why you are so different."

"Light the kettle; and I'll try to tell you." She balanced herself on the edge of the settee. "You say I'm different this afternoon. I'm only different because I'm happy. And I'm happy because of you, because of us, because of everything. You, too?"

"Yes." Her spirits infected him: he, too, laughed.

"Happiness, you see, is our only justification," said the woman who intended running away from her husband. "I've got to make you happy. Otherwise, from the very outset, I fail. And if"—the tiniest note of seriousness crept into her voice—"if I can't make you happy, not just this afternoon, but always—"

"You will," he interrupted. "And I you."

Tea was rather a silent meal. They were content to sit through it, hand touching hand occasionally, their eyes on each other. To each of them it seemed as though, after long wandering, they had come home. For the moment, passion hardly existed. Almost they might have been boy and girl.

"Did you fall in love with me that day with the Mid-Oxfordshire?" she asked.

"I've often wondered."

"It all seems so strange, Ronnie. Not like—like doing wrong."

"We're not going to do anything wrong."

"We are. That's the strangest part of it."

To the man, too, it was all strange, strange and fantastic beyond belief. He could not imagine himself the same Cavendish who had so long wrestled against the inculcated traditions of his upbringing, of his profession; he could not visualize himself potential sinner against society. Sin was a bodily thing; and he wanted no more of this radiant, dimpling creature than to hear the happy laughter in her voice.

So, for a little while, those two remade their rose-bubble of enchantment, forgetful alike of the problems put behind them and the greater problems yet to be faced.

But at last Aliette said, "Let's be sensible."

"Not this afternoon." He tried to take both her hands, but her hands eluded him.

"Don't!" Her eyes darkled. "We mustn't play any more." And after a pause, she asked him: "I wonder exactly how much you really need me?"

"More than any man ever needed any woman."

"You're quite, quite sure?"

"Absolutely."

"Then," she laughed, a little low laugh deep in the throat; for she knew that her elusion had thrilled him to passion, and the knowledge was very sweet, "will you please tell me, man, what you're going to do about me?"

"Do about you?" His meditative drawl stimulated a newborn impishness in her.

"Yes—do about me."

"Why—run away with you, if you'll let me."

"Where to?"

"Anywhere."

"Shall I be allowed to take any luggage?"

"Of course."

"Then we can't very well run away this afternoon."

"No. I suppose we can't," he muttered; and the impishness in her chuckled to see the puzzled thoughts chase themselves across his forehead.

How boyish he was—she thought—how utterly unlike the conventional unconventional lover. The maternal instinct awakened in her heart, and went out to the boy in him. She wanted to pat his head, to say: "Never mind, Ronnie. I'll arrange everything. You sha'n't be worried." Then she remembered that he wasn't a boy; that he was a man, her man.

The man in him burst out: "I wish to God that you needn't go back—"

"Go back?" His outburst frightened her.

"To his house—"

"But I must go back—for a day or two."

"Why should you?" His eyes were flame. "I hate it. I hate the idea of your being under his roof."

"Jealous?" she soothed, still afraid.

"Yes. I suppose I am jealous."

"Is that fair? There isn't anything to be jealous about."

"Forgive me!" His hand gripped her knee. "But I can't bear his being your husband even in name. Aliette, kiss me."

"No." She knew that she must not yield to him. "No. We've got to be sensible. We've got to make plans."

"We can make plans to-morrow."

"We can't. Don't you see that when I go back to—to his house this evening, I'll have to tell him? It wouldn't be straight if I didn't. We've got to be straight, haven't we?"

"Yes." The flame went out of his eyes, leaving them cold and hard as agate. "We've got to be straight. But—telling him isn't your job. It's mine." He heaved himself up from the settee; and she had her first glimpse of a different Ronnie—a fighting Ronnie, chin protruded, lips set. "My job," he repeated.

"I'm not Andromeda. I don't want a Perseus to free me from the dragon." She tried chaff; but chaff left him unmoved. She tried argument; but argument only strengthened the resolve in him. Finally she said:

"There's no need to say much. Hector knows everything—except your name."

"You told him?" There was no anger in the phrase.

"Everything except your name. We had a quarrel. After I got home last Monday. He offered to let me divorce him if—if I'd promise there was no one else." She, too, rose—her face, for all its fineness, obstinate as her lover's. "Of course, I couldn't promise that. So to-night, I shall just tell him—the rest."

Gilbert Frankau

The tall man and the little woman faced each other in silence: each equally determined to carry, right from the beginning, the other's burden.

"It doesn't seem right, somehow or other," Ronnie said at last. "He might—might hurt you."

"Hurt me!" laughed Aliette. "Nothing, nobody in the world can hurt me now. Except you. And you will hurt me if you insist. Don't insist, Ronnie."

"Very well." His hands, thrilling to passion once again, clasped her waist. He kissed her; and this time she did not seek to elude him. For now she knew her power, the power which all women exercise over imaginative lovers; knew that, at her least word, he would loose her—fearful lest, by not loosing, he forfeit the greater gift.

And all through the half-hour which followed, that power, that fear was on Ronnie. He was afraid of forfeiting this Aliette who had let him hold her in his arms; who had let him press his lips to hers in passion; but who, admitting her love for him, could yet sit aloof—a goddess with a time-table.

"I shall take Caroline," she said. "You don't mind?"

He only wanted to take Aliette, there and then; to kiss those rounded wrists, those arms bare to the elbow, that scarlet mouth, those cheeks ivory as curds, the smooth forehead under its loops of shining hair.

"Kiss me!" he whispered. "Kiss me!"

"Ronnie!" She put down the time-table. "Don't let's do anything we might—might regret. Remember that to-night, and perhaps for many nights, I must sleep under his roof."

He yielded again; and a few minutes later she prepared to leave him. The plans they had meant to make were still chaotic—chaotic as her mind.

She realized, as she pinned on her hat, as she let him help her into her coat, that the sweet hour had been full of danger, that—had Ronnie been less chivalrous, more the man and less the boy—she might have given way to him. The realization made her very humble; and in her humility she began to doubt herself.

"You—you've been very good to me," she said; and then, the vivid lashes veiling her vivid eyes, her low voice trembling into shyness: "That's why

141

there's just one—one favor I must ask you."

"Favors! Between us!" He took her ungloved hands, and pressed them to his lips.

"Yes, dear. It's about—about your mother."

"Julia!" His tone hardened. "But we discussed all that last time."

"We mustn't hurt her more than we can help. We must tell her the truth, before—before we do anything. She's a woman, and perhaps—perhaps she'll understand—"

"Aliette—" He hesitated; and her intuition leaped to the cause.

"You—you haven't quarreled with her?"

Her intuition startled him into reply: "Yes. We have quarreled. But I can't tell you anything about it."

She drew away from him, and her eyes grew sorrowful. "Did you quarrel because of anything she said to you about me?"

Again he hesitated; again her intuition leaped to the truth. "I've been afraid you might. Something told me, that morning in the park, that she must have guessed. I can't come between you and your mother. You mustn't quarrel with her on my account. Whatever she may have said, you must go to her, tell her everything, and ask her—if she can—to forgive—"

"Never!" The very humility angered him. "Never! It's not for her to forgive, but for me—"

"Then it was because of me that you quarreled?"

"Yes."

"Foolish man!" It hurt her desperately to think that his mother should have understood so little; but she knew that she must conceal the hurt. "As if I'd let you quarrel with any one, least of all your mother, on my account. You'll go to her, won't you? You'll tell her that I—that I don't ask for any recognition—"

Rudely, obstinately, he interrupted her: "Of course she must recognize you. Either she's on our side or she's against us."

"Ronnie"—her eyes suffused with tears—"Ronnie, I told you we'd got to be happy with one another. You make me unhappy—when you speak like that.

You make me feel like a thief. You do want me to be happy, don't you?"

"Yes. Always." His anger vanished. Bending down, he tried to kiss the tears from her eyes. "Always, darling."

"Then won't you"—she was in his arms now; the warmth, the perfume, the very unhappiness of her a fresh thrill—"won't you grant me this one favor? It's the only favor I'll ever ask."

"How can I?"

"So easily. Just go to her. She's your mother. She loves you, she understands you. But she may not understand—about me. She may think that I'm just—just a dissolute woman. That doesn't matter. Tell her that it doesn't matter. Tell her that I don't want to keep you from her; that until—until we're properly married, you'll be as free to go to her as if"—he could hardly hear the last words—"as if you'd taken any—any ordinary mistress."

"Don't, don't!" He strained her to him, fiercely protective. "You're not to speak of yourself like that."

"Why not?" She lifted a face brave despite her tears. "It's true. Don't let's funk things. From the day I come to you till the day Hector sets me free I shall be your mistress. You mustn't expect your mother or any one else to take a different view. But I'll be so happy, man; so much happier than I've ever been in my life before—if only you'll make it up with your mother. You will, won't you? Promise me."

"Tell me," he whispered, and his lips trembled, "is this thing so vital to your happiness?"

"Yes," she whispered back.

"Then—it shall be as you wish." His arms were still round her; and she felt herself weakening—weakening. She felt herself all exhausted—all a limpness in his arms.

"Sweetheart," his voice was hoarse in her ears, "don't go. I want you so much. Every day, every night without you is misery."

"Ronnie—Ronnie! Don't tempt me—"

Feverishly her ungloved hands fondled him; feverishly her arms looped his neck, drawing his face down to hers. She could see, under the gray-gold of his hair, the great vein throbbing on his forehead, the dart and pulse of passion in his eyes. His lips, trembling still, fastened on her mouth. The kiss was torment. Feverishly her mouth clung to his; feverishly, blent in ecstasy, fire feeding flame, they clung to one another—till, at last, half fainting, she tore herself away.

"Don't!" she stammered. "Don't torture me, don't tempt me any more. Don't let me think—either now or ever—that this love of ours is only—only physical. Because, if I thought that, I'd kill myself."

And a moment afterwards, she was gone.

Chapter XII

1

Ponto the Dane, a piebald hummock of utter contentment, slapped his vast stern on the sands; woke; and rose to his haunches.

At gaze into the sun-dazzle, Ponto's slitty eyes could just discern the twin rock buttresses of Chilworth Cove, the sea-water eddying translucent between them, and, forging through the sea-water, a man's head. White birds, which Ponto after one or two dignified experiments had decided uncatchable, strutted the beach or circled lazily round the buttresses. His mistress slept, sun-bonneted in her long deck-chair, a smile on her lips.

"This," mused the great dog, "is a very pleasant place."

"This," dreamed the great dog's mistress, "is paradise."

Chilworth Cove lies far from the track of motor char-à-bancs in the unspoiled West Country. Inshore from its tongue of hot gold sands, the wild flowers riot; and back along the fritillary-haunted pathway through the wild flowers, Chilworth Ghyll leads to Chilworth Port—a handful of thatch-roofed, pink-washed cottages whereon the clematis spreads its purple stars and the honeysuckle droops coral clusters for the loudly-questing bee.

Once the sea filled the Ghyll; once, from the ancient well-head midway of the streetless "port," men drew water for their ships; once seafarers in hose and doublet with strange oaths and stranger tales on their lips would sit drinking in the parlor of the ancient alehouse. But to-day never a ship and hardly a "foreigner" comes where Chill Down upswells warm-breasted as a woman to the blue and Chill Common sweeps wave on wave of heathered ridges to a houseless horizon.

This summer, indeed, only three "foreigners"—the man forging overarm to seaward, the drowsy dog, and the dreaming lady—had visited the port: for the square-faced, square-hipped Devonian woman, busied at the moment with the setting-out of curdled cream and other homely fare in their pink-washed cottage, was no "foreigner"—but a port woman by birth, as the alehouse well knew.

And if the alehouse sometimes speculated why "Martha Staley's daughter,

145

her who had the good place in Lunnon, should have brought her 'folk' to the port"—who cared? Not Ronnie! Not Aliette! For them, London with all its harassing memories had faded into that remote past before they possessed one another, before flaming June and flaming love alike combined to teach them a delight so exquisite that it seemed to both as though paradise itself could hold no rarer in its offering.

They had been in paradise a full month; and never for a moment had either of them regretted their hurried flight, their abandoned schemes. The past was dead, the future still unborn; they lived only for the all-sufficing present, two human beings fulfilling one another in isolation from their kind.

"Ronnie is happy," dreamed Aliette. "Happy as I am."

Yet even dreaming, she knew her own happiness the greater. She, risking most, gained the most from her risking; she—once that first inevitable fear of revulsion which is the portion of every woman who, disappointed in one man, seeks consolation with another, proved phantom—had been content to surrender herself, body, brain, and soul, to the call of matehood; to pour out all that was best hers, of beauty, of selflessness, of tender thought and reckless caring, at Ronnie's feet; knowing each gift a thousand times recompensed by the slightest touch of his hand on her hair, the lightest brushing of his lips against her cheeks—knowing herself no longer a woman, but very womanhood, eternal essence distilled eternally from the fruit of Eden-tree for manhood's completion.

And, "Poor Ronnie," she dreamed, "he can never be happy as I am. He thinks I am the same Aliette—he does not realize the miracle."

For, of a surety, if ever love wrought a miracle, it was on this woman. She who, in her mateless fastidiousness, had schooled herself to the poise of a virgin Artemis, became, mated, the very Venus Anadyomene, Venus of foam and of sun-glints, rose-flushed for adoration between the roses and the sea. And in the hush of moon-pale midnights, when the clematis-blossoms showed as black butterflies against their diamonded window-panes, when the ripples beyond the Ghyll murmured like tired children asleep, she—to whom, mateless, the nights had been emptier even than the days—became night's own goddess-girl, subduing man's passion to merest instrument of her love.

The dreaming lady stirred, murmuring through dreams; and the smile faded from her lips.

Sometimes, even to paradise—as black ships seen through a golden haze to seaward—came dark visions of the past. Of Julia Cavendish, her son's unanswered letter crumpled in unrelenting fingers; of Mollie and her James; of the mullioned house at Clyst Fullerford; of the stiff bow-fronted library at Lancaster Gate; and of the man in that library, the man whose thin lips muttered: "So it was that briefless fool Cavendish you would have married, had I given you your freedom. Very good! Go to him now, if you dare. You're not my property. I can't force you to stop here. But if you leave this house, remember that you're still Mrs. Hector Brunton, not Mrs. Ronald Cavendish. Remember that you're taking a risk, a biggish risk."

That risk, all in a sweet madness, the dreaming lady and the man forging back to her through the translucent water, had taken within twelve hours; hurriedly; almost planlessly; instinctively as Ponto, who, let loose by a mischievous boy from his kennel in Westbourne Street, nosed his way to the door of Brunton's house just as Aliette and Caroline Staley stepped into the loaded taxi, and, spying the portmanteau, set up such a howl that in sheer self-defense they let him clamber in between them.

"And that," thought Aliette, waking from dreams to find a huge wet nose nuzzling her hand, "was the maddest thing I did in all that one mad day."

Then she, too, sat at gaze into the sun-dazzle; till her lover's head rounded the translucent pool below the buttresses; till he came up the hot sands toward her—the sea-light in his hair, his browned shoulders dripping from the sea.

2

Meanwhile, five hours away along the shining track beyond Chill Common, seven million exiles from paradise plied their harassed harassing earth-days in London City.

The Love-Story of Aliette Brunton

Of all those seven millions only three people knew exactly what had happened; and only two—Julia Cavendish and Benjamin Bunce—the fugitives' address. Even Mollie, who had been overnighting with friends at Richmond during those few hours when her sister decided on flight, had been told—officially—nothing.

But Mollie, from the first moment when she glanced at the incoherent scrawl Lennard handed her on her return, had suspected the worst. With her, Hector's reassurances, given over the telephone from his chambers, that "Alie had suddenly made up her mind to take a holiday," went for nothing.

"Rather unexpected, wasn't it?" she said; and then, remembering the scene in the drawing-room: "On the whole, Hector, I think I'd better take a holiday, too."

Hector, with a terse, "Of course, you must do what you think best," rang off; and the girl, now thoroughly perturbed, telephoned to Betty Masterman, her oldest school-friend, demanding hospitality.

"Nothing wrong, I hope?" said Betty.

"No, dear. Nothing. Only Alie's had to go away, and I can't very well stop here without a chaperon."

Betty Masterman was a comforting creature who neither asked nor demanded confidences; but the interview with James Wilberforce hurt. It took Mollie three days to summon up enough courage to notify him of her new address; and when, throwing up his afternoon's work in Norfolk Street, he came to call at the little conventionally-furnished flat, it seemed to the girl as though they could never again be frank with one another; as though her very greeting, "Hello, James! Rotten of Alie to take a holiday, right in the middle of the season, isn't it?" were a deliberate lie.

And his answer, "Oh, well, it's rather stuffy in town, these days," made any discussion of the topic nearest her heart impossible. "For, of course," thought the girl, "Jimmy knows that Aliette's run away from Hector."

As a matter of fact, Jimmy had not previously suspected any connection between Aliette Brunton's sudden departure from Lancaster Gate and the news, previously imparted to him by Benjamin Bunce, that "Mr. Cavendish had been called out of town and might not be back for some days." It was, Jimmy said to himself, rather weird of old Ronnie to buzz off in the middle of the sessions; but then old Ronnie always had been rather weird, a peculiar kind of chap, pretty reticent about his private affairs.

But subconsciously, the moment Mollie spoke of her sister, the solicitor's mind connected the two disappearances. At first blush, the connection seemed incredible. "Old Ronnie" was "as straight as they make 'em"; and "H. B.'s wife a regular Puritan."

All the same, James Wilberforce—just to reassure himself—would have liked to ask a question or two, to take Mollie's summary of evidence. He wanted, for instance, to ask her if she knew her sister's address.

Something restrained him from asking the question; but while he was taking tea his brain suddenly remembered a little twist of Ronnie's mouth when Julia Cavendish had mentioned Aliette's name during his lunch at Bruton Street. Scarcely noticed at the time, that remembered twist of the clean-shaven lips called up other memories; Ronald and Aliette at Key Hatch, playing patters at Queen's, shaking hands in Hyde Park.

"But it's absurd," thought the big red solicitor, "absurd! I'd lay twenty to one against it. A hundred to one!" And, looking at Mollie across the tea-table, he forgot her sister.

That afternoon the girl seemed more than ever desirable, just the sort of wife he was looking for. He liked the way she bobbed her dark hair, the cotton frock she was wearing, her strong white hands and arms; he liked being alone with her in this little room with its fumed oak furniture, its red wall-paper, its general air of coziness. He would have liked, very much, to kiss that full red mouth. But more than anything else, he liked this new shyness, this very hopeful shyness, which had replaced her old self-confidence.

"What's the matter with you this afternoon, Mollie?" he chaffed her. "Got the hump about anything?"

"No. I'm a bit tired; that's all."

"Nothing worrying you?"

"Nothing much."

And again—vaguely—the solicitor in Wilberforce grew nervous.

"Damn it all," he thought, "supposing my suspicions *are* right. Suppose those two have gone off together. It's fifty to one against, but still—"

The instinct to gamble on that fifty-to-one chance (it had been a hundred to one half an hour since), to propose and have done with it, came to him. But his caution subdued the instinct. The world, his world, was a pretty censorious place; and if one's father were almost a cert. for his baronetcy, if one were junior partner in a firm so entirely *sans reproche* with the king's proctor as Wilberforce, Wilberforce & Cartwright—well, one just couldn't afford to take even thousand-to-one gambles on one's future wife's social position.

The entrance of Betty, a thin golden-haired grass-widow, very much *à la mode* from her trim feet to her modulated voice, tided over the awkward interview.

That night, however, Mollie Fullerford—least sentimental of the modern young—cried herself to sleep.

3

Tears are not fashionable in Pump Court; but that melancholy individual, Benjamin Bunce, very nearly followed Mollie Fullerford's example, when "young Mr. Wilberforce"—anxious only to allay his suspicions—called at Ronnie's chambers next morning.

"I'm sure I don't know what to do, sir," wailed Benjamin. "Here's a couple of good briefs come in; and my instructions is not to send anything on to him. No, sir, I'm afraid I can't give you his address. I'm not allowed to give any one his address—except Mr. David Patterson. And that only if Mr. David Patterson asks me for it."

"David Patterson!" exclaimed the solicitor.

"Yes, sir. Mr. Brunton's—Mr. Hector Brunton's—clerk."

"Good God!" said a young man whose ruddy complexion had gone suddenly white. "Good God!" And he walked out of the door, as Benjamin subsequently described it, "as though he'd been lifting the elbow ever since

150

breakfast."

4

James Wilberforce did not gossip; nevertheless, within a week of the flight for paradise, rumor—the amazing omniscient rumor of London—began to weave, spider-like, her intangible filaments. As yet, rumor was unconfirmed: only a vague web of talk, spun from boudoir to drawing-room, from drawing-room to club, from club to Fleet Street, from Fleet Street to the Griffin.

And in the center of the web, watching it a-weave, sat Aliette's husband.

More than once, friends, those maddeningly tactful friends of the successful, touched on rumor; but none of them, not even Hector's father, succeeded in extracting a syllable. "My wife," said Hector Brunton, K.C, to his friends, "has not been feeling very well lately. I've sent her out of town for a bit of a holiday."

At first the mere mention of Aliette's name enraged him; aroused in him a cruelty so melodramatic, so virulent that, for a full three days, he went in fear of becoming a murderer. He knew that he could find "the guilty pair" easily enough: Cavendish's clerk—Aliette's brief note told him—would give his solicitors their address. But even without Cavendish's clerk it would be simple to trace them. You couldn't lug a twelve-stone dog round the London railway termini without attracting the attention of at least half a hundred involuntary private detectives!

Somehow (comedy and tragedy blend strangely in the heart of a man!) the idea of Ponto's accompanying his wife's elopement seemed in Brunton's eyes the culminating insult, a last intolerable outrage on the domestic decencies. He, Hector, had given Aliette that dog; and, though he hated the beast himself, he grudged it to Cavendish. To his enraged mind, the dog turned symbol of his betrayal. He had been betrayed by a dishonest woman. If Aliette had possessed any sense of honesty, she would have left Ponto behind: as she had left all his other gifts—the pearl necklace, the jeweled wrist-watch, the gray ostrich-feather fan.

The Love-Story of Aliette Brunton

Then, hot on the heels of rage, came remorse—remorse, not for his cruelty, not for his infidelities, but only for the crass stupidity with which he believed himself to have handled the situation. He might have known the woman better than to attempt bluff. He ought to have pleaded with her. Or locked her in her bedroom. On no account ought he to have gone down to the courts next morning. Why hadn't he telephoned Mollie to return that very night? Why hadn't he wired to Clyst Fullerford for Aliette's mother?

Self-pity succeeded. He pictured himself the injured husband; and, his heart softening towards Aliette, vowed "that seducer Cavendish should suffer."

But Cavendish's sufferings did not suffice his imagination. Why should Cavendish alone suffer? Why should either the woman or the man get off scotfree? Why shouldn't both of them be made to suffer—damnably—as damnably as he himself was suffering?

For, surely as love made paradise of Chilworth Cove, so surely did lust fashion hell at Lancaster Gate.

From this hell in which—as Brunton imagined—the loss of a woman, and not the loss of his own self-esteem furnished the flame, Brunton's only escape was work; and into work he flung himself, as a scalded child into cold water, only to find the agony redoubled on emergence. For though his work—eight, ten, and sometimes sixteen hours a day of the tensest mental concentration—did momentarily banish introspection; always, his work concluded, came the Furies.

In the night, they came—like evil old women—lashing him, sleepless, from room to room of that huge silent house, mocking him, mocking him. "Only wait," mocked the Furies. "She'll come back. Perhaps she's on her way home at this very moment. She'll soon tire of Cavendish—of Cavendish."

Brunton tried to scream back at them (he knew, even before they showed him his face in the mirror of his dressing-room, that the scream could not pass his lips), "I wouldn't have her back. I wouldn't, I tell you—I wouldn't. She's a loose woman. An adulteress."

"Oh, yes, you would," answered the Furies. "Oh, yes, you would. If she

152

came into this house now—if she rang the front door-bell—listen! listen hard! didn't you hear a bell, Brunton?—if she offered herself to you, you'd take her. It's three years, Brunton. Three years since you went into that room. Think of her, Brunton. Think of her—her hair unbound—her arms open to receive—Cavendish!"

And by day, when the evil old women slept, men mocked at him—voicelessly. All men—so it seemed to him—knew his shame. All men! Lennard and the chauffeur, so smooth-faced, so efficient, grinning behind smug hands: the acquaintances at his clubs: his co-barristers, lunching either side of him at Middle Temple Hall: his subservient clerk: his respectful clients—all these knew him for the deserted bull, for the male incapable of authority, for the public cuckold. Even the impassive pseudo-friendly judges who gave him his verdicts were wise to his cuckoldry.

Curiously enough, in all that month of June, Brunton never lost a case. Possible defeats, probable compromises, doubtful prosecution, or still more doubtful defense—every legal battle he fought ended in sweeping victory. Treasury briefs, consultations, and demands for his "opinion" avalanched on his chambers in King's Bench Walk. Fleet Street echoed and reëchoed his name; till it appeared as though the herd, the damned hypocritical herd who fawned openly on his public success so that they might gloat the more on his secret failure, twitted him in very malice with the prospects of a knighthood, of a judgeship, of a safe seat at the next election.

More and more, as the days went by, he saw himself as the deserted bull; and, so seeing, swore that he would teach the whole herd a lesson. The herd had its rules, its shibboleths; but he was above all rules, above all shibboleths. Let the herd murmur if it dared. His wife and her lover could rot in the mire they had pashed for themselves. The lone bull would not even deign to horn their flanks.

So, arrogance and cruelty in his secret heart; lash-marks of the Furies red across his secret loins; feigning himself unhurt, uncaring; feigning himself ignorant; feigning even solicitude for the health of his absent wife, Hector Brunton went his conquering conquered way.

Chapter XIII

1

In the heart of Julia Cavendish—those earliest days—was neither hatred nor cruelty; only a terrible numbness as from a blow.

Ronnie, her own son, had struck her! At first she could not bring herself to believe the happening real. His letter, read and reread, conveyed nothing.

But soon the letter grew real enough—so real that Julia's imagination, peering between the lines, could actually see him with the woman who had inspired it; with the woman who had ruined her boy's career.

Her first impulse was to go to them, to go swiftly; to say to the woman, "It's not too late—even now. Return to your husband—give my son back to me."

Yet every traditional instinct in Julia fought against that solution. All her life she had schooled herself to the belief that adultery—in a woman—was the unforgivable sin. Men, of course, were never guilty of "adultery," only of "lapses." Modern society, so pitifully lax, so given over to the sentimental impulse, might forgive both parties. Julia Cavendish could not. She, in her eugenic wisdom, knew that individual sin—in a woman—must earn individual punishment. Mrs. Brunton, therefore, could not return to her husband. But if Mrs. Brunton did not return, how could Mrs. Brunton give back Ronnie?

Mrs. Brunton probably took the ordinary tolerant view about divorce; the view that she, Julia, had spent a lifetime in combating. Not that her own public position on the divorce question counted! At any moment since Ronnie's birth she would have sacrificed more than public position for him. But this, this was a question of beliefs. Love might urge forgiveness but how could love countenance sin—a deadly sin?

For a week that stubborn old doctrine of deadly sin, which Julia had imbibed with a bookish Christianity—the same bookish "Christianity" which still tolerates the ghastly word "heretic," continued to harden her heart as it blinded her intellect; for a week she held on, with a tenacity almost Hebraic, to the fixed idea of the woman taken in adultery.

Then, as the numbness of the blow warmed into pain, her heart softened, and her intellect—momentarily freed by sorrow from the blindness of all formal faiths—saw a ray of light.

Admit, just for argument's sake, that a husband was entitled to put away his guilty wife; and suppose that the guilty man were willing to marry her. What then? Could one doom the guilty parties to a perpetual living in sin?

But the ray of light petered out, leaving her in even blacker darkness, because—by the beam of it—she had seen herself already drifted so far away from her old beliefs as to countenance not only divorce but the remarriage of divorced parties.

All the same, mother-love still urged her to forgive: so that, for a full week, she went about her house (a lonely house, it seemed now; all the charm of the years gone out of it) in a positive stupor of intellectual and religious bewilderment. She asked herself: "Does anything matter except my boy's happiness, my boy's career? Does anything really count except love? Isn't love—and love alone—the true teaching of Christianity!" But she found no answer to her questions. Honesty said: "It's a matter of principle; judge the case as though it were a stranger's, not the case of your own son."

Nevertheless the argument of the individual case persisted. Memory recalled her son's statement about Aliette's relationship to her husband. If those two—the woman to whom she had taken such an instinctive liking and the man she had deemed, at first sight, capable of cruelty—were husband and wife only in name, didn't the case alter? "No!" said formal religion. "Yes!" said the mother in Julia Cavendish.

She remembered a phrase of Aliette's: "I have no children, worse luck." That was hardly the phrase of a loose woman, of a harpy. Suppose this woman really loved Ronnie?

But that brought back the old jealousy. How could Aliette really love Ronnie? She, his mother, would have held her right hand in the flames rather than jeopardize her son's career—as Aliette had jeopardized it.

Whereupon the novelist's imagination in Julia started to activity. She pictured—knowing little of the law—a crowd of clients besieging Ronnie's chambers, only to be told that "the eminent Mr. Cavendish" could not take their cases; and—thoroughly frightened at the heroic version of Benjamin

Bunce and those few dusty briefs which Ronald had abandoned—sent for her secretary, the blank-faced Mrs. Sanderson, whom she told to ring up Sir Peter Wilberforce.

But Sir Peter was in Paris; and James deputized in his stead.

"Do you know what she wants to see him about?" asked James's secretary on the telephone.

"It's about her will, I think," answered Julia's.

2

Jimmy Wilberforce, who had not seen Mollie since his talk with Bunce and spent four sleepless nights in consequence, set out for that interview with the uncomfortable foreboding that the "old lady's will" was only a pretext for discussing the old lady's son. And the foreboding justified itself before he had been with her ten minutes.

"I suppose," said Julia, eying him across the Empire desk of her work-room, "that you, as Ronnie's best friend, are very much in his confidence?"

"How do you mean?" prevaricated the big red lawyer. "About his financial affairs?" He laughed, tapping the document between them. "Ronald isn't the sort of chap who'd borrow on his—er—expectations."

"I was not referring to his financial affairs," retorted Julia stiffly. "If you, as my son's best friend, and as the son of my own legal adviser, do not understand the matter to which I allude, the conversation need go no further."

Jimmy looked at his client, and noticed—for the first time since entering the little box of a room—how she had aged, how ill, how ill at ease, how unhappy she appeared. Jimmy, the man rather than the solicitor, was feeling very far from happy himself; and unhappiness, being a completely new experience, keyed him to unusual sympathy.

"We're in the same boat," he thought. "Poor old lady! I wonder how much she knows. Ronnie had no right to run away with H. B.'s wife. The harm it's done already! His mother looks quite broken up about it. And I—I can't marry Mollie."

"Mrs. Cavendish," he said, "I don't pretend to be as fond of your son as you are. I'm rather a selfish chap, I'm afraid. But if there's anything, any affair in which I can be of assistance to you—you've only to ask me."

She asked him, pointblank: "Do you know my son's where-abouts?"

He answered, "No. I didn't even know that he'd gone away, till his clerk told me."

Julia hesitated. "I'm speaking to you in absolute confidence?"

"Of course."

"Then please tell me: Have you heard any—any rumors?"

Jimmy chewed the cud for ten full seconds before replying: "You mean—about a certain lady?"

"I mean precisely that."

"So far, none." Now it was Jimmy's turn to hesitate. "But, speaking entirely in confidence, there are bound to be rumors—if he stays away much longer."

"You know nothing for certain then?"

"Officially—nothing." The solicitor inspected his finger nails. "But I'm afraid that, unofficially, I know a good deal."

"Including the name of the lady?"

"Including the name of the lady!"

Julia's heart sank. Wilberforce could not be alone in his knowledge of the truth. And that meant—publicity! "Tell me, Mr. Wilberforce," she went on, "before we go any further: Is a barrister who has been co-respondent in a divorce case disbarred from further practice?"

"So she knows everything," thought Jimmy, and discarded finesse. "On that point I can reassure you. Even if the petitioner were himself a barrister, it would make no difference."

"You made inquiries then?"

"Yes."

"May I ask why?" Julia's manner stiffened again. The conversation was unutterably distasteful: but she had been alone with her thoughts so long that even the most distasteful of conversations seemed preferable to further silence.

"Because"—the man, moved by a similar impulse, laid all his cards, faced, on the table—"because the sister of the certain lady is a—a very great friend of mine."

"And if"—remembering the meeting in Hyde Park, the novelist's mind jumped instanter to its conclusion—"if the divorce we mentioned were to take place, it would make a difference to the outcome of that friendship?"

"I"—Jimmy stammered—"I'm afraid so."

Remembering Ronnie's letter, Julia Cavendish felt aware of a new pride in her son. Ronnie might have been guilty of a "lapse": but at least he had not been weak. For it was weak, pitifully weak, almost caddishly weak of a man even to contemplate ending his friendship with a girl because of a scandal in her family.

"I'm sorry to tell you then," she said, "officially, that your unofficial knowledge is perfectly correct. I have incontrovertible proof—a letter from him—that my son has run away with Hector Brunton's wife, and that they are now waiting for him to serve them with divorce-papers."

Jimmy Wilberforce's brown eyes darkened with pain. It had been bad enough to know the truth himself; but to hear it from some one else seemed for the moment unbearable.

"That," went on his client, "is why I wanted to see your father. Perhaps I'd better wait till he returns from Paris. You, obviously, will be a little—shall we say prejudiced?"

There are certain instants in a man's life when he comprehends his own character with revolting clarity. Such an instant those last words brought to the solicitor. In the light of them he saw himself as poor friend, as worse lover. He felt he could never again look Ronald or Mollie in the face.

"I hope your father will be back soon." continued Julia. "Naturally I'm rather anxious for his advice."

"Mrs. Cavendish"—Jimmy, contrary to her expectation, made no effort to go—"if I gave you the impression of prejudice by what I said just now, I'm sorry. My father will be away for at least another week. Meanwhile, I beg you to forget my own—er—personal interest in this matter; and to look upon me as—as a friend. You and Ronnie are in trouble; let me help you both to the best of my ability. Do you, by any chance, know Ronnie's address? If so, won't you, in strict confidence, let me have it?"

"I don't think I ought to do that without his permission," said Julia. "But I shall be very grateful for your advice. Tell me—I'm afraid I'm rather ignorant, wilfully ignorant perhaps, about these matters—how are divorces"—she stumbled over the word—"arranged?"

And James Wilberforce told her, in exact legal parlance, the whole nauseating procedure of the English courts. He spoke of orders for restitution, of "hotel evidence," of letters written at the dictation of solicitors, of damages and alimony, and of the king's proctor. Finally—and at this the whole soul of Julia Cavendish sickened—to illustrate a point, he told her the inside history of the Carrington case; how Carrington, in order to blacken his wife's name, had committed perjury in an undefended divorce-case, and how—for fear lest she should forfeit her freedom to marry the man she loved—Carrington's wife had been forced to endure the slander.

Jimmy's client sifted the whole information for some time.

"So you mean," she said at last, "that in this country any husband and wife who—'know the ropes,' I think, was your phrase—and possess sufficient money to fee a firm like your own, can secure a divorce with almost as little trouble as they can secure a marriage-license."

"I mean precisely that," replied Jimmy Wilberforce. "Given the mutual desire to undo their marriage, the law—properly worked—puts no obstacle in the way."

"But if, as in this Carrington business, the desire is not mutual. What then?"

"Then, of course, there are difficulties. Especially if it is the woman who wants her freedom. In our courts, you see, a husband is still his wife's legal owner; a woman merely her husband's chattel. A wife, against a husband unwilling to be divorced, must prove not only infidelity but cruelty—in the legal sense. And it has been held, over and over again, that infidelities—on the husband's part—are not cruelties. Cruelties—legally speaking—imply a

159

damage to the wife's health." Jimmy reverted, once more, to the inside history of the Carrington case.

Julia Cavendish, too, thought of Carrington when she said:

"Mr. Wilberforce, let us be open with each other. My son's letter is quite frank. He says that he and Mrs. Brunton have run away together; that her husband knows all about it; that they are waiting for him to 'file his petition.' What happens if he refuses?"

"That," protested Wilberforce, "is hardly on the cards. A man of Hector Brunton's social status would never behave like Carrington."

"I agree." Julia, who had been feeling for an idea, broached it very tentatively. "All the same, Mr. Wilberforce, I flatter myself that my knowledge of human nature is not often at fault. I met Hector Brunton once; and I summed him up. Believe me, he's not quite—not quite normal where the sex is concerned. And with abnormals, the normal course of action can never be absolutely relied upon. You realize, of course, my—shall we say difficulties?—in making up my mind. It would help me considerably if I were certain of the course this man Brunton intended to adopt. Could you—do you think—ascertain it for me?"

"I'm afraid"—all the legal caution in Wilberforce's nature repelled the suggestion—"that with the best will in the world I couldn't do that. Brunton is a K.C.—a very important K.C. If, by any chance, he decides to wait a month or two—But really, Mrs. Cavendish, with all due deference to your knowledge of human nature, I don't think we need anticipate any trouble from Brunton. All we have to do—you and I—is to await events; to minimize the scandal as far as we can; and to watch over your son's interests until such time as he returns to London."

The solicitor excused himself, rose, and shook hands. "You can rely upon me, you know," he smiled.

But, once more solitary, Julia Cavendish felt that neither on James Wilberforce nor on any other lawyer could she place reliance. To lawyers, matrimony was a contract; to her it was a holy sacrament. Scandal, unpopularity, she could face; but not her own conscience. And conscience already made her accessory to the sin of adultery!

All her prejudices against divorce returned fourfold, submerging her intellect as in slime. After Wilberforce's revelations, the holy institution of matrimony seemed the unholiest of legal farces.

She rang for Kate and ordered her to bring tea. "I'm at home to nobody," said Julia; and all afternoon she sat brooding, love and beliefs at war in her mind. All afternoon, her mind pictured Ronnie; the happy babydom, the fine youth, the clean manhood of him. All afternoon her love strove to acquit him before the tribunal of her beliefs.

And as day waned the romantic in her began to see something splendid in him, some courage akin to her own.

But in the woman she could, as yet, see no courage. The woman had sinned, sinned the deadly sin. Her, one could never forgive!

And yet—and yet—how could a mother abandon her son?

Suppose her son married this sinner? Stubbornly her mind tried to picture Aliette married to Ronnie. Stubbornly conscience repelled the picture. "She is Aliette Brunton," said Julia's beliefs. "She can never be Aliette Cavendish."

Then imagination put back the clock of her own years so that she saw herself thirty again. At thirty one had illusions; one had one's fastidiousnesses. And Brunton was no husband for a fastidious woman. Brunton might easily be a man such as Wilberforce had hinted of; an unfaithful husband against whom his wife possessed no legal remedy. What then?

"Even then," said Julia's beliefs, "she should have endured—as you, too, must endure."

"Yet how can you endure?" asked love. "How can you side with a stranger against your own boy?"

"Soon," answered beliefs, "you must face your God. How splendid if, on that day, you can declare to Him: 'I, like You, sacrificed my only son.'"

But love said: "God and Love are one."

And in that one instant of thought Julia Cavendish crossed her mental Rubicon. Formal religion went by the board. Be he saint or sinner, sordid or splendid, she, Julia Cavendish, would stick by her boy.

3

Now Julia was all impatience. Let the divorce-papers be served without delay! Let Brunton do his worst!

But Wilberforce, summoned next morning, begged her not to be precipitate. "Let us wait," said Wilberforce, "till Brunton shows his hand. At least let us wait till public rumor confirms private information."

Reluctantly Julia took his advice; and the slow days went by. Inaction chafed her. She did not weaken, but she suffered. Love needed the spur of service. Moreover, the old beliefs, scotched, were not yet slain. Conscience whispered to her in the long wakeful nights: "This is intellectual dishonesty. If it were any other than Ronnie, would you be willing to forgive?"

Her son's letter she did not answer. Time and again she took pen in hand; but always instinct, the instinct of parental dominance, restrained her. She had held the reins of her son's life so long that she still lusted to teach him a lesson. Since he had been a fool; since he had allowed the sentimental impulse to unbalance him in his duty toward her, let him write again. Besides, what could she say to him? It was not in her to slobber. When she wrote, it must be with some definite offer of help. To Julia, love without service always implied a certain hypocrisy: and that one concept, though every other seemed to have disintegrated under the stress of circumstance, her set mentality refused to change.

So she waited—ailing, fearful, lonely in her crowded life; thinking always of her son; blaming herself for their quarrel; blaming herself for inaction; her heart humble; her head high among the herd of men.

For as yet rumor knew nothing certain. The herd still patronized Bruton Street: you still met there, on a Saturday afternoon, the literary folk, the financial folk, the clergy, the politicians, and the soldiers. To the outward eye, no tiniest detail of social life in that exquisitely tended house had altered. Friends, acquaintances, casual visitors—so far, one hardly missed a face. Even the ambassadorial Bruntons came, in semi-state, trailing with them the ugly

162

unmarried daughter of Sir Simeon's first marriage and the two blithe flappers of his second.

Nevertheless, Julia was conscious of a growing tension.

Already—or so it seemed to her watchful imagination—the herd sniffed a taint. Dot Fancourt's eyes were an unspoken question. Lady Simeon exaggerated, ever so slightly, her smile of greeting. Paul Flower's inquiries after Ronnie—no one who knew Julia Cavendish ever forgot to make that inquiry—held the semblance of a leer. Others of her circle, saying: "And how's the son?" appeared as though they were anxious not to be answered.

Here and there, too, a clergyman or a politician excused his spouse with a strained, "My wife sends a thousand apologies. She wanted so much to come with me; but her health has been rather troublesome this week. Oh, no, dear lady! Nothing serious. Nothing serious, I assure you."

4

On the first of July, Sir John and Lady Bentham (of the Bank of England) gave a rather solemn family lunch-party, at which—rarest of occasions!—the four sisters Wixton met under one roof.

Looking at her three juniors—at Clementina, ample of breast and bustle, her chin duplicated and triplicated by age, her eyes piercing under their polished crystal lenses; at May Robinson, whose scrawny widowhood was alternately devoted to good works and the cultivation of her St. John's Wood garden; at Alice Edwards, typically the Anglo-Indian woman, her complexion faded but her joviality unimpaired, her blue-eyed golden-haired Lucy in attendance, but her livery husband abandoned in Cheltenham—it came to Julia, seated beside her gray-haired host at the head of the table, that families were a curse. Never a united tribe, to-day the Wixtons seemed more at variance than ever. Julia resented May's pseudo-intimate chatter and the tactless pryings of Alice. Clementina she had always abhorred. And when Lucy tried to question her about Ronnie, her resentment reached fever-point.

For, of course—said Julia's imagination—when the family knew about Ronnie, they would gloat. Clementina, always envious of her treasure, would be in the seventh heaven at his downfall. May would weep a "Poor Julia! I always told her that she spoiled that boy." And Alice would chuckle: "It's just like Simla. Married women are always the worst."

How soon would the family know? Ronnie's secret had been well kept; but it couldn't be kept a secret much longer. Had Sir John, perhaps, heard something already?

Julia's mind wandered away from the family to Chilworth Cove. She had never seen the place, but intuition told her that it must be beautiful; and she found herself craving, suddenly, furiously, in that stuffy Cromwell Road mansion, for beauty, for the sea and the sunlight.

*

Perhaps, though, it was Sir John's confidences about *his* son which impelled the homing mother to stop her electric brougham at the Cromwell Road post-office; and write, with unsteady fingers, those six words: "Would my presence be unwelcome? MATER."

Chapter XIV

1

"Man—you're glad she's coming?"

"If her coming means that she is on our side; yes."

It was ten o'clock of a great July day. From outside, through the low foliaged casement of Honeysuckle Cottage, sounded the drone of a bee, the whine and splash of the well-bucket, and Caroline Staley's loud-voiced chaffering with a fisherman. Within, the lovers faced each other across the debris of a Gargantuan breakfast.

Seen, white-frocked, in the sun-moted coolth of that low whitewashed room, Aliette looked utterly the girl. Happiness had wiped clean the slate of her desolate years. Her cheeks, her eyes, her whole personality glowed with the sheer joy of matehood. Sunlight and sea-light had goldened—ever so faintly—the luster of her bared arms, the bared nape under her vivid hair.

Ronnie, too, had youthened. Gone, or almost gone from his face, was the semi-monastic seriousness. Constantly, now, smiles played about his full lips; constantly, his light-blue eyes held the semblance of a twinkle. One hardly noticed the gray in his hair for the tawn of it. Lean still, to-day his leanness was that of an athlete in training. Under his browned skin, when they bathed together, the muscles rippled like a panther's. As he rose, flanneled, from the table, it seemed almost as though happiness had added the proverbial cubit to his stature.

He came over to her and kissed the palm of her outstretched hand, her wrist, the curls at her temple.

"This afternoon," he said, "our honeymoon ends."

She laughed—but there was something of sadness in the laughter. "Man, don't be immoral. Honeymoons are legal. This hasn't been legal. It's been—"

"Heaven," he suggested.

"Yes." She took his hand. "All that—and more. But all the same, we're outcasts. We've got to realize that the world, our world, won't forgive us for having been in heaven."

Sotto voce, he consigned the world to perdition. Aloud, he answered,

165

"They'll forgive us all right. As soon as H. B. makes up his mind to do the right thing. I expect that's what's at the bottom of the mater's wire."

"Do you?" Intimacy had made this great difference in their relationship: that they could talk of Hector dispassionately enough. "Do you? I wish I were sure. He's a peculiar man. Very obstinate and rather cruel. He may make—difficulties."

"He'll make no difficulties."

Aliette changed the topic. For a week past, the vague possibility of Hector's abiding by his threat had been frightening her. Once, even, she had precisely perceived the social ostracism such a course might entail. But in the sunshine and sea-shine of Chilworth Cove, social ostracism seemed a very tiny price to pay for happiness so great as theirs.

The first fine madness, the glamor of the grand passion was still on her, still on them both. Julia's telegram, which—cycle-forwarded across eight miles of common-land from Chilton Junction—threw the tiny port into a state of seething curiosity, excited its recipients hardly at all. Selfish with the sublime selfishness of mating-time, they regarded the threatened irruption of a mundane personality into paradise as the merest episode.

Nevertheless, as she watched the innkeeper's pony-cart, Ronnie at its reins, rattle away between the pink-washed cottages, slow to a walk up the white road, and disappear among the heathery ridges at sky-line, Aliette grew conscious of a deep abiding joy that—whatever else of harm she might bring into her lover's life—at least she had not separated him from his mother.

And all morning, all afternoon, busied with Caroline Staley in preparation for their guest, that joy warded every apprehension from her mind.

2

But in the heart of Ronald Cavendish, setting out alone on his eight-mile journey for the station, was no joy. To him, it seemed as though he were definitely abandoning happiness, definitely leaving it behind. Mentally and physically obsessed with Aliette, he could anticipate no pleasure in again seeing his mother. Indeed, he could hardly visualize his mother at all.

Gradually, though, as the brown pony ambled its uneager way along the white and empty track among the heather, the image of Julia's face, the sound of Julia's voice came back to him; and he, too, knew joy at the prospect of reconciliation.

Looking back on their quarrel, it appeared to him that he had been rather brutal. "After all," he thought, "one could hardly have expected her to understand. I'm glad Alie insisted on my writing that letter. I wonder if the mater'll be looking well. I hope she'll like Alie. She's sure to like Alie."

Then, from thinking of his mother and the woman he loved, he glided into thought of the world in which they must all three live till Brunton's decree had been obtained and made absolute. It would be—he mused—a bit difficult, rather a rough time.

Aliette's "funny idea" that Brunton might try "the dog-in-the-manger trick," Aliette's lover dismissed—much in the way that Jimmy Wilberforce had dismissed it—as "not on the cards." All the same, the lawyer in him did begin to find it curious that Brunton's solicitors should have dilly-dallied so long in communicating through Benjamin Bunce that the citations were ready for service.

"The mater's sure to have some news," he thought; and by the time his pony topped the ridge from which one sees, three miles away at the foot of the slope, the red roofs and shining rails of Chilton Junction, he felt quite excited about her arrival.

Always strong in the every-day relationship of man to man, but never—until now—decisive in his dealings with woman, Ronnie knew himself rather anxious for Julia's advice. Socially, the period between divorce and remarriage must have many drawbacks. "The mater's" guidance, at such a time, might be most useful.

Of the heart-searchings, of the contest between her love and her beliefs, which even now (as the slow train jolted her, maidless, uncomfortable, in her crowded first-class compartment, out of Andover) still nagged at the intellect of Julia Cavendish, her son had never an inkling. From his point of view, their quarrel—for his share in which he had already apologized by letter—appeared infinitely more important than "the mater's silly prejudice about divorce." Most important, of course, would be "how the mater would hit it off with Aliette."

Ronnie drove on till he made the Chilton Arms; and there, stabling his pony, ordered himself an early luncheon.

The luncheon—solitary cold beef and lukewarm beer—made him realize that it was more than six weeks since he had mealed alone; and from that realization thought traveled—almost automatically—to his rooms in Jermyn Street, to Pump Court, to the past which had been London and the future which must still be London. Smoking, he began to consider the various problems of return.

Where, how, and on what were he and Aliette to live?

Of Aliette's finances, beyond one confided fact that "she had never taken an allowance from "H.," her lover knew nothing whatever. She might, for all he cared, possess five hundred a year or ten thousand. But his own professional income, excluding the four hundred a year from his mother, barely touched the former figure; and since he was by no means the kind of creature who could consent to live on a woman's money, however desperately he might be in love with her, the housing problem alone—Moses Moffatt, officially, sheltered only bachelors—would need more than a little solving.

Consideration of this, and other mundane factors in their somewhat bizarre situation, fretted Ronnie's mind. He could not help feeling, as he drove slowly to the station, how much wiser it would have been if he and Alie had talked these things over before he started. His mother, who liked practical women, might not understand that Alie and he had been too madly happy to bother about every-day affairs. "But by Jove!" he said to himself; "by Jove, we have been happy."

He hitched the brown pony to the railings and strode through the waiting-room. That afternoon Chilton Junction seemed less of a junction than ever. A few rustics, a few milk-cans, two porters, and the miniature of a bookstall occupied its "down" platform; its "up" showed as a stretch of deserted gravel, from either end of which the hot rails ran straight into pasture.

Looking Londonward along those narrowing rails, remembering how, six weeks since, they had carried him into paradise, Ronald Cavendish understood—for the merest fraction of a second—his mother's sacrifice.

"Damn decent of the old lady to come down," he thought, seeing, still far away across the pastures, the leisured smoke-plume of her train.

3

Julia Cavendish—having ascertained from her latest *vis-à-vis*, a burly cattle-dealer in brown leggings and a black bowler hat, that her journey at last neared its destination—closed the novel she had been pretending to read, straightened her hat, and prepared to meet both culprits with stern Victorian condescension.

That Aliette would not accompany Ronnie to the station did not cross his mother's mind. All the way down from Waterloo she had been apprehensive, doubtful of her own rectitude, conscious of a growing antagonism toward "that woman." "That woman," of course, would be furious at the interruption of her amour.

Even the prospect of seeing Ronnie once more could not lighten the cloud of jealousy and self-distrust which Julia felt hovering—like evil birds—about her head. Viewed in retrospect, the five hours of journeying were a nightmare. Viewed prospectively, arrival would be the ugliest of awakenings. She felt ill; ill and old and out-of-date.

But the first glimpse of her son sent all Julia's evil birds flying. As the train steamed in, she saw him craning his eyes at its windows; saw that he was alone, that he was sun-bronzed, flanneled like a schoolboy. Her heart thumped—painfully, joyfully—at the knowledge that he had espied her, that he was loping along after her carriage, just as she remembered him loping along the platform at Winchester, in his cricket-flannels, twenty years ago. Then the train stopped; and he swung the carriage door open, handed her out.

"My luggage—" began Julia; but got no further with the sentence; because

Ronnie, her Ronnie, who had never, even as a boy, caressed his mother in public, just put an arm round her shoulders and, kissing her, whispered: "By jingo, mater, it is ripping to see you."

A porter got her trunk and her handbag out of the train. Another porter put them into the pony-cart. Julia, for once in her life, forgot to thank them. Tears, tears she dared not shed, twitched her wrinkled eyelids; her mouth had dried up; her thin knees tottered. She could only cling, cling with all the strength of one weak arm, to Ronnie. He was her son, her only son—and she, in her stupid pride, had thought to let prejudice come between them. Her jealousy of "that woman" disappeared. The happiness, the health, the rejuvenation of Ronnie were sufficient justification, in her eyes, for Aliette. No worthless woman could have put those sunny words into her boy's mouth, that sun-bronze on his cheeks!

Ronnie, too, was moved almost to tears. The first sight of his mother, reacting on the emotions of the past weeks, struck him to consciousness of his love for her. She needed his protection more than ever before. She looked so frail, so suffering. She had suffered—because of him, because of Aliette. His heart went out to both women—in pity, in self-condemnation.

He helped her into the trap (it no longer surprised her to find they were alone) and said: "I'm afraid it's not very comfortable. That cushion's for your back. We'll have some tea at the Arms before we start."

She managed to answer: "Yes, dear. I think I would like some tea." To herself she said: "I wonder which of them thought about giving me tea, about bringing this cushion."

Ronnie clambered up; took the reins; and tipped the porters. In silence, they drove to the inn.

There the hot tea and the hot buttered toast, which he coaxed her to eat, brought back a little of Julia's courage; but the waitress, popping—eager-faced at sight of strangers—in and out of the coffee-room, made free speech impossible. Perforce they confined conversation to generalities. He, she said, "looked extraordinarily well." She, he said, "looked the least bit tired." The lunch on the train, she told him, had been "execrable." The drive to the

Cove, he told her, was a "good eight miles" and they would have to "take things easy" because of the luggage. Ought they, he asked, to have ordered her a car? Oh, no—she smiled, she preferred the trap: it would give them more time to talk.

"I rather expected you'd bring Smithers," mentioned Ronnie.

"I didn't think a maid—advisable," declared Julia.

He paid for her tea, and they set off again—each silently uncertain of the other, each silently and socially constrained. But at last, as they drew clear of the town, Julia conquered constraint.

"And how is Aliette?" she asked quietly.

All the way down in the train she had intended to speak both to and of "that woman" as "Mrs. Brunton"; but since seeing Ronnie she knew that she could never even think in terms of "Mrs. Brunton" or of "that woman" again. Sinner in the eyes of the world, in the eyes of the mother whose boy she had made so happy, Hector Brunton's guilty wife was already a saint.

"Quite well." His quietness matched her own.

"I'm glad."

And suddenly, impetuously, he burst out:

"Mater, she's so wonderful."

Now mother and son were alone in a world of sky and heather; and the brown pony, as though aware of impending confidences, slowed to a walk. She put a tremulous hand on his driving arm.

"Tell me—the whole story," said Julia.

His fingers loosed the reins; and that afternoon, as the brown pony ambled toward the sea, he told her the full tale of his love for Aliette, of his love for both of them: till, listening, it seemed to Julia Cavendish as though never before had she understood the heart of her son.

And that afternoon, for the first time in all her sixty years, she—whose lifelong struggle had been to cramp life in the bonds of formal religion—saw that formal religion at its very highest could only be a code for slaves, for the weak and the ignorant. For the soul of a free individual, for the strong and the wise of the earth, no formalities—whether of religion, of law, or of social observances—could exist.

The individual souls of the wise and the strong brooked no earthly master. Lonely arbiters of heaven and of hell, their own gods, their own priests and lawgivers, only love could control them, only conscience guide.

Ignorantly, blindly, she, Julia Cavendish, had sought to fetter the free souls, the wise and the strong. And behold! in the very person of her own son they had broken loose from her fetters. Ronnie, her own dearly-beloved son, was of the free! All that her formal religion had preached him wrong, love had shown him to be right; and with love had come both strength and wisdom, so that he had followed his conscience into the freedom which her ignorance would have denied him.

For that Ronnie's conscience was as clear, as limpid-clear of sin as it had been in boyhood, Julia—listening to him—could not doubt. Nor, hugging that certainty, could she doubt Aliette. Love was justified of both by the sheer test of happiness. As well accuse the birds of deadly sin as these two who, moved by an impulse so overwhelming that to deny it would have been a denial of their very natures, had—mated.

4

Aliette, shading her eyes from the sun, watched the pony-cart top sky-line, and crawl leisurely down-hill. At sight of it, her heart misgave her. Every tradition in which she had been reared, all her social sense and all her love for Ronnie warned her that the meeting with Ronnie's mother would be, at its best, awkward—and its worst, disastrous.

In Chilworth Cove, with only Caroline Staley for confidante of their secret (and Caroline, from the first, had been definitely partizan, loyalty itself), she had grown so accustomed to thinking of herself as Ronnie's wife, that it was quite a shock to perceive, with the approach of a being from her own world (a woman who, however much she might pretend sympathy, must be, in her heart, hostile), their exact relationship.

"I'm her son's mistress," thought Aliette; and suddenly seeing herself and her lover through the eyes of the ordinary world, realized the tragedy of those who, knowing themselves not guilty at the bar of their own consciences, can nevertheless sympathize with the many who condemn them. Which is perhaps the heaviest cross that any woman can be forced to carry!

Ponto, darting hot-foot out of Honeysuckle Cottage at the sound of wheels, banished further introspection. Aliette just had time to grab the great hound by the collar as the brown pony, eager for his evening hay, came trotting up; and was still holding him, her bared forearm tense with the effort, when the trap drew to the door. So that—as it happened—the exact greeting of the "harpy" to the mother whose boy she had stolen was, "I do hope you're not frightened of dogs, Mrs. Cavendish," and the mother's to the harpy, "Not in the very least. That's Ponto, I presume. Ronnie's told me about him."

There is, after all, something to be said for a social code which enables people to carry off difficult situations with an air of complete insouciance! Julia Cavendish stepped down from the dilapidated conveyance; shook hands; admitted that she would like to get tidy; and followed her hostess's lithe figure down a whitewashed passage, up one flight of rather crazy staircase, into a low-ceiled bedroom, obviously scrubbed out that day. The room was very plainly furnished, yet it had about it the particular atmosphere which indicates, as between one woman and another: "We expected you. We made preparations for you."

"I'm afraid it isn't up to much," said Aliette shyly. "But we've put a writing-table under the window—just in case."

Julia Cavendish looked at the table, at the pens and the ink-pot and the jar of flowers on the table; Julia Cavendish looked at the little shy woman, so gorgeous in her mating beauty, so socially correct in her shyness; and the "Mrs. Brunton, this is a very serious position" with which—ten hours since—she had firmly made up her mind to open their conversation, vanished into the limbo of unuttered sentences.

"I'm afraid," said Julia Cavendish, "that this visit is rather—an intrusion."

"It is I who am the intruder," answered Aliette simply; and then, seeing that Julia, who had seated herself on the side of the bed, was fumbling at the unaccustomed task of removing her own hat: "Can't I help?"

"Thank you, my dear," said Julia.

Caroline Staley, bringing hot water, knocked; deposited her copper jug by the washhand-stand; and departed with the unspoken thought, "Better leave they two alone for a while."

And, for a while, "they two" scrutinized one another in silence—the elder woman still seated; the younger, diffident, very uncertain of what next to say, upright beside her.

At last the younger woman said, "You must be tired after your journey. You'd like to change into a tea-gown, wouldn't you? Caroline is quite a good maid. I'll send her and your box up." She made a movement to go, but the elder woman restrained her.

"I think I'd rather talk first. We've got a good many things to talk about, haven't we? Won't you sit down?" Julia patted the clean counterpane in further invitation.

"You're very kind, Mrs. Cavendish." Aliette, still standing, shook her head ever so slightly, as one refusing a gift. "Too kind. And I'm glad you've forgiven Ronnie. But you needn't, really you needn't forgive me. You came to see your son, not your son's"—she hesitated—"lady-love. I'm quite willing to—to efface myself as long as you're here." She smiled proudly. "Though, as it's rather a tiny cottage, you mustn't mind seeing me occasionally."

Her favorite word "Rubbish!" rose to Julia's lips; but was instantly repressed. Proud herself, she could both respect and sympathize with the pride in the other.

"I'm wondering," she said after a pause, "just how much my son's lady-love loves my son."

At that, Aliette's eyes suffused. But she could make no reply, and Julia went on:

"My dear, do you think I don't know how much you care for him? Do you think I don't realize that you have made him happy? Happier than I ever did. Won't you make me happy too? Won't you try and care, just a little, for me—for Ronnie's mother?"

"Don't, please don't." The proud lips trembled. "It hurts me that you—that you—" And suddenly, impulsively, Aliette was on her knees—her head bowed, her shoulders shaking to the sobs that had broken pride.

"I love him"—the words, tear-choked, were scarcely audible—"I adore him. I'd kill myself to-morrow if I thought it would be for Ronnie's good. I never meant, I never meant to come between you and him. I never intended that you"—the brown head lifted, the brown eyes gazed up into Julia's blue—"that you should have to know me until—until things were put right. You needn't—after this. I'll be quite content—if you'll let him come to me—sometimes—to take a little house—to wait for him. I don't want you to be—mixed up in things you hate. I don't want to—to flaunt myself with your son."

Said Julia Cavendish, speaking stiffly lest the tears blind her: "You haven't answered my question, Aliette. I may call you Aliette, mayn't I? You haven't yet told me whether you could care for—Ronnie's mother?"

For answer, Aliette took one of the old hands between her two youthful ones; and, bowing her head again, kissed it.

"You oughtn't to forgive me. You oughtn't to call me Aliette," whispered "that woman."

"Ronnie will be so furious with me if he thinks I've made you cry," whispered back Ronnie's mother; and leaning forward, took "that woman" in her arms.

*

What those two said to one another, in the hushed half-hour while Ronnie waited for them in the tiny garden and Caroline Staley busied herself over the kitchen fire, only the bees, droning ceaselessly round the clematis, overheard.

5

It was very late for Chilworth Cove: past ten o'clock of a dull heavy night: the stars veiled: the purr of a torpid sea coming faint down the Ghyll. One by one the lights in the village windows had been extinguished. But light still poured from the windows of Honeysuckle Cottage; and through the light-motes, the smoke of a man's cigar outcurled in blue seashell whorls that hung long-time—meditative as the man—in the windless quiet.

Ronald Cavendish threw the butt of his cigar after the smoke-whorls, and turned to the two women in the room.

"The mater's right," he said. "We must make some move. But it's no earthly use writing to Jimmy. Jimmy can't help us. The only thing to be done is for me to go up to town and see H. B. myself."

Ever since Caroline had cleared away dinner, they had been discussing the problem of Brunton's inactivity. To Aliette, pride-bound, feeling herself—despite the new alliance with Julia Cavendish—still guilty, still the interloper, it seemed best that they should wait. Silently resenting, yet chiding herself all the while for her resentment, the whole discussion, she had held herself, whenever possible, aloof from it.

But now she could hold aloof no longer. No coward in her own love; willing, for herself, to take any and all risks; the suggested meeting filled her with apprehension for Ronnie.

"I beg you not to do that," she said.

"Why not?" Ronnie laughed. "He can't eat me."

"I'd so much rather you didn't. Perhaps he's only waiting because of some difficulty, some legal difficulty. Wouldn't it be better if I wrote to him again, if we both wrote to him? After all, we mustn't forget that"—she stumbled over the phrase—"we're in the wrong."

"Writing won't do any good," pronounced Julia. "Ninety-nine letters out of every hundred are perfectly futile. The hundredth—is usually an irrevocable mistake."

The novelist, rather pleased with the epigram, sat back in her basketwork chair. For the first time since her quarrel with Ronnie, she had regained that peculiar power of mental detachment—of seeing real personalities, her own included, as characters in a book—which is the exclusive property of the literary temperament.

"All the same," she went on, "I can't help feeling that a personal interview would be risky. It might only exacerbate the position."

Gilbert Frankau

"Risky or not," said a determined Ronnie, "it's the only possible thing to be done. Unless H. B. files his petition at once, we shall have to wait the best part of a year before we can get married. And remember, we haven't only ourselves to consider—there's Aliette's family. They'll have to be told sooner or later. Think how much easier it would be if we could tell them that everything was properly arranged."

Julia's newly-regained detachment deserted her. Turning to Aliette, she asked nervously:

"But don't your parents know? Haven't you written to them?"

"Not yet." Beyond the lamplight, the younger woman's face showed scarcely an emotion. "It seemed so useless. You see, I'm not an only child. There'll be no forgiveness—on their side. Mollie may stand by me. But Eva won't. Mother and Andrew will take Eva's advice. They only cared for my brothers. When my brothers were killed, it was just as if everything had gone out of their lives." And she added—pathetically, thought Julia Cavendish, who, loving her own son more than anything in the world, always found difficulty in realizing how frail is the average tie between parents and grown-up daughters: "Mother's rather fond of Eva's children."

"Still, we have to consider them," interrupted Aliette's, lover. "We don't want them to hear the news from—the other side. I think you should write to them, Alie. Mollie I'll go and see myself. Jimmy's sure to know her address. I wonder if she and Jimmy are engaged—"

"Your friend Wilberforce," interrupted Julia, "may be an excellent solicitor; but he's an extremely selfish young man."

"What makes you say that?" asked Aliette; and as Julia did not reply, "Has he spoken to you—about my sister?"

"He has." Julia's voice was rather grim.

"And is—what we've done—going to make any difference?"

"I think not. But if it does," the suspicion of a twinkle gleamed in the blue eyes, "if it does, my dear, your sister will owe you a great debt of gratitude for—running away with my son. That kind of man," definitely, "is no use."

"I've been rather worried about Mollie," began Aliette, whose decision not

177

to await her sister's return had been the most difficult of all the decisions she took in those few hours before she bolted from Lancaster Gate. "That letter of mine—"

She broke off the sentence, divining nevertheless that her letter—meant as a precise document—must have been incoherent to the last degree; divining how impossible a situation her selfishness must have created for Mollie. "I am selfish," she said to herself. "Utterly selfish! I deserve no consideration. And yet these two consider only me."

"Never mind about Mollie." Stubbornly—for now that his mother had joined forces with them it seemed more than ever necessary that they should bring Brunton swiftly to reason—Ronald Cavendish returned to his point. "The question is: When do I go up to town? In my opinion, the sooner the better. Once I have seen H. B., we shall at least know where we stand."

"And suppose," faltered Aliette, "suppose he refuses to see you?"

"He won't."

"Suppose he refuses to do anything?"

"You needn't be afraid of that. A man in his position is bound to take action. If he doesn't—"

"If he doesn't," broke in Julia, "we must fight him. We three." She rose from the creaky chair; and Aliette, seeing the determination, the courage in those old eyes, felt suddenly ashamed of her own weakness. "Meanwhile, I think I'll go to bed. Your maid promised to wait up for me."

Kissing "that woman" good night, Ronnie's mother whispered: "Don't try to overpersuade him. If he feels it is right—he must be allowed to go."

6

Very early next morning, before dawn lightened to palest rose behind the clematis blossoms, the woman who had left her husband, waking with her lover's arms about her, prayed voicelessly to that God whose priests would henceforth bar her from His communion, that Ronnie's love might endure to the end.

For now, Aliette was afraid.

Chapter XV

1

Two days subsequent to his mother's arrival at Chilworth Cove, Ronald Cavendish set out for London.

Aliette, masking her anxiety, drove him to the station; and for nearly an hour after the slow train left Chilton Junction he visualized nothing except her pale, exquisite face and the wistful smile in her brown eyes. Looking back, it seemed to him that those eyes had been very close to tears. Thinking of her, imagination roused all the tenderness, all the fighting instinct in him.

But gradually, as the lush countryside slid by, Ronnie's mind recovered a little of its legal function; and he began to map out, as carefully as he could, his plan of campaign.

The fear lest Brunton should refuse to take any action still hardly troubled him. To one of his public school training, it appeared utterly incredible that a man in Brunton's position, childless and without religious scruples, should refuse to set free a wife who obviously did not care for him, and for whom (equally obviously, as it seemed) he did not himself care. Sheer caddishness of that description was the prerogative of rank outsiders like Carrington.

Nevertheless, Ronnie's instinct dictated caution. It would he best, he thought, to see Jimmy immediately on his arrival in London; and to ascertain from Jimmy how far his flight with Aliette had become public knowledge. Possibly, if there had been no open scandal, Brunton might hold his hand till after the long vacation. Scandal, whether at the bar or elsewhere, never did any one any good.

And at that, Ronald Cavendish knew apprehension. His brain, hitherto blinded by the grand passion, began to see the ordinary point of view, the point of view he himself might have adopted towards their case a twelvemonth since. "Rather sordid," he would have considered the whole business, "rather hard luck on the husband." And so thinking, he imagined the bare legal tale as it might one day appear in the press. Commonplace enough! Mrs. Smith had left Mr. Smith, and was living in open adultery with Mr. Jones. Mr. Smith asked for a divorce; produced the usual evidence;

179

secured the usual decree.

He tried to put apprehension away from him. He said to himself, "As if a little publicity mattered; as if anything mattered except her freedom." All the same, he knew that publicity would matter, that publicity would hurt Aliette and hurt his mother. "Damnable," he thought; "damnable that the law should take so little cognizance of the personal equation!"

And London, seen in the hot sunlight of a July afternoon as his taxi crawled over Waterloo Bridge, only intensified the unimportance of the individual. The isolation of Chilworth, the paradise of enchantment which love and Aliette had made for him at Chilworth, seemed a million miles removed from this peopled city. He recognized himself one of the herd again, forced to think as the herd, to act as the herd dictated. Moses Moffatt's face, smiling most confidential of welcomes at the green door in Jermyn Street, typified the herd point of view—the basement point of view—the feeling that, potentially, one was a mere co-respondent.

While the man was unpacking for him in the bare ascetic bedroom, Ronnie rang up Wilberforce, Wilberforce & Cartwright; and got through to Jimmy. Jimmy on the telephone sounded cold, serious, dignified. Only after some persuasion would he consent to dine at the club.

"And by the way," asked Ronnie, "do you happen to know if Mollie Fullerford's in town?"

"Why?"

"I've got a letter for her."

"From her sister?"

"Yes."

"I'll give you her address this evening," said James Wilberforce, and replaced his receiver.

2

The Lustrum is one of those semi-social, semi-political clubs which combine sound cookery, a cellar beyond reproach, and a chairman of the utmost distinction, with the architectural style of a Turkish bath and the gloom of a family mausoleum. A tape-machine ticks by the glass-doored porter's box in the hall; an enormous gold-framed oil of Mr. Asquith stares down the red marble staircase; English waiters—last of their breed—move in unhurried dignity through the vast dining-room; while "members bringing guests" are subject to rules so complicated that even the honorary secretary—who takes most of the credit for the paid secretary's work when he appears before a somnolent committee—has been known to infringe them.

The constraint of this atmosphere weighed so heavily on the friends as to make immediate conversation impossible. Only after a bottle of the Lustrum's pre-war Pommard, a glass apiece of the Lustrum's '68 port, and the third of a cigar consumed over coffee in the stuffy guest-room, did Jimmy Wilberforce manage:

"Old chap, I'm afraid this is a devil of a mess. You've seen your mater, I suppose!"

"Seen her!" Ronnie smiled—and then, cautiously: "Didn't you know that she was staying with us?"

"Us?" Wilberforce repeated the word. "You mean—"

"With myself and Aliette."

Wilberforce's eyes narrowed. He took the tawny cigar from under his auburn mustache, and scrutinized it a longish while before saying:

"Tell me, then: why are you in town?"

"Primarily to see H. B. We've waited quite long enough for him to make a move."

The matter-of-fact tone annoyed Wilberforce. Despite his resolves not to let the personal issue between himself and Aliette's sister cloud impersonal judgment, that issue had been recurring to his mind all through the dreary bachelor dinner. For six weeks Mollie had been on the defensive with him, unseizable if not unapproachable; for six weeks he had been wavering between the strong desire to "go gently till this damn mess was cleared up," and the fear of what "Society" would think about the match. Therefore, it irritated him that Ronnie should speak about the whole affair as though running away with another man's wife were an every-day occurrence, as though he, Ronnie, were the injured party.

"Rather an unwise move, don't you think?" he said.

"Unwise! One can't let him go on shilly-shallying like this."

"If you've got it into your head that you're going to bully Hector Brunton into giving Mrs. Brunton her freedom," retorted Jimmy, "I should give up the idea"; and he added: "I should have thought your best plan would be to lie doggo. After all, you must remember that he's the aggrieved party."

"If you feel that way about it," Ronnie's eyes kindled to anger, "we won't discuss the matter further."

At that Wilberforce became the solicitor.

"My dear fellow," he began, assuming his father's blandness, "do be reasonable. Don't think I fail to understand your feelings. I know you well enough to realize that you wouldn't have acted as you have acted without imagining yourself justified. Very possibly you are justified. Very possibly there are circumstances—I hold no brief for H. B. All I want to do is to help you and your mother. And so if you come to me for advice, I am bound to tell you exactly what I think. It's for Brunton to move, not you."

"He's had plenty of time. And I'm sick of waiting."

"Then why don't you get some mutual friend to see him? That's the usual thing."

Ronnie rose from the deep saddle-bag chair. His instinct was all for a row. Unreasonably, with the divine unreason of a lover, he had expected sympathy; instead he had met a wall, a wall of misunderstanding between himself and his best friend. "Damn Jimmy," he thought. "Jimmy's common sense ought to tell him that this isn't the usual thing."

And suddenly Aliette's lover realized that Jimmy's common sense had told him nothing, that Jimmy's very common sense prevented him from understanding the peculiar relationship between Aliette and her legal owner. He wanted to tell Jimmy the truth about that relationship; but his training, the code of decent reticence, every tradition of public schooldom restrained him. Decency suggested that neither then to James Wilberforce, nor eventually in court, could he make public the matrimonial position between

Aliette and Hector. "Tongue-tied!" he thought. "Even if I were an orator, in *her* defense I should always be tongue-tied."

Nevertheless, his anger relented.

"Except yourself, Jimmy," he went on, "there's no mutual friend who could act for us; and I can't ask you to act because of your firm's relations with him. Therefore, I'm going to do the job myself."

There was almost admiration in the other's "You always were a plucky devil."

"Plucky! I don't see anything plucky in it."

"Supposing H. B. cuts up rough?"

"Why should he? He's in the wrong, and he knows it."

"All the more reason." Wilberforce, too, rose. Watching his friend carefully, he saw that their conversation had aroused him to fighting-pitch; and Ronnie at fighting-pitch—as Jimmy remembered from their Oxford days—was capable of being a rather desperate person.

"Don't you cut up rough, old man," he continued. "There'll be quite enough trouble without a police-court case into the bargain."

"You needn't be afraid, Jimmy." Ronnie controlled himself. "I'll manage to keep my temper with the fellow. By the way, you don't feel there's any chance of his refusing to file his petition, do you?"

"Hardly. H. B. isn't a religious chap, or anything of that sort. He might go for damages, of course."

"We could settle that before we went into court."

They simmered down; sat down; relit cigars; and began to discuss the legal aspect of the case which each felt sure that Brunton must eventually bring; finally deciding that Wilberforce, Wilberforce & Cartwright could not, under the special circumstances, act for either party.

"J. J. W. would be your best man," said James.

So interested did they become in the professional issue that it was nearly midnight before Ronnie said, "By the way, I'd almost forgotten to ask you for Mollie Fullerford's address"; and Wilberforce, "Do you really think it's advisable for you to go and see her?"

"Advisable! How do you mean?"

The two friends faced one another in silence, each constrained by the peculiar diffidence of their class, the diffidence which makes the discussion of women, and especially of their own women, so terribly difficult to decent Englishmen.

At last Wilberforce said: "You see, old chap, if this case comes on, I'm afraid it will be a big shock to her. H. B. might call her as a witness. Pretty rough on a girl, being dragged into"—he hesitated—"this sort of thing."

"Yes, rotten. We'll have to keep her name out." Ronnie, too, hesitated. "She hasn't said anything to you, I suppose?"

"No, but I feel she knows." The red man nearly blushed. "I say, you'll be decent about breaking things, won't you? You'll let her down lightly. Mollie's jolly fond of her sister, and—er—you mustn't mind my saying it—her sister hasn't behaved over-well in this business—leaving her all by herself at Brunton's."

"My fault, Jimmy. It was I who persuaded Aliette not to wait. But I promise you, I'll see that Brunton keeps Mollie Fullerford's name out of the affair.

"By the way," added Ronnie casually, "you remember something you said to me just before we went into court in the Ellerson case?" A pause. "Does that still hold good? What I mean is this. I should never forgive myself if I thought that this—this trouble of mine—"

"I'm not that sort of cad," retorted James Wilberforce hotly. But all the same, walking home through the night, he realized once more—with revolting clarity—himself. Which self-knowledge is no bad discipline for the James Wilberforces of this world!

3

Ronnie, too, walked home from the Lustrum. The interview with Wilberforce had clarified his mind; he foresaw now exactly how his world would regard the case. The foreknowledge hardened his determination to see Brunton. He must see Brunton. Brunton must be brought to immediate action. Otherwise—

Gilbert Frankau

Resolutely the man strove to put that "otherwise" away from him. But the "otherwise" kept on intruding. Suppose Aliette's legal owner refused to take any action at all? Carrington had waited five years.

And that night, his first bereft of her, alone and sleepless at Jermyn Street, Aliette's lover began to conceive a hatred of Aliette's legal owner. The Wixton imagination, always most active in darkness, showed him pictures of Brunton, of the sandy hair, the cold gray eyes, the feet in their big boots. Tossing sleepless on his tumbled pillows, imagination bade him remember that once—long ago though it must have been—Brunton had actually—

Horrors, physical horrors, capered and sarabanded before his eyes, rousing the blood-lust in him—the old blood-lust experienced four years since. He remembered, just as sleep overtook him, the face of a Turk he had killed. His squadron was charging. Behind him, he heard the galloping stamp of shod hoofs on desert, the creak of saddlery, the jingle of accoutrements, the curses of his men; in front of him rose a face, the face of the Turk, bearded above dirty linen. The face was afraid; he could see the face twitch as he fired. Only as he fired, the face changed—became the face of Hector Brunton.

4

"I'm afraid you didn't sleep very well last night, sir," said Moses Moffatt, serving the usual faultless rashers in Ronnie's beige-papered sitting-room.

"What makes you say that?" Ronnie, clear-eyed after his morning tub, looked across the breakfast-table.

"Well, sir," Moses Moffatt smiled deprecatingly, "if you don't mind my mentioning it, the missus and me heard you calling out in your sleep."

"Is that so? I'm sorry if I disturbed you."

Ronnie, remembering his dream only very vaguely, ate his breakfast; skimmed through the "Morning Post"; took his top-hat, and sauntered downstairs into Jermyn Street.

It had not yet struck ten. Fishmongers were still swilling down their marbles. The usual early morning crowd had emerged into sunshine from the Piccadilly Tube. Ronnie swung past them down the Haymarket.

185

The Love-Story of Aliette Brunton

The asphalt of London, the cars, the buses, and the taxicabs seemed more than ever alien after the sea and the solitude of Chilworth Cove. He felt like a stranger in a strange, hostile city. Only as he emerged through Northumberland Avenue upon the Embankment did London seem home again; only as he turned leftward from the river into the Temple did there come over him the full realization of the issue at stake.

In his chambers at Pump Court nothing had altered. Tho other three barristers were, as usual, away; Benjamin Bunce, as usual, pottering among the foolscaps. The little clerk's watery eyes lit with curiosity at sight of the returning wanderer.

"There were papers," hinted Benjamin, "there was correspondence."

Benjamin's employer glanced at the taped documents on the table, at the unopened letters. "They can wait," he said. "Has Mr. Brunton's clerk inquired for my address?"

"No, sir."

"You're sure?"

"Quite sure, sir."

"Very good. I'll ring when I want you."

The clerk—a thousand unanswered questions seething in his soul—withdrew.

Ronnie hung his hat behind the door, and began striding up and down the book-shelved room. Here, he remembered, he had first tried to reason out his feelings for Aliette. Here, just before the Ellerson case, he had almost decided it his duty to give her up. And now, now—in fact if not in law—Aliette was actually his.

For a little while he dreamed of her, but soon the professional atmosphere of Pump Court infected him; and he began to see their case impersonally—as a "case." In law, unless Brunton acted, they had no remedy. His whole career, Aliette's whole happiness, their whole future lives depended on the clemency of Aliette's legal owner. Neither the old divorce-laws nor the proposed divorce-reforms could help them. Whatever wrongs Aliette might have suffered at her husband's hands in the past, she had forfeited those rights by running away; and only her husband could set her free. Would Brunton set her free? That was the whole issue. Best face it out of hand!

Ronnie pressed the bell on his desk, and the clerk popped through the door.

"Bunce, I want you to go over to Mr. Brunton's chambers. Ask Mr. Brunton's clerk if he can see me before he goes into court. You can say that it is on a private matter, and rather important."

Bunce—Ms curiosity satisfied—sidled out.

Waiting for Brunton's decision, Cavendish knew both curiosity and fear. Suppose Brunton refused even to discuss the matter?

And Brunton did refuse. The message Benjamin brought back was perfectly definite, perfectly courteous. He, Benjamin, had seen Mr. Brunton's clerk, David Patterson, and Mr. Brunton had sent word by Mr. Patterson to say that he was very sorry not to be able to see Mr. Cavendish, but that he was extremely busy and would be busy all day.

"Funk!" thought Ronnie; and remembered suddenly how Brunton had avoided the war. Brunton's refusal to see him was sheer cowardice. Rage kindled in his mind. For the flash of a second, he saw red. He *would* see Brunton. Damn it all, he *would* see him. How dared Brunton shelter behind a clerk! But it would be no use trying to force his way into Brunton's chambers. Brunton would be in court. Very well, then, he would wait for him; wait till the court adjourned; wait, if necessary, all day.

"Won't you look through your letters, sir?" reminded Bunce.

Ronnie tried to look through his letters; tried to examine the few briefs which had come in during his absence. But his legal mind refused to concentrate. Between his mind and his correspondence, between his mind and his briefs, rage hung a scarlet and impenetrable curtain.

5

That morning, yet another legal brain refused to concentrate on its immediate business.

All through the long hours in the stuffy court-room, Hector Brunton, K.C., was conscious of the Furies. "Cavendish," whispered the Furies, "Cavendish has come back." He tried to dismiss the fellow from his mind, to attack the case in hand. But again and again the witnesses under cross-examination eluded him. Instead of the faces in the witness-box, he saw Cavendish's face—the face of his wife. And when—his cross-examinations concluded—the court adjourned for luncheon, those two faces were still before his eyes, mocking him, mocking him.

"God's curse on them," he thought. "God's curse on both of them. I'll not see Cavendish. Let them lie in the bed they made for themselves. Let the adulterer and the adulteress rot together."

Angrily Brunton disrobed; angrily he left the law courts and made across Fleet Street toward King's Bench Walk. Even David Patterson, dour, heavy-jowled as the K.C. himself; who followed, brief-bag slung over his shoulder, at a respectful distance; was awed at his employer's obvious fury.

The K.C. strode rapidly, his hands behind his back, his head lowered, down Middle Temple Lane, through Elm Court, through Fig Tree Court, into the big graveled square of the Walk, and diagonally across the Walk to his chambers.

Suddenly his head lifted. There, at the steps of his chambers, waiting for him, obviously waiting for him, stood Cavendish. For the fraction of a second Brunton, K.C., hesitated in his stride.

Ronnie, watching, saw that hesitation; saw his man come on again, head low, eyes on the pavement; and knew instinctively that Brunton would pretend not to recognize him, would try to push past him up the stone stairway. Resolutely, he planted himself across the stairway; and in that one second of time before they met face to face, the vision he had seen in the darkness of overnight flashed through his mind. Then he had his enemy in front of him, and was saying quietly:

"I'd like a word with you, Brunton."

The K.C. tried to pass; but Ronnie stood his ground.

"I'm afraid I'm too busy to see you to-day, Cavendish." The voice sounded courteous enough; but a glance, a glance of insane rage, darted snake-like from behind the gray pupils. Brunton's great jowl twitched; the veins on his forehead were steel cords.

"The matter is rather urgent." Ronnie, watching the approach of David Patterson, lowered his tone. "I sha'n't keep you a minute. Unless, of course," the tone rose, "you prefer that our discussion should take place in public."

The fire in his blue eyes beat down the snake in Brunton's gray; and, without another word, Ronnie accompanied his man up the stairway, along the corridor into his chambers.

David Patterson made as if to follow, but Brunton barked over one shoulder, "I sha'n't need you," and the two of them were alone.

"And now," began the K.C., standing foursquare in front of his empty fireplace, "I shall be glad to know the reason of this unwarrantable intrusion."

"You know the reason as well as I do." The red mist still hung before Ronnie's eyes. He had forgotten the "legal position": he wanted to strike Brunton; to strike him across the sneering face. Only the code, the public school code of restraint, held him back.

"I haven't the slightest idea why you should force your way into my chambers. Perhaps you will condescend to explain." Brunton, too, felt the code on him—heavy, like a net hampering his limbs. He wanted to free himself from the net; wanted to lash out at the man who had stolen Aliette, to destroy him.

"I came to ask you," Ronnie's lips hardly moved, "how much longer you intend to delay."

"Delay what?"

"Your petition."

"What petition?"

"Your petition for divorce."

"That's my business." Brunton laughed—a harsh, bitter laugh, low in the throat.

"And mine."

"I fail to see the connection."

Ronnie's fists clenched. "Apparently you take me for a fool."

Brunton laughed again. "No. Only for a thief."

With an effort, Ronnie thrust his hands into his pockets. "I didn't come here to bandy words with you. All I want to know is how soon you intend filing your petition."

"When I choose." Rage mastered Aliette's husband. "And if I don't choose—never."

Now Ronnie laughed—contemptuously. "You may be able to browbeat a woman in the box, but you can't browbeat me. I want an answer to my question. How soon do you intend to file your petition? This isn't only your business. It's mine—mine and—"

"Kindly keep my wife out of this discussion," snarled Brunton. "Your question is a damned insult, and your presence here an infernal outrage. Neither you nor God Almighty can make me file the petition you refer to."

For a full minute the pair faced each other, tense, wordless, self-control fighting against instincts, instincts fighting against self-control. Then Brunton's nerve snapped.

"I hate the very sight of you," he shouted. "Will you get out? Or have I got to throw you out?"

"Don't make a fool of yourself," said Ronnie; and his voice was ice. "If it comes to violence I sha'n't be the one who'll get the worst of it."

He took a step forward, and the K.C. recoiled before him.

"Answer my question, Brunton."

"I'll see you to hell first, Cavendish."

And suddenly the red mist thickened to blood-color before Ronnie's eyes. He wanted to kill Brunton. Killing would be the easiest way to deal with Brunton—far the easiest way. His hands clenched in his trouser-pockets; he itched to take his hands out of his pockets, to dash them in those cold gray eyes, to seize that heavy jowl, to tear the life out of it.

And then, in a flash, his legal mind saw the consequences of that killing. The blood-red mist vanished. Swiftly his mood changed. He began to plead, to plead desperately, not for his own sake, but for Aliette's. He said:

"We're being selfish. It isn't of ourselves we have to think. Think of her position if you don't take action."

"She should have thought of my position before she ran away with you," retorted the other. "I tell you, I'm not going to be hustled; and I'm not going to be bullied. I'll take action when I choose; and not a minute before. Nothing that you, nothing that she, nothing that anybody else can do will persuade me to say one word further on this subject. Now, will you go?"

And Ronnie went, realizing himself powerless. As he passed through the doorway he gave one glance at his adversary. His adversary still stood, like a bull at bay, against the empty grate; but the look in his adversary's eyes—a look which Ronnie could not fathom—was not the brave look of the bull; rather was it compound of fear and obstinacy, of injured pride and of determination for revenge; the look of the weak man who knows himself in the wrong, yet means to persist in his wrongdoing.

*

Surely as night follows day in the firmament, so surely does reaction follow action in imaginative man. Ronald Cavendish's mind, as he crossed King's Bench Walk after his interview with Hector Brunton, was almost a blank. Reaction wiped out every detail of that interview. He remembered only Brunton's words, "I'll take action when I choose."

Twice—the mad purpose of killing Brunton mastering him once more—he tried to turn back. But his feet carried him on, carried him away from Brunton, across the Walk to his own chambers. There, at least, was sanctuary—sanctuary from crime against the herd.

For the herd, even his dazed mind knew, would not countenance his killing Brunton. Brunton was within his herd-rights, within the law; while they, he and Aliette, having broken the herd-rights, were outlaws. Still weak from reaction, he visioned the consequences of that outlawry; visioned Brunton relentless, Aliette without a friend.

Till gradually, thinking of Aliette, his manhood came back to him. Let Brunton do his damnedest. Let them be outlaws. Even in their outlawry they would possess one another. Soon, Brunton would be brought to reason.

Meanwhile, even if he were not soon brought to reason, they, the outlaws, would find people to stand by them; people like his mother. And at that, abruptly, Ronnie remembered the letter Aliette had written to her sister, the promise he had made to Jimmy.

Somehow it needed more courage than he had required in facing Aliette's husband to lift the telephone and make his appointment with Mollie!

6

Over a snack of luncheon—snatched late and hastily at a little uncomfortable coffee-shop near the Griffin—Ronnie's usual calm returned. He realized that he had made a fool of himself in going to see Brunton; that Jimmy, after all, had been right. Confound Brunton! Brunton's "dog-in-the-manger" attitude would not endure, could not endure. Even Carrington had given way in the long run. It was only a question of patience. Still, he would have to break things very gently to Aliette's sister.

Betty Masterman was out; and Mollie received her sister's lover alone in the little red-papered sitting-room which seemed so cozy to the Philistine mind of James Wilberforce.

"It's nice of you to call," she said perfunctorily. The voice might have been that of Aliette, of the socially poised Aliette as Ronnie first remembered her: but the girl's violet eyes were stern with suspicion; her red lips showed unsmiling, uncompromising.

"Won't you sit down?" she went on.

"Thanks. I sha'n't keep you very long." Always impossibly shy with women, the man did not know how to begin.

"You've got some message for me," the girl prompted "Some message from—"

"From your sister."

She seated herself, avoiding his eyes.

"Your sister and I," he began bruskly—

And in those four words—even without the halting explanation which followed—it seemed to Mollie Fullerford that she knew the whole story. But she was not going to help him out. Why should she? The story—carefully though he told it—revolted her. She felt hot; hot and dirty and ashamed. Hurt, too, as though the healed scars of her bodily wounds were opening afresh. All the suspicions of the past weeks, all her still-smoldering resentment that Aliette should have let her return unwarned to Hector's house, all her balked love for James Wilberforce, harshened Mollie's judgment. She saw Cavendish no longer a "sober-sides" but a hypocrite; and so seeing, hated him for his imagined hypocrisy.

"You see," he concluded, "it wasn't Aliette's fault. I mean the running away in a hurry. You mustn't condemn her. I was to blame for that. I was to blame, from beginning to end."

"Of course," said that Mollie who had once thought "most women rotters." "It's always the man who's to blame."

Nevertheless her judgment softened. "After all," she thought, "he isn't beating about the bush. He's being perfectly straight with me." And she discovered to her great surprise that it was not their having run away together which had been hurting her, but their omission to take her into their confidence.

Ronnie, trying to guess the verdict behind those averted eyes, drew Aliette's letter from his pocket; and handed it over without another word. Watching her open the envelope, watching her as she read, he saw her fingers tremble, her violet eyes suffuse.

"And have you seen Hector?" she asked at last.

"Yes. I saw him this morning."

"What did he say?"

Ronnie hesitated to tell the brutal truth; and the girl repeated her question, adding:

"Of course he's going to divorce her."

"I'm afraid, Miss Fullerford, that it's not going to be quite so easy as that."

"You don't mean to say that he isn't going to—?"

"He says he hasn't made up his mind—"

"But"—the girl was stammering now—"that's absolutely caddish. Hector's a gentleman. Alie's been perfectly straight with him. Besides, even if he had been badly treated, he couldn't, couldn't possibly—"

And suddenly the full possibilities of Hector's persisting in a refusal to take action grew visible to the girl's mind. She braced herself to meet those possibilities; the personal consequences of them. She forced herself to ask:

"Have you seen Mr. Wilberforce?"

"Yes. Last night."

"Did you ask his advice?"

"Yes."

"What was it?"

"To do nothing. To wait."

At that, thought of her own love affair obsessed the girl's mind. She visualized James, there, in the very chair which Cavendish occupied. Remembering a thousand unspoken hesitancies of James, she saw only too clearly the reason of those hesitancies.

"How long has Mr. Wilberforce known about—about you and my sister?"

"Some weeks, I believe."

"You're sure?" The wounds hurt again, hurt desperately. James ought to have told her. "He never said a word—to me." She could have borne it better from James than from Cavendish.

"Of course he couldn't tell you anything about it, Miss Fullerford. It was a secret, a professional secret. My mother told him—"

"Your mother?"

"Yes, my mother. She's with Aliette now." His voice softened. "She's on our side. You'll be on our side, too? Won't you? You won't let this—this contretemps come between you and your sister? I'm not asking anything for myself—but it's pretty rough luck on Alie."

Mollie's decision crystallized. "I can't go back on Alie," she thought. "Whatever happens I mustn't go back on Alie." She remembered their conversation at Moor Park; remembered herself saying, "I don't believe divorce is wrong."

"Yes," she said, and held out her hand. "I shall stand by Alie whatever happens. Will you tell her that? And say I'll write in a day or two. I don't feel like—like writing to her at the moment."

Ronnie clasped her hand, and rose to go. He would have liked to thank her; he would have liked to say something more about Jimmy. But instinct restrained him. Perhaps, after all, she didn't care for Jimmy; perhaps the pallor of her cheeks, the drooped corners of her full red mouth were all for Alie.

7

And next day Ronald Cavendish went back to Chilworth Cove. All the long train journey he was aware, growingly aware, of Aliette. Brunton and the herd, Wilberforce and Mollie receded into the background of his thoughts. He said to himself:

"Let Brunton do his worst. Aliette and I have our love, each other."

Love, all said and done, was the only issue. As for Brunton, they would face him together, face him with courage high and hearts unflinching. Courage! Courage and love! Weaponed with those two defenses, he and his mate, his mother at their side, could battle down the onslaught of any disaster.

Chapter XVI

1

On a gray afternoon of October, Julia Cavendish sat alone in her drawing-room at Bruton Street.

She was often alone now. That curious "London" which an eclectic woman of means can gather about herself by the time she reaches sixty had begun to desert. Brunton had done nothing; but already scandal, "the scandal of Julia Cavendish's son and Hector Brunton's wife," was spreading: and although people were "very sorry for Mrs. Cavendish," still, "one had to be careful where one went," "one couldn't exactly countenance that sort of thing." So the clergymen and the politicians, the schoolmasters with their wives and the young soldiers with their fiancés came but sparingly, the embassy folk not at all. Only the "Ritz crowd," who thought the whole affair rather amusing; real Society, which could afford to ignore what it did not actually know; and, of course, the literary folk still visited.

Julia Cavendish treated the disaffections of her circle—scanty as yet, for the holidays scattered the scandalmongers—with contempt. In the months since her visit to Chilworth, much of her outlook on life had altered. The Victorian and the traditionalist in her were dead, the formally religious woman convert to a kindlier creed. Even literature slumbered. Literature, the sort of literature she had hitherto written, the stereotyped social romances of her earlier books, seemed so puny in comparison with the great tragedy of her son!

Seated there in the old familiar drawing-room, her embroidery-frame at her elbow, a clean fire at her feet, the light from the standard-lamp glowing on her worn features, Julia tried, as she was always trying now, to find some happy ending to the tragedy—peace for her son, reward for Aliette's courage.

For Aliette *had* been courageous—divinely courageous as it appeared to Julia—that afternoon at Chilworth Cove when Ronnie broke his bad news. Her own heart had failed a little; but not Aliette's. Aliette said—Julia could still remember the look in her eyes when she spoke: "You're not to worry for my sake, either of you. I shall be perfectly happy so long as you and Ronnie don't fret. If only Ronnie's career doesn't suffer—"

She, Ronnie's mother, had wanted to fight; had wanted the lovers to return to Bruton Street with her, to defy Brunton openly. After that one little failure of courage, her whole temperament cried out for combat. Fighting, she felt, was now the only course. But Aliette had counseled delay. Aliette had persuaded her to leave them at Chilworth, to go back alone to Bruton Street. And at Bruton Street she had stayed all summer.

It had been foolish to stay all summer at Bruton Street; she perceived that now. She ought to have taken her usual holiday. She ought to have listened to the advice of her "medicine-man," who, still maintaining the need for rest, was vague, unsatisfactory, disturbing.

The parlormaid, entering to make up the fire, startled her mistress.

"I wish you'd come in more quietly, Kate," said Julia irritably.

"I'm sorry, madam. Shall I bring your tea?"

"No, not yet."

Julia resumed her reverie. Was there no way by which the man whose obstinacy stood between her son and his happiness might be brought to bay? Apparently none. Sir Peter Wilberforce could only suggest that "the lady might pledge her husband's credit to such an extent that he had to take action"—and that Aliette refused to do.

Dot Fancourt, whom she had also consulted, finding him incredibly stupid, incredibly weak, was all for "letting sleeping dogs lie." *He* seemed to have no spirit; and she would have been grateful to him for spirit. She felt old; terribly old and weak; prescient, every now and then, of death.

This occasional prescience frightened her. The formal religion to which she had so long clung provided only a personal and a selfish consolation for death. She wanted an impersonal, an unselfish consolation; realizing that she would never be happy to leave this world unless she could leave Ronnie happy in it. Materially, of course, she had already provided for him: all her fortune would be his. But that did not suffice. Before death claimed her she must find some sword to sever his Gordian knot.

The Love-Story of Aliette Brunton

So Julia, alone in her quiet house; Julia, the literature all gone out of her, her mind busied with the actual happenings of life; while Brunton, lost in the holiday mists of the long vacation, gave never a sign; and rumor, spider-like, wove its intangible filaments to close and closer mesh.

2

That very afternoon—October 11 it was, the day before the autumn session of the law courts began—Aliette and her lover walked in Kensington Gardens. Even as Julia's, much of their attitude toward life had altered in the past months. The first grandly onrushing wave of the grand passion, the wave which swept them both from safe moorings into outlawry, had spent itself. They were still lovers; but now, with love, comradeship mingled. A comradeship of mutual suffering—knit closer as the days went by.

For, in love's despite, since training and inherited traditions alike unfitted them for the rôle they played, both suffered.

To Aliette, lonely no longer, Ronnie's comradeship compensated for so much that, as yet, the social disadvantages of their position hardly mattered. Only every now and then, in lonely-waking night-hours when full perception of the thing she had done shimmered black for a moment through the rosy veils of affection, did her heart grow faint at the thought of perpetual ostracism from her kind. At other times, her sufferings, her self-torturings were all for Ronnie.

Ronnie, she knew, chafed at his defeat. Ronnie had grown to hate Brunton. Ronnie—for her sake—wanted social position, success. Ronnie loathed the illegal fact that they had had to register as "Mr. and Mrs. Cavendish and maid" at the quiet Kensington hotel, whither Moses Moffatt's shibboleth of "bachelor chambers" drove them on their return from Chilworth.

But Ronnie had other frets—money-frets—on that October afternoon when they strolled under the browning trees.

They strolled lover-like, arm in arm; and Ponto the Dane, incongruous appanage of their elopement, followed leisurely. Aliette was all in furs, soft furs that cloaked her from the cream of her chin to the slimness of her ankles. Above the furs her face showed happy, glowing with a new youth, a new softness.

"Man," she said suddenly, "do you realize that we are two thoroughly unpractical people?"

"Are we?" He pressed her arm. "Does it matter very much?"

"Of course it matters." She paused, and went on shyly: "Don't you understand that I've been living with you for three months, and that so far I haven't contributed a single penny to the—to the establishment?"

"How absurd you are!" He tried to brush the matter aside; but that she refused to allow.

"I ought to contribute something, you know. I'm not quite penniless."

"You're not going to pay my hotel bill," he parried: a little stubbornly, she thought.

"Why not? What's mine is yours."

They walked on in silence for a minute or two. Then Ronnie said:

"I'm afraid I can't quite see things that way, Alie. I suppose I'm a bit old-fashioned in my ideas. But it does seem to me that the man's responsible—" He bit off the sentence.

"I hate you to talk like that." There was a little of the old temper in Aliette's voice. "We must be sensible about money."

"Oh, don't let's bother this afternoon," he coaxed.

"But we must bother. Ronnie, be frank with me. What are we living on?"

"Oh, all sorts of things. The Jermyn Street rent; my earnings, such as they are; a bit of money I'd got saved up."

"And," she added, "the allowance your mother makes you. I wonder if we ought to take that."

"I don't see why we shouldn't. She always has made me an allowance. But of course I shouldn't like to ask her for more."

"Naturally." Aliette's brow creased. "Let's think. I've got about three hundred and fifty a year of my own. Your allowance is four. That makes seven hundred and fifty. How much is that a week?"

The Love-Story of Aliette Brunton

"Fifteen pounds," laughed Ronnie, remembering a phrase of his mother's, "No woman's financial mind covers more than seven days."

"And our hotel bill last week was twenty."

At that, the man began to feel thoroughly uncomfortable. His mind shied away from the topic. But the woman pursued it resolutely.

"We'll have to find a cheaper hotel."

"It seems rotten luck on you; the present one is uncomfortable enough. Besides," he brightened visibly, "there ought to be briefs coming in now."

"Man, you're a great optimist." There was an undercurrent of criticism in Aliette's voice, of a criticism which Ronnie felt he could not fairly resent; because already he had begun to divine the professional consequences of Brunton's enmity. Only the day before, James Wilberforce had dropped a hint—the barest hint, but sufficient to indicate which way the financial wind might blow.

"I suppose I am rather an optimist," he admitted; and for the moment they dropped the subject, reverting, as they nearly always did in their walks together, to the main problem.

"H. B. ought to be back any day now," said Ronnie, "and when he does come back, he'll simply have to file his petition."

But to-day she would have none of the problem.

"Don't let us discuss that. After all, nothing that H. does or doesn't do can really hurt us." She looked up into his eyes. "We've got each other."

"I don't mind for myself, Alie. It's you I'm thinking of. Of course we won't talk about him if you don't want to."

By now they were through Kensington Gardens, and passing the herbaceous border at Victoria Gate. They stopped to inspect the flowers. Two gardeners were at work, clearing away the wreckage of summer. The climbing roses and the clematis had withered, but dahlias still flaunted scarlet and crimson against the high dark of the shrubbery.

They walked on, silent, the dog pottering at heel; and inclined half-right across Hyde Park.

"Do you remember—" began Aliette.

"What, dear?" he prompted.

"Oh, nothing. Only I was just thinking. Mollie and I came this way, that morning we met at church parade. It seems such a long time ago."

"Am I as dull as all that?" he chaffed her. "Are you getting bored with me?"

"Bored with you!" Her voice thrilled. "Oh, man, man, you don't understand a bit. You're everything in the world to me. The only thing that ever makes me really frightened is the thought of forfeiting your love. That's because I'm happy—happy. You don't know, no man ever does know, what happiness means to a woman; how utterly miserable she can be. I was miserable with H.—miserable. Luxuries don't help—when one's unhappy. When I look back on my life before I met you, I wonder I didn't"—she hesitated—"I didn't do something desperate. I suppose I didn't know how miserable I really was. I don't suppose any woman in my position ever does know, till some man teaches her—"

"And now?" he broke in.

"Now, I'm absolutely happy. Honestly, I don't care a bit about the legal position—as you call it. What does it matter whether we're legally married or not? What does it matter whether people want to know us or whether they don't? I don't care," she ended almost defiantly; "I don't care a bit so long as I've got you; so long as we're right with our own consciences."

And really, when Aliette looks back on those unsettled days, it astonishes her how little she did care for the rest of the world. Even her parents' attitude seemed of no importance.

3

For outwardly the Fullerfords had taken up a very determined attitude.

At Clyst Fullerford Aliette's name was scarcely mentioned. The people who had known Aliette since cradle-days, the pleasant Devonshire people busied with their pleasant trivial country round, still called neighborly as of yore; but they no longer inquired of Andrew Fullerford, nor of Andrew's wife, after the health of Mrs. Brunton. Somehow rumor, unconfirmed yet accurate in the main, had penetrated to every corner of the county; and though the pleasant people pretended to ignore rumor, at least until such time as rumor's story should be substantiated by the London papers, still they thought it "safer" not to mention Aliette when they visited the long, low house of the mullioned windows.

Ever since the death of the Fullerford boys in France, the house with the mullioned windows had been sad. But now it seemed more than sad—a home of utter tragedy, despite its tended gardens and its deft servants. The stags' heads and the foxes' masks on its walls only enhanced its gloom. Its empty stables typified empty hearts; hearts of a man and a woman whose sons might not inherit.

Mollie, in that long August and longer September, found the place unbearable. Yet she was afraid to leave it; afraid to leave Andrew and Marie alone. Her father aged hourly; his gray-lashed mouth used to quiver with pain whenever he looked across the dinner-table at his wife. To the girl, who did not understand that Aliette's abandonment of her husband had evoked between these two the old specter of religious differences, both parents appeared incredibly unforgiving, incredibly out of their century.

Yet, had it not been for that specter, it is more than possible that the puisne judge would have relented toward his "erring daughter." Under certain circumstances he might even have helped her to secure her freedom. For although Aliette had outraged both his legal sense and his sense of propriety; although she had admittedly broken the oath sworn at a Protestant altar; yet the lapse of the years had so softened Andrew's Protestantism, left it so broadly tolerant, so much more of an ideal than a religion, that he considered, as many latter-day Protestants do consider, almost every tenet of his church open to the argument of the individual case.

The judge, moreover, was instinctively aware that Aliette's relations to Hector might furnish exactly that individual case necessary for her justification. But in view of his wife's obvious misery, Andrew felt himself incapable of forgiveness.

To Marie Fullerford—and this her husband realized—from that very first moment when she opened Aliette's letter of confession, it had seemed as though the Roman Catholic Church, the church from whose rigid discipline she had revolted to marry Andrew, were taking its revenge for the long-ago apostasy.

After one heartbroken conversation with her husband, she withdrew into contemplation. Hour after hour she used to sit in her own little room, remembering and regretting the faith of her childhood. Marie could no more go back to that faith! The Church, the surely-disciplined authoritative Church of Rome, would have none of her. And she would have given so much in her present distress for the comfort of Rome!

The spiritual uncertainty of Protestantism frightened her with its easy-going tolerance. She saw the doctrine of the English Church as a broad-pathed quagmire, through which one trod with individual and uncertain steps toward an individual and uncertain heaven; while Roman Catholicism, knowing neither tolerance nor uncertainty, indicated the only road, the safe and the narrow road to constitutional bliss.

Constantly Marie Fullerford tried to recall her old courage, the individual fortitude which had broken her loose from Roman Catholicism. But the old fortitude would not return. She yearned in her weakness for the guidance of the priest, for the infallible laws, for the infallible dogmas of an infallible hierarchy.

Her spiritual knees ached, and the hard hassock of Protestantism could not rest them. Stumbling, she desired to cast the heavy pack of her doubts at the feet of a father-confessor—of a father-confessor who would give one orders, definite commands: "Let your daughter sin no more. Let her return to her husband, expiate her offenses." No doubting there! No leaving of the individual case to individual judgment!

And yet—and yet Aliette's mother could not bring herself to answer Aliette's confession in the spirit of Rome. She herself had been so long free, so long undisciplined, that she wanted, desperately, to find the solution of this problem by the aid of that very love in which she had given herself to Andrew.

At last, in her uncertainty, she consulted with her eldest daughter.

Eva, without the slightest hesitation, forbade any answer at all. The colonel's lady, always adverse to her juniors, sided from the first definitely with Hector. Aliette, opined Eva, had brought disgrace upon the entire family. No fact that Mollie, no argument that her husband could adduce in the culprit's favor, availed to bend Mrs. Harold Martin's domestic rigidity; a rigidity socketed home on the two unshifting rocks of personal dislike and personal rectitude.

4

Meanwhile Moor Park, though spiritually less troubled than Clyst Fullerford, failed egregiously in presenting a united front to its domestic troubles. Hector, returning thither from a lonely holiday in Scotland, found Rear-Admiral Billy in quarter-deck mood, and the Rev. Adrian—invited for obvious reasons to dine without his Margery—uncomfortably silent through an interminable meal.

Purposely the admiral had staved off discussion of the matter at heart until the mastodontic dining-table should be cleared of its food. Now—the port decanter being in its third circulation—he drew back his chair from the board, screwed a cigar firmly between his bearded lips, and began:

"Well, Hector, you've had a couple of months to make up your mind. What are you going to do about Alie?"

The K.C. looked straight into his father's unjovial eyes and retorted:

"As I told you before I left, sir"—"sir" between the admiral and his sons always betokened trouble,—"I'm not going to do anything."

"Dog-in-the-manger, eh?" rumbled the old man to his beard.

"You can take it that way if you like, sir."

"Pretty rough on your wife, ain't it? Adrian thinks—"

"Adrian is not his brother's keeper."

There intervened a considerable silence, during which the parson scrutinized the lawyer. "Hector's nature," pondered the Rev. Adrian, "has not altered much since he was a boy. He's a reticent fellow, is Hector. Sullen, too. Resents any one interfering in his affairs—even if it's for his own good."

But the parson could see that, in outward appearance, Hector *had* altered. He looked less corpulent, less certain of himself, more inclined to bluster. His sandy hair had thinned nearly to baldness.

"I haven't the slightest wish to interfere"—Adrian, except in his episcopalian wife's presence, was a very human being,—"but really it does seem to me that your duty is either to use every means in your power to get your wife back, or else to set her free. You can't play the matrimonial Micawber."

"I tell you," the K.C. fidgeted in his chair, "I don't want your advice. This is my own affair and nobody else's."

"That be sugared for a tale." The admiral unscrewed his cigar from his mouth, and waved it fiercely before his eldest son's eyes. "That be sugared for a tale, Hector. A man's marriage concerns his whole family. I was talking to Simeon only the other day, and he said it was perfectly impossible for any one in your position—"

"I've heard that argument before," said Aliette's legal owner, "and I can't say that it appeals to me. I fail to see why Uncle Simeon or his wife should presume to pass judgment on what I choose or don't choose to do." He made a movement to break off the discussion, refrained, and continued. "Since you have reopened the subject, sir, I think it would be as well if I explained my views once and for all. My views are that I fail to see any reason why I should take my wife back, or any obligation to set her free to marry her lover. What he and she did, they did with their eyes open. Let them abide by the consequences."

"But, blast it all!" broke in the admiral, "a fellow must behave like a gentleman."

"I refuse to admit that a man must behave like a gentleman to a wife who forgets to behave herself like a lady." The lawyer reached for the cigar-box, and kindled a weed.

"Come, come, Hector." The parson, who had seen life, put his professional prejudices on one side. "It really isn't as bad as that. Mind you, I'm not making any excuses for Aliette. But, even admitting that she's behaved badly to you, does that furnish you with any justification for behaving badly to her?"

"And mind you, my boy," the father elaborated his younger son's argument, "people aren't like they used to be about this sort of thing. There's deuced little prejudice against divorce these days. We must go with the times. We must go with the times. God knows I'm an intolerant old devil; but, thank God, I can still take a broad-minded view where the sex is concerned."

"It's easy enough for you to be broad-minded, sir," interpolated the K.C.; "she's not your wife."

"Fond of her still, eh?" rambled the old man shrewdly. Hector Brunton kept silence, but his eyes showed that the shot had gone home.

"You've asked her to return to you, I suppose?" said the Rev. Adrian, pouncing on this new hare like a religious beagle.

"Certainly not." The coincidence of the two ideas exasperated Hector. For two months he had been hardening himself to meet this very ordeal; and already, curse it! he felt himself growing soft. Dimly the voice of conscience told him that his father and brother were in the right. Socially he recognized that he was taking up an impossible position. Nevertheless, as an individual, he intended sticking to that position. All the obstinacy, all the weakness in him combined to reject the obvious solution. Why the devil *should* he divorce Aliette? *He* still wanted Aliette—wanted her physically—craved for her with a desire so overpowering that, at times, it drove him almost mad.

"Quite apart from your wife's reputation, you know," the admiral returned to his oratorial quarter-deck, "you've got to consider your own. People don't look too kindly on a man who allows his missus to live openly with some one else. And then, both you and he being in the same profession! Take it from me, my boy, it won't do you any good."

"It won't do *him* any good," said Hector viciously. "If I've any influence with the benchers, I'll get the fellow disbarred before the year's out; and if I can't get him disbarred at least I'll take"—he snarled—"other steps."

At the snarl, Adrian lost his temper.

"I've been trying to talk to you like a brother, Hector," he rapped out, "not like a parson. If you came to me as a parson, I should be bound to tell you that your attitude isn't Christian at all. It's—damn it!—it's Hebraic. An eye for an eye, and a tooth for a tooth."

The elder brother turned on his junior.

"Christianity," he sneered. "Is that your Christianity? Free love!"

The junior fidgeted with his white collar.

"We'll leave my Christianity out of the discussion, if you please."

The admiral, also a little hot under the shirt, intervened again.

"Christianity or no Christianity, I maintain that you're putting yourself in the wrong. Alie's a decent enough little woman. She's always played the game with you. Even when she ran away with this fellow, she told you about it before she went. She did tell you, didn't she?"

"Yes."

"What did *you* say?"

"I told her she could go if she wanted to."

"You didn't try to restrain her?"

"No. I didn't."

"Why not? If you felt so strongly about her going off as you pretend to now, why didn't you lock her up in her bedroom? Why didn't you go and see this man Cavendish—knock his head off?"

Infuriated, Hector rose to his feet.

"I have no wish to be disrespectful, sir," he said to his father, "but my decision is final. I refuse to discuss this matter a minute longer." And to his brother, "As for you, Adrian, I'll thank you not to interfere." Then he moved from the table, swung open the door, and clumped heavily upstairs to his bedroom.

*

Left alone, the rear-admiral turned to his younger son.

"How's the new baby, Adrian?"

"Getting on splendidly, father."

"Good." The bearded lips chewed at their cigar for a full minute. "A pity Hector's wife didn't have any kids."

"A great pity, father."

207

Chapter XVII

1

Another month of outlawry went by.

The dahlias in Hyde Park died, cut down by the frost; and with the death of them there came over Aliette that keen longing for the countryside in winter-time which only English hunting people know. She used to dream about hunting; about Miracle, striding full gallop across hedged fields, steadying himself for his leap, flying his fence, landing, galloping on.

But Miracle—Hector's gift—was lost to her, as hunting was lost, and nearly every social amenity which made up existence before she met Ronnie. Between a hunting-season and a hunting-season, she had "dropped out of things"; had become one of those illegally-mated women whom our church neglects, our law despises, and our press dares only ignore.

The Aliettes of England! The women whose sole excuse for illegal matehood is love! There are half a million such in Great Britain to-day: women whose only crime is that, craving happiness, they have taken their happiness in defiance of some male.

They are of all classes, our Aliettes. You will find them alike in our West End and in our slums, in little lost cottages beneath whose windows the sea moans all day long, and in prim suburban villas where the milk-cart clatters on asphalt roads and cap-and-aproned servants gossip of a morning under the peeky laburnum. You will find them—and always with them, the one man, the mate they have chosen—in Chelsea studios, on Cornish farms and Yorkshire moorlands, in Glasgow and in Ramsgate, in a thousand stuffy apartments of Inner London, and in a hundred unsuspicious boarding-houses of that middle fringe which is neither Inner London nor Suburbia.

These women—who crave neither "free love" nor the "right to motherhood" but only the right to married happiness—are the bond-slaves of our national hypocrisy. Sometimes their own strength, sometimes death, sometimes money, sometimes the clemency of their legal owners sets them free. But, for the most part, they live, year after year, in outlawry; live

208

uncomplaining, faithful to that mate they have taken, bringing up with loving care and a wise tenderness those children whom—even should their parents ultimately marry—our law stamps "bastard" from birth to death.

Meanwhile our priests, our politicians, our lawgivers, and all the self-righteous Pharisees who have never known the hells of unhappy marriage, harden their smug hearts; and neither man nor woman in England may claim release from a drunkard, from a lunatic, from a criminal, or from any of those thousand and one miseries which wreck the human soul.

2

Powolney Mansions—four impossible Victorian dwelling-places, converted into one impossible Georgian boarding-house of that middle fringe which is neither Inner London nor Outer Suburbia—front a quiet road half-way between the Baron's Court and West Kensington Stations.

"Queen's" being the limit of Aliette's London, it was natural enough that her deliberate mind, casting about for some less expensive abode than their hotel near the park, should remember the neighborhood, and search it for a hiding-place.

Natural enough, too, was that instinct for a hiding-place, in a woman who had no desire to parade her unmated self before the herd, and no craving for unnecessary martyrdom.

At the Mansions, six guineas a week (and three extra for Caroline Staley) provided a bed-sitting-room, complete with a double-bedstead of squeaking brass, a hard sofa, two harder chairs, a so-called armchair, a writing-table, three steel engravings of the eighteen-eighties, and a shilling-in-the-slot gas-stove. The six guineas also provided meals, served by dingily uniformed waitresses in a crowded communal dining-room—and "congenial society."

This "congenial society" did not—as the society to which Aliette had been accustomed—shift its habitat with the seasons; except for an occasional fortnight in Margate or Clacton, it clung limpet-like to the Mansions.

Moreover, as the pair discovered within three days, it was eclectic as well as cliquey—containing gentlefolk and ungentle-folk; workers and idlers;

bounders and the unbounding. Of the first were two pathetic spinsters who knitted all day before the untended fire in the vast untended drawing-room, remembering, as lost souls might remember paradise, the bygone millennium of cheap eggs and cheap income-tax. Of the last were an Anglo-Indian family, looking for, and never finding, "a nice easily-run flat." Item, were three foreigners, vague creatures from vague places, who never seemed to have anything to do, and never seemed to go to bed; one prosperous commercial traveler who "liked the sociability"; one ruined squire who had furnished his own room and hoarded the remnants of a pre-war cellar in its undusted cupboard; and three mothers of no known social position, whose daughters, dingy at breakfast, grew demure by lunch-time, and—communal tea included—sallied forth with mysterious "dancing-partners" to return mouse-footed in the early dawn. An understrapper from the Belgian consulate, and a plantation overseer on leave from the Federated Malay States completed the tally of "Monsieur Mayer's guests.

"A fine gossipy lot, Miss Aliette," judged Caroline Staley, her loyalty a little strained by, though proof against, her surroundings. "While as for they maids—"

But the "congenial society" of Powolney Mansions gossiped—the aloof Aliette knew—neither more nor less than the society she had abandoned. For—try as one would to hide one's self—awkward meetings were inevitable.

Never a woman of easy friendships, Hector Brunton's wife before her elopement had possessed three distinct sets of cordial acquaintances—the "Moor Park lot," the "London lot," and the "Clyst Fullerford lot," as she phrased them. Of these, the "Clyst Fullerford lot" and the "Moor Park lot" (barring Colonel Sanders, the M.F.H., who, apparently untouched by gossip, greeted her, at walk with Ronnie down St. James's Street, in his cheeriest voice as "dear Mrs. Brunton") might, except for an occasional letter forwarded from Lancaster Gate via Mollie, have inhabited the moon.

And with the "London lot" one never quite knew how one stood. Bachelor barristers inevitably lifted the hat and smiled. Hugh Spillcroft, meeting one alone at Harrods, invited one to tea with him and proffered a tentative sympathy which one gently but firmly rebuffed. Mrs. Needham, also encountered on a shopping expedition, pretended the most tactful ignorance, but forbore to inquire after one's husband. Sir Siegfried and Lady Moss, passing in their Rolls-Royce, looked politically the other way. Hector's particular friends one, of course, avoided; and, since she made no overture, one also avoided—a little hurt, perhaps, at the ingratitude—Mary O'Riordan.

Taking it all round—as Julia Cavendish put it on one of those frequent afternoons when, always preannounced by telephone, the lovers came to tea with her—the situation held "little hope and less comfort."

"And it'll get worse," said that indomitable old woman; "it's bound to get worse if you persist in hiding yourselves, if you go on refusing to meet anybody. Don't you see, my dear," she turned on Aliette with a little of her former brusquerie, "that you're playing right into your husband's hands? Don't make any mistake about him. He knows exactly where you are; and, so long as there's no open scandal, so long as you remain tucked away in that abominable boarding-house, he'll leave you there. Whereas, if you'll only make the scandal an open one, public opinion will force him to act. Take it from me, the only thing to be done is to flaunt yourselves."

"Flaunt?" said Aliette.

"Yes! Flaunt yourselves!" repeated Ronnie's mother, rather pleased with the literary expression.

"I rather agree," said Ronnie. "That's the way Belfield broke Carrington. Dash it, we can't go on lying doggo forever. It isn't fair to Alie."

Since their move to Powolney Mansions, Ronnie had begun to realize the exact difference in the world's treatment of a man's "lapse" and a woman's "adultery"; to perceive that he apparently was to be allowed to go on with his avocation, scanty though the emoluments of that avocation were becoming, as though nothing had happened; that his clubs and almost every house he had visited while a bachelor were still open to him as an unmarried husband, so long as the world, officially, knew nothing of his "unmarried wife."

"Never mind me, I'm quite"—Aliette glanced round the comfortable drawing-room, so unlike the spinster-haunted wilderness of the

Mansions—"resigned to my temporary fate."

"Rubbish!" retorted Julia; and went on to elaborate the plan that they should move from Baron's Court as soon as ever they could find some residence, the more expensive the better, in Inner London.

"You must be seen everywhere," she went on. "You must entertain and be entertained. In a word, Aliette—like Mrs. Carrington—must afficher herself as Mrs. Cavendish. Never mind what it costs. I'll finance you."

But Aliette's whole nature recoiled from Julia's scheme.

She, had it not been for Ronnie's career, would have been more than content to wait a year, two years, a whole lifetime for freedom. Her idea—she told them—was to take some little cottage, not too far removed from London; so that "Ronnie could come down every week-end."

Nevertheless, since any hope of freedom was tantalizing, because now, always and always stronger, there mounted in her the conviction that one day she would have a child by Ronnie, Aliette so far weakened from her resolution against "the flaunting policy" as to accept Julia's invitation, telephoned next day, to share her box for the first night of Patrick O'Riordan's "Khorassan."

3

Ronnie's "wife," though too proud to make the first move, often wondered why Mary O'Riordan, eager enough to accept her championing in a similar situation, should have taken so little trouble to reciprocate, now that reciprocation was so obviously indicated: but, dressing for the theater in the unkindly bedroom whose harsh lights made her needlessly afraid of the mirror, she decided that sheer delicacy alone had restrained her old school-friend from getting into touch; and anticipated their inevitable meeting without a qualm. It would be nervous work, displaying one's self in Julia Cavendish's box before a "first-night" audience (unwise work, thought Aliette, unwise of Ronnie and his mother to have been so persistent); but Mary's presence would at least furnish a guarantee against complete ostracism. Whatever other people might do, she could rely on Mary's visiting their box in theentr'acte, on Mary's going out of her way to demonstrate sympathy.

"Looking forward to it, darling?" interrupted Ronnie, entering with the usual perfunctory knock from the bathroom, where he had been doing his best to shave, for the second time that day, in lukewarm water.

"Not exactly." Aliette dismissed her maid.

"Why not?"

"Oh, I don't know. It seems all wrong, somehow or other. And suppose"—she hesitated—"suppose people are nasty?"

"They won't be," assured Ronnie, through the shirt into which he was struggling. "You're too sensitive about the whole thing. One or two people may snub us. But what's a snub or so, if only we can force H. B. to move?"

"But"—she hesitated again—"snubs hurt, man." Thinking of various slights already endured, her eyes suffused, and she had difficulty in keeping back the tears.

"Nobody shall hurt you." He came quickly across the room; put his arms round her; and kissed, very tenderly, the smooth skin behind her ears, her bared shoulders.

"Oh, yes, they will. Not even you can prevent that. Women in my position are bound to get hurt. All the time! But it doesn't hurt much"—she looked up into his eyes, and smiled away the tears from her own;—"it doesn't really hurt at all so long as I've got you."

Nevertheless, as they raced through their execrable meal in the empty dining-room, Aliette knew herself face to face with an ordeal. And the ordeal waxed more and more terrible in anticipation as the electric brougham, which Julia had insisted on sending to Baron's Court for them, rolled toward Bruton Street.

She sat wordlessly, her hand clasped in Ronnie's, staring wide-eyed at the buses, the taxicabs, and the private cars which passed or overtook them. It was as though every soul in London, all the people in those buses, those taxicabs, and those private cars, were hostile to her; as though she were a woman apart from all other women, outcast indeed. She wanted to say to her man: "Must we do this unwise thing? Must we? Can't we turn back? Can't we go on hiding ourselves?" But she said nothing, only clung the closer to his responsive hand.

4

Literary folk can be peculiarly childish; which is perhaps the reason why great authors are usually little men.

One part of Julia's mind—as she waited for Ronnie and Aliette to fetch her—positively grinned with mischief in anticipation of the new adventure, "defying Society." That part of her felt very much the heroine, a female knight-errant about to do lusty tilt against the dragon "Convention." But, in the main, her mood was retrospective.

"Curious," she thought, looking back at her dead self; "curious how entirely my views have changed." And she remembered the reactionary stubbornness of her anti-divorce article for "The Contemplatory," her delight at the stir which that article had created, her delusions that it might "help to stem the flood of post-war immorality."

Now even the closing sentence, "Until humanity learns to discipline the sentimental impulse, there can be no hope of matrimonial reconstruction," rang false in the auditorium of experience. She yearned suddenly to rewrite that sentence, to substitute "the lustful impulse" for "the sentimental impulse." But the written word, alas, could not be revoked.

Then, vaguely she visioned herself writing a new article—perhaps a new book—some pronouncement, anyway, which should contradict and counteract her old doctrine. And from that, her creative mind—as though linking story to moral—started in to examine the individual case of her son and Aliette.

The front door-bell rang; and Julia heard Ronnie's voice in the hall.

"Where's Aliette?" she asked, as he entered.

"Waiting in the brougham. By Jove, mater, you look like a stage duchess."

"Do I?" She blushed a little at his chaff, knowing it merited by the super-splendor of her attire; by the sable-and-brocade opera-cloak and the black velvet thereunder, by the coronal of diamond wheat-ears which banded her graying hair, and the Louis Seize buckles on her elegant shoes. Once more the heroine of an adventure, she picked her long white gloves and her bejeweled hand-bag from the dining-room table; and followed her son, through the front door which Kate held open for them, into the brougham.

Aliette, she greeted with a rare pressure of the hand and the still rarer compliment, "You're looking radiant to-night, my dear."

Kate closed the door on the three of them; and the electric brougham rolled off through Bruton Street into Bond Street; through Bond Street into Piccadilly. Julia did not appear in the least nervous. She began to talk of Patrick O'Riordan—a little contemptuously, as was her wont when dealing with stage-folk, against whom she cherished a prejudice almost puritanical.

"Patrick O'Riordan," opined Julia, "was a poorish play-wright; but of course he had money to play with. Not his own money. Naturally. People in the theater never did speculate with their own money. Lord Letchingbury was behind the show. Dot said Letchingbury had put up ten thousand." Followed a Rabelaisian reference to Letchingbury's penchant for Mary O'Riordan, which horrified Aliette, who had always imagined Mary, except for her one lapse, virtuous; and landed them in the queue of vehicles making for the illuminated portico of the Capitol Theater.

As the brougham crawled near and nearer to the lights which blazed their one word "Khorassan," it seemed to Aliette that she was about to plunge into a stream of icy water. Her heart contracted at mere sight of the furred opera-cloaks, of the smoothly-coiffured heads and the shiny top-hats under the portico. For a moment, fear had its way with her; the impulse to flight overwhelmed her courage. Then she looked at Ronnie; and saw that his face was set, that his chin protruded ever so slightly for sign of determination. Julia Cavendish, the wheat-ears glimmering like a crown in her hair, sat bolt upright, unflinching.

All said and done—thought Aliette—the risk, the big social risk, was Julia's. If, for her sake, Julia Cavendish could dare to jeopardize her entire circle, she, Aliette, must not prove unworthy of the offering. Her red lips pursed—even as they had pursed long ago when she and Ronnie waited for hounds to give tongue beyond Parson's Brook; and, head equally high, she followed the diamond wheat-ears out of the brougham, through the crowd under the portico, and into the theater.

Passing the box-office, she saw Julia smile at an old man with drooping gray mustaches and a reddish face, blue-lined above a bulging shirt-front.

Dot Fancourt shambled hesitantly across the few feet of carpet; shook hands; whispered "Surely this is very unwise"; and vanished downstairs toward the stalls.

"Old coward!" thought Julia; and her thirty-year-old friendship for the editor of "The Contemplatory" exploded in a red puff of rage.

Ronnie, noticing Dot's evasion, felt his color heighten. He handed their ticket to an attendant, and took Aliette's arm protectively as the three of them passed round the circular corridor into their box.

"You sit there, dear." Julia indicated the most conspicuous seat. "And I'll sit beside you."

Aliette, throwing the opera-cloak back from her shoulders, looked down across the house. To her imagination, the whole auditorium was a blur of eyes; hostile eyes, thousands upon thousands of them, some furtively upturned, some staring unabashed, some taking cover behind the gleam of opera-glasses.

Julia, too, looked downward; but her eyes saw every face, every dress, every gesture of every personage in the crowded stalls and in the opposite boxes, clear-cut and sharp as a photograph. Obviously the appearance of her party had created a sensation. Lady Cynthia Barberus and Miss Elizabeth Cattistock, making a conspicuous and loud-voiced entrance down the center gangway, stopped in mid-career blocking the Ellersons, Paul Flower, and Sir Siegfried with his fat Lady Moss. Lady Cynthia did not smile; Elizabeth Cattistock did—maliciously. Paul Flower gave an astounded grin; and nudged Dot Fancourt, who was already seated next to that inveterate first-nighter, Sir Peter Wilberforce. Dot whispered something to Sir Peter, who kept his attention rigidly on the curtain.

Various other people whom Julia knew more or less intimately, after one swift glance at the box, also kept their attention on that curtain; talking together, low-voiced.

And suddenly Julia grew aware that the white-gloved fingers of the woman beside her were gripping the ledge of their box as though it had been the arm of a dentist's chair, that the eyes of the woman beside her were focused as the eyes of a sleep-walker on the third row of the stalls. Instinctively, her own glance followed the line; and following, envisaged Aliette's husband.

To Julia, the female knight-errant a-tilt against the dragon "Convention," the presence of the Brunton family—for they were all there, Sir Simeon with his ambassadress, Rear-Admiral Billy, two of Sir Simeon's daughters by his first wife, and Hector—should have been the crown of her adventure; but to Julia Cavendish, society-woman, the happening was rather a shock. For the society-woman in her could not quite prevent herself from sympathizing with the peculiar position of Sir Simeon and Lady Brunton. Sympathy, however, turned to rage when they deliberately looked up at the box, and, with equal deliberation, looked away.

The two daughters did not look up; and the admiral gave no sign either of recognition or of partizanship. But Hector, at a word from his uncle, stared and continued to stare across the house.

Ronnie, perceiving the stare, deliberately drew his chair closer to Aliette's; and the momentary panic stilled in her mind. Her fingers loosened their grip on the velvet ledge; her eyes were no longer the vacant eyes of a sleep-walker. Coolly now she faced her husband's ill-mannered stare; coolly she forced a smile to her lips, and, pretending to examine her program, managed an aimless remark.

The pretense of nonchalance deceived even Hector. Hector turned to his cousin Moira and tried to talk with her. But hardly a word came to his lips. His heart thudded under the stiff of his shirt-front. He felt himself surrounded, pent in a cage, pent to sitting-posture. He wanted to heave himself upright, to smash the cage, to scatter the people surrounding him.

"Confound them!" he thought, "they all know. All these first-nighters know. Of set purpose, she has done me this shame."

Once again he saw himself as the lone bull, the lone bull before the scornful herd. He wanted to gore with his horns, to lash out with his hoofs; for his eyes—averted from the box—still held their picture: the two disdainful women, the tall disdainful man between them.

"Pretty bad form, *I* think," said Moira sympathetically.

"Curse her sympathy!" thought Hector.

5

The preliminary music neared its ending; and the first part of Aliette's ordeal, even more terrible than she had anticipated, was almost over by the time that Mary O'Riordan billowed her imposing way to the front of the stage-box. Other people followed, but Mary's hoydenish bulk, draped in the gold and scarlet of some super-Wagnerian goddess, dwarfed them to the insignificance of pygmies.

Aliette's heart, still numb from its effort at self-control, gave one pleasurable beat at sight of her friend. She smiled across the house at Mary. Their eyes met, clashed. And in that moment, the house darkled.

*

The curtain had been up a full three minutes before Aliette realized that those blue eyes of Mary's intended the cut direct. Realizing, every nerve in her tense body throbbed with resentment at the ingratitude. Mary to cut her! Mary of all people! Mary, by whose side she had stood stanch through a year of trouble! Mary, whose affair with Letchingbury provided the very money which sent up the curtain, which bought the scenery and paid the actors of "Khorassan"!

Gradually, the first throbs of Aliette's resentment subsided, leaving her every nerve a living pain. Mary's ingratitude hurt, hurt. "Most women are awful rotters"; Mollie's words, uttered long ago at Moor Park, came back to her.

She tried to distract her mind with the play; but O'Riordan's play—poor, thinly-poetic stuff, indifferently mouthed by mummers whose sole claim to their salary was their supping-acquaintance with the fringe of Society—failed to hold her thoughts. Her thoughts hovered between the enemy audience, blur of heads below, and the two friends, her only friends in a hostile world, on either side.

Thinking of their loyalty, Aliette no longer shrank from her ordeal. Her heart swelled, resolute against all hostility. It became two hearts: the one, warm and throbbing with partizanship for the stark old lady beside her, the old lady who had never turned a hair since they entered the theater, and for the "old lady's" son, for the man whose love was a rock: the other, icy-cold, almost beatless, frozen to contempt.

What a farce was this social game! As if the world's hostility mattered! One played one's little part on the stage of life, played it as best one might to the prompting of conscience, till the curtain fell, as it was falling now to a subdued rattle of perfunctory applause and the usual "snatched" calls.

Aliette felt Ronnie's fingers tighten on her own, relax. The house lights went up.

"Letchingbury will lose his money," remarked Julia calmly. "O'Riordan's poetic drama is merely an excuse for bad poetry and no drama. By the way, that is Letchingbury, isn't it?" She looked across at the stage-box; and Ronnie, looking with her, saw a young man, blond, with a receding chin and a receding forehead.

"Yes. That's Letchingbury all right," he said. "And, by the way, Alie, isn't that your friend, Mrs. O'Riordan?"

"I should hardly call her my friend," answered Aliette, a little bitterly; and steeled herself to look down at the stalls. Hector's was already empty. The remainder of the Brunton party sat perfectly rigid. Sir Peter Wilberforce, remembering himself one of Julia Cavendish's executors, managed a surreptitious nod. Dot Fancourt, like Hector, had escaped. Various dramatic critics, sidling their way out of the stalls toward the bar, bowed to Julia as though nothing out of the ordinary had occurred. Mary O'Riordan retired ostentatiously to the back of her box.

Aliette panicked again. Suppose Ronnie left her? Suppose Ronnie and

The Love-Story of Aliette Brunton

Hector met—in public? But Ronnie, for all his obtuser mind, divined that his women-folk were under fire; and that duty forbade him to desert. He whispered to her:

"Not so bad as you anticipated, eh? Of course one can't expect the Bruntons to be exactly cordial."

"I wish they hadn't been here," whispered back Aliette. "It makes things so much worse."

"Rubbish!" interrupted Julia. "It's the best thing that could possibly have happened. He'll have to bring his action after this, or be the laughing-stock of Mayfair."

While the auditorium emptied and filled again, Julia, her head erect, her hands quiet, talked on—as though the lack of Dot's usual visit to her box were of no moment. Ronnie, every fiber in him furious, played up to her. But Aliette could not speak. In her, social instincts were at war with conscience. Feeling herself definitely in the wrong toward society, yet definitely in the right toward her own soul, feeling terribly afraid, yet terribly courageous, striving desperately to wrench out the iron of resentment from her mind, striving piteously to forget the hurt of the wound which Mary O'Riordan had dealt her, she played her game in dumb show. And furtively, fearfully, as the music for the second act began, she watched for Hector's return.

But Hector did not return. Even when the house lights went out and the curtain rose again, Aliette could see that his stall remained empty. Subconsciously she knew that he had fled the theater.

The second act of "Khorassan" dragged to its undramatic climax. Once again those three faced the eyes of the audience. Now, more than ever, it seemed to Aliette, still sitting rigid in the forefront of Julia's box, as though all eyes were hostile, as though the entire house, and with it her entire social world, had decided to ostracize them.

All through that overlong *entr'acte*, she sat speechless; her brown pupils hard and bright; her white shoulders squared above the black sequined dress; her pale face, her red lips set to an almost sullen determination. And, as the *entr'acte* ended, those hard brown pupils fell to devisaging Mary O'Riordan.

Till, visibly ill at ease, the cow-eyes under Mary's mop of gold hair turned away.

But it gave Aliette no pleasure to realize that, hurt, she had retaliated.

6

Everybody in front of the curtain and everybody behind the curtain knew—as it fell—that Patrick O'Riordan's poetic drama, "Khorassan," was a proved failure. Nevertheless, the audience, as is the polite custom of first-night audiences, applauded; and called on the author, white-faced in the glare of the footlights, for a speech.

"And in the morning," thought Julia Cavendish satirically, "we shall read of the great service rendered by Patrick O'Riordan via Letchingbury's bank-account, to art; and of the pressing need for more revivals of the poetic drama."

Julia could not help being a little pleased at the play's failure; in a way it mitigated her own. For that *she* had failed, lamentably, in her adventure, Ronnie's mother realized even better than Aliette. Hold her head high as she might, this consciousness of disaster persisted all through O'Riordan's overlong speech. The literary childishness went out of her, leaving the woman of the world conscious that she had done the foolish thing, that she had flaunted her son and her son's mistress before that little section of society which is a London first-night. Society, of course, had averted its face! Remained, therefore, only the assurance that Aliette's husband had seen the flaunting, and so must surely be forced into action.

"Poor Aliette," thought Julia. "Poor Ronnie." Her mind was all a weakness toward them, all a strength against the world. For herself, she needed no comforting; but them she wanted to take in her arms, to mother.

O'Riordan's speech ended. The house clapped, and emptied. The three left their box; and Ronnie—reluctantly leaving Julia and Aliette in the foyer—went off in search of the electric brougham.

Waiting in the crowd, both women knew themselves on show, the dual cynosure of a hundred furtive glances. People seemed anxious to escape without the need for recognizing them. The few smiles were frigid, standoffish—all for Julia, none for her companion. Hector's aunt, jostling by, cut the pair dead.

Aliette tried to think, "It doesn't matter; it doesn't matter a bit"; she tried to hold herself upright, to cut rather than be cut, to preserve—outwardly at least—the semblance of a dignity. But inwardly she knew herself all one tremble of undignified panic. If only one person, just one person in that jostling mob, would be really decent! If only Ronnie would be quicker with their carriage!

Then simultaneously both women grew aware that a face, one kindly face, was smiling at them, was making its way toward them through the crowd. Simultaneously they recognized the face—Hermione Ellerson's.

"My dear, I've been trying to catch your eye all the evening," called Hermione to Aliette. "But you wouldn't look at me. Why don't you come and see us? I want you to see our new house. Curzon Street, 24. In the telephone-book."

Hermione was swept away before Aliette could collect her wits for reply: and a moment afterward they saw, beyond the crowd, Ronnie signaling the arrival of their brougham.

7

"It was decent of Hermione, frightfully decent, especially as she's a kind of relation of Hector's. All the same, I don't think I'll go and see her."

Aliette, disrobed, sat staring into the gas-fire of their Powolney Mansions bedroom.

"Why not?" asked a shirt-sleeved Ronnie.

She turned to him, and her face showed very pale.

"Man, it's all so hopeless."

"It isn't. It isn't a bit hopeless. The mater's right. H. B. must act now."

"He won't, and even if he does—Oh, don't you see that I've—that I've ruined you! I've ruined your career. I've ruined you both."

"Rubbish!" There was something of his mother's brusquerie in the man's tone.

"It isn't rubbish." The woman was deadly in her calm. "It's the absolute truth. Don't let us deceive ourselves."

He tried to take her in his arms; but she rose, eluding him. "Don't, Ronnie! Let's be sensible; it's high time. We—you and I and your mother—have made a mistake. A mistake that's almost irretrievable. There's only one thing to be done now—"

"And that is?" He had never known her in this mood. She seemed utterly different from the sensitive Aliette of a few hours since; almost unloving, hard, purposeful, resolute.

"And that is?" he repeated.

"I must leave you."

At her words Ronnie's heart stopped beating as though some giant had put a finger on it. For one fraction of a second, love vanished utterly; almost, he hated her.

"Yes," went on Aliette, "I must leave you. It's the only way, I'll take a little cottage. Somewhere not too far from London. And you—you must go and live with your mother."

His heart began beating again, faintly.

"But why?" he managed. "Why?"

"Because that's the only way to stop people from talking. If they know that you're at Bruton Street, that I'm not at Bruton Street, then," she was faltering now, faltering in her firm purpose, and she knew that she must not falter; "then they'll think that your mother didn't know anything when she invited us to-night."

He came toward her: and she felt her momentary determination weaken; felt herself powerless to do the right. He put his hands on her shoulders, and looked her deep in the eyes. Then he smiled, the quaint, whimsical smile she loved best.

"You're not serious, Alie?"

"I am," she faltered, "desperately serious. You'll let me have my cottage, won't you?"

"You know I won't." He had her in his arms now. "You know that I won't consent to anything so absurd." He bent to kiss her. "Darling, don't let's lose our pluck. It's been a rotten evening for you. Rotten! I know that."

"It's not of myself that I'm thinking."

"I know that, too. I'm not thinking for myself, either. I'm trying to think for both of us, for all three of us. We've got to see this thing through. Together."

"Together!" The word weakened her still further.

"Yes, together." He followed up his advantage. "Life's a fight. A hard fight. You mustn't desert."

"And you"—her voice, as she lay motionless in his arms, was almost inaudible—"you think I'm worth fighting for?"

"More than anything in the world. But I wish"—a little he, too, faltered, his fears for her sake making him afraid—"I wish that people didn't hurt you so."

She stirred in his arms; and her face upturned to his.

"Man," she said, her eyes shining, "I'm not afraid of anything people can do to me. Nobody except you could ever really hurt me. I—I didn't mean to desert; only just to efface myself. Won't you let me efface myself? Until—until Hector divorces me. It's the right thing—the best thing. Really it is."

"Right or wrong," said Ronnie, "we'll see this business through—see it through together—even if it lasts all our lives."

*

Aliette, seeing the fighting-fire in those blue eyes, seeing the stubborn set of that protruded jaw, knew her momentary determination beaten to the ground.

Chapter XVIII

1

Within one week of its first launching, "Khorassan" sank, leaving hardly a ripple, into the deep pool of theatrical failures. But for weeks and weeks thereafter, that shallow pool which is West End society rippled furiously to the stone which Julia Cavendish had thrown into it when she attended Patrick O'Riordan's first-night accompanied by her son and Aliette.

Some of the consequences of that stone-throwing were explained to Ronnie's "wife" when—overpersuaded from her decision not to visit Hermione—she called at the little black-carpeted, Chinese-papered, orange-curtained box of a house in Curzon Street.

Hermione, her willowy figure supine on an enormous sofa, her dark eyes glinting with a sympathetic curiosity not entirely bereft of humor, extended one ringless hand with a laughed "Well, my dear, you really have put your foot into it this time. Your in-laws are perfectly furious."

Aliette laughed in reply (no one ever took Hermione quite seriously); possessed herself of a luxurious chair before the luxurious fire, and admitted:

"It was rather a faux pas, wasn't it?"

"I'm not so sure of that." Hermione's smooth brows crinkled in thought. "I'm not at all so sure of that. It's quite on the cards, I think, that it'll lead to something. Sir Simeon told me, only last night, how perfectly impossible it was for such a state of affairs to go on."

She rose from the sofa; and, coming over to the fire, took the vast pouffe in front of it. "Poor darling! It's rotten for you."

Aliette stiffened at the suggestion of sympathy. "I'm quite happy, thank you."

"Are you? I'm so glad." Hermione edged the pouffe closer. "My dear, you have surprised the clan. None of us imagined you capable of a really-truly love-affair. Why, you're the last person in the world—"

"Please, Hermione, don't let's discuss me."

"But I want to discuss you. I think you're perfectly marvelous. How on

225

earth you ever had the nerve. And from a husband like Hector!" Ellerson's wife paused to warm her expressive hands at the fire. "I never did like Hector. Strong, silent men always bore me to distraction. But Ronnie Cavendish is a perfect dear."

It was the first time that any one except his mother had been personal about Ronnie, and Aliette felt herself blushing at the mere mention of his name. She wanted to shoo Hermione away from the topic; but Hermione, like some obstinate butterfly, returned always to the forbidden flower. Hermione wanted "to know everything." Hermione hinted herself more than ready to be profuse in sympathy—if only the other would be profuse in confidences. Even the presence of an exiguous Belgian butler, carrying exiguous French tea-cups on an exiguous Russian silver tray, failed to distract Hermione from her purpose.

Ellerson's wife had been discussing *l'affaire Aliette* with Lady Cynthia Barberus, with Miss Elizabeth Cattistock, with many another mannequin of the "Ritz crowd"; and they had jointly come to the conclusion that it was abominable, "perfectly abominable," "a return to feminine slavery" for any man to behave as Hector Brunton was behaving. If only "dear Alie" would tell them how they could help her!

Aliette, however—who, in her safety, had always rather despised Lady Cynthia and Lady Cynthia's associates,—could not bring herself to seek alliance with them in her danger. Her fastidiousness resented the "Ritz crowd's" partizanship. Trying her best to be grateful, she could not stifle the instinct that Hermione's "sympathy" was the sympathy of an idle, over-sexed woman, inspired rather by sensational and illicit novelty than by reasoned understanding.

But even oversensitive Aliette could not misjudge the real understanding, the real sympathy of Hermione's husband.

That tall, casually-groomed, blond-haired youth came in just as the guest was perpending departure; offered her a large hand; and said nothing whatever to complicate a difficult situation. My Lord Arthur merely opined that he was sorry to be late for tea, that he hoped Aliette would come and see them again, that she must dine and do a show with them as soon as ever they got back from the Riviera, and that she must bring—he said this with extraordinary tact—anybody she liked to make a fourth at the party. Lord Arthur, in fact, without mentioning Ronnie's name, made it quite clear on which side of the social fence both he and his wife purposed to sit.

For by now the various sections of that complicated community which is social London had grown conscious of the Cavendish-Brunton fence. People had begun to comprehend that *l'affaire Aliette* was serious, and that one would have to sit either on Aliette's side, on Hector's side, or on the fence itself. So that if Aliette had been less old-fashioned, in the best sense of that much-abused word; if Aliette's lover had been less shy, less reticent, less aloof from his kind; and if Julia Cavendish had only been a little less certain, that victory was already won—there is little doubt that other houses besides 24 Curzon Street would have opened their doors.

Social London, you see, was in a state of moral flux. Cadogan Square, Belgravia, and Knightsbridge still clung rigidly to the tenets of the Victorian past. But for Mayfair, parts of Kensington, and the more artistic suburbs, matrimonial issues had assumed a new aspect since the war. Actually, a tide of freer thinking on the sex question had begun to sweep over the whole of England. Happiness had not yet come to be acknowledged the only possible basis of monogamy, but divorce reform was no longer only in the air—it was more or less on the table of the House.

And to divorce reformers Hector Brunton's attitude appeared almost as indefensible as it did to those who, not yet in revolt against the old tenets of indissoluble matrimony, found it hard to stomach a man's permitting his wife to live unsued in open adultery.

2

Julia Cavendish tried to explain these post-war matrimonial issues to Dot Fancourt, when he called at Bruton Street to remonstrate with her about "the very serious blunder" she had committed. But Dot, willing enough to open his columns in "The Contemplatory" for an intellectual threshing out of such issues, could not face them in real life. A social cowardliness, essentially editorial, obsessed his failing mentality.

"My dear," he argued, "it isn't as if you were a nobody. Nobodies can afford experiments. You can't. You're a Cavendish. You have a position, an eminent position in the scholastic world, in the world of society, and in the world of letters. Therefore you, of all people, have least right, especially in times like the present, to countenance matrimonial bolshevism."

Julia Cavendish put down her embroidery-frame, and faced her quondam friend squarely. Ever since their meeting in the foyer of the Capitol Theater, she had been seeing him with new eyes, seeing only his weakness, the insufficiency and the inefficiency of him. That he meant his advice kindly and for the best, she knew. Nevertheless, he had wrecked their friendship; failed her when she most needed him. The disloyalty stung her to bitterness.

"The fact that I married a Cavendish," she said, "is neither here nor there. My position, such as it is, is one which I attained for myself. If, by siding with my own son, I jeopardize it—"

"But, my dear, why jeopardize it at all? You're being so unwise. You won't do your son any good by quarreling with your friends."

"Apparently I have no friends." The Biblical phrase about the broken reed crossed Julia's mind. "If I had friends, they would stand by me and mine; not try to avoid us in public."

"You're very unfair." Dot rose irritably, and began shambling up and down the room. "Terribly unfair. Can't you understand how I hated seeing you—messed up in this sort of thing?"

She fired up at that. "One defends one's own, Dot."

And for an hour after Dot had gone, the words rang in Julia's mind. "One defends one's own—at all costs—however hard the battle."

For her, battle grew harder as the days went by. One by one she argued out the issue with her protesting friends, convincing few, antagonizing many. Her family, however—always a little jealous of "the immaculate Ronald"—Julia met not with argument but with shock tactics.

Clementina, calling, breasted and bustled for fray, accompanied by Sir

Gilbert Frankau

John, in his best Bank of England blacks, who admitted that "they had heard things" and pressed to know if there was any truth in "the things they had heard," received a direct "My dear Clementina, if your husband means that you've been informed of my son's running away with Hector Brunton's wife, and that Hector Brunton is going to divorce her, you've been informed correctly"; while Alice, writing a dutiful letter from Cheltenham, received a typescript reply—to the same effect—which cut her Anglo-Indian sense of etiquette to the quick.

As for May who, relinquishing the expensive good works and still more expensive garden of her house in Abbey Road, called unattended and found Julia alone; she returned to St. John's Wood with the firm conviction that her "poor dear sister" must have been "got at by some of those dreadful writing people," and bombarded her, for nearly a week, with pamphlets on "The Sin of Divorce."

Meanwhile, regular callers at Bruton Street grew rarer and rarer; until Paul Flower, busy rewriting some of his earlier books for American admirers and utterly unable to discuss anything else, almost monopolized the once-crowded drawing-room. Paul, engrossed with pre-war literature, became in those days Julia's best refuge from post-war life. He succeeded—sometimes for hours together—in stimulating her creative imagination.

And since, to a literary craftswoman, the creative imagination is only as the first nip to a confirmed toper, Paul Flower soon succeeded in more than this—in arousing the actual creative instinct: so that the creative instinct awoke and demanded work.

Gradually Julia grew hungry for the pen, for the long and lonely hours when the creative mind is as God, fashioning puppets for His pleasure. But always, when Paul Flower had left her, her imagination switched back from literature to life.

"The man Brunton," said imagination, "is not beaten. He'll bring no action. He is working, working secretly, to ruin your boy's career."

3

And indeed, during those few days which preceded the close of the autumn sessions, it did not require his mother's imagination to perceive that some curious and sinister influence must be at work against Ronald Cavendish in the quiet quadrangles and the gray-pinnacled courts either side the Griffin.

From the unwigged Mr. Justice Mallory, sipping the port of midday adjournment in his private room behind King's Bench Seven, to melancholious Benjamin Bunce, perusing his "Law Times" at Groom's coffee-shop in Fleet Street, the whole "legal world" was aware that "H. B. meant to make trouble." Alike in Middle and in Inner Temple halls, in robing-rooms, in chambers, in corridors, and in offices, wheresoever and whensoever barristers or solicitors foregathered to talk "shop," one heard the buzz of dignified curiosity, rumors of instant citation, of citation delayed.

Meanwhile Ronnie, growing less and less inclined to intimacy with his fellow-lawyers as he grew more and more conscious of their interest in him, visited Pump Court with a regularity which held more of bravado than of necessity. The flow of his briefs, never broad, had dwindled to the tiniest trickle. Barring the work he still did for Wilberforce, Wilberforce & Cartwright, he foresaw almost complete idleness at the Hilary sessions.

The foresight, financially, frightened him. Never a spendthrift, his own needs, small though they were, had to be met. His savings and the Jermyn Street rent, paid six months in advance, were almost exhausted. The idea of borrowing from his mother did not appeal; and to let Aliette bear her part in the "family" expenses was unthinkable.

But even Ronnie failed to realize the full extent of his financial shipwreck until that afternoon just before Christmas when James Wilberforce, preannounced by telephone, strode into the duck's-egg-green paneled chambers, and, having made certain that they could not be overheard, plumped his long bulk into the dilapidated armchair with a diffident, "Old chap, I've come on a devilish unpleasant mission."

The barrister did not answer; and after a constrained pause the solicitor went on, picking each word as though fearful of its giving offense: "Pater would have come and seen you himself. But he thought, you and me being pals, that perhaps I'd better be the one. You see, being your mother's executor, and, so to speak, a friend of the family, pater's always tried to do everything he could for you—"

"You needn't say any more," interrupted Ronnie. "I quite understand. You've come to tell me I'm not to expect any further briefs from Wilberforce, Wilberforce & Cartwright."

"Hardly that," prevaricated Jimmy. "But the fact is—you know how I hate beating about the bush—pater's afraid of offending Brunton. We've got the big Furlmere divorce case coming on fairly soon. 'Bout the end of January, I expect. We're pretty high up on the list. Furlmere insisted on H. B. leading for us. We sent round the brief to him in the usual way, and of course he had to accept it. But when he took our retainer, his clerk, that fellow Patterson, hinted—mind you, he only hinted—that if there were any question of 'a certain gentleman' acting as junior to him, 'Mr. Brunton' would not appear in court when the case came on."

"But surely you had no idea—"

"Of briefing you as junior? Of course not. I shouldn't be such an incredible ass. Still, straws show which way the wind blows. And we simply can't afford to quarrel with H. B. Not till the Furlmere case is over, anyway."

The friends looked at each other for one silent minute. Outside, a thin rain had begun to patter on the flagstones. Within the room darkled. Ronnie clicked on the table-lamp, and began to scrawl with vagrant pencil on the blotting-paper.

"I'm not quarreling with your position, Jimmy," he said at last. "Tell your pater I'd do the same if I were he."

Jimmy's voice softened. "Old man, I don't want to interfere. But I do wish you'd arrange for some mutual friend to see Brunton. Take it from me, he's going on playing dog-in-the-manger. And he can do you a hell of a lot of harm."

"Let him!" Ronnie's jaw set. "If this is going to be a fight between us, it may as well be a fight to a finish. I don't propose asking favors, even by proxy. If he thinks he's going to succeed in driving me out of the bar—"

"No one's suggested your leaving the bar. In fact"—Jimmy began to stammer, as a man making offer of a gift which is almost certain to be refused—"another thing I came round to see you about was—"

The sentence refused to complete itself: and Jimmy started a new one. "As you know, our partners, the Cartwrights, do quite a lot of work that never comes into the High Court at all; criminal stuff, county courts, and all that sort of thing. If you'd care to accept their briefs—"

Again the sentence refused to complete itself; again the two friends looked at one another in silence. Then the barrister said:

"A bit of a come-down, isn't it? Almost as bad as 'taking soup.'"

This allusion to the practice of young and briefless barristers, who sit all day long in the criminal courts waiting their chance to defend any prisoners that may be allotted to them, made Ronnie's friend squirm.

"Hang it all, it isn't as bad as that. John Cartwright's quite a good sort. And a big criminal case brings other work. Anyway, think it over, and let me know." Jimmy rose to go. "And by the way, will you give my regards to the little lady? Tell her how sorry I am about the whole thing and that I'm sure it'll all come out right in the long run."

At the door, James Wilberforce turned; and, coming back, extended a hand. "Buck up, old boy," he mumbled rather shamefacedly.

Left alone, Ronnie sat for a long while, scrawling on the blotting-pad.

"After all," he thought, "it was pretty decent of Jimmy to send Alie that message. I wonder why he did it. I wonder whether he's still keen on Mollie. Jolly rough luck on him if he is. Curse that fellow Brunton! He's stirred up a pretty kettle of fish."

And from that he fell to evil-tempered rumination—in which his newly-aroused ambition for legal success played no small rôle—finally deciding, *faute de mieux*, to accept the work offered.

Chapter XIX

1

Every year, toward the end of November, Betty Masterman had been accustomed to receive an invitation to spend Christmas at Clyst Fullerford. This year, to her surprise, she received a long, carefully-worded letter in Mollie's childish handwriting: a letter which contained the unusual suggestion that Mollie should spend Christmas with her. "My dear," wrote the girl, "I simply daren't ask you down here. It's too utterly dull for words."

Betty, nothing if not extravagant, wired back an immediate answer; and met her friend, two days before Christmas eve, in the holiday bustle at Waterloo station.

"Mollie," greeted the grass-widow, "you look like a ghost. What on earth's happened to you since the summer?"

But it was not until Betty's "daily woman" had completed her hasty washing up of the dinner things, and they sat alone in front of the gas-fire in the little red-papered sitting-room, that Mollie answered the question.

"Betty dear," she said, puffing a vague cigarette. "I'm feeling too rotten for words. Nothing seems to go right with me these days."

Betty's experienced eyes sparkled with laughter. "Give sorrow words," she quoted chaffingly; and then, a note of seriousness in her voice, "What's the trouble? The sister or the Wilberforce man?"

"You've heard something then?"

"Only gossip." The other trod carefully. "But of course I'm not quite a fool. I thought when you came rushing round here from Lancaster Gate that something must have gone pretty wrong."

"Everything's gone wrong." Mollie repeated the inevitable slogan, of post-war youth, "Everything. You remember Ronald Cavendish—"

"I've met him once or twice."

"Well, Alie's run away from Hector—"

"And run away to Cavendish."

"You did know then?"

"My dear, everybody knows." Betty considered the position. "Still, that's their affair, isn't it? Why should you worry about it? There'll be a divorce, I suppose, and after that they'll get married."

"That's just the trouble."

"How do you mean?"

"Apparently, Hector's refused to divorce Alie."

"Oh!"

The pair inspected one another across the mellow firelight. After a long pause, the elder said:

"You're not much of a pal, Mollie. You've only told me half the story."

Mollie Fullerford blushed. Her reticent virginity revolted from the idea of confessing herself, to Betty, in love with James Wilberforce. Yet that she was in love with the man, most uncomfortably in love with him, Mollie knew. Despite all her efforts to maintain the pose of the modern young, the pose of cold-blooded mate-selection, she had failed as lamentably as most others of her kind to control nature. Nature and the modern creed refused to be reconciled. She realized now that she wanted—exclusively—James. She wanted to belong to him; she wanted him to belong to her; she wanted him—and no other—to father her children.

That last thought rekindled Mollie's blushes. Succeed as she might in curbing her tongue, she could not curb her feelings. She fell to wondering if Jimmy would ask her to marry him, to speculating whether, even if their friendship so abruptly broken off should be renewed (as she had subconsciously hoped it would be renewed when she invited herself to London), whether, even if Jimmy did ask her to marry him, she would be capable of sacrificing Aliette. Would she not be forced to make conditions—conditions that no man in Jimmy's position could possibly accept? Would she not be forced to say: "If I marry you, you'll have to let me receive my sister and my sister's lover"?

"How about the Wilberforce man?" Betty's words interrupted reverie. "Does he know you're in town?"

"Yes," admitted Mollie.

"You still write to each other then?"

"Only occasionally."

"My dear, how exciting! When did you hear from him last?"

But at that Aliette's sister broke off the conversation with a wry "Betty, I simply won't be cross-examined."

"You needn't get ratty, dear thing," retorted the grass-widow. "I don't want to pry into your secrets. But"—she rustled up from her chair, and made a movement to begin undressing—"if he *should* write that he's coming to see you, for goodness' sake try and make yourself look a little less of a 'patient Griselda.' What about face-massage? I know a man in Sloane Street who's simply wonderful!"

2

Aliette, whom Mollie visited next day, was even more shocked than Betty Masterman at the change in her sister's appearance. The girl seemed utterly altered, utterly different from the fancy-free maiden of Moor Park. She came into the connubial room nervously; almost forgot to kiss; entirely forgot to inquire after Ronnie; refused to take off her hat, and sat down on the edge of the hard sofa gingerly as though it had been an omnibus seat.

"Rather awful, isn't it?" Aliette, with a comprehensive glance at her surroundings, broke the social ice. "You mustn't mind."

"I don't mind. But it is rather awful." A pause. "I suppose you had to do it, Alie?"

"Do what? Come and live here?"

"No. The whole thing." Aliette did not answer, and her sister went on. "I wish you hadn't had to. It's been simply rotten at home. Mother and dad—" She broke off, biting her lip. "*They* aren't so bad really; it's Eva who's putrid."

"Eva never did like either of us."

For the first time in their lives, the sisters felt shy with one another. Caroline Staley, entering, broad-hipped, a smile on her full lips and a tea-tray in her large hands, noticed the tension.

"My, Miss Mollie!" ejaculated the tactful Caroline, "but you aren't looking yourself at all. You ought to take that hat off and lie down awhile."

Tea relaxed the tension; but made intimate conversation no easier. Between them and their old intimacy rose—as it seemed—insurmountable barriers. It was Mollie who, involuntarily, pulled those barriers down.

"I say," she asked abruptly, "isn't Hector going to do anything?"

"I'm afraid not."

"Doesn't it make you frightfully unhappy?"

"Only for Ronnie's sake."

Mollie did her best to restrain indignation. Woman-like, she could not help blaming Ronnie for the whole occurrence. Girl-like, she could not quite divine the immensity of passion behind her sister's steady eyes; till, somehow infected by that passion, her thoughts veered to James. Suppose James had been married. Married to a lunatic, say, or a drunkard? Tied to some rotten wife, for instance, a wife who made him unhappy? Suppose that James had said to her, "Mollie, let's cut the painter"?

And suddenly Mollie's indignation passed, leaving her contrite.

"Alie," she said, "I ought to have come up to town before. I oughtn't to have left you alone all this time. I'm afraid I've been"—she faltered—"rather a beast about the whole thing."

"You haven't." Aliette came across to the sofa, and took her sister's hand. "It's been simply wonderful of you to forgive our thoughtlessness, our lack of consideration—"

"Oh, that!" interrupted Mollie. "I wasn't thinking about that." She fell silent; and again, to her contrite mind, the romance of Aliette and Ronnie assumed a personal significance.

So this was love—thought the girl—the real thing! Love without orange-blossom, without wedding-presents. Love so gloriously reckless of material considerations that it could exist in and defy the most sordid surroundings, the completest ostracism from one's kind.

"It's you who are wonderful," said Mollie.

And all that afternoon, as conversation grew easier between them, as she learned from a hesitant Aliette of the real Hector and the real Ronnie, of the snubs one had to put up with, and of the sympathy which was even harder than the snubs to bear, of the petty, almost indecent economies to be anticipated now that Ronnie's professional income looked like failing (soon it might be necessary to sacrifice Ponto, whose board and lodging at a near-by stable cost fifteen shillings a week), the girl, continually testing her own affection for James on the touchstone of Aliette's love for Ronnie, could not but find it a little lacking in that spirit of service which is truest comradeship.

"But where *is* Ronnie?" she asked, as they kissed au revoir.

"With his mother, I expect," smiled Aliette. "He said, when you phoned last night, that we'd probably like to be alone."

3

"Rather decent of Cavendish, leaving us alone like that," thought Mollie, waiting—befurred to the eyes—on the drafty platform at Baron's Court station.

Strangely affected by her sister's revelations, she found herself as the train got under way—comparing Ronnie with James; not, she had to admit, entirely to James's advantage.

It was all very well—went on thought—being in love with James, but why should one be in love with James? One ought to be jolly angry with the man. Taking it all round, he had behaved disgracefully. James had "shied off" because he couldn't face a little scandal; had written the coldest, unfriendliest letters.

"James, in fact," decided the girl, "doesn't care a button for me, and I'm a little fool to let myself care for him."

But when, arrived at the flat, Betty Masterman, with a malicious pout of her red lips, imparted the news that "the Wilberforce man" had rung up to suggest himself for tea on the following afternoon, Mollie Fullerford's mental dignity gave way to an ardor of anticipation which made her feel—as she expressed it to herself just before falling asleep—"a perfect little idiot"; and when, next afternoon—to all outward appearances his undisturbed self—Jimmy was heralded into the sitting-room, the girl felt extraordinarily grateful to the "man in Sloane Street" under whose ministrations she had spent the morning.

All the same, she felt uncommonly nervous. Watching her James as he arranged his long bulk in the most comfortable of the three chairs, handing him his tea, listening to the easy flow of small talk between him and Betty, Mollie found it impossible to realize that this could be the creature about whose physical and mental qualities her imagination had woven its tissue of dreams. That he and she were participators in a tragic romance; that if he asked her to marry him (and she knew subconsciously, even though consciously denying the possibility, that he *would* ask her) she would have to refuse—seemed possibilities connected rather with the heroine of some magazine story than with her own demure self.

Tea finished, Betty made the telephone in her bedroom an excuse to leave the pair alone; clicked the door on them; and pattered away in her high-heeled shoes.

"You're not looking as well as you were when I saw you last," managed Wilberforce, after a minute's self-conscious silence.

"Aren't I?" Mollie would have given a good deal to run away from him, to run after Betty.

"No. You haven't been ill or anything, have you?"

"Ill!" She forced a smile to her lips. "Rather not. I've been quite all right."

They gazed at each other. Then, abruptly, Jimmy said:

"Mollie, what's happened to us?"

"To *us*?" she queried shyly.

"Yes; to you and me." The man paused, plunged in. "We were such frightfully good pals last summer, and now it seems as though"—another pause—"we don't hit things off a bit."

"Is that my fault or yours?" There was scarcely a hint of their old camaraderie in the girl's sulky voice.

"Mine, I suppose," he sulked back.

"Well, isn't it?" she shot at him; and at that all the self-realizations, all the heart-searchings and heart-burnings in James Wilberforce blew to one bright point of clear flame, melting his reserve as the blow-pipe melts cast iron.

"Mollie," he blurted out, "you know how I hate beating about the bush. Let's be open with one another. Let's admit that something has happened." He leaned forward in his chair, both hands on his knees. "But you aren't going to let that something make any difference, are you?"

His method irritated her to abruptness.

"You *are* beating about the bush, Jimmy. Why not be straight?"

"I'm trying to be straight." His hands clenched. "But it's jolly difficult. You see, there are some things that—well, that one doesn't discuss with girls."

"Isn't that rather rot nowadays?" retorted Mollie, hating herself for the slang.

"I don't think it's rot. I think there are a good many subjects a man doesn't want to discuss with—with a girl he—er—cares about."

"Then he does care," thought Mollie; and felt her heart leap to the thought. Outwardly she made pretense of considering his sentence; her brows crinkled. Inwardly she pretended herself still vexed with him. She said to herself, "He mustn't see that I care. He must be taught his lesson."

"You're a bit old-fashioned, aren't you, Jimmy?" she prevaricated at last.

"Perhaps I am." Affection made him suddenly the schoolboy. "But it's devilish awkward, isn't it; this—this business about your sister?"

"Awkward!" Mollie's loyalty stiffened her to discard prevarication. "I don't think it's awkward. I think it's jolly rough luck on Aliette and Mr. Cavendish. Hector knows perfectly well they'd get married if he'd only set her free. I think Hector's a cad. Alie told him everything before she went. He knows jolly well she'll never go back to him. Why should she? A man doesn't own a woman for ever and ever just because he happens to marry her."

The speech roused Jimmy to an unwonted height of imagination. He saw himself marrying Mollie, quarreling with Mollie; saw Mollie running away from him, as Aliette had run away from Hector.

"So if *you* married a man, you wouldn't consider yourself tied to him for life?"

"Certainly not. Not if he didn't behave decently."

The girl's eyes were brave enough, but a shiver of apprehension ran through her body. She thought: "He couldn't care for anybody who said that sort of thing to him." Jimmy seemed to be considering her statement, weighing it up. It came to her instinctively that they were at the crisis of their lives.

"And if he behaved well to you?" The words seemed fraught with meaning.

"Why, then"—she could feel herself shivering, shivering from the soles of her feet to the roots of her bobbed hair—"then—there wouldn't be any need for me to run away from him."

Their eyes met; brown eyes searching violet. Their eyes lit with mutual understanding. Self-consciousness deserted her; deserted them both. She was conscious of him—close to her—seizing her hands—speaking rapidly, unrestrainedly:

"I've been a rotter—an absolute rotter, darling. I ought to have warned you the moment I found out. I ought to have told you that it didn't make any difference. It hasn't, it can't make any difference, not the slightest difference. Nothing that your sister may have done, may do, can affect us one way or the other. It's you I want to marry, not your sister."

"Jimmy!"

He was conscious of his arms round her—of his lips on hers—of her yielding to his kisses—returning them.

The gush of Jimmy's passion, of her own, frightened the girl. Somehow she freed herself from his kisses; and stood upright, tremulous, blushing a little, stammering a little, altogether incoherent.

"Jimmy, you mustn't, you oughtn't to. It isn't fair to me. It's not fair to Alie."

"What's she got to do with it?" Mollie could see the big vein on her lover's forehead throb to each syllable. "What's she got to do with us?"

"Everything." For a moment the girl felt herself the stronger. "Everything. It isn't fair. Can't you see why it isn't fair? How can I marry you?" Her voice broke. "How can I take my happiness while Alie's an outcast? She *is* an outcast. You wouldn't, you couldn't let her come to our wedding."

"Then you care for your sister more than you care for me?" interrupted

Wilberforce, shirking the issue.

"I don't! I don't!" Strength had gone out of Mollie; she felt herself weak, incapable. "It isn't that. It isn't that a bit. Only I can't take my happiness while Alie's miserable. She is miserable, though she won't admit it. Don't you see how rotten it would be of me if I married you—with things as they are?"

"No, I don't." Her recalcitrance angered him.

"You must. Jimmy," softly, "you do want me to be happy with you, don't you?"

"Of course I want you to be happy with me." His anger relented. "I'd do anything in the world to make you happy."

"Would you, dear?"

"Rather. Only tell me what it is."

"It's only Alie." Loyalty strung her to the sacrifice. "Only Alie. Can't you do something for her? You're a lawyer; you know how these things are managed. Oh, do, please do something to help her, to help"—the young voice dwindled to a whisper—"to help both of us. Jimmy, I do want to marry you. I want to marry you most awfully. But I simply can't even promise to marry you with things as they are. It wouldn't be decent of me. Honestly it wouldn't. It wouldn't be decent of either of us. It wouldn't be playing the game."

They faced each other, half in love and half in hostility.

"You really mean that, Mollie?"

"Yes, I really mean it."

"And if I *could* manage to do anything?"

"If you only could"—she smiled into his eyes—"there wouldn't be a thing in the world to keep us apart."

Jimmy took the girl in his arms; and again she let herself answer his kisses. "I'll move heaven and earth and the lord chancellor," vowed James Wilberforce to that sleek bobbed head.

4

Betty Masterman, returning, dressed for some mysterious dinner, on the stroke of seven, found a Mollie who could not decide herself happy or unhappy; a Mollie whose lips still tingled from her lover's kisses—but whose eyes still shone with the tears shed in loyalty to her sister.

Chapter XX

1

Before, and even during the war, Christmas day at Bruton Street used to be rather a function. On that day, Julia, still the feudalist in her domestic policy, was wont to rise earlier than usual, to distribute gifts among her servants, to proceed to church, lunch in some state, and during the afternoon receive such of her friends as had not left town.

This Christmas, Brunton's continued obduracy made functions impossible. Waking late to the subdued glimmer of the bed-lamp, to the presence of her maid and the tea-tray, Julia was conscious of depression. Her night had been restless, haunted by the specter of defeat. The "flaunting policy" had failed! Depression grew. The idea of distributing presents, of her servants' formal thanks, fretted her. Fretted her, too, the thought that this would be the first Nativity on which she had ever missed going to church.

But gradually, as she bathed, as her maid swathed her in a long purple velvet tea-gown, Julia's vitality began to revive. A little of the Christmas spirit entered into her. She recognized for how much she had to be thankful; for ample means, for well-trained servants, for a well-tended house, for a mind still confident of its powers, for a conscience assured in its right-doing, for a son who adored her and whom she adored, and, lastly but not least, for work still to be accomplished.

This certainty of work to come, of a creative task dim-visualized as yet, but already quickening in the womb of her mentality, had been newly-vivid during the restless night; so that she was now assured—with that assurance which only the craftswoman possesses—of another book shortly to be born from her pen. "My last book, perhaps!" she thought; and dreaded, in anticipation, the labor of that book-bearing.

The distribution of the presents tired her. Depression returned with the physical fatigue of being gracious. But, once the little ceremony was over and she sat waiting for Ronnie and Aliette in the square box of a work-room, the old lady grew almost fey with the prescience of coming triumph. She, Julia Cavendish, might die, but even in her dying she would not be defeated. By her own unaided strength, by the very steel of her spirit, she would beat down all obstacles—the labors of book-bearing, the obduracy of Aliette's husband, the defections of their friends.

And—in that moment of feyness—Julia knew that the unwritten book, her own death, and her son's future were mysteriously intertwined; that the only sword which could sever the Gordian knot of Hector Brunton's obduracy was the sword of the written word. But as yet her knowledge was all nebulous, the merest protoplasm of a plan.

2

Aliette, that Christmas morning, had not even the semblance of a plan. Ever since her visit to Hermione she had been growingly aware of strain, of a strange morbidity. Increasingly she felt resentful of her position. Increasingly she reproached herself for the *impasse* in Ronnie's career.

The lack of a real home affected her almost to breaking-point. In her hyper-sensitive mind, Powolney Mansions had become symbolical of their joint lives. They were "boarding-house people"; and even that only under false pretenses.

So far, she had managed to conceal her mental state from Ronnie. Yet she was aware, dimly, of occasional unkindnesses to him, of a tiny retrogression from the standard of happiness which she had laid down for them both. "I'm failing him," she used to think; "I'm failing him—dragging him down."

London in holiday-time accentuated this feeling of failure. Caroline Staley had departed to Devonshire for a week; and a slatternly maid brought them their tea, their lukewarm "hot water." Ronnie, kept waiting half an hour for his bath, gashed his chin with his razor, and soothed the resultant ill-temper with one of the cheap cigarettes to which he had lately taken. Breakfast, in the stuffy communal dining-room, was as cold as the perfunctory Christmas wishes of their fellow-boarders.

Ponto, developing a cough, had been sent to the vet's. Ronnie, kindling his pipe, suggested that they should "look up the hound." Aliette refused and he went off by himself.

Aliette returned to their room, and surveyed its untidiness with a shudder. "I'm the wrong sort of woman for Ronnie," she said to herself. "I'm not a bit domesticated." And from that, thought switched automatically to the other side of domesticity. Imagination pictured some old-fashioned Christmas in some old-fashioned country cottage; herself mistress of a real home; Ronnie a father; he and she and "they" church-going along snow-powdered roads; their return to a board loaded with goodies. Almost, in that moment, imagination heard the laughter of unborn children.

But the moment passed, and she knew herself still childless. "Better childless," she thought bitterly; and tried, for a whole wretched hour, to bring order into the chaos of their unfriendly room; dusting and redusting the melancholy furniture; hanging and rehanging hats and dresses; finally, in sheer desperate need of distraction, plying Caroline Staley's little wire brush on a pair of white suéde shoes she found hidden away in a corner of the wardrobe.

There was dust on the shoes; and, here and there under the dust, a speck of mud. A wire brush—thought Aliette—could cleanse dust and mud from shoes. But no brush could cleanse the mud and the dust from one's mind. Mind—what was mind? Her very soul felt itself besmirched. A Hermione's curiosity, a Mary O'Riordan's ingratitude, the snubs of a Lady Siegfried Moss—all these were flecks, undeserved yet ineradicable, upon the white surface of one's purity.

She finished cleaning the shoes, and put them aside. Yet the symbolism of them remained with her. It seemed a bitter and a cruel thing that she must drag her feet through so much mire, that the wheels of all the world's traffic must bespatter her because—because she had gone to her mate openly and not in secret.

"Not for our sin," she thought, "the penalty; but for the candor of our sinning"; and so fell to resenting the hypocrisy of a country which winks tolerant eyes at "dancing-partners," "tame cats," "best boys," "fancy-men," and all the ragtag and bobtail of clandestine lovers whom England excuses, tolerates, and even finds romantic. "Only for women such as I am," thought

Aliette, "for those of us who go openly to our one lover, can England find neither excuse nor toleration."

"Nothing much wrong with the hound," pronounced a returning Ronnie; and then, noticing the unhappiness in his lady's eyes, "Anything the matter, darling?"

"No. Nothing in particular."

Silently Aliette changed her gown, pinned on her hat, and let him help her with her furs. Silently they made their way downstairs. Outside it was foggy. From the hideous hall-lamp, still illuminated, hung a sprig of grimy mistletoe. Aliette looked up at the thing. "I hate Christmas in London," she said.

As they waited for their train in the chill West Kensington station, Ronnie, too, grew unhappy.

"Poor darling! I wish I could afford taxis," he said; and throughout the journey to Bruton Street—thinking of their long-ago taxi-ride from "Queen's"—a depression almost physical constrained both to silence.

The arrival at Bruton Street minimized a little of the morning's depression. Julia was in her old form, jovially dictatorial. They had brought presents for her: from Ronnie, a plain gold penholder, such as she always used; from Aliette, a trifle of embroidery. Her present, newly-written, lay in an envelope on her writing-desk. She gave it to Aliette with the command, "Don't open it till we've had lunch," just as Kate came in to ask if she should bring in the meal.

3

The "lunch," laid—Aliette noticed—for five, consisted of grilled soles, turkey with cranberry sauce, plum-pudding with cream and brandy, mince-pies, and the whole old-fashioned indigestible paraphernalia. Holly decked the Venetian wall-lights; mistletoe hung from the chandelier. But there were ghosts at the feast. Try as they three might to be cheerful, each felt conscious of awkwardness.

After the servants had left the room, Julia, breaking the rules of her "medicine-man," took a glass of brandy and a cigarette.

"You haven't even looked at my Christmas present," she said to Aliette; and she would have liked to add, if the words had not seemed so ill-omened, "I sha'n't give you one at all next year, if you don't take more interest in it."

Aliette reached for her hand-bag (which she had hung, a habit of hers, on the back of her chair) and took out the envelope Julia had given her before luncheon. Throughout the meal she had been dreading this moment, because, obviously, the envelope contained a check—and she hated the idea of accepting a check from Ronnie's mother. Slitting the flap with her fruit-knife, picking out the stamped paper, she saw at a glance that the check was for five hundred pounds. Her heart leaped. Five hundred pounds meant freedom from Powolney Mansions, the possibility of taking some little abode where she and Ronnie could be happy. Then reluctance overwhelmed her.

"It's too good of you," she protested. "But I can't, really I can't take all this money."

"Rubbish!" snapped Julia in her bruskest manner. "Why shouldn't you take money from me? All my money really belongs to Ronnie. If his father had had any sense he'd have left it to him. Besides, you need it. You can't go on staying at that appalling boarding-house for ever."

"But we can't take it! Can we, man?" Aliette's eyes appealed to Ronnie; who said, trying to be gay: "You mustn't rob yourself for us, mater."

"I'm not robbing myself. Sir Peter sold three of the Little Overdine properties a fortnight ago."

"Did he, though? Whom to?"

"The tenants."

"Really!"

Ensued an awkward silence, during which Ronnie stared at the check, Julia at her "daughter-in-law," and Aliette at the pair of them.

"You need it more than I do," reiterated Julia at last.

"But don't you see," Aliette's voice was very gentle, "It's just because we do need this money that we oughtn't to take it?"

"You're two very stubborn young people," said Julia, half in anger and half good-humoredly. "But as it's Christmas day, and as I'm nearly old enough to be Aliette's grand-mother, you'll have to humor me." She took the check in her own hands, and returned it to Aliette's bag, which she closed with a little snap of decision—at the precise moment when Kate announced "Mr. Paul Flower."

The distinguished litterateur entered languidly; extended both flabby hands to his hostess; and allowed himself to be persuaded into drinking a glass of port.

"My dear Paul," remonstrated Julia, glad of the interruption, "you were invited for luncheon, and it's now nearly half-past three."

"My dear Julia,"—the new-comer raised his glass to the light, and inspected the ruby glow of the wine with some care—"after all these years you ought to know that I never take luncheon."

"Not even on Christmas day?" put in Aliette.

"No, dear lady, not even on Christmas day." Paul began to be epigrammatic; striving to convince them that Christmas was an essentially pagan function, and that paganism was the fount of all true art. "More especially of my own art," he went on, pulverizing an imaginary object between thumb and forefinger; and immediately became so Rabelaisian that it needed all Julia's tact to prevent him from narrating his pet story of the American lady who had visited him in Mount Street, "because Texas, Mr. Flower, has no literature."

"These literary people," thought Aliette, listening to him, "are all peculiar." Yet undoubtedly Paul Flower's harmless egotism had relieved an awkward situation.

It was nearly a quarter past four by the time that the party eventually moved upstairs to the drawing-room; nearly five before Julia Cavendish, whose brain had been singularly active since Paul's arrival, succeeded in leaving him alone with Aliette while she and Ronnie "went off to the library for a little chat."

"Ronnie," she said to him as soon as they were alone, "you won't let her send back that check, will you?"

"Not if you're bent on our keeping it. But I say," his eyes were troubled, "are you sure it's the right time to sell out the Rutland farms?"

"I'm positive. And Ronnie," she rose from her desk and laid a hand on his arm, "you'll let me make that allowance eight hundred now, won't you?"

"I'd rather not, somehow."

"Why not?"

"Oh, I don't know. Alie wouldn't like it."

"You needn't tell her."

"We haven't got any secrets from each other."

"H'm." Julia spoke slowly. "That may make things rather difficult." She sat down again, and began to fidget with the gold pen he had given her. "Young Wilberforce came to see me yesterday," she said abruptly.

"Jimmy? What did he have to say?"

"A great deal." Julia laughed nervously. "It appears that he's sounded Brunton."

"The dickens he has!" Ronnie's brain leaped to the inevitable conclusion. "I suppose that's the result of Mollie's arrival in London."

"Probably." The mother eyed her son. "'Cherchez la femme' is not a bad rule when one sits in judgment on the Jimmy Wilberforces of this world. However, we can't afford to leave any stone unturned."

"No, I suppose not. Still, I hate people going behind my back. Alie would be furious if she knew."

"Then don't tell her. Not that there's anything to tell. Brunton refused to discuss the matter. But"—again Julia fell to playing with the penholder—"Wilberforce made the suggestion—mind you, it's only a suggestion—that I should try to get into touch with the admiral."

"I don't see how that could do any good." Ronnie's forehead wrinkled with thought. "Besides, Aliette would never consent. She'd think it undignified."

"Need we consult her?" Now Julia trod very gingerly. "Need we tell her anything about it until I've either failed or succeeded?"

Her son rose from his chair, and took two strides up and down the little room. "Aliette wouldn't like it," he repeated stubbornly.

"But it's for her good."

"I don't see that the admiral could do anything."

"He might have some influence with his son."

Ronald sat down again. All the literary Wixton in him urged acceptance of the plan. All the schoolmaster Cavendish urged refusal. "It would be going behind her back," he said at last. "It wouldn't be fair. She ought to be consulted first."

"And suppose she refuses?" A little of the old dominance crept into Julia's voice. "Suppose she refuses? What are we to do then? Ronnie," the tone rose, "don't you see that it's our duty, our absolute duty? I don't want to be unkind, but the social position gets more impossible every day. Unless something is done, and done quickly, it'll take the pair of you all your lives to live down the scandal."

"I know." His blue eyes saddened. "But there are worse things than scandal. There's," he seemed to be searching in his mind for a word, "there's disloyalty."

"Don't be obstinate." She summoned up all her strength to beat down his opposition. "Do trust me. Do let me write to the admiral. I used to know him years ago. That might help."

"Yes. But suppose it doesn't! Suppose you fail? Suppose Alie finds out?"

"If I fail, we shall be no worse off than when I started. As for Aliette finding out, you can tell her if you like. Only don't tell her till afterwards."

"You're sure it can't do any harm?"

"Quite sure. You won't tell her?"

"All right, mater. But don't ask me to take the extra allowance."

"Very well. That shall be as *you* wish."

They came back, a little guilty, to the drawing-room. Aliette was laughing. Hearing her laugh, it seemed to Ronnie as though the tension of the morning had relaxed.

4

But the tension between them did not relax; rather, in those few days which followed Christmas, they came nearer to quarreling than ever before. The paying in of Julia's check raised the money question again. Ronnie wanted Aliette to use it immediately, to buy herself some clothes, to take a holiday. Aliette demurred.

"We can't stay here forever," she protested, eying the scratched wall-paper of their bedroom.

"I know, darling. But a boarding-house has its advantages. If we were to take a flat, who'd do the housework?"

"Caroline and I could manage that easily between us."

"I'd hate to see you doing housework."

"I might be some use scrubbing floors. I'm none at the moment."

"You are."

"I'm not. I'm only a drag on you."

So the game went on—the fact of their not being legally married and the sense of isolated responsibility which each felt for the other's happiness, making mountains out of every molehill.

Chapter XXI

1

Ever since the contretemps at Patrick O'Riordan's first-night—although his sense of family solidarity would have given much to admit his eldest son entirely in the right—Rear-Admiral Billy's sense of chivalry had been troubling him. From whatever angle he considered Hector's conduct, the cruelty of it was apparent. Moreover, he and Aliette had always been "jolly good pals," and he hated "parting brass-rags with the little woman" who, all said and done, had been perfectly "aboveboard."

Nor was it only this "aboveboardness" on the part of his daughter-in-law which worried the admiral, but the knowledge, acquired quite fortuitously, and therefore relegated to the background of his memory, of his son's first infidelity to her.

Always a religious man, though never a formal religionist, Rear-Admiral Billy worshiped a god of his own in his own way. But this god—a peculiar combination of the laws of cricket, navy discipline, family feeling, and sheer sentimentalism—found in Julia Cavendish's short, carefully worded note so insoluble a problem that within half an hour of its arrival the admiral sent his stable-boy on a bicycle to summon Adrian.

Adrian mounted his cock-throppled nag and rode over to Moor Park. Said Adrian, who knew his father better than most sons: "Naturally, sir, you won't go?"

Whereupon Adrian's father, after damning the episcopalian eyes for narrow-minded bigotry, dashed off a characteristic scrawl to say that, he "would take pleasure in calling on Mrs. Cavendish on the following Monday, December 30, at 3:30 P.M."

2

It was exactly twenty-five years since "the young Mrs. Cavendish," whose second novel had already laid the foundation-stone of her literary reputation, danced the old-fashioned waltz with Commander Brunton of her Majesty's China Squadron, newly returned from foreign service; but the pleasant

252

bygone meeting came back clearly to Julia's mind as she rose from her sofa to welcome the bearded figure in the cutaway coat and sponge-bag trousers.

This present meeting, both felt, was not going to be pleasant. On the contrary, it was going to be very awkward: its purpose presenting a social stile over which even their good breeding and the similarity of their castes must inevitably stumble.

However, after a good deal of finesse on Julia's part, and various high-falutin compliments from her visitor, the admiral managed to stumble over it first, with a gallant:

"Mrs. Cavendish, I fancy I've a pretty shrewd idea why you sent for me."

"It's nice of you to come to the point, admiral," said an equally gallant Julia; and then, taking opportunity by the forelock, "Your son isn't behaving very well, is he?"

The father in Rear-Admiral Billy bristled. "He's behaving within his rights. Your son hasn't behaved over-well, either."

"If you think that," the mother in Julia met brusquerie with brusquerie, "why did you come and see me?"

The sailor in Rear-Admiral Billy cuddled his beard. "Damned if I know why I came," he ejaculated. "We can't do anything, either of us. Young people are the very deuce. I don't know what your son's like, but mine's as obstinate as a mule."

"You've spoken to your son then?" The novelist in Julia could not restrain a smile at her opponent's incapacity as a diplomat.

"Spoken to him? Of course I've spoken to him. I've done nothing else but speak to him." The sailor waxed confidential. "But what's the use? Sons don't care a cuss about their fathers nowadays, nor about their mothers, either."

"I'm sure mine does."

"Don't you believe it. None of 'em care about their parents. They call us 'Victorians'—whatever that may mean. Ungrateful young puppies!"

Seeing her man mollified and disposed for confidences, Julia thought it best to let him "return to his muttons" in his own way.

"Nice little woman, Aliette," he said, apropos of nothing in particular. "Not like these up-to-date hussies."

"A charming woman, I call her."

"Pity her kicking over the traces like this."

"You're sorry for her, then?"

"Sorry for her? Of course I'm sorry for her. I'm sorry for any woman who makes a hash of things. But that"—the disciplinarian, finding that the luxurious room and the pleasant creature on the sofa were both affecting his judgment, momentarily revolted—"that don't alter facts. Marriage is marriage; and if your son runs away with my son's wife, you can't expect me to sympathize with either of 'em."

"But surely," Julia nearly purred, "surely, my dear admiral—sympathy apart—your son doesn't intend—"

"My dear lady,"—the disciplinarian in Billy subsided—"if I only knew what my son did intend, I might be able to help you. Whenever I try to talk to him about this business, he just shuts me up. What has your son got to say?"

And suddenly both of them began to laugh. Old age, the greatest tie in the world, made them for the moment peculiarly comrades. In the light of that comradeship, the young, even their own young, seemed less pathetic than to be envied. "After all," they thought, "it's all very sad; but it's worse for us than for them. They do get some fun out of these affairs. We don't. We only get the trouble; and we're too old for troubles."

"It isn't so much the scandal I mind," broke in the admiral, voicing their mutual idea; "it's the damned upset of the whole business. I like a quiet life, you know. And that seems the one thing one simply can't get nowadays. Not for love nor money."

For fully ten minutes they wandered away from the purpose in hand; discussing first their own era, then his profession, then her profession.

"Talking about books," said the admiral, "give me Surtees."

Truth to tell, the pair were rather enjoying themselves. Both belonged to the conversational school of an earlier day; and the flow of conversation was so satisfactory that—finally—it needed all Julia's strength of will, all her love for her son, to interpolate a crisp, "We don't seem to have come to any decision. You will try and do something, won't you, admiral?"

The sailor interrupted himself sufficiently to manage a courteous, "But, my dear lady, what *can* I do?"

"Couldn't you talk to your son again? Couldn't you tell him that he's doing himself just as much harm as he's doing his wife?"

"I *have* told him that. He says he doesn't care."

"And your other son? You have another son, haven't you, a clergyman?"

"Oh, Adrian! Adrian's no good to us. Hector doesn't like him. Still,"—after all, thought the admiral, one really ought to do something for a woman who lived in Bruton Street—"I might get him to talk to Hector. I might even have another talk with Hector myself. But I'm afraid it'll be quite useless. You see, Mrs. Cavendish, neither of my sons is a man of the world. That's the whole trouble. Alie isn't a woman of the world, either. Between men and women of the world, these situations don't occur. At least, they didn't in our day. Not often."

"I rather agree with you. Still, we have to take life as we find it."

"Exactly, exactly." The old man waved a hairy-backed hand. "Nobody can say that I'm old-fashioned. Divorce don't mean what it did in my young days. And besides—I'm devilish fond of little Alie."

"Then I can rely upon your help?" smiled Ronnie's mother.

"Absolutely, dear lady, absolutely."

Ringing the bell for Kate to see her guest out, Julia Cavendish felt that she had at last found an ally; but the feeling was tinged with apprehension—reticence, she gathered, not being the admiral's strong point.

3

The admiral, making his way up Bruton Street, and along Berkeley Street toward his club, felt not only apprehensive but a trifle foolish. He had intended to be so very much on his dignity, so very much on his guard. Instead of which—

"That's a damn clever woman," he said to himself, half in admiration, half in annoyance. "An infernally clever woman. Wormed everything out of me, she did, just as if I'd been an innocent snotty. Not that I ever met an innocent snotty. Confound it, I've let myself in for something this trip. Have another talk with Hector! Made me promise that, she did."

For frankly, the admiral funked the idea of having another talk with Hector. One never knew how to tackle Hector. "Hector was such a damned unreasonable dumb-faced puppy!"

Cruising along Piccadilly, a mid-Victorian figure in the inevitable top-hat, with the inevitable white spats and the inevitable malacca cane, the admiral wondered whether he hadn't better get Simeon to tackle Hector, Adrian to tackle Hector, any one other than himself to tackle Hector—and so wondering, nearly rammed Hector's wife.

The meeting, completely unexpected, entirely unavoidable, flurried the parties. But the sailor recovered his wits first; and Aliette, wavering between the impulse to pass on without bowing and the desire to smile and fly, knew herself cornered. Automatically she extended a hand, which her father-in-law squeezed in a firm clasp.

"Hello, my dear, whither away?" he asked in his bluffest, heartiest manner.

"Nowhere in particular," answered Aliette shyly.

"Then you can walk me as far as the club." He took her arm and steered her masterfully along the pavement. It flashed across his mind, "Bless her heart, she didn't want to recognize me. After all, she is a lady. She is one of us."

"Quaint—our meeting this afternoon," he volunteered aloud.

"Why this afternoon, Billy?"

Billy thought, guiltily, "Perhaps I oughtn't to tell her," but the words were out of his mouth before thought could restrain them: "Because I've just come from Bruton Street."

"Bruton Street!" She panicked at that; and tried to release her arm. "Billy, I'm sure you oughtn't to be seen walking with me."

"Stuff and nonsense, my dear! Stuff and nonsense!" The old man, gripping her arm all the tighter, lowered his voice in conspiratorial sympathy. "We ain't either of us criminals. Why shouldn't we be seen walking together?

Besides, you and I've got to have a little chat. Between you and me and the gatepost, Mrs. Cavendish has been asking my advice about things. Naturally, I had to tell her that I thought you'd behaved pretty badly to Hector. Still," he patted her arm blatantly, "that's no reason why Hector should behave badly to you, is it?"

And for a full five minutes—all the way from Devonshire House to the door of his club—chivalry had its way with Rear-Admiral Billy Brunton. He called her his "dear Alie," he assured her that he'd "fix up the whole business," and that she was to "rely upon him." He even managed to remember that she would like news of Miracle, and to inquire after Ponto.

Listening, Aliette's heart warmed. Billy seemed so hopeful, so sympathetic. And she needed both hope and sympathy that afternoon: for latterly the tension between her and Ronnie had become almost unbearable, vitiating every hour, accentuating the loneliness of outlawry, till outlawry—in comparison with retrogression from their standard of happiness—appeared only a trivial sorrow.

They arrived at the club. "Tell you what you'd better do," said Billy, "you'd better come in and drink a dish of tea. We've got a ladies room at the Jag-and-Bottle these days. Too early for a cocktail, I'm afraid. That's what you need. You're looking peaky."

"You're a dear, Billy," retorted Aliette, at last disengaging her arm. "But you mustn't be a silly dear. You know perfectly well that you can't take me in there"; and, cutting short the old man's protests, she bolted.

4

As he watched his daughter-in-law's fur-coated figure, the little shoes thereunder and the little hat a-top, recede from view up Piccadilly, chivalry still had its way with the sailor's sentimental soul. He had promised Julia Cavendish that he would tackle Hector—and, by jingo, he would tackle Hector.

So, navy discipline and the laws of cricket alike allotting him the role of knight-errant, he drew a fat watch from his fob-pocket, consulted it, waved the malacca at a crawling taxi-driver, ordered him peremptorily: "The Temple, Embankment entrance," and stepped aboard.

The admiral anchored his taxi on the Embankment; strode through the gates, up Middle Temple Lane, and across King's Bench Walk. David Patterson, rising superciliously from the desk in the outer office of Brunton's chambers to inquire a stranger's business in vacation-time, encountered a curt, "Tell my son that his father wants to see him," and disappeared within.

"What the devil does he want?" Hector Brunton looked up from a letter he was studying; rose to his big feet, and straddled himself before the fire as his subdued clerk ushered his father through the doorway.

"This is an unexpected honor, sir," said Hector Brunton, K.C.

The old man took off his top-hat, laid it among the papers on the desk; retained his malacca; and sat himself down pompously on an imitation mahogany chair.

"I've come to talk to you about your wife," he began tactlessly; and without more ado plunged into a recital of his interview with Julia Cavendish and his chance meeting with Aliette, concluding: "And if you take my advice, the best thing you can do is to start an action for divorce."

"As I told you before, sir," broke in the K.C., who had listened with restrained anger to his father's recital, "I regret I cannot take that advice." The hands trembled behind his back. "If I may say so, I consider that you've put me entirely in the wrong by calling on Mrs. Cavendish."

"Oh, you do, do you?" The old man, already sufficiently excited for one afternoon by his interview with the two ladies, felt his temper getting the better of him. "You do, do you? Well, I don't. Mrs. Cavendish is a very delightful woman. A woman of the world."

"Is that all you came to tell me, sir?" Hector's gray eyes smoldered.

"No, sir." The senior service beard bristled. "I came to have this matter out once and for all. I came to tell you that you're not behaving like a gentleman."

"So you said before, sir. And I repeat the answer I gave you then. I see no reason why I should behave like a gentleman to a wife who hasn't behaved like a lady."

"Two blacks don't make a white, Hector."

"Possibly." The K.C. gathered up the tails of his morning-coat, and sat down, as though to terminate the discussion.

But the old man, gloved hands glued on the handle of the malacca, stuck to his guns. "Black's black and white's white," he rumbled dogmatically. "You won't whitewash yourself by throwing mud at your wife. I didn't want to go and see the Cavendish woman. I've always stood by my own and I always shall, so long as they stand by me. A man's first duty is to his family."

"Exactly my opinion, sir."

"Then why not act on it?" The admiral fumed. "D'you think this business is doing me any good? D'you think it's nice for Adrian, or Simeon, or Simeon's wife, to hear you talked about all over London—"

"A man has his rights and I mean to assert mine. Let London talk if it likes." Aliette's husband spoke resolutely enough, yet he was conscious of a tremor in his voice. More and more now the thought of Aliette made him feel uncertain of himself. "Let London talk!" he repeated. "My wife's made a fool of me. She and young Cavendish between them have dragged my name in the dirt. May I remind you, sir, that it's your name, too—"

"All the more reason, then, to drag it out of the dirt. You won't do that by continuing to behave"—the sailor's rage got the better of him—"like a cad."

At that, Hector Brunton forgot himself. His left hand thumped furiously on the desk. "You tell *me* I'm behaving like a cad, sir. What about this bastard Cavendish! What about the man who seduced my wife from her allegiance? He's the gentleman, I presume. Well—let the gentleman keep his strumpet—"

"By God, Hector"—the old man's eyes blazed,—"you area cad."

The K.C. quaked at the red fury in his father's look. Weakly he tried to take refuge in silence; but the next words—words uttered almost of their own volition—stung him out of silence.

"Who are you to talk of keeping strumpets?"

"Sir—"

"Be quiet, sir. D'you take me for a fool? D'you think I don't know—d'you think London doesn't know"—the admiral's gall mastered him completely—"about the strumpet you kept—kept without your wife's knowledge—kept in luxury for two years while other men were being killed—"

"Really, sir, I protest—"

"Protest then, and be damned to you. That's all you lawyers are fit for—protesting. Christ Almighty, you're worse than parsons. Talk of your rights, would you? Precious good care you took not to fight for other people's rights when you had a chance. Why, even Adrian—"

"I fail to see, sir—" Hector Brunton's face whitened, as the face of a man hit by a bullet whitens, at the taunt.

"You fail to see a good many things, sir." The admiral reached for his hat. "Allow me to tell you one of them—that the man who permits his wife to live with somebody else without taking any steps to get rid of her, is a common or garden *pimp*."

And the senior service, having said considerably more than it intended, marched out of the door.

5

Left alone, the K.C.'s first feeling was relief. During the last weeks he had grown more and more resentful of his father's interference. And now he had finished with his father for good.

Nevertheless, the taunt about his war-service rankled. Rankled, too, the admiral's last sentence, "Get rid of her." "God, if only I could get her back," thought Hector; and so thinking, remembered, as born orators will remember past speeches, his opening in the Ellerson case, his impassioned defense of woman's right to free citizenship.

Then he remembered Reneé. Reneé had returned to England. How the devil had his father found out about Reneé? Aliette, of course! Aliette must have told his father about Reneé.

Hector's gorge rose. He took a cigar from the box on his desk, lit it, and began to stride slowly up and down the book-lined room. Alternatively he visioned Reneé, greedy, compliant, satisfying to nausea, and Aliette—Aliette the ultra-fastidious, infinitely unsatisfying. His marriage to a woman of Aliette's temperament had been a mistake. A mistake! Best cut one's loss—best get rid of her. Best comply with his father's wishes. And yet—how desirable, how infernally and eternally desirable was Aliette.

The mood passed, leaving only rage in its wake. Curse Aliette! Curse his father! Curse the Cavendishes! How they would laugh if he yielded. They were all persecuting him, trying to break him. And "They sha'n't break me," he muttered; his teeth biting on the cigar till they met through the sodden leaf. "They sha'n't break me."

Hector returned to his desk, and tried to absorb himself once more in study. But his mind refused its office. It seemed to him as though there were a ghost in the room, the ghost of his wife. "I wonder if she ever thinks of me. I wonder if she ever sees me—as I see her," he thought. "As I am seeing her now."

6

That afternoon, however, there was no picture of her legal owner in Aliette's mind. For months he had been receding further and further into the background of her thoughts, till now he had become more a menace than a man. It surprised her, as she walked slowly up Piccadilly after her meeting with Hector's father, to realize how little Hector had ever mattered, how much—always—Ronnie. Ronnie would be glad perhaps, to hear of her meeting with the admiral.

"Dear old Billy!" she thought, "dear old Billy!" And thinking about him, a rare tinge of selfishness streaked her altruism. Suppose Billy succeeded! Suppose Hector really did set her free! How wonderful to be "respectable" again—to be done with the make-believe "Mrs. Cavendish" of Powolney Mansions, to be really and truly and legally Ronnie's! Always Ronnie had been splendid, loyalest of lovers; and yet—and yet—even in the shelter of a lover's arms one was conscious of outlawry, of the world's ostracism. What if, soon perhaps, the lover's arms were to be a husband's?

But at that, illusions burst as bubbles in the breeze. Once more the tension of the past days strung Aliette's mind to misery. She was an outlaw, a woman apart—a woman ostracized—worse, a woman who had failed her mate. Memory, killing illusions, cast itself back, remembering and exaggerating her every little unloving word, her every little unloving gesture, blaming her for them. "My fault," thought Aliette, "mine and mine only. I have been selfish to him. Utterly selfish. I've been—like I used to be with Hector."

Thought threw up its line, horrified at the comparison; and, abruptly conscious of every-day life, Aliette found herself in Berkeley Square. Automatically she turned down Bruton Street.

The mere name of the street—newly-painted in black block letters on gray stone—reminded her again of Billy, of Billy's visit to Julia Cavendish. At whose instigation, his own or hers, had the admiral visited Ronnie's mother? Hope rose again; but now, with hope, mingled despair. Had she so far failed Ronnie as to have forfeited his confidence?

Still walking automatically, Aliette found herself facing the mahogany door of Julia's house, and rang the bell.

"Yes," said Kate, "Mrs. Cavendish was at home, and alone. Would Mrs. Ronnie" (it was an understood thing in the basement of Bruton Street that Aliette should be referred to as "Mrs. Ronnie") "like some tea?"

"Thank you, Kate. That would be very nice." Aliette, unannounced, went slowly up the print-hung staircase; tapped on the drawing-room door; heard a faint "Come in"; and turned the handle.

Ronnie's mother lay on the sofa. She looked white, exhausted; but her lips framed themselves to a smile.

"I may come in, mayn't I?" Aliette's misery increased at the sight of her hostess's pallor. "Kate's promised to bring me some tea. I'm not disturbing you, am I?"

"My dear, you're always welcome. Come and sit here by me." Julia made place on the sofa, and Aliette sat down.

"I wonder why she came this afternoon," mused the elder woman. "I wonder if, by any chance, she can have found out. Awkward, if she *has* found it. Very awkward." But there was no tremor of guilt in her, "How's Ronnie?"

"Quite well, thank you."

"And you?"

"Oh, I'm all right. A little worried, that's all."

"Worried? What about?"

"Oh, various things."

Kate, bringing the tea, interrupted their conversation. Watching Aliette as she drank, Julia saw that the hands, usually so steady, trembled. "Can't you tell me about the worries?" she said kindly.

"There's nothing—really." Aliette's voice trembled as her hands. "Only I—I—met Hector's father just now. And somehow—it rather made me realize—my position."

"Did he tell you," Julia's courage fought with her fatigue, "that he'd been to see me?"

"He did." Aliette put down her tea-cup on the little mahogany stand. "May I know—did you send for him?"

"Yes. I sent for him." A smile. "You mustn't be angry with me."

"But why—why wasn't I told about it?"

"Then you are angry?" Another smile.

"Not angry. Only a little hurt."

"Hurt! Why? It was done in your interests." The old eyes looked into the young. "We thought that, if we consulted you, you mightn't allow it."

"We! Then Ronnie"—the young eyes looked into the old—"Ronnie knew. And he never told me—he never told me."

"It wasn't Ronnie's fault." Julia laid a hand on Aliette's shoulder.

At the touch, it seemed to the younger woman as though all the misery of the past days stabbed to one dagger-point of pain. Jealousy wrenched at her tongue. She wanted to cry out, "Oh, you're cruel, cruel. Why can't you tell me the truth, the truth?" But the pain stabbed her dumb; stabbed and stabbed till her mind was one unbearable tension of self-torture. Ronnie no longer loved her. Ronnie only wanted to do his duty by her. And it was her own fault, her very own, ownest fault, for not having loved him enough.

And then, suddenly, the tension snapped—leaving her weak, defenseless.

"You're so good—so much too good to me," faltered Aliette. "So infinitely better than I deserve. If only—if only I hadn't brought all this trouble into your life."

"Nonsense, child," said Julia bruskly—for, despite her own weariness, she recognized hysterics in the other's voice.

"It isn't nonsense. I've brought you only troubles—troubles."

"Don't be foolish. The troubles, as you call them, are nothing. Nothing at all in comparison with Ronnie's happiness."

"Happiness!" Now hysteria was blatant in the other's every word. "Happiness! How *can* I make him happy? I can't—can't even make a home for him. All I've done is to—to let him keep me—in a—in a boarding-house."

"You're overtired, child. Overwrought. Otherwise you wouldn't talk like that." The brusquerie had given place to a quiet understanding tenderness; the hand tightened on Aliette's shoulder. "I tell you, you have brought happiness into our lives. Into Ronnie's life and into mine. Nothing that either of us could ever do—"

"But I'm not worth it. I'm not worth it." Tear-choked, Aliette seized Julia's hand and pressed it to her lips. "I've been rotten—rotten to your son. That's why he didn't tell me about Billy."

"Rubbish!" Resolutely the elder woman withdrew her hand. "Utter rubbish! It was entirely my fault that you weren't told about the admiral."

"Your fault?" A ray of hope illumined the brown eyes.

"Yes. Ronnie wanted you to know. But I overpersuaded him."

Silently the blue eyes held the brown, till—gradually—self-control came back to Aliette; till—gradually—she realized the tension gone from her brain.

"I'm sorry," she began. "I don't often make scenes."

"My dear"—exhausted, Julia lay back on the cushions—"you needn't apologize. No one understands better than I that life isn't altogether easy for you. But don't lose your pluck. Believe me, it'll all come out right now that we have the admiral on our side."

"Billy hasn't much influence over Hector." There was no fear, only certainty in the statement. "Hector's so vain. It's his vanity, only his vanity that prevents him from giving me my freedom."

"One day he'll be forced to give you your freedom. But," of a sudden, anxiety crept into Julia's tired voice, "if he doesn't? What if he doesn't give you your freedom, child?"

"Even if he doesn't,"—proudly, all the misery of the past days forgotten, Aliette took up the unspoken challenge—"even if he never does,"—proudly, all her being resuffused with happy courage, she rose to her feet—"it will make no difference. Whatever happens, I shall always be your son's—I shall always be Ronnie's."

And bending down, she sealed the promise with a farewell kiss—a kiss whose memory lingered with Julia long after Aliette had gone, comforting her against the prescience which had prompted that unspoken challenge, even against the prescience of death.

Chapter XXII

1

Even average people, when obsessed by the grand passion—which is a far rarer passion among Anglo-Saxons than Anglo-Saxon novelists would have us believe—cannot be judged by average standards. Such are as surely bound to the wheels of terror as to the wheels of courage. In such, strength and weakness, misery and ecstasy, love's heaven and love's hell, mingle as wax and honey in the comb. For the grand passion is the sublime exaggerator of human emotion, the indefinable complex of the soul.

So, to Aliette, returning from her interview with Julia, it seemed as though London's self had altered its countenance, as though every face encountered on her homeward way spoke of her own newly-regained happiness. Her momentary change of feeling toward Ronnie had been trivial; an undercurrent of misunderstanding rather than an overt quarrel. Yet the relief of knowing it over was tremendous.

She found him huddled in the armchair before the gas-fire; Ponto, surreptitiously introduced into Powolney Mansions, couched at his feet. He rose as she entered; and the great dog, wagging a delighted stern, rose with him. In a flash of new insight, she saw how alike they were: the big man and the big dog—devoted both, both asking only kindness. And whimsically she thought: "I've been unkind to both of them. I ought to have gone to see Ponto when he was ill. I ought never to have let myself drift away, even in thought, from Ronnie."

As always, Ponto nuzzled his great head against her knee; Ronnie, as always, kissed her. But that night, as never since Chilworth nights, Aliette answered Ronnie's kisses, giving him all her confidence, all her tenderness.

"No more quarrels, man. No more secrets," she whispered drowsily, falling to sleep in his arms.

"Quarrels, darling?" he whispered back. "We couldn't really quarrel—you and I."

And after that, for many a day, their rose-bubble of enchantment—the frail yet impermeable magic of the grand passion—reblew itself about those twain, isolating them from their fellows, making even Powolney Mansions a paradise.

For many a day neither spiritual nor material troubles clouded the bright mirror of their joint happiness. Scarcely conscious of the discomforts in which they lived; utterly unconscious of the nascent hostility—a hostility based on some rumor which had arisen none knew whence and was tending none knew whither—among their fellow-boarders; careless alike of financial difficulties, of outlawry, and of ostracism, they went their way among their uncaring kind.

The high courts were closed; and so far, despite the promises of John Cartwright, neither county nor police courts afforded Ronnie a single brief. Wherefore he and Aliette made holiday together, with London for their playground. Wandering, Ponto at heel, her streets and her parks, her squares and her terraces, they knew the keen radium of London's morning, her smoke-gray half-lights, the red-gold radiance of her dimmed sunsets, the first out-twinkle of her street-lamps, faintly green against a faintly violet sky, her high evening arcs, and the long lit saffron parallels of her mysterious nights.

And one day, wandering casually beside London's river, wandering, to be exact, through Fulham and over Putney Bridge, they knew that, by sheerest accident, they had found them a home.

To a Lady Hermione or a Lady Cynthia, Embankment House, a great red building-block which overlooks the Thames, would have been the last word in discomfort. Except for the automatic lift (into which Ronnie, Aliette, Ponto, and the uniformed porter who showed them over, squeezed only as asparagus into a tin), and the gas-cooker left in the tiny top-floor kitchen by an absconding tenant, no luxuries whatsoever ameliorated the bareness of Flat 27, Block B. It was, in fact, hardly more than the model working-man's tenement of its original builder's dream. But since it possessed five tolerable rooms, the possibility of installing a geyser bath, and, above all things, its own front door, they decided instantaneously on its acquirement, seeking out the secretary of the house and paying the requisite deposit of a quarter's rent that very afternoon.

The Love-Story of Aliette Brunton

So excited were both at the prospect of domestic privacy, so engrossed with their plans for expending Julia's Christmas present to best advantage, that two incidents which—at any other time—would have been of immense importance, passed almost unnoticed. The first of these incidents was Rear-Admiral Billy's written confession of failure, and the second—"the scandal of Powolney Mansions." For the rumor which had arisen none knew whence, the rumor that "Mrs. Cavendish wasn't really Mrs. Cavendish at all, but the wife of a well-known society man who refused to divorce her," at last blew so strongly that *Monsieur* (who before the war would have called himself *Herr*) Mayer, proprietor of the Mansions, felt himself finally obliged to take notice of it.

"Of course, I ask you no questions, Mr. Cavendish," said Monsieur Mayer, seated undistinguished at the dusty desk in his private office. "Of course I ask you and your wife no questions. Your private affairs are your private affairs. But in a boarding-house it is not always possible to keep one's private affairs private; and there has been talk, much talk. That Miss Greenwell, she who have No. 26, and pay less than any one in the house, she gossip all the time. She gossip about you and Mrs. Cavendish. For my part," he waved a deprecatory hand, "I know it is only gossip. I make no suggestion. To me, so long as you pay your bill at the end of the week, it is all right."

To which Ronnie, in his most cautious legal manner, retorted:

"If Miss Greenwell or any of your other guests wish to make imputations against myself or my wife, I shall be glad if they will make them to me personally"—and promptly gave a fortnight's notice.

"Dash the fellow's impertinence." he laughed to Aliette, when he reported the interview. "There's no law in England to stop you from calling yourself Mrs. Cavendish." But Aliette, looking up from the wall-paper pattern-book she was studying, did not laugh; because intuitively she knew the power behind Miss Greenwell's throne.

"Hector's doing," she thought. "Somehow or other he must have put the tale about." And in that moment, for the first time, she began to despise her legal owner.

There was neither fear nor hate in her despising; only disdain and a crystallization of courage. That Hector should try to hurt her man financially seemed unsporting enough; but this latest secret effort to drive them shelterless into the streets of London put him, in her eyes, definitely beyond the pale.

All the same, for the last fortnight of their stay, "Mr. and Mrs. Cavendish" more than ever eschewed the public apartments and "congenial society" of Powolney Mansions.

2

Meanwhile, for the only character in our story who was not directly concerned with the feud of the Bruntons and the Cavendishes—to wit, Betty Masterman—the average metropolitan life went on. Betty Masterman, however, treating her self-invited guest with that lavish hospitality which provides bed and board without asking even companionship in exchange, lunching out, dining out, dancing and theatering, visiting and being visited by a horde of acquaintances, knew a good deal more about the progress of the feud than she confided to Mollie, and vastly more than Mollie confided to her.

Betty knew, for instance, that Hector Brunton, had it not been for the now full-blown scandal of his wife's desertion, would have been offered his knighthood; that Julia Cavendish, for the identical reason, had not been made a dame of the British Empire; that Dot Fancourt who, it was rumored, had been captured in betrothal by a middle-aged spinster of markedly reactionary views, never tired of lamenting "dear Julia's mistaken devotion to her son"; and that Sir Peter Wilberforce, whose baronetcy had been duly announced in the New Year's honors, was more than anxious that *his* son should get married.

To the grass-widow, it must be confessed, the feud itself seemed as petty as its ramifications ludicrous. Her own affair—the affair of the known husband who wrote every month from Toowoomba, Queensland, and the unknown lover who wrote almost every day from Queen's Gate, London—had always been one of those semi-public secrets which leave no speck upon the escutcheon. Aliette's method, therefor, appeared in her estimation foolish—though not quite so unnecessarily foolish as the scruples which prevented Mollie Fullerford from accepting the obvious heart and equally obvious hand of her Jimmy.

"Sorry, dear," Betty used to say, "but I can't see it. Either you're in love with the man or you're not. If you are in love with him, why on earth don't you marry him? He's got plenty of money; you've got a little money; and until you're tired of one another it ought to be ideal."

"You needn't be so beastly cynical," Mollie, ignorant of Queen's Gate, used to protest. "Just because your own marriage wasn't a success, there's no reason why mine shouldn't be. But I'm not going to marry Jimmy until he's arranged things between Alie and her husband."

"Suppose he can't arrange them, my dear?"

"Of course he can arrange them if he really wants to. He's a lawyer."

"You absolutely refuse to marry him until he does?"

"Absolutely."

Despite which repeated assurance, Mollie Fullerford knew that her decision weakened daily. It was all very well to pretend to Jimmy when he called, as he constantly did call, that there could be no hope for him until her wishes had been carried out; all very well, for the moment, to be reluctant in hand-clasps, grudging with kisses. But "that sort of thing" couldn't go on. It wasn't—Aliette's phrase—"dignified."

And besides—she felt herself growing far too fond of Jimmy for half-love. She wanted Jimmy; wanted him very badly; wanted him worse than she had ever wanted anything in her life. In point of fact—it had come to that now—she couldn't "jolly well live without Jimmy"; and would undoubtedly have yielded to Jimmy's persistence before the spring, had it not been for Eva Martin's interference.

That resolute lady of the cold blue eyes, the fading gold hair, and the hard unpleasant hands came to London early in January with the avowed intention of "putting matters straight once and for all." With Aliette, invited to luncheon at the Ladies' Army and Navy Club (irreverently known as "Arms and Necks" to junior subalterns), she failed completely, Ronnie's "wife" refusing, tight-lipped, even to discuss the situation. But with Mollie the sisterly machinations attained, in some slight degree, their trouble-making objective.

"You see, my dear," said the colonel's lady, "you're such a child that one really oughtn't to take you into one's confidence at all. But unfortunately this sort of thing can't be glossed over. In a way, I need hardly tell you, I'm very sorry for poor Alie. When I compare my own Harold with her Hector, I realize Hector's inferiority. All the same,"—this last with both elbows firmly on the tea-table—"the only course to be pursued, believe me, is for Aliette to return to her husband."

"But that would be perfectly beastly," retorted Mollie, the mild antagonism she had always felt for Eva turning to intensest dislike.

"Beastly or not," decided the colonel's lady, with some asperity, "it's the only thing to be done." And she added, with that bitter-sweetness which made Colonel Harold Martin look back upon the western front during the great war as the only peaceful place he had ever known: "Let me remind you, dear child, that there isn't only Alie to be considered. There are your own chances. You'll want to be getting married one of these days, and naturally, no man in a good position—"

The sentence trailed off into a silence as suggestive as the atmosphere Eva left behind her when she trailed out of Betty Masterman's flat; so strengthening the girl's weakened decision that Jimmy Wilberforce, who dropped in half an hour later to plead his own and his baronet father's cause, found himself confronted with a white face, a pair of haggard eyes, and the tense ultimatum, "Jimmy, I'll marry you the day Hector sets Alie free, but not a day before."

Chapter XXIII

1

England has not yet quite forgotten the "Bournemouth Tragedy" during which Hector Brunton, who led for the Crown, first became known to the public as the "hanging prosecutor."

The charge against Mrs. Cairns was murder; and for days no newspaper dared to omit a single comma from its reports of the case. For days Hector's bewigged photograph blazed on the back page of the "Daily Mail" and the front page of the "Sunday Pictorial"; for days England abandoned itself to the raptest scrutiny of Dr. Spilsbury's and other experts' evidence anent the poisonous properties of a certain arsenical face lotion with which—the "hanging prosecutor" alleged—Mrs. Cairns had doctored her dead husband's whisky; and to speculations, ruminations, discussions, and wagers as to the probable fate of Mrs. Cairns.

During those days, that epitome of England, Powolney Mansions, oblivious alike of reconstruction, strikes, German indemnities, the Irish question, and the "scandal of Mr. and Mrs. Cavendish," demanded only to know whether Mrs. Cairns would dare to face Hector Brunton's cross-examination; whether, cross-examination concluded, Hector Brunton would succeed in securing a verdict of "guilty" against Mrs. Cairns; and whether Mrs. Cairns, having been found guilty, would be hanged by the neck until she was dead or incarcerated for the period of her natural life—which period, Miss Greenwell informed Monsieur Mayer, was limited to twenty years with the remission of one quarter the sentence for good conduct.

"She'll be out in fifteen years," said Miss Greenwell, when, some ten days after the conclusion of the trial, the home secretary's remission of the death penalty was duly announced, "and she'll still be a young woman."

"I," retorted Monsieur Mayer, "do not believe that she was guilty at all. If it had not been for 'Ector Brunton—"

"And that reminds me," began Miss Greenwell—but by then the lovers were already away.

272

2

Consciously and subconsciously, the success and the réclame of the "hanging prosecutor" infuriated Ronnie. Always he hated the man, but now, every time he saw H. B.'s face staring at him from the newspapers, a new thought, the thought of his own meagerly employed talents, talents of which he had begun to feel more and more surely confident, rankled. Even in the "ridiculous flat" (he and Aliette christened it the "ridiculous flat" in the same way that Orientals always refer to their most cherished possessions as things of no account) he felt himself a failure.

Yet the flat's self was an indubitable success—a home of their own—very symbol of mated unity.

Julia Cavendish herself, too weak, with a curious lethargy of which Heron Baynet alone knew the exact cause, to pay more than one visit to Flat 27, Block B, Embankment House, admitted it "passable." At her suggestion Aliette had decided on using a beige wall-paper, almost identical with the one at Jermyn Street, throughout; on Ronnie's Chippendale and Ronnie's eighteenth century engravings (removed almost by force from Moses Moffatt's) for the tiny flame-curtained dining-room. Ronnie's ascetic bedroom furniture she relegated to Caroline Staley, providing him in its stead with hanging-cupboards craftily and cheaply contrived in the wall-spaces either side his dressing-room fireplace.

For the sitting-room (christened by Aliette the "parlor"), the tiniest box of French simplicity combined with English comfort; and for their communal chamber, with its tester bed and its short purple curtains, Julia's Christmas check provided the adornment. But it was only by adding some of her own income that Aliette, faced with and realizing for the first time the petty troubles of home-making with one servant, could install the electric kitchenette, the Canadian "cook's table," the gas-fires and the tiled hearths, the Califont hot-water system which functioned automatically as soon as one turned the taps, the Hoover vacuum-sweeper, and all those other labor-saving devices which people who really need them can never afford.

Despite all of which, the "ridiculous flat" had its discomforts, not least of them being the impossibility of sleeping Ponto on the exiguous premises.

"Man," asked Aliette dubiously, as they finally drove away, luggage on taxi, from a curiously incurious Powolney Mansions, "what are we going to do with him?"

"The Lord knows, my dear," laughed Ronnie. "People who elope have no right to take Great Danes with them."

"I suppose we ought to get rid of him. He's very expensive."

However, neither of them had the heart to part with the beast; and eventually they found quarters for him in a little side-street off the Hammersmith Road.

3

From their very first meal together, faultlessly cooked and faultlessly served by Caroline Staley—as glad as she to be free from boarding-housedom; all through February and well into March, Aliette's home-life was one long ecstasy, marred only by her growing anxiety about Julia's health and a vague suspicion that Ronnie "worried." Looking back from the safe coziness of the "ridiculous flat" on the long months they had wasted in Powolney Mansions, it seemed impossible that they should ever have been "boarding-house people," ever have tolerated the uncleanliness, the unhomeliness, the gossip, and the monotony of Monsieur Mayer's establishment.

And by the end of March even Ronnie's "worries" seemed to have disappeared. For John Cartwright's promises had more than materialized; and though the briefs were rarely marked higher than "Two guineas," the work they entailed kept Ronnie from brooding.

Despite his whimsical grumblings at being forced to leave her alone all day, Aliette knew that her man, growing hourly more ambitious for success, saw prospects of it in this strange employment. Coming back of a late afternoon, he would lounge into the parlor, kiss her, accept the tea Caroline Staley never failed to bring him, light his pipe, and talk at length about his petty triumphs at the Old Bailey or Brixton.

Once, even, he showed her his name in a press-report, with a smiled "I'm getting quite a reputation among the criminal classes. Soon there won't be a pickpocket within the metropolitan radius who doesn't regard me as his only hope of salvation. They call me 'Cut Cavendish,' I believe. Hope you haven't had too dull a day, darling."

But Aliette's days were never dull. The hours when Ronnie was away from her "defending his pickpockets" passed all too swiftly for accomplishment of the manifold trivialities which ministered to his comfort. Literally "she never had a moment to sit down."

So soon as he had left for his chambers (he hated seeing her do housework, and so she used to maintain the pretense of idleness until she heard the front door close, and the gate of the automatic lift clink to behind him), Caroline Staley—grown, as all servants, somewhat dictatorial in her old age—would demand help in the making of the bed, demand that her mistress sally forth to wrangle with the milkman or impress upon the butcher the alien origin of the previous day's joint.

These wrangles provided Aliette, hitherto immune from the petty worries of the average woman and now almost completely isolated from her kind, with a certain amusement. Returned from them, she helped lay her own table for luncheon; and, luncheon over, busied herself with the darning of stockings, with the cleaning of special pieces of silver, or with some other of the thousand and one tasks which your really class-conscious domestic, whose master is waited on hand and foot, always manages to leave to her master's wife. So that if, as at least once a week, Aliette felt it her duty to visit Julia Cavendish, it meant a rush for tube or omnibus, and a second rush homewards in time to dress for dinner—"dressing for dinner" being a shibboleth on which both lovers insisted as their "last relic of respectability."

And even if her days had been dull, the evenings would have made their dullness worth while. Those evenings! Their one servant abed. She and her man alone together, isolated high above London—solitary—safe—not even the telephone to connect them with their kind: Ronnie, pipe between his lips, his face tired yet happy in the glow of the fire, his long limbs outstretched, his lips moving rarely to speech; Aliette, some unread novel on her lap, the light of the reading-lamp a-shimmer on her dimpled shoulders, on the vivid of her hair and the vivid of her eyes; Aliette, pleasantly wearied of body, pleasantly vacuous of thought, speaking rarely as her mate, utterly happy in his silent company, so happy that all the terrors of her past life with Hector seemed like a nightmare dreamed long since in girlhood and remembered in maturity only as foolishness.

Nevertheless, as London March blew chilly toward London April, Aliette again grew fearful. Try as she would to elude them, moments came when she craved so desperately for maternity that Ronnie's very passion seemed a reproach. And in those moments her imagination fashioned itself children—a boy-child and a girl-child—Dennis and Etta—dream-babies who would bind her man to her forever and forever.

Ronnie, too, had his moments of fear, of hope, of dreamery. But for the most part they were a silent couple; and only once did either give voice to their secret thoughts. Then it was Ronnie, who said with one of his whimsical smiles:

"You've no idea, Alie, what an orator I'm getting to be. If only I could get one really big case. A murder trial, for instance. But one needs luck for that!"

So the equable days went by.

4

April came; and, to Aliette, the fret of spring. More and more with every opening bud, with every deepening of the green leaf-haze along the river-bank below her windows, she yearned for children—for Ronnie's children. Her body gave no sign; but already, as though for warning, her mind was pregnant with a new power, the power of prophetic imagination which comes only to the isolated.

Sometimes—as when, after one of Mollie's rare visits, it showed her sister married to Wilberforce—this new power pleased Aliette; sometimes, playing about Hector, it frightened her. But always it made her restless; so that, abandoning more and more of her household duties to Caroline Staley, she walked again with Ponto, as she had walked in the old days when Ronnie was not yet hers.

Fulham Park knew the pair of them—and Barnes Common—and Putney Heath. Down the myriad streets that lead away from the river to the unexplored south of London they wandered as far as Shadwell Wood and Coombe Wood and Richmond Park. And always, from those walks, Aliette returned thoughtful; for now, as imagination pictured more and more clearly the fate of Dennis and of Etta should those dream-children be at last made real, there waxed in her the determination to strike the one last possible blow for legal freedom.

Hitherto pride, and to a certain extent the fear of still further exasperating him, had prevented her from making any personal move in Hector's direction. Hitherto she had acquiesced in the policy that others—Ronnie, Julia, the admiral, James Wilberforce—should fight for her. But all these had failed!

And, "Surely," thought Aliette, "surely it is my duty to conquer this pride, to put aside these fears, to meet him face to face."

But, despite the assurances of the imaginative power—which showed her herself resolute against Hector, reasoning with Hector, remonstrating with Hector, finally shaming Hector into giving her her freedom—Aliette could not bring herself to ask even the favor of an interview. Three separate times she sat down to the little satin-wood desk in the parlor, three separate times she took pen in hand; but each time determination failed at mere sight of the first uncompromising "Dear" on the tinted note-paper. Pride and her disdain for the man, courage and fear alike forbade her to cross that Rubicon.

"I'm a fool," she said to herself, "a fool and a funk. For Ronnie's sake, for the sake of Ronnie's mother, even for my own sake I ought to write. But I can't—I just can't." And the pen would drop from her nerveless fingers, leaving her soul prey to that utter despondency which only the prophetically imaginative suffer.

Meanwhile, the imaginative powers of another woman—powers so infinitely better trained than Aliette's that their least effort could formulate the written word—were concentrating on Hector Brunton. To Julia Cavendish, ever since the Bournemouth Tragedy, the mere name had become an obsession. Despite her growing prescience of death, despite the lethargy which every day made more potent over her limbs, the old lady's mind throbbed with activity. That tiniest protoplasm of a plan which she had conceived on Christmas day spored under her thoughts as coral-blossoms spore under the sea; till her brain, mistress of the written word, saw itself join issue with the brain of Hector Brunton, master of the word spoken—and defeat it.

"There is one weapon," thought Julia Cavendish, "one sure weapon with which I can pierce his armor." Yet somehow her hand tarried in the forging of that weapon, as though the moment were not yet come.

5

The "ridiculous flat" held one supreme joy—the finest view which a Londoner may have of London. From its parlor window, of a day, one could survey all the city—from Putney Church to St. Paul's, from Chiswick Mall where once red-heeled gallants tripped it with the ladies of St. James's, to Keats's Hampstead and the dim blue of Highgate.

At that window, on an April evening, Aliette and her lover stood to contemplate the pageant which Thames and town proffered nightly for their delight. Dusk had fallen, masking the river-pageant with a cloak of indigo and silver. Northward, a saffron shimmer under murky skies, lay London. Westward, the river dwindled out between its fringing lamps to darkness and the misty fields.

"Time for bed," said Ronnie practically. He made to close the curtains, but Aliette restrained him.

"Not yet, man."

"Why? Aren't you sleepy?"

Aliette made no answer. She seemed to have forgotten his presence. Her eyes were all for the pageant below; her ears all for the faint hum of the city which mounted, drowsily murmurous, to their high apartment. And after a little while, knowing the need for solitude upon her, Ronnie tiptoed away.

Aliette was hardly conscious of his going. It seemed to her as though—in that moment—she were aloof from him, from all men; as though her soul, wandering free, mingled with myriads of other souls whom night had liberated from their earthly bodies to hover above the city.

The little French clock on the mantelpiece ticked and ticked. Hardly she heard it ticking. The earthly minutes passed and passed, flowing under her, flowing away into the ocean of time as the river-flood flows away into the oceans of the sea. From below came sound of London's clocks chiming the quarters.

Thought died in her brain. Only the imaginative power was alive. Imagination's self died. Only her soul was alive. And, with her soul, she dreamed a dream.

She dreamed that her letter to Hector had been written, that Hector had answered it. She saw herself setting out to meet him. He had sent his car to fetch her from Embankment House. She saw herself stepping into the car. It was their old car; but the man whose back she could see through the plate-glass of the cabriolet was not their old chauffeur. "I wonder what his name is," she thought.

The car set out, noiseless. It left Embankment House behind; it crossed Putney Bridge. It came, between miles and miles of utterly empty streets, into London. A peculiar grayness, neither of the night nor of the day, a peculiar silence, almost a silence of death, brooded over London. No lights gleamed from its ghostly houses; no feet, no wheels echoed on its ghostly paving.

The car spun on, noiseless—beyond the ghostly gray into ghostly green—and now it seemed to Aliette as though the time were twilight-time; as though she were in Hyde Park; as though in a few minutes she would make the remembered door in Lancaster Gate.

"Hector's house," she thought. And the thought frightened her. She wanted not to go to Hector. She wanted Ronnie—her Ronnie. But the car spun on.

Now, faltering and afraid, she stood before the door of her husband's house. Now the door opened; and Lennard, subservient as ever, led her into the recollected hall.

Lennard vanished; and suddenly Aliette's soul knew its dream for dream.

Then the dream grew real again. Fearful and alone she stood in the chill vastness of that shadowy hall among the recollected furniture. She felt her breasts throbbing under the thin frock, felt her knees tremble as she grasped the door-handle of Hector's study.

No lights burned in the study. It was all gray, gray as the streets without. Hector was not there—only a face—a huge, cruel, unrelenting face.

"So you've come back," it said.

She moved toward the face, across the gray carpet that gave back no sound to her feet. But she could not speak with the face. Between her and the face—as a great sheet of glass—slid silence, the interminable unbearable silence of dreams. Through the glass, Aliette could see every pore in the great face, every hair of its head; but she might not speak with it, nor it with her. Then a voice, a voice as of very conscience, cried out in her: "Your strength against its strength. Your will against its will."

She felt her will beat out from her as wings beat, beat and batter at the glass between them. The glass of silence slid away; and she knew the face for Hector's. She said to it:

"Hector, I haven't come back. I'm never coming back."

"You shall," said the face, Hector's face; and now, under the face, she knew feet, her husband's feet.

At that, terror, the hopeless panic of dreams, gripped her soul by the throat, choking down speech. It seemed to her that she stood naked in that gray and silent room.

But now, as a momentary beam through the grayness, another face—the face of her lover—was added to their silent company. And again, "Your will against its will," said the voice.

Terror's fingers unclutched from her throat, so that her will spoke, "I shall never come back, Hector."

The face writhed at the words as a face in pain; and suddenly, knowing herself its master, she knew pity for the face, pity for the thing she had done. Till once more she heard the inner voice whisper: "No pity. Your strength against its strength. Your will against its will."

"But I love you," pleaded Hector. "I need you."

She said to him, "My children need me, Hector. Set me free."

And once more the glass of the silences slid between them; once more the interminable, unbearable silence of dreams held her speechless.

*

Tap, tap, tap. Who was that knocking on Hector's door? It must be Ronnie. Tap, tap, tap. Ronnie mustn't come in. Ronnie mustn't find her and Hector alone together.

The glass darkled. Behind the glass Aliette could see Hector's face blur and blur. The face vanished. She was alone, alone in Hector's study. She was cold, desperately cold through all her limbs.

Tap, tap, tap. She heard a voice, a human voice: "Mr. Cavendish, Mr. Cavendish. Are you there, Mr. Cavendish? You're wanted on the 'phone, Mr. Cavendish."

Chapter XXIV

1

Abruptly, as the strung ball snaps back to its wooden cup, Aliette's soul returned to its body.

Waking, she knew that she had fallen asleep by the open window; that somebody was knocking on the outer door of the flat, somebody who called insistently, "Mr. Cavendish, Mr. Cavendish. I've a message for you, Mr. Cavendish."

Her heart thumping, her head still muzzy with dreams, Aliette ran across the sitting-room, out into the hall; unchained, unlatched the door. The night-porter stood before her. His shirt was open at the neck; she could see the veins in his throat throb to his words: "Is your husband awake, madam? He's wanted on the telephone. His mother's house. It's very urgent."

"Mr. Cavendish is asleep." Aliette's heart still thumped, but she spoke quietly enough. "I'll go and wake him. Wait here, please."

She darted back to the door of their bedroom; knocked; opened. The light by the bed still burned, showing her lover's face just roused from the pillow.

"Am I wanted?" he asked.

"Yes, dear." Aliette controlled her nerves. "Bruton Street's asking for you on the telephone. I'm afraid your mother's been taken ill."

"I'll be down in a second." He was out of bed and into his dressing-gown before she could stop him. She thought, "If it's bad news, he'll have to go to Bruton Street. He'll have to get dressed." She said, "You'd better get some clothes on. I'll go down and find out exactly what's the matter."

After a second's hesitation, he decided, "You're right"; and made for his dressing-room. Aliette went back to the outer door. The night-porter still waited. She asked him, "Who telephoned?"

"A servant, I think."

"Did she say why she wanted to speak to my husband?"

"No. Only that it was very urgent."

"Is the lift still working?"

"Yes, madam."

"Then I'll come down immediately."

Aliette's mind, as she followed the slippered man along the cold stone corridor to the lift-shaft, worked rapidly. If Julia Cavendish had been taken ill—and obviously Julia Cavendish must have been taken ill—the sooner she and Ronnie got to Bruton Street the better.

She asked the porter, "What's the time?"

He told her, "Three o'clock."

"Can you get me a taxi?"

"I'll do my best, madam."

The lift was working badly. The slowness fretted her imagination. Suppose Julia Cavendish were—more than ill; suppose she were—dead?

At last they reached the ground-floor. The night porter, flinging back the iron gates, let her out and made for the street. Aliette, running to the telephone-box, picked up the receiver.

"I want to speak to Mr. Cavendish, Mr. Ronald Cavendish. Is that Mr. Cavendish?" Kate's voice sounded stupid, excitable, over the wire.

"No, it's Mrs. Cavendish. Is that Kate?"

"Yes, Mrs. Ronnie."

"Mr. Cavendish will be down in a minute. What's the matter?"

"Mrs. Cavendish has been taken ill. She's very bad indeed. She told us to telephone for Mr. Ronnie."

"You telephoned for a doctor?"

"Oh yes, Mrs. Ronnie. We did that first thing. But Sir Heron's out of town."

"Then you should have telephoned to another doctor."

"We never thought of that." Obviously the maid had lost her head. "We thought we'd better telephone Mr. Ronnie first. That's what she said we was to do."

"Wait." Aliette thought swiftly. "Isn't there a doctor in Bruton Street?"

"Oh yes, Mrs. Ronnie. Dr. Redbank."

"You'd better send for him immediately. Don't waste time telephoning. Go yourself. . . . And, Kate, you can tell Mrs. Cavendish that Mr. Ronald and myself will be round in less than half an hour. Can you give me any idea what's the matter with Mrs. Cavendish?"

"I don't know, Mrs. Ronnie, but Smithers says she's very bad indeed. Smithers says she woke up with her mouth full of blood. Smithers says she doesn't know how she managed to ring her bell—"

The parlor-maid would have gone on talking, but Aliette cut her short with a curt: "You're to go and fetch the doctor, Kate. You're to go and fetch him at once. Do you understand?"

"Yes, Mrs. Ronnie."

Aliette hung up the receiver; turned to find Ronnie, apparently full dressed, at her side; explained things to him in three terse sentences; saw his face blanch; ran for the lift; swung-to the lift-gate; pressed the automatic button; reached her own floor, her own flat; twitched a fur coat from its peg; remembered something Mollie had once told her about hemorrhages; darted into the kitchen; snatched what she wanted from the refrigerator; wrapped a dish-cloth about it; darted back to the lift.

Downstairs, Ronnie waited impatiently. "The taxi's here," he said.

They leaped into the taxi.

2

The shock of unexpected ill-news held both lovers rigid, speechless, as their vehicle, an old one, rattled and bumped over Putney Bridge; and when at last Aliette spoke it was of those trivial things with which human beings console themselves against the threat of disaster. "How on earth did you manage to get dressed so quickly?"

"The old school trick." Ronnie masked his anxiety with the semblance of a laugh. "Trousers and an overcoat." But sheer anxiety forced the next words to his lips. "What do you think can have happened?"

"From what Kate said, it sounded as though your mother had had a hemorrhage."

"A hemorrhage," repeated Ronnie. And then, under his breath, as though trying to convince himself, "But she can't have had a hemorrhage."

The taxi rattled on down a gray and empty King's Road, bringing back to Aliette's mind the memory of that other drive she had taken in vision-land.

"What's that?" asked Ronnie suddenly, pointing to the dish-cloth at her feet.

"Ice. There's just a chance they won't have any."

They swung out of King's Road into Sloane Street. Under the lights of Knightsbridge, Ronnie, looking sideways at his mate, marveled at the composure of her face; marveled that her brain should have acted so swiftly in crisis. His own brain felt impotent, dumb. His heart hung like a nodule of ice in his breast. The nodule of ice sank into his bowels, turning his bowels to water. The Wixton imagination pictured his mother helpless, in agony. He thought, "Suppose we're too late. My God, suppose we're too late."

"I don't expect there's any immediate danger." Aliette, fighting for her own composure, guessed the unspoken thought in her lover's mind. "Servants always exaggerate."

Ronnie wrenched down the window, leaned out. "Hurry," he called to the driver, "hurry." The old taxi rattled to speed. Hyde Park corner flashed by—Piccadilly.

"Don't worry, dear," Aliette managed to whisper. "The doctor will be there by now."

Ronnie sat silent. It seemed as though, for the moment, he had forgotten her presence. Nor could she be angry with him for that forgetting. "His mother," she thought; "his mother!"

At last they made Bruton Street. Outside the open front door, waiting for them, stood Kate. Kate, the immaculate cap-and-aproned Kate, was in tears. "Oh, Mr. Ronnie," she sobbed, "I'm so glad you've come. I'm so glad you've come."

"Doctor here?" Julia Cavendish's son, usually so affable with servants, snapped out his question as though he had been speaking to a defaulter.

"Yes, Mr. Ronnie. I fetched him myself. He's with your mother now. He wants cook to go out and get some ice, but cook don't know," the domestically precise English vanished under stress of emergency, "where to get no ice."

"Lucky you thought of bringing some." Abruptly, rudely almost, Ronnie snatched the dish-cloth from Aliette's hand; and she watched him disappear, three at a bound, up the green-carpeted stairs.

"Kate," she said quietly, "tell the taxi-driver to stop his engine and wait. We may want him for something."

3

Ronnie, a little out of breath, found himself, on the second landing, confronted at the closed door of his mother's bedroom by his mother's woman, Smithers. Smithers was still in her dressing-gown—her hair disheveled, but her black eyes unpanicked.

"You can't go in, sir. The doctor's with her."

"I've got the ice." He made to push past the woman, but she put a hand on his arm.

"I'll take it to him, sir. Your mother said you wasn't to go in."

"Why not?"

"Because of the blood. After the doctor came, she said you wasn't to see her till I'd put clean sheets on the bed. It's a hemorrhage, sir."

"I know. Let me go in." Again Ronnie tried to push past the woman. Again she restrained him. Her black eyes seemed strangely hostile, resolute.

"It's a hemorrhage," she repeated fiercely, "and it's her own fault. Time and again I've told her she ought to heed what Sir Heron said. But she wouldn't. She wouldn't give in." Then, accusingly, "Because she didn't want you and Mrs. Ronnie to know."

"Know what?"

"That she had the consumption."

"Consumption!" The word struck Ronnie like the lash of a whip. He saw accusation—an accusation of selfishness—in the woman's hostile eyes. Those eyes knew his whole story. He wanted to say to them: "We hadn't an idea. Honestly, we hadn't the slightest idea." Sir Heron Baynet's reported diagnosis recurred to his mind. "She isn't ill, but she has a tendency to illness." Either the specialist had made a mistake, or else— He realized, with a heart-rending clarity, that Julia must have purposely concealed her danger, because—because of his own troubles.

The bedroom door opened noiselessly, and a clean-shaven intellectual face inspected him through gold-rimmed glasses.

"Are you the patient's son?" asked Dr. Redbank; and then, seeing the dish-cloth in Ronnie's hand, "Is that the ice?"

"Yes. Can I come in?"

"If you like. But please understand she mustn't talk."

Ronnie followed the man into the bedroom, and closed the door quietly behind him.

Save for the glow of the bed-lamp, the room was in darkness. Making his way round the foot of the bed, Julia's son saw, in the light of that one lamp—the shade of it was crimson, crimson as those telltale marks on his mother's pillow—his mother's face.

The face lay on the stained pillow, pallid, motionless, the hair awry, the mouth half-open as though in pain. On the chin and on the half-open lips, blood clots showed like brown stains. But the blue eyes were wide open. Motionless in their sockets, they recognized him.

Stooping down, Ronnie saw that Julia would have spoken. Remembering the doctor's warning, he said: "You're not to talk, mater. I'm here. Aliette's here. It's quite all right." It seemed to him as though the blue eyes understood. They closed wearily; and a sigh, almost a sigh of relief, came through the half-opened lips. He thought, standing there by the bedside: "I am powerless. Powerless to help. I can do nothing. Nothing. Why doesn't the doctor do something? Why did he want that ice?"

Then, glancing toward the shadowy fireplace, Ronnie saw the doctor at work; heard the faint smash-smash of the poker handle on ice in a cloth. The doctor came to the bedside. He felt the doctor's hand on his arm; heard his authoritative whisper, "Hold this for me, please"; and found himself grasping a soap-basin.

The soap-basin was full of crushed ice, of the ice Aliette had remembered to bring. The doctor had been crushing the ice. Now he was feeding the ice to his patient. Piece by little piece he fed it—fed it between those half-open lips.

Through interminable minutes Ronnie, holding the soap-basin, watched. At last the doctor said: "One more piece, Mrs. Cavendish, just one more piece. It'll do you good." His mother tried to shake her head in refusal, but Dr. Redbank insisted. "There, that will do."

Somehow Julia's son knew her immediate danger over. For the first time he could hear her breathing. Faint, irregular breathing. "She's asleep, isn't she?" he whispered, looking down at the closed eyes.

But at that, the eyes opened again. His mother seemed to be searching—searching for him about the darkness of the room. He bent over her, and it appeared to him that her pupils moved. "Is there anything you want, mater?" he asked, forgetful of the doctor's warning. The eyes turned in their sockets.

Following their glance, Ronnie saw, beside the bed-lamp, a handkerchief—a stained handkerchief. Scarcely conscious of his action, he fumbled in the pocket of the overcoat he was still wearing, found his own handkerchief, dipped it in the soap-basin, and wiped the blood-clots from his mother's lips. Faintly, the lips murmured: "Smithers—want Smithers—want clean sheets."

"*Please* don't talk, Mrs. Cavendish," interrupted the doctor's voice.

"You're all right now, mater." Ronnie grasped the situation. "Quite all right. *I* know exactly what you want done. *I'll* tell Smithers for you." "She'd like her maid," he whispered to the doctor. "She'd like clean pillow-cases."

"Of course she would." The answer sounded loud, almost cheerful. "Of course, she'd like clean pillow-cases. But not for another half-hour, Mrs. Cavendish. I want you to rest. I must insist on your resting."

Julia's eyes closed.

"We shall have to have a hospital-nurse," whispered Dr. Redbank. "If you'll stay with her I'll go and telephone for one." He tiptoed from the room, leaving mother and son alone.

For a long time, hours as it seemed, Ronnie stood watchful. His mother must be asleep—safe—out of pain. A great rush of gratitude, gratitude to some unknown deity, overwhelmed him. Quietly he drew a chair to the bedside. Quietly he sat down. But the faint noise disturbed the woman on the bed. Her eyelids fluttered; and she tried to speak—indistinctly, incoherently, choking on each word.

"Ronnie,"—her first thoughts, as always, were for him—"did I—frighten—you?"

"Mater," he implored, "please don't try and talk. If there's anything you want, just look at it, and I'll get it for you.'"

"Ice," she choked, "more ice."

Every movement of her lips frightened him, but he managed to keep fear out of his voice.

"Good for you. I'll get it."

He took the basin of ice from the bed-table, and fed it to her bit by bit, slowly, as Dr. Redbank had done.

The touch of her lips on his fingers almost unnerved him. The lips were so weak, so loving, so piteously grateful as—piece by piece—they sucked down the melting pellets. Controlling himself for her sake, Ronnie realized a little of the self-control, of the unselfishness which had so long locked those weak lips from revealing their own danger. And again, at that realization, he felt his heart melting, even as the ice melted.

"Good man!" It was the doctor—whispering. "She can't have too much of that. I've sent your taxi for the nurse. It's her first hemorrhage, I suppose?"

"Yes—as far as I know."

"H'm. I thought so. Frightening things, hemorrhages. But there's no cause for immediate alarm. I'll wait till the nurse comes, and give her a second injection. You'd better go down and look after your wife."

On the landing, Smithers still waited. "Is she better, sir?" asked Smithers.

"Much better, Smithers. She's out of danger. But you can't go in yet."

Tiptoeing downstairs, Ronald Cavendish knew that the woman was watching him—blaming him. Half-way down, he hesitated. "I can't face Alie," he thought. "I can't face Alie." Then he turned, tiptoed upstairs again.

Together, in silence, the son and the servant waited outside the mother's door.

4

Aliette, too, waited—waited downstairs in the dining-room where Kate had insisted on lighting a fire for her—waited and waited while the slow half-hours went by. She felt weary; but there was no sleep in her weariness. Her ears, keyed to acutest tension, magnified every whisper in the house of illness; Dr. Redbank's feet in the hall, the jar of the front door, the taxi chugging away, the faint creak of carpeted stairs, the fainter clink of crockery in the basement.

At four o'clock Kate came in with a pot of coffee; at half-past, Smithers to ask if the nurse had arrived. Aliette suffered both maids to go without question. In that well-ordered home she felt herself the useless stranger. Her muscles yearned to be of use, to be doing something, anything, for Julia. "I owe her so much," she thought; "such a debt of gratitude."

The impotence of her muscles stung her mind. Her mind ached with memories, memories of Julia, of her brusk kindliness, of her courage. "I wonder if she knew," thought Aliette. And at that, painfully, her mind conjured up the "scene" she had made—Julia comforting her—Julia's unspoken challenge—her own promise. "She knew then," thought Aliette. "She must have known. That was why she wanted to be certain—of me."

At last the nurse arrived. At last Ronnie, tired out, white-faced, and unshaven, left his post on the landing and joined her.

She asked him, "How is she?"

"Better. Much better. She's asleep."

"Isn't there anything I can do?"

"No, dear, nothing." His voice seemed curiously toneless, and after two or three nervous puffs at a cigarette he again went upstairs.

Another half-hour went by. Already Aliette could see hints of dawn behind the dining-room curtains. Now, knowing danger averted, her mind reacted. She wanted desperately to sleep. Her eyes closed wearily. But her ears were still keen to sound. She heard the doctor's feet and Ronnie's creep cautiously downstairs, heard their whispered colloquy at the dining-room door, woke from her brief doze before they could open it.

"I do hope you haven't been frightened." Dr. Redbank smiled professionally at the pale pretty woman by the fireside. "I hear we have to thank your thoughtfulness for the ice. Most useful it was, too. I have assured your husband that there is no cause for immediate alarm."

"You're sure, doctor?"

"Quite sure. However, as I understand that your mother-in-law's regular attendant is away, I purpose looking in tomorrow, or rather this morning, at about half-past ten. Meanwhile, you must keep her quiet; and, of course, no solid food." He shook hands with her; and went out, accompanied by Ronnie. Aliette, still sleepy, heard the front door close gently behind him.

"Good man, that," said Ronnie, returning. He sat down heavily at the table, and tried to light himself another cigarette. But his hands trembled. The smoke seemed to stifle him.

"Won't you have some coffee?" she asked, suddenly wide awake, and as suddenly aware of the misery in his eyes.

"Thanks dear, not yet."

Rising, she laid a hand on his arm.

"Man," she ventured, "was it very terrible?"

"Dreadful." His voice, usually so controlled, shook on the word, jangling her overwrought nerves to breaking strain. "She's dying. Dying."

"But the doctor said—"

"Never mind the doctor. I know. And Alie," a sob tore at his diaphragm, "it's my fault."

"*Your* fault?" Awfully, she guessed his meaning.

"Yes."

Her hand dropped from his arm, and they stared at one another in silence.

"Tell me," she said at last.

"No. Not now. Not yet." The remoteness of his eyes frightened her.

"I'd rather know," she pleaded; and again, "Why is it your fault? How can

291

it be your fault?"

"I'd rather not tell you." Once more she caught that frightening remoteness in his eyes—in his very voice. Then, awfully, his reserve broke. "She knew all the time, Alie."

"Knew what?" There was no need for her question.

"That she had consumption. That her only hope was to go away. She only stayed on in London for—for," the words choked in his throat, "my sake."

Minutes passed. Through the chinks in the curtains Aliette could see dawn growing and growing. Her mouth ached to comfort him; but she dared not speak. Her eyes ached for tears; but she dared not shed a tear. Superstition tortured her mind—it seemed to her as though, Biblically, their sin had found them out. Then resolutely, remembering the promise sealed by her own lips to the dying, she put superstition from her.

"Not your fault," she said at last. "Not even *our* fault. Ronnie—believe me—even if she did know that she—that she was very ill—she knew that you and I loved her, that we couldn't, either of us, do without her. She's—she's not going to die. Not with us, both of us, to nurse her—to look after her."

"Alie—you—you believe there's a chance?" He rose from the table; and she saw that the remoteness had gone from his eyes.

"Chance!" she smiled at him. "Chance! It's not a question of chance, man. We'll *make* her get well."

And with those words, Aliette knew that she had paid a little of her debt to them both.

Chapter XXV

1

Miraculously, as it seemed to her comforted son, death stayed its hand from Julia Cavendish.

For three days and nights of morphia she drowsed away the effects of that first hemorrhage. Heron Baynet, returning hot-foot to Harley Street on his secretary's telegram, insisted—despite the fact that he was a consultant—on ousting Dr. Redbank; on taking over the entire conduct of the case in person.

A year ago the little keen scientist of the lined face, the fine forehead, and the shining eye-glasses had suspected, warned, begged his distinguished patient to let him radiograph her lungs;—mentioned the possibility of a diabetic complication—advised Switzerland. Now perhaps his advice, and the one slender chance of life it offered, would be taken.

"How she tricked me!" he used to ruminate, looking down at the tired face on the smooth pillow. "How she fought me!" For although in his heart Sir Heron both pitied and admired this woman whose stubbornness and stamina had so long eluded his aid, it gave him a certain satisfaction, not altogether professional, to feel that she would now be completely in his power. Yet—would she be completely in his power? Already, on the fourth day of her illness, he sensed the stubbornness and the false stamina of stubbornness renewing themselves in her; already he perceived that his medical fight would be two-fold—against his patient as well as against her disease.

"I suppose you're pleased," she managed to stammer. "You warned me that this might happen if I refused to take your advice." And after he had given her the morphia injection, "The less I have of that stuff, the better. If I'm going to die, I'd rather die with my brain clear."

"You're not going to die yet awhile," retorted the specialist. "Not if you refrain from talking, lie perfectly still, and get away into the country as soon as you're fit to be moved."

Julia smiled up at him without moving her head. "I congratulate you on your bedside manner, Sir Heron, but you needn't be professional with me.

My case is hopeless. It always has been hopeless. You haven't forgotten our compact, I hope? You won't tell my son or my son's wife more than is absolutely necessary?"

"Of course I won't tell your son," he humored her; "not if you'll consent to go to sleep."

"But I don't want to go to sleep."

"Oh yes, you do. Besides, if you go on talking, you'll have another hemorrhage."

That seemed to frighten her. "Very well," she said, closing her eyes, for already the morphia was pouring wave on wave of lassitude through her body. "Very well, I won't talk. Do you think you can manage to keep me alive for six months? It's rather important. I've got work to do."

Thinking her brain already under the influence of the drug, he humored her again. "We'll see about that in the morning. Meanwhile I shouldn't worry. Your daughter-in-law and your secretary between them will be able to manage quite well until you're up and about again."

"It isn't that sort of work," began Julia Cavendish; and pretended to fall asleep.

This pretense of falling asleep was a trick, learned from the drug. One had only, Julia discovered, to pretend sleep, and nurse or doctor left one entirely alone. Alone with one's dreams. Very curious, very pleasant dreams hers were, too. All about a book. A book called—Now what had she intended to call the book?—"Man's—Man's—Man's Law." Yes—that was the title. If only—one took—enough morphia—one could write—like—like de Quincey.

"I mustn't let them give me too much, though," thought Julia; and fell really asleep.

2

For Aliette those first four days of her "mother-in-law's" illness were almost happy. At Julia's particular request, both lovers had abandoned the "ridiculous flat," to take up their abode in Bruton Street; and the sense of self-sacrifice—for it was a sacrifice to abandon the little home where she had been so safe and face the inevitable difficulties of her anomalous position in Julia's household—seemed yet another chance of repaying her debt.

Work (she found enormously to do) saved her from overmuch introspection. Julia, the feudalist, had never learned domestic decentralization; her daily secretary, Mrs. Sanderson, a gray-haired gentlewoman with tortoise-shell spectacles and a diffidence which only just avoided crass stupidity, had become a typewriter-thumping automaton; her cook was a mere obedient preparer of ordered meals, and even Kate seemed incapable of performing the simplest household duty on her own initiative. Resultantly there devolved on Aliette, seated of a morning in the novelist's work-room, the manifold activities of a strenuous celebrity, a housekeeper, a woman of property, and an information bureau. For, of course, everybody wanted information about the celebrity's health.

The telephone and the telegrams were a curse. The press association rang, apologetically, twice a day. The Northcliffe press, commandingly, once. Julia's American publishers cabled almost hourly; and hourly, scandal for the moment forgotten, one or other of her private acquaintances quested for news of her. Even Dot Fancourt rallied gallantly to the receiver. While as for the three other sisters Wixton and their appanages, one would have imagined them afflicted to the verge of suicide.

Of an evening, Ronnie helped Aliette to deal with the "family"; but by day she had to cope with them single-handed. The "family" were never satisfied with Mrs. Sanderson's report; the "family" demanded to speak with the hospital nurse; the "family," barred by Sir Heron's instructions from visiting, demanded to speak with Sir Heron himself. Soon Aliette began to recognize their voices—Sir John Bentham, courteous if a little aloof; Lady Clementina, full-throated and fussy; May Robinson, piteous and protestant out of the depths of St. John's Wood; Alice Edwards, distantly jovial on the trunk-line from Cheltenham. "How they must be hating me," Aliette used to think.

On the afternoon of the fifth day, Julia—having coaxed permission from a reluctant nurse—sent down word that her "daughter-in-law" was to come up.

"You won't stay with her long, will you, ma'am?" said Smithers, permanently on guard at the bedroom door. (Mysteriously, since Aliette had moved to Bruton Street, the social sense of the basement had substituted "ma'am" for Mrs. Ronnie.) "The doctor says the less she talks, the better."

Aliette passed into the bedroom; and heard a weak voice say, "Leave us alone please, nurse."

Nurse—a pleasant-faced creature very much impressed at finding herself in charge of so literary an invalid—made her exit to a stiff rustle of starched linen. Aliette moved across to the bedside. Sunshine illuminated the elegance of the room, slanting down in dust-motes from the three open windows on to the écru pile carpet. Among Julia's cut-glass toilet-ware on the porphyry Empire wash-table showed none of the paraphernalia of sickness. The pillow-propped figure on the low mahogany and gold bedstead seemed, to the visitor, rather that of a resting than of a dying woman. A frilled boudoir-cap hid Julia's hair; a padded bed-jacket of crimson silk swathed her shoulders.

"I suppose I gave you all a rare fright," she said, thinking how well she had staged the little scene.

"We were rather frightened." Aliette took a chair, obviously arranged for her, at the bedside; and began to talk aimlessly of this and that.

But Julia soon interrupted the aimless phrases. "Are my servants behaving themselves?" she asked. "Are they making you and Ronnie really comfortable? I told Smithers to maid you. I hope she's been doing it properly."

"Beautifully," prevaricated Aliette.

"You're sure you wouldn't rather have your own maid? You could shut up the flat easily enough. You don't mind coming to live with me, do you? It's," the weak voice betrayed the first sign of emotion, "it's bound to be a little difficult for you, but I'm not quite up to running things myself yet. And Mrs. Sanderson is a fool."

"Of course I don't mind. It's wonderful to feel that I can be of some use at last."

Aliette did her best to prevent the patient from talking; but Julia Cavendish, feudalist, wanted to know a thousand domestic details. Whether cook was being economical? Whether the new kitchen-maid promised to be a success? If Mrs. Sanderson had remembered to take carbon-copies of important correspondence? Whether the "family" had been very troublesome?

"Families are bad enough when one's well. They're impossible in illness," pronounced Julia. "I'm always glad my husband died abroad. One day I must tell you about Ronnie's father." She relapsed into silence, closing her eyes; and Aliette thought she had fallen asleep. But in a moment the eyes opened again. "Talking of families, my dear, how is your sister?"

"Mollie? Oh, Mollie's gone back to Devonshire."

"Is she engaged to young Wilberforce?"

"No. I don't think so."

"What a pity!"

The nurse, tapping discreetly, announced it "time for Mrs. Cavendish's medicine"; and the invalid closed the interview with a weak, "If the family call, for heaven's sake keep them out of my room."

3

On the seventh day after the hemorrhage, Aliette's ordeal at the hands of the Wixton family began.

Sir John and his lady, dissatisfied with the meager information afforded them on the telephone, called in person to insist upon seeing "some one in authority." But Julia's bell had rung four times during the night, and nurse was lying down.

"Surely there's a day-nurse?" fussed Clementina.

"No, m'lady. Only Mrs. Ronnie, m'lady." Kate, erect and correct at the front door, watched the pair of them whisper together; heard them decide after some hesitation that they would like to see "Mrs. Ronald Cavendish"; and showed them upstairs into the drawing-room.

Rising to receive her guests, Aliette was humorously aware of Sir John's discomfort. She could almost read behind his keen brown eyes the thought, "So this is the little lady there's been all the trouble about, is it? Rather good-looking. I wonder what the deuce one ought to call her, Mrs. Cavendish

297

or Mrs. Brunton?"

"How do you do—er—how do you do?" he compromised. "And how is your illustrious patient? I'm sure it's most kind of you to look after my sister-in-law. Very kind indeed."

But there was little compromise about the breasted Clementina. *Her* greeting, *her* scrutiny, her omission to shake hands, were definitely hostile. In attitude she resembled nothing so much as a virtuous English lady visiting the questionable quarter of Cairo. Aliette, her sense of humor fighting against her resentment, invited the pair of them to sit down, and offered propitiatory tea.

"Please don't trouble," retorted the female of the species Bentham. "We've had tea. And besides, we wouldn't think of disturbing you. As a matter of fact, it was my husband's idea that we should look in for a moment to get first-hand news about dear Julia. In a few days, I presume, we shall be able to see her ourselves."

That "dear Julia" made Aliette wholly resentful. "Ronnie's mother," she began stiffly, observing, not without a certain malicious satisfaction, how Lady Bentham writhed at the phrase, "is going on as well as we can possibly expect. But I'm afraid it will be some time before Sir Heron will allow her to receive visitors."

"But surely her sister—" protested Sir John.

"Not even her sister, I'm afraid," decided Aliette; and Julia, informed of the Bentham defeat, chuckled audibly.

But the interview, for all Julia's chuckles, left its scar on Aliette's sensitive pride—as did her talk with May Robinson.

The tea-broker's scrawny widow called two days later in her 1908 Panhard; accepted tea, and stayed for a full three quarters of an hour gossiping about her sister's symptoms. May, far from being outwardly hostile, positively beamed with that particular brand of offensive condescension which only those whose lives are devoted to good works know how to assume toward "fallen sisters." With her every non-committal word, the untempted widow contrived to suggest, "Considering what a thoroughly bad woman you must be, I think it remarkable, entirely remarkable and praiseworthy, not to say Christian of you, to have given up your fast life so as to look after my poor dear sister in her illness." Luckily for May, Paul Flower arrived just in time to prevent Aliette from losing her temper!

Alice Edwards's visit, however—for reasons that can be imagined, she did not bring her daughter with her—passed off easily enough. "I never was any good in a sick-room," said the Anglo-Indian lady brightly.

Followed, to Aliette's surprise, the admiral, who, calling to leave formal cards, heard that she was at home and insisted upon seeing her. The sailor only stayed his Victorian quarter of an hour; managed, however, although Aliette did her best to restrain him, to thrust a good Georgian foot into the conversational plate with his "That boy of mine's putting you in a rotten position, me dear. But it ain't my fault."

"Billy," Aliette, seeing his sorrowful face, could not refrain from laughing, "you've got no tact. Of course I know it isn't your fault. I've never really thanked you for what you tried to do for me."

"Me dear," retorted the admiral, "it's no laughing matter. Honestly, I'm sorry I ever sired the fellow. But never you mind; just you keep your courage up, and it'll all come out right in the long run."

"I'm keeping my courage up all right," said Aliette, still laughing; for, somehow or other, Julia's illness had made her own affairs seem rather petty.

4

After ten days of bed, the patient insisted on seeing Mrs. Sanderson.

"Sir Heron advises a few months in the country," she told that secretarial automaton. "I shall take a furnished house; the bigger the better. You'd better write to Hampton's and ask for particulars. It mustn't be more than forty miles from town, so that my son can run down for week-ends. You'll have to come with me, and I shall take all the servants."

"Sir Heron says we must humor her," said Aliette, consulting Ronnie over dinner. "He says that if she wants a big house, she must have a big house. Nurse seems to think Sussex would be the best place."

"But, Alie, is she really fit to be moved?"

"Sir Heron says he wouldn't risk it with any one else, but that with her constitution it's the best thing we can do."

Ronnie agreed. His mother's recovery appeared so rapid, her good spirits were so infectious, that he had already persuaded himself of her ultimate cure. Of the diabetic complication, definitely diagnosed at last, neither he nor Aliette was informed, nurse and specialist being alike constrained to secrecy by a patient whose brain had begun to function so masterfully, even under the reduced doses of morphia, that they were afraid to cross her will.

For now that the hemorrhage had eliminated all possibility of self-deception from her imagination; now that she realized—despite Sir Heron's confident reassurances—how at the best she could only live two years, at the worst a bare six months, the plan, the final plan for Aliette's release, had taken concrete shape in Julia's brain. Wilberforce's revelations about the Carrington case had stuck in her memory. Carrington, according to Wilberforce, had been broken by the press. She, Julia, wielded a more enduring weapon.

It was strange, very strange, to lie there, on one's own bed, surrounded by one's own cherished furniture; and knowing one's self doomed, yet know one's self capable of wielding a weapon—could one but forge it—which would outlast death itself. Yet could she, an ill woman, a woman who had never known the financial need for working swiftly, hope to forge her weapon, her sword of the written word, within six months? "Yes," she decided, ruminating one late afternoon behind the warm darkness of closed eyelids, "yes, it can just be done."

There and then she wanted to begin. Then and there, opening her eyes, she attempted to untuck the bedclothes. But her arms, weak, almost powerless, refused their task. Even as she moved them, the ghost of a remembered pain stabbed at her left lung; and, frightened by remembrance of past agony, she desisted. "Not yet," she thought, "not yet. I must rest for another week, perhaps for another fortnight. Fresh air might cure these lungs of mine, and make me well again. What a fool I am to deceive myself! That must be the consumption. Consumption always cheats its victims with the hope of life."

300

And she fell to remembering Aubrey Beardsley, to comparing herself with him, to conjuring up mental pictures of his "handkerchief-parties," as he used to call them, when he would break off in the midst of some gay anecdote, rush—silk pressed to mouth—from the room, and return, gayer than ever, to carry on the game of make-believe with his cronies. "Brave!" mused Julia, "but I mustn't be brave like that. For Ronnie's sake I must husband every ounce of my strength. Above all, I must find a house in the country."

The taking of that country-house, even though it had to be accomplished by proxy, served in no small way to distract her mind from gloomier thoughts. Mrs. Sanderson's inquiry had brought many answers, and Julia used to sit up in bed of a morning, her secretary in attendance, buff "particulars" from the house-agent's littered like cards on the heavily embroidered eiderdown. These perused, she would send for Aliette. "Take a car," she used to say. "Charge it to my account. The brougham's too slow for long journeys. This lot," handing over a packet of slips, "look as though they might do. All the rest are hopeless."

For the best part of a week, Aliette motored about the southern counties. April was almost May; the blossomed countryside a dream of green and white beauty. Rushing lonely through the sunlit air, hedges, fields, and orchards streaming by, it seemed impossible that any breathing creature should be near to death. Her mood expanded to the expanding summer, so that she forgot her personal troubles, too, in the sheer fun of her quest, and enjoyed every minute of it, from the setting-out of midday to the evening consultations with her "mother-in-law" and Ronnie about the places she had seen.

Finally, their choice narrowed itself down to two places—one, a modern mansion perched high on the slopes that overlook Reigate and Dorking; the other, an old-fashioned brown stone house roofed with great slabs of Sussex slate, midway between Horsham and the sea.

"Let it be Sussex," decided Julia; and to Daffadillies, as the brown stone house called itself, some fortnight later, they went.

5

Even to die in, Daffadillies was marvelous. No roads, save the one road through the woodlands by which the recumbent Julia and her nurse motored, gave access to that great house set high above terraced gardens. On three sides of it—east, west, and north—great oaks baffled the winds; southward were no trees, only slope on slope of field and farm-land, ramparted in middle distance by the bosoming downs.

Day-long, the wise brown southward-gazing face of Daffadillies trapped the sunshine in its high gabled windows; day-long, whiffs of the sparkling sea blew tempered across twenty miles of kindly earth into that vast oak-floored room, with the four-poster bed and the Jacobean furniture, which Aliette at her very first visit had mentally chosen for the invalid.

In that Sussex home quiet reigned like a sleeping princess. The balustered staircases gave back scarcely a sound to the sedulous feet of Julia'a serving-women. Neither from the brown-paneled dining-room nor from the book-lined library could any whisper of voice arise to where, had she so willed it, the invalid might have dreamed away her summer in country peace, hearing only the swish and click of the mower on the tennis-lawn, the snap and cut of gardeners' shears among the shrubberies.

But it was not for dreams, rather for their accomplishment, that Julia had taken Daffadillies. Aliette, bringing Ponto on the evening train, found her in the highest fettle, curiously awake.

"My dear," she smiled, "this place is ideal. Ideal! You've done wonders."

"Then the journey didn't tire you?"

"Not a bit. I feel quite well. So well, in fact, that I've told nurse she needn't sleep in my room to-night."

"But suppose you were taken ill?"

"I sha'n't be taken ill." Something of the old mastery was back in Julia's voice. "If I am, I can always ring for Smithers." And she touched the two electric pushes, one for the light and the other for the bell, which nurse had arranged under her pillow; smiling at her own astuteness when—her morphia refused—the watchers withdrew for the night. Then she waited, ears tense, eyes wide open, heart throbbing in anticipation of its deed.

Smithers, acting on instructions, had set out her writing-things on the desk under the vast curtained window. A night-light burned on the bed-table. Across the glow of the night-light she saw her traveling ink-pot, the gold pen which Ronnie had given her for Christmas, the leather manuscript-box with its store of foolscap and sharpened pencils.

"Was it safe to begin?" If only she could be certain that nurse and Smithers were in bed.

At last she heard the pair of them whispering to one another in the corridor; at last she heard them separate, heard their doors close; and after yet another interminable quarter of an hour the house grew utterly quiet.

"Now," she said to herself, "now"; and very carefully, very quietly, very fearful of waking the woman in the next room, her wasted hands untucked the bedclothes. Very quietly her wasted limbs released themselves from the sheets; very quietly her feet touched the carpet. Then, surreptitious as a schoolboy breaking bounds—a tottering figure of courage in her cambric nightgown,—she stole toward her desk.

She could never reach that desk! She felt her legs, weak after their unaccustomed effort, wobble under her like loose springs. The dim room spun. A breeze rustled the cretonne curtains, chilling her to the bone, terrifying her for her own frailty. Quivering, she reached the desk; clung to it. The dim room ceased its spinning. Quivering still, she took two blocks of manuscript-paper from the leather-lined basket; and tottered back to the bed.

Pencils! She had forgotten to bring pencils. She must go back—all those miles from her bed to her desk, from her desk to her bed. She tottered to the desk. It seemed as though she would never win her way back to the safety of those distant sheets, those distant pillows.

Somehow, the pencils clutched in her trembling fingers, she had reached the bed. Faintness overwhelmed her. The weak wire springs that were her limbs sank under the weight of her body. Her body was a flaccid torment, sinking down by the bed. Her heart yearned to give up its struggle. Her brain told her to ring for Smithers. Smithers would lift her gently, so gently, put her to rest between those waiting sheets.

Somehow she had climbed into bed; somehow she had covered her aching body. On the eiderdown, two oblong patches of white, lay the paper.

For a full five minutes, exhausted, fearful with a thousand fears, Julia Cavendish watched those two white oblongs. But gradually her fears subsided. Gradually her brain conquered the exhaustion of her body.

She began to think, as literary craftsfolk think, in words. "'Man's Law,'" she thought; "'The story of a great wrong.' I wonder if I need that second title."

The night-light sputtered, expired. Sleep began to beat, soft-winged, on her eyelids. Her brain fought with sleep in the darkness, fought sleep away from her.

Wide-eyed in the silent darkness she thought, "I must have light—light for the forging of my weapon." Her hands groped for the two electric pushes under her pillow; found them. Her hands panicked lest they should press the bell-push in mistake, and so waken Smithers. Her hands remembered the light-switch pear-shaped. She drew the light-switch from under the pillow; pressed it.

Light glinted on Julia Cavendish's wasted hands, on the virgin manuscript-blocks and the sharpened pencils, on the runkled bed and the wadded jacket at bed-foot. Painfully she reached for the jacket; painfully, afraid for her lung, she managed to drape it about her shoulders; painfully she arranged a pillow to prop her back; painfully she took paper, a pencil; and, drawing up her knees to support the manuscript-block, began.

"God," she prayed, "give me strength for the forging of this last weapon."

*

It seemed to Julia Cavendish that she had scarcely set pencil to paper when the first bird-twitter from dewy lawns warned her to abandon work; to make, once again, that supreme effort from bed to desk, from desk to bed; to smooth away with trembling fingers all signs of her surreptitious task, and lay herself down to get what sleep she might before Smithers brought her morning medicine.

Chapter XXVI

1

Only those who have tended their loved ones through long illnesses know how at such times hour slides into hour, eventless save for the notches on the temperature-chart, for the slight recoveries or the slight relapses of the patient, for the doctor's cautious warnings or the nurse's hopeful cheeriness; how wary nights are but the interludes between weary days.

But night after night at Daffadillies, while her watchers slept, unwearied and warier than they, Julia's brain clocked away its eventful hours; and dawn after wakeful dawn her weary hands added their carefully-hidden sheets to the pile of penciled manuscript in the leather-lined basket.

"Nurse," she used to say of a morning, "I haven't slept quite as well as usual. After I've had my breakfast I think a little doze would do me good." After lunch, too, she liked to doze, and sometimes even after tea. "It's the best thing for her," said nurse. "She's getting better. Quite soon she'll be able to get up."

And indeed to all of them, not only to nurse, but to Smithers and Mrs. Sanderson, to Aliette and to Ronnie, who came down every week-end with better and better news of the work for which John Cartwright had briefed him, it seemed as though eventually she must get well. Already she talked of returning to Bruton Street for the autumn, of wintering on the Riviera. "That hemorrhage," she pronounced, "was a blessing in disguise. This rest is doing me the good in the world. I feel like a two-year-old."

Her assumed high spirits deceived everybody. Even Sir Heron Baynet, who motored down one evening, felt the slender chance possible. "Let her get up," he told Aliette over dinner. "Let her come downstairs if she feels like it."

But Julia, on that first visit, refused to get up. She and she alone at Daffadillies knew, with that mysterious prescience of the doomed, that death had only consented to stand off for a period; that only by husbanding every ounce of her strength could she hope to run the full race with him. So far, in that race, she was well ahead. But inevitably there would be setbacks, stumbles and faintings, when death would close up his distance.

The Love-Story of Aliette Brunton

It was a fascinating race, yet terrible—this secret course which she and her pencil ran nightly, for her son's sake, against the ultimate doom. Times came when she tasted the very foreknowledge of victory; times when despondency took her by the shrunken throat, when it seemed as though not even the supremest effort of her pencil could outrun those cellules of consumption, those tiny implacable burrowers into the shrinking lung-tissue, which spored with every breath she drew.

Once for twenty-four whole hours she relapsed into black despair. "Man's Law"—so alive through so many wonderful nights—was dead in her brain. Her body, too, was dying. She would perish, leaving her sword unforged, Ronnie's Gordian knot unsevered.

Then, and then only, did Julia Cavendish decide to get up.

"I feel I need some distraction," she told Sir Heron on his next visit. "A little literary work. It'll take my mind off things. Just a few rough notes for a new book."

The physician, after much protest, yielded; and next afternoon Julia, duly dressed by the adoring Smithers and helped to a cushioned chair at the window by a proud nurse, sent for Aliette, who came bringing a great armful of flowers from the garden, and—Aliette gone—for Mrs. Sanderson, to whom, under pledge of secrecy and with the threat of instant dismissal should the secret be revealed, she confided the penciled contents of her manuscript-box.

2

May drifted into June. Forty miles away London seethed with strikes, with rumors of a general election, and with Hector Brunton's viciously victorious prosecution of three fraudulent bank directors. At Daffadillies brooded peace.

Once more, typed, "Man's Law" grew alive. Once more, by daylight now, Julia ran her race with death. From half-past ten to half-past one she would sit at her desk by the open window—resentful of the faintest noise, of the slightest interruption, resentful even of the medicines which kept those tiny cellules at bay. At half-past one would come Mrs. Sanderson, her face an

306

unhappy mask; then lunch; and, lunch over, sleep. Every afternoon nurse and Smithers would carry the invalid down the wide staircase to take tea with Aliette and Ponto, either in the book-shelved morning-room, or under the big cedar, whose branches just shadowed the base-line of the tennis-court.

At those tea-parties Julia was curiously inquisitive. Habitually she would steer conversation into personal channels, putting question after question to Aliette—about her marriage with Hector, about her family, about her elopement; till it seemed to the younger woman, shrinking from the frankness of those questions, as though the elder were striving to probe every secret of her life. But the probing was never unkindly; and after Julia had retired to her room, Aliette, lonely in the hush of Sussex sunsets that splashed warm gold on the gabled brown of the great house, mused much for love of this marvelously valiant old lady whose very valiance had beaten down death.

For actually, listening to the courage in Julia's voice, it was impossible to imagine that voice forever silent. Even the second hemorrhage, so slight that only the patient divined its full significance, failed to dissipate Aliette's confidence.

Those nights, Hector's wife dreamed no more of Hector. Her dreams were all of Ronnie; of Ronnie, solitary from Monday night to Friday in the ridiculous flat where Caroline Staley still tended his sparse requirements; of Ronnie, very loving, very confident of ultimate success.

Latterly more than one important case—cases that brought publicity rather than fees—had been put in Ronnie's way; and Julia, reading his name in the papers, would gloat a little, seeing him already famous.

With her son, too, whenever he visited them, Julia had grown curiously inquisitive, cross-examining him by the hour together about the work he had done during the week, about the intricacies of the law, about various prominent members of his profession. But when he grew inquisitive about her work, Ronnie's mother always pleaded tiredness.

"I'm only playing at things," she used to say. "Don't worry me to tell you about my scribbling."

3

The love of a man for a woman, and of a woman for her mate are very blind, very selfish, when compared with the love of a mother for her son. Every week, as June flamed into July, as her fears for Julia subsided, as the fret of London dwindled into memory and the country wove its soothing spells more and more surely about her consciousness; every week-end when she drove to welcome her lover at the little wayside station which served Daffadillies, Aliette grew more and more radiant, more and more akin to the woman of a year ago, the woman whose kisses had made paradise of Chilworth Cove.

Here, under the ramparting downs, even as then by the creaming beaches, no harsh breeze from the outer world blew cold to wither the crimson flowers of their lonely happiness. Even as at Chilworth, no strangers came nigh them. Friends, acquaintances, her chagrined family—Julia banned them all. The rare visitors from neighboring places had to content their curiosity with leaving cards. The press, satisfied of convalescence, left them undisturbed. Miraculously the telephone had ceased to ring.

So while in the high rooms and on the smooth lawns of Daffadillies Julia worked undistracted, glad that her loved ones, all unknowing what they did, should make high holiday, Ronnie and Aliette, careless of Hector, careless of scandal, careless of ostracism, played man and wife: until, since no word, no thought, no living creature reminded them of reality, their play grew truth and they forgot.

In this, their second honeymoon-time, their second oasis of make-believe in the desert of unmarried life, Daffadillies became very "Joyous Gard," love's castle whence they rode out together—every week-end—on hired nags—into fairyland. Southward to the downs or eastward into the weald they rode; and wonderful it was once again to feel even hired horseflesh under them, to recapture for ecstatic moments on swift scurries across sheep-bitten turf the mad inexplicable bliss of their first meeting long and long ago in the hunting-field.

"Man, if only hounds ran in summertime," Aliette would laugh, and crack a playful whip at Ponto lolloping, stern high, beside them.

For if the man and the woman were happy, the huge hound was in his seventh heaven. The great house suited him. His harlequin shape might have been bred to match the gleam and shadows of those stone terraces where—coat silken from the chamois-leather, slitty eyes somnolent yet watchful—he basked in sunshine or bayed the moon till Aliette, fearful for the invalid's comfort, drove him to the stables.

In "Joyous Gard" even Dennis and Etta were forgotten. How could Aliette desire dream-children or any children so long as her present happiness endured? To feel that Ronnie still cared, that the mere touch of her hand could still kindle in him the flames of their early passion; to realize herself responsible for his mother's comfort; to know that at last she was being of real service to both of them—these things suffced the woman.

But the man, subconsciously, still yearned for material success, for the prizes of his profession, for the fame and the emoluments of it. At the woman's touch not only passion but ambition kindled him. If only once, just once, he could meet and defeat, snatch a forensic victory from the "hanging prosecutor."

4

Once again, as July sped, Julia Cavendish stumbled in her race with death. The sustained effort of the past weeks had exhausted her vitality. Her brain wearied of its weapon-forging; and for a week she stayed it from the anvil.

But her brain, once released from its secret task, felt the impulse—as is the habit of creative brains—to burden itself with other tasks. The imaginative power, no longer under definite control, grew fearful, painting devils on every wall. She summoned Sir Heron Baynet from London, questioned and cross-questioned him about her disease. "You're a mind-specialist, *inter alia?*" was one of her questions. "Tell me, do you believe that a healthy mind can triumph over an unhealthy body?"

"It depends on the quality of the mind," Sir Heron humored her. "In your own case, I should say that the sheer will to be cured has done more than all my drugs. But don't overdo the work."

That—since all she now lived for was to bring her work to its conclusion—frightened her but the more. Torn between the desire for work and the fear lest, overworking, she should too soon pay the inevitable penalty, she drove her brain once more to the anvil—hammering, hammering, hammering at her sword of the written word till even Mrs. Sanderson dared to protest with her.

"Your business is to type, not to argue," said Julia grimly; and once again, openly this time, she began to work o' nights—so that it was a novelist nearer than she had ever been to a nervous breakdown who said to her "daughter-in-law" one afternoon as they took their tea in the book-shelved morning-room overlooking the rain-dripped magnificence of the herbaceous borders: "I wonder if I ought to have my family down. They'll be a frightful nuisance, and I sha'n't be able to scribble while they're here. All the same, one has one's duties—"

"I think your first duty is to get quite well," smiled the "daughter-in-law."

"Perhaps you're right, child." Nervously Julia's tired mind broached another of its secret anxieties. "And *your* family? Don't you ever feel the need of them?"

"Mollie wrote last week," answered Aliette, burking the main question.

"Yes, but your father, your mother, that other sister of yours? Don't you ever wish that they'd see reason; that they knew the exact truth; that somebody could tell them the inside story of your married life?" The questions came abruptly from the shawled figure in the easy chair.

"Sometimes. Not that the truth would influence mother. Mother was a Roman Catholic, you know, before she married."

"Ah! I'd nearly forgotten that. It's important, very important, because—" Julia, as though she had said too much, checked herself, leaving the other rather mystified. "Still," she went on, "your mother isn't a Roman Catholic now. She'd forgive you if there were a divorce, if you married my son?"

"Yes. I suppose so." The younger woman brushed away the topic. "But mother and I never cared for one another as you and Ronnie care. Mollie and I were the pals in our family."

"Quite so." A sudden plan formulated itself in Julia's troubled brain. "It must be lonely for you down here," she said after a pause. "Wouldn't you like to have your sister Mollie to stay for a week?"

"But wouldn't she be a nuisance?"

"No. I like having young people about me, and besides, I've a reason—"

Again, as though fearful of betraying herself, Julia checked speech. But the next day and the next, work finished, her mind reverted to its plan.

"We might invite young Wilberforce, too," she suggested when Ronnie came down on the Saturday. "That would make you four for tennis."

"And two for match-making," retorted Ronnie, entirely unsuspicious of his mother's real motive.

Chapter XXVII

1

Jimmy's two-seater was suffering from one of its usual breakdowns. That red-haired young man, instructing his porter to put his bag into a first-class smoker, had no idea of the coil woven about his destiny. Ronnie he had not seen for some weeks; Julia's letter to his firm requesting that "Mr. Wilberforce, Jr., should, if possible, come down and see me" conveyed an invitation to stay the Friday night, but no hint of Mollie's presence at Daffadillies.

Nevertheless, as he watched Victoria Station slide past the lowered windows, the solicitor's thoughts visualized a girl whose letters from Clyst Fullerford showed all too plainly that she meant to insist, despite her love for him, on Aliette's divorce preceding her own marriage. Jimmy had written that girl only a week since, begging her—"for the absolutely last time of asking"—to be reasonable. But the veiled threat brought only the inevitable reply, "You mustn't ask me that. It wouldn't be fair to Alie."

He had apologized for his veiled threat; but the reply to it still rankled. "Really," thought the junior partner in Wilberforce, Wilberforce & Cartwright, "it's getting a bit too thick. I've told her over and over again that I don't care what her sister does. As far as I am concerned, she can go on living with Cavendish till the cows come home. But when it comes to that dear little idiot insisting that I should arrange my prospective sister-in-law's divorce before my own marriage—well, it's enough to try the temper of the lord chief!"

Though temperamentally incapable of a grand passion, the solicitor had long ceased to regard matrimony, in his own particular and individual case, as an unsentimental contract. He wanted the girl; and "Dash it all," he decided, "this thing's got to stop. If necessary, I'll have to run down to Devonshire. I can't wait much longer. She's asking too much of a chap. *I* can't settle this affair of her sister's. Nobody can settle it except H. B. And H. B.'s as obstinate as a mule. Bit of a cad is H. B. Clever devil, though; I wish

312

I had his income."

Ruminating thus, James Wilberforce made Horsham Junction; changed trains; and arrived, still ruminating, at West Water.

"Here, you," he called to the solitary porter, "is there a conveyance of any sort from Daffadillies?"

"Yes, sir. There's a motor; and two ladies, sir."

For a moment, Jimmy's eyes refused to recognize the two lone figures by the ticket-collector's gate of the little wayside platform: Aliette in a dove-gray coat and skirt, floppy straw shading her eyes; and Mollie, hatless, gloveless, almost too obviously unperturbed at his approach. Then, conquering surprise, he took off his hat; shook hands; and was whisked into the tonneau of a dusty car before he could collect his wits.

"Astonished, Jimmy?" smiled the girl, still outwardly unperturbed, as Aliette, hardly restraining a sly chuckle of amusement, climbed up beside the driver.

"I certainly didn't expect—"

"To find me here." Imperturbability gave place to diffidence. "I didn't know *you* were coming down till an hour ago. Perhaps, if I had known, I shouldn't have come."

"That's a jolly remark to one's fiancé."

"I'm not your fiancée."

They were within two miles of Daffadillies before Jimmy ventured his next remark. "Then you haven't changed your mind, dear?"

"Certainly not. And, Jimmy—please behave yourself."

The man—his slight caress eluded—fell into a sulky silence. "Devilish awkward position," he decided—thought of his father's baronetcy, and of the social responsibilities entailed on a family solicitor, weighing heavily on his Philistine mind—"women are the devil!" He felt that he had been trapped; first, into foregathering with Aliette, a situation he had done his best to avoid since the scandal; secondly, into a scene with Mollie; and thirdly, into yet another discussion with that very resolute old lady, Julia Cavendish, about her son's matrimonial troubles.

Nevertheless, the drive soothed him; and by the time they made the stone lodge and the eagle-crowned pillars of the great house, the prospect—scene or no scene—of twenty-four hours in Mollie's company outweighed all other considerations. Moreover, it seemed impossible to associate the foursquare magnificence and tree-girt terraces of Daffadillies with any form of scandal!

"And how *is* Mrs. Cavendish?" he remembered to ask Aliette, as they alighted. "Bucking up, one hears."

"She's ever so much better. She's in the garden to-day."

2

It is one of the tragedies of a long illness that those who live in daily contact with it fail to perceive the changes wrought in their loved one.

James Wilberforce, as he made his way through the long hall and out of the French windows, down the stone steps on to the south lawns, was horrified at the first sight of his client. Only two days since he had read of her, somewhere or other, as "well on her way to recovery." Nearing the shawled figure in the long chair under the cedar-tree, he knew the full inaccuracy of that bulletin. Julia Cavendish had shrunk to a merest vestige of the woman he remembered. The hand she extended to him seemed so frail that he hardly dared clasp it. The gray hair was nearly white; the sunken cheeks hectic; the bloodless lips tremulous. Only in her eyes shone the old dominance.

"Ronnie's coming down by the evening train," said the semblance of his old client. "We're wondering if you'll stay the week-end." A servant whom Jimmy remembered to have seen at Bruton Street brought silver tea-things, a table, a cake-stand, and a hot-water-bottle for the invalid's feet. "My daughter-in-law coddles me," she told him, as Aliette arranged the hot-water-bottle on the foot-rest of the chair and retucked an eiderdown round the thin knees. "But I don't grumble. It's so splendid to feel one's getting well again."

The pathos of that last remark brought tears very close to Jimmy's eyes.

But once Julia had been carried into the house by nurse and Smithers, the young man in the town clothes forgot all about her. He wanted to be alone with Mollie—and the "Brunton woman," confound her, refused to leave them alone.

That tea-time, James Wilberforce learned yet another lesson, to wit, the exact meaning of our ancient saw, "one man's meat is another man's poison." To him Aliette, the exquisite Aliette, was a bore, a nuisance, an interloper. He had never pretended to like Mollie's sister. Now positively he loathed her. Had it not been for the old lady's "daughter-in-law"—Daughter-in-law, forsooth. Why, damn it all, the position was a public disgrace!

Irritably surveying both sisters, Jimmy speculated why on earth Ronald Cavendish should have jeopardized his career for any one so utterly insipid as Aliette. She was insipid, compared with Mollie. Except for her hair. And that, in the sunlight, was red. A rotten red! (Jimmy, like most red-haired people, could not bear the color in others.) As for the pale complexion and the carefully modulated, rather shy voice, he, personally, found them tiresome.

"If only she'd go," he thought; and, at last, making the excuse that it was time for her to meet Ronnie's train, the "Brunton woman," still chuckling, went.

"Isn't Alie a dear?" said Alie's sister, following her with her eyes across the lawn. "Isn't Hector a beast?" And again James Wilberforce was troublesomely aware of his own selfishness.

"What did you think of Mrs. Cavendish?" went on the girl after a pause. "I've only met her once before. She seems rather—rather thin, don't you think?"

"She *is* rather thin," prevaricated Jimmy.

"But you do think she's going to get well, don't you?"

"Let's hope so."

For both the new-comers had seen, though neither of them could speak it, the truth about Julia; and in the light of that truth, their own troubles seemed petty. They didn't want even to speak of themselves. With their eyes, they said to one another: "Not now. Not here. Not just under her windows." With their lips, till Ronnie and Aliette arrived, they made pretense. "She'll get well," they said, sheering away, by mutual consent, from every personal topic.

And this game of make-believe—which only good breeding enabled them to play—endured all through the dinner of which those four partook (Mrs. Sanderson and the hospital-nurse mealed alone) in the paneled room whose heavy gold-framed pictures looked down across vast spaces on the pale oval pool of the candle-lit dining table.

But Ronnie, even taking part in the game, seemed distrait, self-absorbed. Dinner finished and the sisters gone, he poured himself a second glass of port; and, extracting a piece of carefully-clipped newsprint from his waistcoat-pocket, handed it across the table.

"Tell me," he said, "of whom does this remind you?"

James Wilberforce took the proffered paper and scrutinized it carefully before replying: "Well—it's a little like—"

"Like Aliette." Ronnie's self-absorption passed in a flash. "My dear chap, it's the very image of her. Look at those eyes, that mouth. I tell you I got the shock of my life when I opened the 'Evening News' on my way down to-night."

"Really—and who is the lady? Lucy Towers, eh! Screen-star, I suppose."

"Screen-star, you blithering idiot; she's just been arrested for murder."

"By Jove!" Jimmy, whose wits had been wool-gathering, skimmed through the paragraph underneath the photo, and handed it back without further comment. His friend's excitement over the vague resemblance to Aliette—for that Ronnie was excited, quite uncontrollably excited, even the love-lorn solicitor could now see—appeared, to say the least of it, peculiar.

"Jimmy," went on the barrister, his eyes shining, "I'll swear that woman's no murderess."

"You'd better offer to defend her then."

"Wouldn't I like the chance! Look here,"—another newspaper-cutting emerged from Ronnie's pocket,—"that's the chap she's alleged to have murdered. Her husband, apparently. A nice-looking blackguard, too. As far as I can make out, there's another person under arrest for complicity. A man—"

"*Crime passionel*, eh?"

"Possibly." Ronnie folded up both the cuttings and put them carefully back into his pocket. "And from the look of the late Mr. Towers, I can't say they're either of them much to blame." He relapsed into silence; and James Wilberforce realized, in a rare flash of psychological illumination, whither the chance remark had led his excited imagination.

"Talking of murder," he said suddenly. "What would happen if I were to put a bullet into H. B.? There's been many a time when I've wanted to. It makes me mad to feel that that man, or any man, has the power to deny a woman her freedom. It's sheer slavery—our marriage system."

"What the dickens is the matter with you to-night?" James Wilberforce had risen, and placed a restraining hand on his friend's shoulder.

"I'm bothered if I know. Seeing that photograph got on my nerves, I suppose. Funny things—nerves. I never knew what they were till—Hello, what the hell's that?" A bell shrilled loud and long above their heads. "The mater's bell. I hope to Christ there's nothing wrong."

Ronnie sprang from his chair, and they waited a moment or so—as those in invalids' houses do wait on sudden summonses.

But the bell did not ring again, and after a little while appeared Smithers with the news that "Mrs. Cavendish would be very grateful if Mr. Wilberforce would go up and see her, alone, for a few minutes."

3

"I hope you've finished dinner?" Julia Cavendish lay, like a queen in state, on the smoothed bed. To the eyes of James Wilberforce, puzzling their way here and there about the subdued light of the room, she looked almost herself again. "You didn't mind my sending for you?"

"Not in the very least. Isn't that what I came down for?" The solicitor, unpleasantly self-conscious of his own physical bulk, sat down awkwardly beside the weak form on the bed.

The invalid dismissed her nurse. She had intended to postpone Wilberforce's interview till the next morning, to work an hour or so. But her mind was in one of its peculiar turmoils. To any other listener, the tremor in her voice alone would have betrayed the importance, to her plans, of the forthcoming talk.

"I ought to have sent for your father, I suppose," she began. "Have you brought the will with you?"

"Yes. It's in my room. Shall I go and get it?"

"No. There's a copy on my desk. Do you mind handing it to me?"

Obeying, James Wilberforce asked: "Is there anything you want altered?"

"Well—no—not exactly. But tell me, suppose I did want to make certain alterations, would it be necessary for you to draw up an entirely new document, or would this one do?"

"If it was only a minor alteration," said Jimmy, quite unconscious of the thought at the back of his client's head, "we could execute a codicil."

"A codicil." She played with the word. "That's a kind of postscript, isn't it?"

"More or less. But, of course, a codicil has to be properly witnessed." Wilberforce went on to explain the law of last wills and testaments at some length; and the invalid listened carefully. She appeared curiously inquisitive on the subject. and he humored her inquisitiveness till nurse, returning with medicine-glass and bottle, interrupted their conversation.

"I'm sure you're tired," said nurse. "I'm sure you ought to let me settle you down for the night."

"I sha'n't go to sleep for at least another hour. I've a great deal to discuss."

The nurse, realizing the patient in her stubbornest mood, left them alone again; and Julia, apparently satisfied on the subject of her will, began to talk of Ronnie. What did Mr. Wilberforce think of her son's chances at the criminal bar? What hopes were there, in Mr. Wilberforce's opinion, of Brunton's being forced to take action? Would publicity, for instance, the kind of publicity Belfield had used against Carrington, help?

"I shouldn't worry about that till you're better." Jimmy strove to be cheerful.

"But I do worry about it."

"Why? It's only a question of time. H.B.'s bound to come round in the long run."

"I doubt that." Dropped lashes veiled the interest in Julia's eyes. "Not without considerable pressure. He's a cruel man; and if he doesn't want to marry again, I'm afraid there's very little hope. That's why—" She grew thoughtful, silent. Then a new idea seemed to cross her mind. "If he doesn't bring his divorce soon, he won't be able to bring one at all, will he?"

"That depends." Wilberforce laughed. "Divorce judges don't want to know too much in undefended cases."

"That's good." Julia, her mind now more or less at rest about its main problem, lay back among her pillows. So far, apprehensive lest the solicitor should discover her secret, she had gone subtly to work. But there was no subtlety about her next speech:

"Mr. Wilberforce, I suppose you know I'm going to die?"

The directness of those words dumbed Jimmy. Only after the greatest difficulty could he manage the conventional prevarication: "We all of us have to die some day."

"I'm too tired for clichés." The woman on the bed smiled superciliously, whimsically almost. "Death, in my case, is a very near certainty. That's a privileged communication." She smiled again. "You won't tell my son or my daughter-in-law, will you?"

Not knowing how to reply, the man held his peace; and after a little while Julia Cavendish continued: "When the end comes, it will be your father's duty as my executor to go through my papers. I'll telegraph for him if my mind is still clear. But he may not arrive in time. I'd have sent for him to-night instead of for you, if I hadn't been afraid of," she hesitated, "frightening people. I want you to give your father this message. Memorize it carefully, please. Tell him that there will be a letter for him—either for him or for you—I haven't yet made up my mind which. It depends on—on certain circumstances."

With an effort, the frail form raised itself from the pillow and leaned forward. Even in the subdued light, James Wilberforce could see the pearls of sweat beading his client's forehead. Her hands showed blue-white on the sheets. Her blue eyes were an imploring question. "The instructions in that letter will be a sacred trust. Will you give me your promise, your personal promise, that they shall be carried out?"

"Of course, Mrs. Cavendish." Jimmy, moved to a great compassion, took one of the blue-white hands in his own strong clasp. "You can rely upon me."

"Thank you. I can sleep now."

He released her hand; and Julia subsided, eyes closed, among her pillows.

For a moment, Jimmy was terrified. "She's going to die," he thought. "She's going to die to-night!"

But the eyes opened again; and it seemed to Jimmy that they read his unspoken thought. "I'm not going to die yet awhile," said Julia Cavendish. "I'm only sleepy. You might ring for nurse."

Just as the nurse came in, she said to him, "If I write that letter to you instead of to your father, it will be because I feel that you owe me a debt—a debt of gratitude. Scandal's a very small price to pay for—love, Mr. Wilberforce."

4

Once outside Julia's bedroom door, the solicitor took a silk handkerchief from the pocket of his dinner-jacket and pretended to blow his nose. He wanted, in his own elegant phraseology, "to blub like anything." For the moment, his essentially legal mind was off its balance. "I must control myself," he thought; "I mustn't let those people downstairs see."

And perhaps, if Ronnie and Aliette had been in the drawing-room, James Wilberforce might have succeeded in disciplining himself. But Mollie was alone; had been alone for a whole anxious hour.

"Jimmy"—she rose from the sofa as he entered, and her eyes met his across the sudden brightness of the room—"Jimmy, what's the matter? You look as if you'd seen a ghost."

"Nothing's the matter," he said dully.

"You're sure?"

"Quite. She's asleep." He came across the room to her, and they faced one another, all pretense wiped from their eyes.

"Tell me," said the girl at last. "Tell me, is it quite hopeless? Does *she*—does *she* know?"

"Yes. She knows."

"How terrible!" Mollie's voice trembled. "Jimmy, won't you tell me what she said? There might be some way in which I could help—"

"There's only one way in which you can help me, Mollie."

"Don't! Please don't!" Her hands protested. "We mustn't think of ourselves. Not here. Not now."

"Why not!" he said sullenly; and then, sinking heavily into a chair, "I suppose you're right, dear. Life's a rotten mess—"

"Poor Jimmy!" Mollie's voice was very tender. "My poor Jimmy!" She put her hand on his head. He grasped it feverishly; and quite suddenly she knew that her James, her unemotional Philistine of a James, was crying.

*

Thought expired like a candle in the mind of Mollie Fullerford. She was just conscious that Jimmy had risen from his chair—that his hand still grasped hers—that he was leading her through the open windows—over a lawn which felt damp to her thin-shod feet—under a moon-fretted tree—toward the dark of shrubberies.

Somehow they were standing on a bridge; a little rustic bridge, mossy banks and moss-green water below. Her hands on the bridge-rail quivered like the hands of a 'cello player. She was quivering all over, quivering like a restive horse. Jimmy's arm was round her shoulders. He was speaking to her, hoarsely, hysterically, pleading with her; and she knew that the resolution which had held her so long firm against his importunities was weakening; weakening to every jerk of the Adam's apple in his throat.

"Mollie," he pleaded, "I need you. I want you. I can't do without you. I can't wait any longer for you. You must marry me. You must, I tell you, you must."

"Jimmy," she stammered, "Jimmy—please."

"You little idiot!" Suddenly, she grew conscious of an immense anger in him. "You dear, damned little idiot. What good do you think you're doing by refusing to marry me? You're not doing yourself any good. You're not doing me any good. You're not doing your sister any good." Words rushed out of him—faster—faster—always less coherent. "Little fool. Selfish little fool We sha'n't do anybody any good by waiting. Shall we? Answer me, Mollie! Shall we? Shall we do anybody any good?"

Words petered out. He could only strain her to him, crudely, fiercely. She felt her body weakening; felt the inhibitions of a year ebbing like water from, the channels of her mind. His lips sought hers. She yielded her lips to him—yielded herself beaten, to the fierceness of his arms.

"Little idiot, will you marry me?"

"Yes, Jimmy."

Triumphant, he released her; and in that moment his mind, still quivering from the verity of death, knew the verity of love.

Chapter XXVIII

1

Next morning, Saturday, after breakfast, a very subdued Jimmy and Mollie broke the news of their formal engagement. To both of them the events of overnight, remembered in the prosaic day, seemed curiously out of perspective. They had, they decided, "gone off the deep end"; and, being rather casual young people, left it at that, content to enjoy the happiness which their emotional plunge had brought them.

Jimmy, of course, changed his original plan of returning to town by the evening train. The usual notice for the "Daily Telegraph" was drafted, Clyst Fullerford and the baronet communicated with in two conventional letters, and the inevitable bottle of champagne broached for luncheon.

Though Julia did not share that bottle, the engagement was like a draft of wine to her mentality. She felt that the alliance of the Wilberforces with the Fullerfords could only benefit her secret schemes; and, strong in that feeling, put all cerebral turmoils away. On Saturday afternoon, quite undisturbed by the swish and pat from the tennis-court, she worked two hours, and on Sunday morning, three.

Aliette, delighted though she was at her sister's obvious happiness (for some time past she had guessed that only her own peculiar position could be hindering Mollie's chance of matrimony), found it hard to restrain a vague jealousy, a trace of petty resentment. Soon Mollie would be a married woman. Whereas she—

And in Aliette's lover the resentment was tenfold stronger. The utter legality and social correctness of the whole procedure infuriated him. It took all his self-control to make semblance of congratulating the "lucky couple." His overnight absorption in a "vulgar murder-case" seemed absurd. Every time he looked at Aliette, graceful on the tennis-court or dignified across the dinner-table, he said to himself: "If only we could be 'engaged,' if only we could be legally married."

But Monday morning—the two men traveled to London together, leaving Julia at her anvil and the sisters surreptitiously planning trousseaux—brought

The Love-Story of Aliette Brunton

back the nervous excitement of Friday night with a rush. No sooner had Ronnie arrived at Pump Court than Benjamin Bunce—a little soured by the setback suffered in the civil courts, yet tolerably optimistic about the new criminal work—informed him that Mr. John Cartwright had been on the telephone twice before ten o'clock and would be glad of a conference as soon as possible.

"It's about this shooting case at Brixton. Perhaps you've read about it, sir," confided Benjamin; and Ronnie's heart leaped at the confidence.

At twelve o'clock precisely the clerk announced the solicitor, who came in clutching an armful of the Sunday papers, which he flung down on the barrister's table with a curt "Here you are. Here's your murder at last."

For John Cartwright, John Cartwright was phenomenally moved. A man of five-and-fifty, domed of forehead, bald of pate, his black pupils—which possessed the inclination to squint—prominent under rimless eye-glasses of peculiar magnification, he had those thin, unemotional lips, those bony, unemotional hands, which are so often found in the legal profession. But to-day the unemotional lips twitched, and the bony hands were almost feverish in their excitement as they drew a battered pocket-book from the tail of a battered black coat, fumbled for an envelope, and handed it over.

"Read what's in that," said John Cartwright, "and see if it isn't a plum."

"That" turned out to be a letter from the millionaire editor of the "Democratic News," a new Sunday illustrated paper devoted almost exclusively to those readers whom unkind journalists describe, when they foregather with one another, as "the father-of-the-family public."

Bertram Standon—he had so far refused two titles and owned one Derby winner—was apparently much exercised over "this unfortunate woman, Mrs. Towers." "I feel convinced," he wrote to his friend, Sir Peter Wilberforce, Bart., who had turned the letter over to his partner, "that she is more sinned against than sinning; and in the cause of honest justice, no less than in the cause of honest journalism, I have decided that—should the coroner's court bring in a verdict of wilful murder against her or the ex-sailor, Fielding—I will put all my personal resources, and all the resources of my paper, at their

324

disposal. Will you therefore have the case watched on my behalf, and, should the verdict go as I am afraid it will, take any steps you consider necessary."

"A stunt, I should imagine," decided Cartwright, "and not a very new stunt at that. Bottomley, you may remember, once did the same thing. Still, it may not be a stunt. Standon's a curious fellow. Sometimes his heart gets away with his brain. It certainly has in this case."

"You think Lucy Towers and Fielding guilty then?"

"Not a doubt, I should say. Still, that's not our affair. Our job is to give Standon as good a run as we can for his money. The inquest, I see, has been adjourned for a week. When it comes on again you'll have to go down."

"Can't I see the prisoners beforehand?"

"Better not, as I take our instructions."

"But we might get them off at the inquest."

"Where would Bertram Standon's stunt come in if we did?" said John Cartwright satirically, and so closed the interview.

2

During the week which preceded the adjourned inquest on William Towers, Bertram Standon held his journalistic hand; and—Fleet Street being momentarily occupied with the controversy of "Submarines v. Battleships"—no further details of the tragedy became available.

Reperusing the week-end papers of an evening, it seemed to Ronnie that the case against the woman—whose likeness to Aliette waned and waned the more one scrutinized her photograph—looked black enough. Apparently she had shot her husband during an altercation in another man's room. The other man, a sailor who had lost both his arms in the war, was her cousin, and—the reports suggested—her lover.

All the same, the "vulgar murder-case" continued to excite both his personalities: the magisterial Cavendish because of a curious inward conviction—the conviction he had voiced to Wilberforce—that "the woman was no murderess": and the imaginative Wixton because if the coroner's jury found her guilty he might at last get his chance—slim though that chance appeared—of a big forensic victory.

Night after night, therefore, Caroline Staley, who, in the absence of her mistress, had relapsed into the perfect bachelor housekeeper, completely idle from ten to four, and completely assiduous for the rest of the time, left her master at work in the little sitting-room of the "ridiculous flat," studying—with his mother's own concentration—first in his red "Gibson and Weldon," and thereafter at length, the reports of Rex *v.* Lesbini, of Rex *v.* Simpson, of Rex *v.* Greening (in which it is definitely held that, though the sight of adultery committed with his wife gives sufficient provocation for a husband to plead manslaughter, the major accusation must hold good if the woman be only mistress of the accused), and of any other case that might, by the vaguest possibility, have some bearing on the problematic defense of Lucy Towers.

3

On the Saturday, Ronnie, as usual, went down to Daffadillies. Mollie had returned to Clyst Fullerford. Julia and Aliette, informed of the new work, were enthusiastic.

"It'll be a public prosecution, I suppose?" asked Julia.

"Of course. All murder cases are conducted by the director of public prosecutions. But I haven't got the brief yet."

"Not even a watching brief?" put in Aliette.

Ronnie laughed. "Where did you pick up that phrase?"

"In the newspapers, I suppose." Aliette, remembering from whose lips she had last heard the expression, blushed faintly. And next morning, Sunday, the front page of the "Democratic News" again reminded her of Hector.

Standon, nervous lest some of his titled brethren in Fleet Street should appropriate the stunt, devoted his Napoleonic leader-page to "The Quality of Mercy."

Standon dared not, of course, comment on a case which was still "sub judice," but Standon could and did dare to comment at great length on "one-sided justice," on the delays demanded by the police at inquests, on the hardships suffered by those who could not afford "our overpaid silks," and on the crying need of a "public defender."

"Our 'hanging prosecutor,'" howled Standon, "is paid by the state. Who pays for the defense of his victims? Why, even as I write, there lie in Brixton Prison a man and a woman who—for all we know—may be as innocent of the charge brought against them as I am. Next week they will be haled before the coroner. The police will have sifted every vestige of evidence against them. But who will have sifted the evidence in their defense? No one! I ask the great-hearted British people, whose generosity to the weak and unhappy never fails, whether this is justice or a travesty of justice; whether, in any properly constituted community, the very finest legal brains obtainable would not have been placed immediately and without any fee whatsoever entirely at the service of these two unfortunates, who now lie in a felon's cell, hoping against hope, if they are innocent, as I believe them to be innocent, that some public-spirited person will come forward and give them, out of mere charity, money. Money! The shame of it!! The shame of it!!!"

The "silly season," when newsprint gasps for "copy" as a drowning man for air, was already on Fleet Street; and Standon's article, duly garnished with photographs of Lucy Towers, of Bob Fielding, the ex-sailor, and of "Big Bill" Towers, started a controversy which relegated both submarines and battleships to the editorial scrap-heap.

"Mark my words," said John Cartwright, calling for Ronnie on the Tuesday morning, "the Cairns case will be nothing to this one. If by any chance you were to get Lucy Towers off, you'd be a made man."

"But surely,"—for a moment the wild idea that by some amazing piece of fortune Hector Brunton might be briefed for the prosecution crossed Ronnie's mind—"surely, if Standon's out for publicity, he'll never let you brief *me* for the actual trial? He'll have one of the big guns, Marshall Hall or somebody like that."

"No, he won't." John Cartwright chuckled slyly. "Oh no, he won't. He'll make a discovery."

"A discovery?"

"Yes, a young man. 'A new light in the legal firmament—a David to slay Goliath.' That'd look well in the Democratic News.' Besides," Cartwright chuckled again, "Marshall Hall would cost them a week's advertising revenue, and you're Julia Cavendish's son."

"I've no wish to trade on my mother's reputation," said Ronnie stiffly. But, as Cartwright's car came nearer and nearer to the coroner's court, he realized that if by any possible miracle Hector Brunton were briefed for the prosecution, he, Ronald Cavendish, would trade on any one's reputation rather than not be entrusted with the defense.

4

By the peculiar processes of the English legal machine, a man or woman on trial for murder may be required to undergo no less than three ordeals: at the coroner's court, before the magistrate, and finally at the assizes.

Even before Cartwright's car came to a standstill outside the modest building of the coroner's court at Brixton, Ronald Cavendish could see tangible effects of Bertram Standon's publicity. The two bemedaled constables at the door were surrounded by a knot of people, well-dressed for the most part, all equally anxious for admittance to the first ordeal of Lucy Towers, and all equally ready to pay modest baksheesh for the privilege. Various alert youngsters, whose living depended on the news-pictures which their wits and their hand-cameras could snap, hovered—eager for the face of a celebrity—on the pavement. A touch of the theatrical was added to this scene by two sandwich-men, parading boards with the latest slogan of the "Democratic News": "Why not a Public Defender?"

Ronald and Cartwright pushed their way to the door; and—Cartwright having shown his card—were conducted down a long passage into the exiguous court-room. The jury, all males, had already taken their chairs. The coroner, a meek, tubby mid-Victorian fellow with a rosy bald head and a hint of port wine in his rosy cheeks—was just about to sit down.

One of Cartwright's henchmen, sent on in advance, came up, whispering that he had kept them seats at the back of the room. These, unobtrusively, they took.

So far, apparently, the state—to use Standon's phraseology—had not thought it worth while to brief counsel. At the table reserved for the prosecution Ronnie saw only a black-mustached uninterested solicitor and his clerk. The solicitor for the defense, a weak-kneed, unimposing little man, sat at the table opposite, looking even more bored. Only the reporters, bent over their note-books, and the few members of the public who had by now bribed themselves into the room, seemed in any way alive to the enacting of a human tragedy.

Then the coroner whispered something to his clerk, and the prisoners were brought in.

In that moment—despite the photographs—Ronnie thought himself the victim of hallucinations. "It's a dream," he thought; "a crazy nightmare." For the accused woman, accompanied on the one side by a hatchet-faced constable, and on the other by a tall prison-wardress in the blue cloak and cap of her order, might—had it not been for the work-reddened hands, the over-feathered hat and the rusty black coat and skirt—have been Aliette's self. Complexion, figure, carriage, personality, the very voice that answered to her name, showed Lucy Towers the living, breathing double of Hector Brunton's wife. She had the same auburn hair, the same vivid eyes, the identical nose, the identical mouth. There was about her, even, that same shy dignity which, in Ronnie's eyes, distinguished the woman he loved from all other women in the world.

"Not a bad-looking wench," whispered Cartwright.

But the barrister could not answer. Sheer amazement held him speechless. He had no eyes for the other guarded figure, for the pale unshaven young man whose two coat-sleeves hung empty from his broad shoulders. As it was to be throughout the case, so now at the very first glimpse of his client, every instinct urged him to her defense. He forgot Standon, Cartwright, his own career, everything. Seeing, not a woman of the lower orders, presumably the mistress of a common sailor, but his own woman, his Aliette, Aliette on trial for her life, lone save for his aid against a hostile world, he no longer wanted even the coroner's jury to convict her. He wanted her to be free. Free!

And suddenly, he hated the law. The law—policemen, wardress, coroner, jury, the little black-haired Treasury solicitor—wanted to hang this woman, to put a greasy rope round her throat, to let her body drop with one jerk into eternity. Against her, even as against Aliette, the law was hostile. And "They sha'n't hang her," swore Ronnie. "By God, they sha'n't."

With a great effort he pulled his legal wits together and began to follow the evidence. Deadly, damning evidence it was, too. The woman, according to the police, had already confessed.

"Bob didn't do it. I did it," began the confession which a sergeant, thumbing over his note-book, read out in a toneless voice. "Bob is my cousin. He lived in the same house as me and my husband, Bill. Every afternoon I used to go and clean Bob's room for him, because he couldn't do it himself, having no arms. Bill, my husband, didn't like me going to Bob's room. He was jealous of Bob. He didn't like me giving Bob money. This morning Bill told me that if I went to Bob's room again, he would do us both in. I told him I must go and help Bob, because he couldn't feed himself proper. I went to Bob's room about half-past four. I told Bob what my husband had said, and Bob laughed about it. He told me there was an old pistol in the cupboard and that if my husband came, I could pretend to shoot him. Of course Bob was joking. I got him a cup of tea. I was helping him drink the tea when my husband came in. Bill was very angry. He said he was going to thrash Bob, and then thrash me. I got very frightened, and thought of the pistol. Bill had his stick in his hand. I thought he was going to hit Bob with the stick, so I ran to the cupboard. I found the pistol and pointed it at Bill. I told him not to touch Bob. He said, 'That pistol's not loaded. You can't frighten me.' Bob said, 'Don't be a fool, Bill; it is loaded.' I thought Bill was going to strike Bob, so I pulled the trigger. I'm not sorry I killed Bill because I thought he was going to do Bob in. I love Bob very much."

"I love Bob very much." As those last words fell, heavy for all their tonelessness, on the hot hush of the crowded room, Ronald Cavendish knew—with the instinct of the born criminal lawyer—that coroner, jury, and public had already decided on their verdict. He could read condemnation, abhorrence, fear, in every eye that stared and stared at the pale forlorn creature seated motionless between her jailors. "The sailor was her lover," said those condemning eyes. "That was why she killed her rightly jealous husband." But for the armless man whose lips, as he listened, writhed in pain, those eyes held only pity.

Cartwright's voice whispered to his clerk, "You'll get a copy of that, of course," and the inquiry went on.

The police produced Bob Fielding's revolver, the blood-stained bullet, the empty cartridge-case, a plan of the room where the crime had been committed, Bob Fielding's navy record. The black-mustached solicitor called witnesses who had heard the shot, witnesses who had seen the body, one witness, even, who was prepared to swear the crime premeditated.

"More than once I've heard her say," swore Maggie Peterson, a frowzy, blowzy creature whose hands showed like collops of raw meat against her blowzy skirt, "that she wished Bill was dead. And there's others as heard her besides me."

In the case of Lucy Towers, the weak-kneed unimposing solicitor for the defense reserved his cross-examination, but for Fielding, to Ronnie's surprise, he put up a most spirited fight; and despite the prosecution's every effort to implicate the sailor as accessory to the shooting, the jury refused to give a verdict against him. "As if," decided the unimaginative jury, "armless men could fire pistols."

But Lucy Towers they found guilty of murder. "And quite rightly," said John Cartwright, as the woman—with a faint smile in the direction of her released cousin—was led from the room.

5

"All the same, mater, I'll swear that—in intention—Lucy Towers is innocent."

It was Sunday afternoon at Daffadillies, and ever since his arrival Ronnie had been harping on the same topic. But Ronnie found his womenfolk hard to convince. In their eyes, as in the eyes of the public, Fleet Street's report of the inquest, and more particularly Maggie Peterson's evidence, branded Lucy Towers irrevocably murderess.

"Rubbish!" said Julia—it was one of her "good" days—"Rubbish! She's guilty, and she'll either hang or go to jail for life."

"That would be an outrage," answered Ronnie gravely.

"Why?" The novelist laughed. "Lucy Towers shot her husband. She'll never get over that point. Not in England, anyway. In France it's just possible that a sentimental jury would give her their verdict. We, thank heaven, do not indulge in that sort of perverted justice."

Aliette reluctantly sided with Julia.

"But, of course, man," said Aliette, "of course, I'm sorry for the poor creature. Still, whatever her husband did, she had no right to shoot him."

"Not even in self-defense?"

"No, not even in self-defense."

"In defense of an armless man, then?" countered Ronnie; and, so countering, saw in one vivid flash of insight his one and only chance of victory should Cartwright give him the brief.

Chapter XXIX

1

"There is always," says Bertram Standon in his book "How I Fought Fleet Street," "a psychological news-moment. To be premature with news is even worse than to be dilatory with it. The editor who knows when not to publish is worth his weight in gold."

In the Towers-public defender stunt, the proprietor of the "Democratic News" backed his maxim to the limit. Clean through a newsless August, and well into a newsless September, he stirred the pool of the controversy he had started; whipped up every ripple of public interest to a wave of excitement over the guilt or innocence of Lucy Towers; but gave no hint of the rope he, Standon the Magnificent, intended to pull when finally the last act of the great drama should be launched upon London.

Even Ronnie, chafing for his chance, could ascertain no detail of the magnate's intention. Cartwright, pumped whenever etiquette allowed it, only beamed, "Wait and see!" Jimmy, who must have known something, had disappeared into Devonshire. At her second ordeal, the trial before the magistrate, Lucy Towers—still represented by the same unimposing solicitor—reserved her defense and was formally committed for trial at the Old Bailey.

Meanwhile Julia Cavendish worked on.

2

Physically and mentally, as day followed September day, Ronnie's mother felt well—better, indeed, than at any other period of her illness. The weapon of her forging grew sharp and sharper under her hand.

Despite the realization, every time she set pencil to paper, that the candle of her life was burning remorselessly to its socket, that her mind and her body must alike expire at task's completion, she experienced no fear. Her brain, rapt in the creative ecstasy of Julia Cavendish, living novelist, regarded Julia Cavendish, dying woman, from a point of view of the coolest detachment.

The Love-Story of Aliette Brunton

Outwardly, to her watchers, to Ronnie, nurse, Aliette, and Mrs. Sanderson, she played a part; the part of the convalescent. That they, in their ignorance, should believe the part she played to be real, gave to her detachment a whimsical and peculiar happiness.

And always in those days the illusion of immortality sustained her. She used to think, lying weary of work on her great bed: "Like Horace, I shall not utterly die. Dying, I shall leave my Ronnie this sword of the written word. What greater proof of love and service could any son or any god require?"

For now, almost at the end of her race with death, Julia Cavendish knew the conviction of Godhead. The priest-hoisted sectarian idol of her middle years lay shattered into a thousand fragments. In its stead was a spiritual Presence, all-pervading, all-comprehending, all-pardoning: an Individual of Individuals, to whom, freed from the slave-allegiance of the formal churches, each unhampered soul must fight its own unhampered way: a Soul of Souls who—despising no man-made creed—yet demanded more than any creed made of man, even the courage to look on life and death and Himself alike fearlessly.

But to that Godhead the soul of Aliette Brunton had not yet come. Her second honeymoon-time was over; Daffadillies no longer "Joyous Gard"; Ronnie no more the single-minded lover of July. Between them, like a wraith, hovered a man's ambition.

And, "If only—if only I could be with child," thought Aliette. "If only there could be given me one tiny mite of love—one human atom to be wholly mine." For always now—as it seemed—Ronnie and Ronnie's mother grew less and less dependent on her affection. To each was their work: to her only the waiting.

Ronnie's nerves, Ronnie's chafing after success, reminded her of Hector, of the Hector she had married. Every Monday morning, as she drove with him down the odorous country roads to West Water, his talk would be of Lucy Towers: "She's innocent, Alie. I'll swear she's innocent"; "If only I can get that brief, I'll be a made man"; "A made man, I tell you; Cartwright said so."

Rushing back to Daffadillies she used to think: "I'm selfish, selfish. I mustn't stand between him and his career. I must help him—help both of them." But at Daffadillies, demanding no help, resolute over her desk, sat Julia; and Aliette, looking up at the magnolia-sheathed window, would feel lonely; lonelier than ever before; so lonely that not even Ronnie's letters could console her through the desert week.

Yes! even his letters seemed less loving. Through every line of them she could feel the pulse and surge of a new desire—of the desire for success—which, if gratified, must leave her lonelier yet. Once she had cherished his letters at her breasts. But now her very breasts were a reproach; a reproach of childlessness. Once, laying her head among the pillows, she had dreamed of him beside her. But now, every night, her pillows were wet; wet with tears. Strange terrors tore her in the nighttime. She dreamed herself utterly outcast—the woman reproached of her own children—mother indeed, but mother-in-shame.

3

And then suddenly, a bare fortnight before the reopening of the Central Criminal Courts, Ronnie's dreams came true. John Cartwright himself brought round the brief, the long taped document marked on the outside:

Central Criminal Court. Session October.

Rexv.Towers. Brief for the Defense.

Mr. Ronald Cavendish. 50 gns. Conference 5 gns.

Wilberforce, Wilberforce & Cartwright, Norfolk Street.

"Standon jibbed a bit at that fifty," chuckled John. "He said you ought to take the case for nothing, considering the publicity he's going to give you."

"Oh, did he?" Ronnie laughed; but his nerves were quivering. "My whole career," he thought. "Riches—success—fame. It's all in my own hands now. Standon thinks he's overpaid me, does he? Perhaps he has. But I'll give him a run for his money. Fight! By Jove, I'll fight every foot, every inch of the way."

"I shall want an order to see the prisoner," he went on. "And, look here, if Standon's people can find out—" The cautious voice dropped; so that Benjamin Bunce, in the outer office, heard only a vague drone of talk.

"That'll be all right," answered the solicitor; and two days later a very different Ronnie caught the Saturday afternoon train to West Water.

"I'll get her off," he told Julia and Aliette, seated at tea under the cedar. "I'll get her off—or die in the attempt. This is my chance, I tell you. My big chance at last!"

"Optimist!" Julia laughed, a little wearily. "How can you 'get her off'? As far as I can see there's nothing in the woman's favor except that she's a little like our Aliette."

"A little like her! Mater, it's amazing. When I saw her yesterday, in that wretched place at Brixton, I could have sworn it was Alie." And he went on talking, talking, talking of "his chance" till the sun sank behind the cedar-tree; till—Julia, utterly tired out, having been carried into the house—Aliette interrupted him with, "I've been rather worried about her this week. Don't you think we might have Sir Heron down again?"

"We might see what she's got to say about it in the morning," answered Ronnie; but next morning, Sunday, the "Democratic News" drove all thoughts save one from his mind.

At long last, Bertram Standon had launched his journalistic thunderbolt. "Shall Lucy Towers hang?" howled Bertram Standon. "Never—if she be innocent—while we can prevent it. Never—if she be innocent—while there's a dollar in our purse or a sense of pity in our hearts. Let the state pour out the taxpayers' money like water—let the bureaucrats brief their 'hanging prosecutor' if they will. We, so far failing in our efforts to secure the appointment of a public defender, have briefed—out of our own pocket—a defender for Lucy Towers, a young man, an untried man, but a man in whom both we and the unfortunate woman in whose defense he will rise at the Old Bailey have the most unbounded confidence. And who is this young man? He is Ronald Cavendish—son of a woman who is known wherever the English language is spoken, of Julia Cavendish, our greatest woman novelist."

And squeezed away in the "stop press," so inconspicuous that Julia, who did not see the papers till tea-time, was the first of the three to notice it, stood the news: "Brixton Murder. Saturday night. The Crown has briefed Mr. Hector Brunton, K.C., for the prosecution of Lucy Towers."

4

Hector Brunton sat alone in his chambers at King's Bench Walk. Within the dusty book-littered room brooded silence. From without, from under trees already browning for a hint of autumn, sounded the occasional tup-tup of feet on the flagstones, the occasional staccato of a raised voice. The noises fretted Brunton, distracting his attention from the multitudinous papers prepared by the director of public prosecutions in the case of Rex *v.* Towers, which stood piled on his ink-stained desk. "I'm getting jumpy," he thought, turning from the signed and sealed findings of the coroner's jury, through the verbatim reports of the proceedings before the magistrate, to the actual indictment.

Concentrating, the K.C. reread the words of that indictment.

CENTRAL CRIMINAL COURT

THE KING V. LUCY TOWERS

Lucy Towers is charged with the following offense:

Statement of Offense: Homicide.

Particulars of Offence: Lucy Towers on the fifth day of July, in the County of Middlesex, murdered her husband, William Towers, by shooting him with a revolver.

Reading, an expression almost of mania flickered across Brunton's face. Behind the words of the indictment, his mind visualized the actual crime: the woman, some blowzy Messalina of the slums lusting horribly for a mutilated lover: the lover, a puppet in her adulterous arms: the husband, shot down in cold blood because he dared to come between the woman and her desires.

337

A fitting client—thought Brunton—for this other adulterer, this Ronald Cavendish with his gutter-press backing, to defend. But he would defend her in vain!

The K.C.'s long fingers prodded among the papers. Ever since the Cairns case, he had derived—subconsciously—a satisfaction, a secret chop-licking satisfaction, from his title of "hanging prosecutor." It was as though, harrying Mrs. Cairns to her death, he had taken his revenge on all women. And he thought: "Hilda Cairns escaped my rope. Lucy Towers shall not escape it."

Concentrating again, he reread the entire evidence. Outside it grew darker—silent. He switched on the opal-shaded reading-lamp; and sent David Patterson home. It was good—good to be alone with this chess-game of death: Messalina for its queen, his brain the mover of those pawns which would sweep her from the board.

Brunton's gray pupils shrank to pin-points. There were flaws, flaws in the evidence. The chess-board, as prepared by the solicitors for the Crown, lacked one pawn; the pawn of premeditation. Given himself, with his gift of oratory, to defend her, Lucy Towers might escape the black-cap sentence of the murderess.

Now the K. C.'s brain took the other side of the chess-board. He played the queen against himself; played her to the stalemate of "manslaughter." That would be Cavendish's gambit; a reduction of the charge.

But could Cavendish succeed?

For a long time Hector Brunton sat motionless, brooding; a cruel figure in the green glare of the desk-light. Then he drew the proof of Maggie Peterson's evidence from the paper pile; and, recasting it word by word, saw the rope tighten, tighten round his victim's neck, saw her drop feet first through the sliding floor.

God! but it would be good—good to know Cavendish beaten; to know him as incapable of defending this woman as of defending that other.

And at that, abruptly, the K.C.'s concentration snapped. The Furies were on him again, lashing at his loins, lashing him to blood-frenzy. He sprang to his feet; and his chair crashed backward as he sprang. This woman, this Lucy

Towers, must hang. Hang! Between him and his enemy, between him and the man whose body possessed Aliette, she, the Messalina of the slums, stood for a symbol. Destroying the one, he would destroy all three. This was his chance; his chance for revenge.

Vengeance at last! Too long Aliette and Cavendish had eluded him—eluded the torturer.

God! If only he could torture Aliette; torture her, not as he would torture this other woman when she stood before him in the witness-box, but physically. Of what avail was the law—the law that had reprieved Hilda Cairns from the rope, that left Aliette to revel unpunished in the arms of her paramour—the law that gave him, the wronged husband, no remedy for his wrongs save to set the woman who had wronged him free—free to marry her paramour, to flaunt herself as her paramour's wife before an uncensorious world?

The Furies were howling at him: "Don't set her free, Hector Brunton. Don't set her free! Get her back, Hector Brunton! Make her come back to you! Make her submit—submit her cold unyielding body to your hot desires. Make her your slave, your puppet—as the armless man was puppet of the woman you have sworn to hang."

With a great shock of self-disgust, of self-realization, Aliette's husband controlled his distraught brain. But his loins still quivered to memory of the lash; sweat beaded his forehead; his hands, as he lifted the overset chair, felt hot and clammy on the polished rail. For months he had succeeded in forgetfulness; in chasing the Furies from his mind. Work had helped him to forget—and Reneé, Reneé with her red and riotous hair, her facile, faithless sensuality. Other women too—facile, unfastidious.

Christ! but he was tired of it all. Tired! Work and women, women and work—month after month, the same eternal treadmill! Now he was weary; wearied alike of his work and his women. Remained in him only the one desire; the desire for vengeance. That desire he would satisfy. And after that?

What did it matter? He, Hector Brunton, knew the hollowness of all desires. Even in success, even in hatred, even in vengeance, could be no enduring satisfaction.

A great mood of self-pity submerged his mind. Fame, riches, every fruit of his up-reaching—he had won. And the choicest fruits left only a bitterness in his mouth. How could a man enjoy those fruits in loneliness?

Christ! but he was lonely—lonely. He hadn't even a friend. Not one single friend with whom to take counsel! Not one solitary being in all the world who would listen—as a friend listens—to—to the still, small scarce-articulate voice which had begun to whisper in Hector Brunton's soul.

That voice, the still small voice of conscience, was whispering now. "Cruel," it whispered; "cruel. Set her free. Set her free!"

Heavily Hector Brunton sat him down at his desk. His gray pupils stared vacantly at the light. He saw two faces in the light: his wife's face, torture-pale; and the face he imagined Lucy's, heavy-jowled, animal, yet with a hint of soul behind the animal eyes.

The two faces seemed to be pleading with him, pleading for pity. "We have known love," they pleaded, "but you—how should you understand?"

The faces vanished; and in their stead he saw Reneé—insatiate, submissive, her mouth still upcurled for his. "*I am love*," said the mouth of Reneé.

But always the still small voice of conscience whispered in Hector's soul. "Between love and lust," whispered the voice, "between the good and the bad that is in you, between the cruelty that cries for vengeance and the understanding which is pity—choose!"

Chapter XXX

1

For Ronald Cavendish, the fortnight which intervened between his briefing and the Monday of the trial passed like an hour. All that he had ever hoped for seemed at last within reach: and his mind, concentrating, could spare no minute for introspection. Even the personal factor, that Brunton would be his opponent, dwindled into insignificance when compared with the supreme issue of winning; even his belief in his client's spiritual guiltlessness seemed paltry before the difficulties of proving her technically innocent. Yet the belief was there, keying him to effort, making him utterly oblivious of his every-day surroundings.

But all that fortnight Aliette scarcely slept. Dozing or waking, two figures—the figures of Ronnie and of Hector—haunted her thoughts: she saw them, gowned and wigged, fiercely terrible, at death-grips for the soul of a woman—a woman whose face showed white and tormented in the dock—a woman who was no longer Lucy Towers, but herself. Sometimes, too, behind the woman in the dock, she saw Dennis—her dream-son—Dennis whose eyes, Ronnie's own blue eyes, stared accusingly at the mother who had born him to shame.

And all that fortnight, fearful only of interruption, Julia Cavendish worked on. The leather manuscript-box was nearly full. Almost, the weapon of her mind's conceiving had been forged sharp to the point. The watchers at her bedside—even her own son—were no longer quite real. She saw them as dream-folk; queer dear people who ministered to her comforts in the hours when her brain, weary of word-fashioning, rested awhile. Those dream-folk—she knew—all except Ronnie, were growing anxious, doubtful of the part she played to them. They wanted her to send for the "medicine-man." But the "medicine-man" could not help. His part was done. Only courage could help her now—courage and the certainty of that all-pervading Presence, of the Godhead who, watching her as she ran her painful race with physical death, understood.

Vaguely—when her son came to bid her au revoir—Julia Cavendish realized

341

the Presence hovering about the familiar room. Distant church-bells told her that it was a Sunday, that Ronnie must catch the afternoon train for London within the hour.

"Just looked in to see if you were all right, before I toddled off, mater," he said; and hearing his voice she yearned, with a foreknowledged longing acuter than any physical pain, to abandon the part she played for him, to tell him—for his own sake—the truth. But the Presence sustained her; so that she fought back the betraying truth; so that she answered him, gaily, casually, "I'm feeling like a two-year-old, son"; so that she sat upright in her bed—oh, for the comfort to have felt his arms about her shoulders!—and listened for twenty agonized minutes to his talk of "the case."

"You must wish me luck, mater," he said, as he rose to go. "It'll be a terrific fight; but I feel, somehow, that I'm going to win."

"You will win," she answered. "Don't worry about me. I'll be all right. And remember—if by any chance the verdict goes against you—that no man can do more than his best."

Yet after he had kissed her good-by, after the door had closed gently behind him, leaving her alone with her thoughts in the slanting sun-rays of that quiet room, even the knowledge that *she* had done her best, even the conviction of Godhead, failed to comfort Julia Cavendish, mother.

2

The Central Criminal Court of London, though still known as the "Old" Bailey, is the modernest of modern edifices; domed stone without, polished marble within. Were it not for the uniformed police on guard at its narrow portal, and for the particular legal atmosphere which pervades it even out of session-time, you might at first glance take the place for a club-house or a bank building. From the tessellated spaciousness of its ground floor, a central staircase, broad between marble balusters, up-sweeps to an immense landing where witnesses, constables, and barristers foregather outside the various oaken doors which lead into the oak-paneled court-rooms. Below are the cells.

There is nothing theatrical about the Old Bailey. To the highly sensitized mind its aura is the aura of a museum. The very statues which garnish it seem aloof from actual life. Yes here London stages her tensest human dramas; here England dispenses her ultimate justice.

But there was no sense of justice in the mind of Hector Brunton, K.C., as, scornful alike of the crowd and the cameramen, he strode bullheaded through that narrow portal; acknowledged with perfunctory hand the salutes of the constables; and pushed his way up the stairs, diagonally across the landing to the robing-room.

Deliberately the man had made his choice. For the sake of his vengeance on Cavendish, Lucy Towers must die the death. Righteous or unrighteous, he, the "hanging prosecutor" whom no prisoner had yet eluded, meant to secure his verdict. His mind, as he adjusted his robe, his wig and tapes, was the actor's mind, resolute in illusion. Actor-like, his thoughts discarded all truth that might tell in the victim's favor. Actor-like, his thoughts clung to their part; the part which should prove conclusively that this woman, this Lucy Towers, had shot her husband of malice aforethought and for love of another man.

And yet, making his early way through the crowd towards the door of the court—he had no wish to meet with Cavendish face to face in the robing-rooms,—a vision of his wife flashed for one vivid instant through the K.C.'s mind. In that vivid instant, conscience troubled him again. "Was he being cruel to Aliette?" asked conscience. "Was he planning yet another cruelty toward this woman he had never seen, this Lucy Towers?"

"Cavendish defends them both," he thought; and stifled the voice of conscience.

3

Ronald, when Caroline Staley woke him on that first morning of the trial, thought neither of Hector nor of Aliette. Hardly, he thought to himself. To win—and, now that the contest so long anticipated was actually at hand, he felt that not to win outright would be disaster—seemed almost impossible, the forlornest of hopes.

Dressing, breakfasting, making his way to Putney Bridge Station, his mind held only the picture of his client. Visited overnight, the woman—whose likeness to his own woman never failed to strike a responsive chord in Ronnie's heart—had afforded no help. Curiously resigned to an adverse verdict, curiously incurious as to whether that verdict should be murder or manslaughter, the tense clamor of the newspapers and the tense pleading of her counsel left her alike unmoved.

"I'll go into the witness-box if you like, sir," she had consented. "But I don't see what good it'll do. I can only tell them the truth. And I told them that at the police-station. I never was a liar, sir. I did it to save Bob."

"I did it to save Bob!" Those words still echoed in the barrister's ears as he emerged from the gloom of Temple station into sunlight, and turned down the Embankment toward his chambers, where—Bunce, brief and witnesses for the defense being already on their way to the court—John Cartwright alone awaited him.

The solicitor was in his gloomiest mood, thoroughly convinced of Lucy's guilt.

"Unless Brunton fails on the issue of premeditation," he said, "we haven't got a dog's chance. Even if he does fail on that point, she'll get seven years."

At that, poignantly, the human element of the case came home to Ronnie. It seemed to him as though he saw Aliette's self imprisoned, beating out her heart—day after day, month after month, year after year—against the cold walls and the cold bars of a prison-house.

"Not if I can help it," he said hotly.

"Have you decided to put her in the box? H. B.'s a holy terror for cross-examination."

"Of course I shall put her in the box. I'm not afraid of H. B.! Let's be off."

John Cartwright—thinking the tactics hopeless—would have protested; but, realizing from the other's demeanor how much this case meant to him, realizing (Ronnie's matrimonial position was common gossip in the offices of Wilberforce, Wilberforce & Cartwright) more than a little of the secret drama which underlay the public, he kept his own counsel all the way to the Old Bailey. "At any rate," thought John Cartwright, "Standon will get the show he's paying for."

It was fifteen minutes to ten by the time their car made Holborn; ten to when it drew up at the door of the court. Already they could see the forerunners of a crowd. Public sympathy, astutely roused by Standon, had enlisted itself on the side of the accused and of her counsel. In any other country, the little knot of people would have cheered. As it was, they only stared sympathetically while the cameras clicked and the two men disappeared from view.

"I'll see to the witnesses," said Cartwright, as the lift jerked them to the first floor. "You go and get dressed."

In the robing-room Ronnie found Hugh Spillcroft.

"I'm at a loose end," said that genial youth, "so I've come to watch the show. Going to win?"

"If I can," retorted Ronald grimly. "But it's going to be a devil of a job."

They passed out of the robing-room, and threaded their way across the crowded landing toward No. 2 court. By the outer door, its oak and glass guarded by two enormous constables, stood Bob Fielding and various other witnesses. The young sailor's face was gray. His whole body, even the two empty sleeves of the shabby coat, twitched.

"You'll do your best for her, sir?" he stammered. "You'll do your best for Lucy?"

"I'll do my utmost, Fielding," answered the tall, dignified man in the wig and gown, the man who was no longer either Aliette Brunton's lover or Julia Cavendish's son, but only an advocate whose brain, keyed to contest-pitch, resented any and every unnecessary strain on its concentration.

With the various other people who tried to detain him, more especially with Benjamin Bunce and Bertram Standon's secretary, Ronnie's manner was abrupt, irritable to the point of discourtesy. Knowing that he would need it all, he husbanded his self-control against the inevitable face-to-face meeting with Brunton.

"Time to toddle in," reminded Spillcroft.

One of the constables opened for them. Halting just inside the outer door, Ronnie could see, through the glass panels of the inner, the back of the great dock, light oak below, glass-and-iron paneled above; and beyond the dock, on the left of it, the already-occupied jury-box and the projecting canopy of the judge's dais. Then the outer door closed, the inner door opened, and they made their way in.

The domed court was a sight, every seat taken. There were ten tiers of curious heads behind the dock. On the low benches between dock and witness-box; in the high gallery opposite; and even below the gallery, among the bewigged counsel who crowded the benches reserved for the bar, lay spectators packed and packed. At the press table, the reporters sat so close to one another that their right arms could scarcely reach their note-books. But Ronnie had no eyes for the crowd; his eyes were all for his enemy.

Brunton sat very still, like a mastiff on watch, in the far corner of the front bench just below the three unoccupied thrones of the judge's dais. The gray eyes under the gray horsehair, fixed on the jury as though to hypnotize them, did not deign to notice the entrance of counsel for the defense. Nevertheless, Ronnie, taking his seat below the dock at the opposite end of the bench, knew instinctively that Brunton was aware of him.

Sitting, the barrister could no longer see his enemy. Henry Smith-Assher's vast Pickwickian back blocked his view. But the mental vision still remained; and with it, strengthening the will to win, came the first fierce gush of personal hatred.

"His lordship's late," whispered Spillcroft.

Ronnie, controlling himself, settled his back comfortably against the oak; glanced through his brief; and glanced up covertly from his brief at the jury. There were nine men and three women in the box. The men looked to be ordinary orderly citizens, apparently of the shop-keeping class, their faces bovine, their eyes unimaginative. Of the women, two were hard-featured, sour-faced spinsters whom he felt instinctively would be difficult to convince, and the third a fat, good-natured matron of five-and-forty, with a string of false pearls round her ample neck and a feathered hat on her jaunty head. He decided not to challenge any of them.

The click of an opening door disturbed further scrutiny; and a moment later there appeared, on the right of the judge's dais, a man's figure in full court dress—silk stockings on his legs, lace ruffle at his throat, and sword at his side—who ushered in his lordship, robed in the scarlet and ermine of full ceremonial, and, following his lordship, two portly creatures in aldermanic robes, chains of office round their necks.

"Silence!" called the crier of the court.

Rising to his feet, Ronnie felt the tense pull of the crowd. The crowd expected him to speak; expected oratory of him. Supposing he were to fail them! The tongue felt like leather in his mouth. His mind blurred. He forgot every detail of the case. To sit down again, to fumble among the papers on the desk in front of him, was positive relief.

The crier of the court began swearing in the jury. One by one the nine men and the three women rose from their places, answering to their names and to the quaint old formula: "You shall well and truly try, and true deliverance make, between our sovereign lord the king and the prisoner at the bar, whom you shall have in charge, and a true verdict give according to the evidence." Last of all, from the back of the box, answered the fat and friendly matron.

"Quel chapeau!" whispered Hugh Spillcroft from behind; and a second later, as it seemed to Ronnie, he heard the sound of feet moving up the steps below the dock; and caught sight of Lucy's face pale above the pale oak.

Her gaze sought his trustfully; and at that precise moment Ronnie's ears, nervously attuned, were aware of the faintest gasp behind him, of the whistling breath-intake of a man shocked beyond self-control. Turning his head, he saw Brunton; Brunton—gray eyes staring, jowl a-twitch, teeth bit to the underlip.

To Brunton, startled almost out of his wits by the unexpected apparition; to Brunton with his preconceived idea of the blowzy slum-woman, it was as though Aliette herself stood before him; as though the wraith of her had materialized, Banquo-like, to fight for Cavendish. Then, as Lucy Towers, upright between wardress and constable, proud, dignified, aloof with Aliette's own aloofness, her brown head bare, her brown eyes unflinching, her hands—small as Aliette's own—gripping the edge of the dock, smiled down at Ronnie, the last least whisper of conscience was still in the K.C.'s soul; and he swore to himself that the very likeness of this woman to the wife who had deserted him should be her doom. "Vengeance," he thought. "Vengeance indeed!"

The crier of the court was reading the indictment. "Murdered her husband—William Towers—by shooting him," read the crier; and Brunton, watching his victim as a snake watches the bird, saw that her eyes, Aliette's own vivid eyes, were still on Cavendish.

"Prisoner at the bar, do you plead guilty or not guilty?"

"Not guilty, my lord," came Aliette's own shy voice.

And a moment afterwards, cool, self-controlled, pitiless, deadly sure of every deadly word, the "hanging prosecutor" rose to speak.

"My lord and members of the jury"—the man was all actor now, an actor keyed to cold genius by the hot urge of suppressed rage,—"you have already heard the indictment against this woman. It is an indictment on the charge of murder, the penalty for which is death. The actual facts of the case will not, I fancy, be disputed. Let me give them to you as briefly as I can. At about six o'clock on the afternoon of the fifth of July last, a police-constable on duty in Brixton heard the noise of a revolver-shot from No. 25 Laburnum Grove, a block of working-class flats.

"Entering these flats, the constable—as he will tell you in his evidence—found, in a room on the third floor, the prisoner and a man, a certain Robert Fielding, of whom the less said the better. At their feet, a bullet-wound through his heart, lay the dead body of the prisoner's husband, William Towers. In the woman's hand was a smoking revolver, one cartridge of which—and one only—had been fired.

"The constable arrested both the man and the woman. He took them to Brixton police-station. There, Lucy Towers, entirely on her own initiative, made a clean breast of the whole business. Her confession, which you will hear, is—I shall submit—even without the other evidence in possession of the Crown, sufficient to merit the rope."

Now, pausing, Brunton grew aware of his enemy. His enemy was eying him, quietly, dispassionately. For a second his concentration failed. Then, pitiless, the deadly speech flowed on.

"Such, members of the jury, are the actual undeniable facts. The defense has entered a plea of not guilty. After you have heard my evidence—evidence which in my contention proves conclusively not only the commission of this dreadful crime, but its dreadful motive—it will be for you to decide, subject to his lordship's direction, the issue between us.

"And at this point, before I go into the question of motive, I purpose, with his lordship's permission, to give you a brief, a very brief summary of the legal definition of homicide. Our English law divides the crime of homicide into three classes: justifiable or excusable homicide, manslaughter, and murder. It is of this last that I shall ask you, after duly weighing my evidence, to convict Lucy Towers.

"Murder, let me tell you, has been very aptly defined in the few words, 'Murder is unlawful homicide with malice aforethought.' It is the existence of malice which distinguishes this crime from justifiable or excusable homicide and from manslaughter. In order, therefore, to prove to you that this woman murdered her husband, I must demonstrate, as I shall demonstrate, not only that she shot him down with a revolver—a fact which I again remind you is not in dispute—but that she shot him down in cold blood and with malice aforethought. That is to say, that she had actually planned to kill him before—long before—the fifth of July. On this point, quite apart from the point of motive, we have incontrovertible evidence."

Again Brunton paused, conscious of his opponent; again, actor-like, Brunton's part went on.

"Malice aforethought, as his lordship will direct you, entails motive. Now, what was this woman's motive? Why did she kill her husband? Had she, in killing him, some ulterior object? It is my contention," the voice rose, "that she had such an object; that this woman," one gentlemanly finger pointed accusingly at the dock, "when she killed William Towers, her wedded husband, had one object, and one object only in her mind—to free herself from him, to free herself at all and any cost. Why?

"Members of the jury, it will be my duty, my very painful duty, to answer that question by proving that this woman, this Lucy Towers, is not only a murderess but an adulteress; that she had a lover, an illicit lover—none other than Robert Fielding, the very man in whose room this crime, this atrocious crime, was committed. I think"—Brunton's eyes dropped to the brief in front of him, and he began turning over the pages of it—"that after I have read to you the confession, the voluntary confession of the prisoner, you will admit that not only the crime but its motive stands proved, and proved up to the hilt, out of her own mouth."

So far, Ronnie—chin propped on one hand, the other busy with his notes—had listened, unmoved, to his enemy's opening. But now, suddenly, as Brunton read out, emphasizing every word that might tell against her, his client's confession; as he guessed from the very looks of the jury, from the very way in which they craned forward from their box, how deep an impression those words were creating in their minds; his heart misgave him, and he glanced up, as though for confirmation of her innocence, at Lucy.

Lucy Towers was eying Brunton, not as the fascinated bird eyes the snake, but as the slandered eyes the slanderer. In the white of her cheeks, color came and went by fitful flashes. Her mouth kept opening and closing, as though to give Brunton the lie. Once, when the harsh voice mouthed the end of her confession, "I love Bob very much," she would have started to her feet had not the wardress placed a restraining hand on her arm.

But in all that crowded court only Lucy's advocate and the wardress noticed Lucy. Judge, jury, spectators—all watched the "hanging prosecutor." He, and he alone, dominated the court by the sheer amazing flow of his oratory. For now Brunton had thrown aside the legal mask; now his every word came hot from his heart, from that heart which had made its choice between mercy and vengeance.

"My lord," rang the harsh voice, "my lord, members of the jury, can any

350

Gilbert Frankau

statement be more damnable, more damning that those words which I have just read to you? What need have I for eloquence, when this adulteress, this fallen woman," again his hand shot out, pointing to the prisoner in the dock, "whom my learned friend for the defense would have you find not guilty, has proved herself, out of her own mouth, Robert Fielding's strumpet? What need have I of witnesses to prove the malice, the lecherous malice which inspired this crime? What mitigation can any counsel put before you?

"Will he say that this crime was an accident? That it was an act of self-defense? Accident! This was no accident. Self-defense! This was no act of self-defense. It was murder, members of the jury, deliberate, cold-blooded murder.

"What need have I of witnesses? Yet I have witnesses—not one witness, but many witnesses—a witness who will prove to you that for weeks, for months, nay, for years before the perpetration of this crime, Robert Fielding had been amorous of his cousin—witnesses who will testify that this woman, almost since the day of her marriage, had been on the worst possible terms with her murdered husband—witnesses, unimpeachable, independent witnesses to whom she has admitted, not once but a dozen times, that she wished her husband dead.

"Members of the jury, we do not live in an age of miracles. When you know, as you already do know, that those wishes came true, and came true by her own hand—when you hear, as you will hear, of her clandestine visits, at dead of night to her lover's room—you will say to yourself, as I say to you now, 'This was no accident; no act of self-defense: this was murder, murder premotived and premeditated, the murder which our justice punishes with death.'

"A life for a life, your lordship. A life for a life, members of the jury. That is the penalty which, on behalf of the Crown, I shall demand against this woman whom counsel for the defense would have you find not guilty of any crime whatsoever."

Slowly Hector Brunton's eyes turned from the woman in the dock toward his enemy; till even Ronnie shrank before the vindictive fury in those gray and glimmering pupils.

"This is the man," muttered the voiceless soul behind those grayly glimmering eyes, "this is the man who stole your woman; the man who dares defend this other adulteress against you." But the words, the words planned overnight, never faltered on Brunton's lips. For all his fury, his legal mind, functioning automatically, missed never a point.

The clock-hands crept on and on. In the packed courtroom was no sound save the scratch of the shorthand-writers' fountain pens, the tap-tap of the gentlemanly fingers on the oak, the harsh interminable harangue. Till at last the harangue slowed to its peroration; and passion ebbed from Brunton's voice, leaving it once more cool, deadly, pitiless.

"If I," rang the cool, deadly voice, "if I, the paid advocate of the Crown, have spoken in anger, rarely it is just anger. Surely, in this England of ours, adultery which leads to murder—as this woman's adultery has led to murder—will find none to excuse, none to condone it. Surely, the quality of mercy was overstrained when another court let this woman's paramour go free.

"Members of the jury, that woman in the dock, that adulteress, shot her husband. She shot him down in cold blood, of malice aforethought and after due deliberation. It is for you, as just citizens, to see that she does not escape the uttermost penalty of her guilt."

The harsh voice ceased.

Brunton, with one last glance at the woman in the dock, a glance commingled of fear and triumph—for now, once again, he saw her as Aliette, a ghost siding with the man who had betrayed him—sat down; and Henry Smith-Assher, rising, began to call the stereotyped, commonplace evidence entrusted to a junior counsel.

Ronnie hardly listened. The production of the revolver, the testimony of the constable who had made the arrest, the plan of the room—none of these mattered. Mattered only Brunton—Brunton whose eyes never left the jury—Brunton whose deadly oratory had closed every loophole of escape save one.

But just before the luncheon interval, when the sergeant who had taken down Lucy's statement kissed the book and began his tale in the usual toneless voice of the police, Cartwright—watching counsel for the defense—saw his hands busy with the pencil; and knew that—luncheon interval over—the real fight would begin.

4

Usually barristers at the Old Bailey lunch communally in the mess-room; sometimes in private, with the judge. But to-day no invitation came from his tactful lordship; and, since Brunton might be in the mess-room, Ronnie elected for the near-by "George."

Emerging disrobed from the court, Hugh Spillcroft on his one side and Cartwright on his other, he was again aware of the crowd. The little knot of idlers had increased. On the opposite side of the road, newspaper placards—black on red of the "Evening Standard," black on white of the "Evening News," black on green of the "Westminster Gazette," already flaunted their slogans: "TOWERS CASE: SPEECH FOR THE CROWN." "HANGING PROSECUTOR OPENS TOWERS CASE." "TRIAL OF LUCY TOWERS BEGUN."

The placards worried Ronnie; they seemed to accentuate the forlornness of his cause. All through their hasty meal, snatched at a corner-table of the crowded chop-house, he felt himself growing more and more nervous, less and less confident of success. Spillcroft's conversation and Cartwright's irritated him. Their interest was so coldly legal. They spoke of Lucy Towers, of himself and Brunton, as men who have betted well within their means speak of race-horses.

"H. B.'ll have you on toast if he proves adultery," decided Spillcroft.

"Do as you like, of course; but I shouldn't risk putting the woman in the box," urged Cartwright. "I should plead 'manslaughter' and have done with it."

"Thanks for the suggestion," fumed Ronnie. "I thought I was being paid to *fight*."

"Good for you! Try one of these." Cartwright, laughing, offered him a small cigar: "Nothing like tobacco for a fighting man."

Smoking, Ronnie visualized Brunton, gray eyes staring, jowl a-twitch, teeth bit to the under lip; Brunton as he had seen him when Lucy Towers first entered the dock. And visualizing, realizing the shock that amazing likeness must have been, he could not help admiring the man. Brunton, startled at the very moment of tensest concentration, had yet managed to make the speech of his life, missing never a legal point in two hours of impassioned argument. How could he, the poor orator, compete with such a man; how prove any flaw in the "hanging prosecutor's" thesis that Lucy Towers, adulteress, shot her husband so that she might marry her paramour?

"Ten minutes to two," said Cartwright, paying the bill.

5

Reëntering the crowded court, Ronnie saw that Brunton was already seated. The K.C., turning from conference with his junior, darted one look at his opponent; that same look, compound of fear and obstinacy, of injured pride and determination for revenge, of the weak man who knows himself in the wrong and means to persist in his wrong-doing, which Ronnie had noted on the day when he pleaded for Aliette's freedom.

Forcibly the personal issue obtruded on Ronnie's mind; and he could not help speculating, as Mr. Justice Heber took his seat, whether that ermined figure, whose gleaming spectacles turned this way and that, to the police-sergeant reëntering the box, to the jury, to Henry Smith-Assher rising to continue his examination-in-chief, and lastly to the motionless woman in the dock, knew anything of the fight for another woman's freedom, of the private quarrel between counsel for the prosecution and counsel for the defense.

"May we take it, then," Henry Smith-Assher fidgeted with the tapes round his bull-neck, "that the accused's statement was entirely voluntary?"

"Entirely," answered the witness, obviously honest, and as obviously convinced of the prisoner's guilt.

"Thank you, sergeant, that's all I have to ask you."

Henry Smith-Assher subsided; and Ronnie—his voice vibrating with suppressed nerves, but all issues save the immediate driven from his mind—rose to cross-examine.

"I want you to tell me, sergeant, whether the original suggestion that the accused should make a statement came from you or from her?"

"From the accused."

"You cautioned her, of course?"

"Yes."

"Did she, at the time she made the statement, appear much upset?"

"Considerably, I should say."

"Ah." Ronnie—one hand spread-eagled on his brief, jingled with the other at the coins in his trouser-pocket. "Then I should not, perhaps, be putting it too strongly if I suggested that at the time she made this so-called confession the accused was in a state of hysteria?"

"She was considerably upset," repeated the witness stolidly.

"Was she crying?"

"Well—"

"Answer the question, please."

"She might have been crying."

"H'm." Again the coins jingled in the trouser-pocket. "Did you gather from her general demeanor that the accused was attempting to tell you the exact truth?"

"Yes."

"And, coming to the last words of her statement, 'I love Bob very much,' did you gather from the way accused made that statement that Robert Fielding was her lover, in the accepted sense of the word?"

The uniformed witness hesitated; and Ronnie, his nerves for the moment forgotten, took advantage of the hesitation. "I want you to tell his lordship and the jury, sergeant, whether, when the accused volunteered this statement to you, the impression made on your mind was the impression that she had been guilty of adultery with her cousin, Robert Fielding."

"I can't say I thought very much about it."

"You can't say you thought very much about it? Exactly. Didn't you think, perhaps, as any reasoning man would think, that all the accused meant to imply was that she was very fond of her cousin?"

"Yes. I suppose so."

"Thank you. I'll take that answer."

The next witnesses were the medical experts—Dr. Spilsbury and Dr. Wilcox. Them Ronnie did not cross-examine. But as Maggie Peterson, answering instantly to the call of her name, flounced through the glass doors and made her defiant way past the reporters' table to the box, John Cartwright—watching counsel for the defense as a trainer watches his man in the ring—saw his mouth set, his chin protrude. And John Cartwright thought, "I wonder if I was right about briefing Cavendish. I wish I knew what he was driving at with that last cross-examination. I wonder what he'll make of this witness. From the look in H. B.'s eyes, she's the crux of his case."

Lucy Towers, too, seemed to realize the importance of Maggie Peterson's evidence. Again, as during Brunton's opening, aloofness went from her. She leaned forward from the dock.

"You're a married woman, Mrs. Peterson?" Hector Brunton in person rose to examine the blowzy black-eyed creature who had just kissed the well-thumbed book.

"I am."

"And at the time when Lucy Towers shot her husband you were living at 25 Laburnum Grove?"

"I was."

"Could you tell us the date of the shooting?"

"The fifth of July."

"Were you actually in the house when the crime took place?"

"I was not." The patness of the cockney woman's answers warned Ronnie that she must have been coached in her part. It seemed to him, listening to her every carefully-pronounced syllable, that a purpose, a definite, a personal, and a premeditated purpose, underlay them.

"For how long before the fifth of July had you been living at Laburnum Grove?" went on Brunton.

"Two years."

"Had you known Mr. and Mrs. Towers for some considerable time?"

"I had. And Bob Fielding."

"Confine yourself to answering my questions, please. For how long had you know William Towers and his wife?"

"Eighteen months. Ever since they came to live at the Grove."

The K.C. paused, and looked warningly at the jury before putting his next question. "Then can you tell us, of your own knowledge, whether, during those eighteen months, the accused was on good terms with her husband?"

The woman—purposely as it appeared to Ronnie—hesitated; and Brunton, leaning forward, altered his formula. "Did they, as husband and wife, get on well with one another?"

"Well, I shouldn't like to say they was on the best of terms."

"Were they on bad terms?"

"Yuss." The voice, hitherto so careful, lapsed into slum cockney. "Yuss. She was a bad wife to Bill, was Lucy. Never did nothing for him."

At that his lordship made as though to put a question, and the examiner changed his line. "Now I want to ask you: have you ever heard the dead man complain about his wife?"

"Not till Bob Fielding came to live at the Grove."

"But after Robert Fielding came, he did complain about her?"

"Yuss, often."

"Can you tell us the sort of thing he used to say?"

"Yuss. He said that he could never get nothing done because she was always muckin' about with Bob."

With any other examiner except Brunton, the coarse phrase would have elicited laughter from the spectators. But Brunton was taking no chances. Quickly he carried on his witness's story.

"You gathered then, I take it, that William Towers was not satisfied with his wife's behavior?"

"Satisfied?" The black eyes under the feathered hat glinted. "Nah. He wasn't never satisfied, with 'er. Not after Bob Fielding came to the Grove."

"Would you describe William Towers as jealous of Robert Fielding?"

"Nah. Not jealous, but suspicious."

"Suspicious, eh? Had he, to your knowledge, any reasons for that suspicion? Have you personally, for instance, ever seen any act on the part of the accused which might give rise to suspicion in her husband's mind?"

"Well—" Again it seemed to Ronnie, weighing every inflection of the cockney voice, that both the hesitant monosyllable and the answer which followed it were premeditated. "Well, I've seen her going to 'is room often enough."

"Whose room?"

"Bob Fielding's."

Brunton paused to study his brief; and in that pause it came home to Ronnie that the whole atmosphere of the court was hostile. The domed place seemed charged with psychical electricity. He could actually feel the currents of fear and prejudice tingling between the motionless jury and the motionless figure in the dock. Looking at his client, he saw that her lips moved, as though in dumb, unavailing protest.

"And these visits"—the "hanging prosecutor" did not even look up from his brief,—"were they paid by night or by day?"

"She was alwus going to 'im."

"By night as well as by day?"

"Yuss. By night as well as by day."

"What time of the night?"

"All hours of the night."

"You're certain on that point?" Now Brunton looked at his witness.

"Yuss, certain."

"Then can you give us any particular date on which you actually saw the accused woman go into Bob Fielding's room late at night?"

"She went there about half-past nine on the night of July 4th."

"And did you see her come out?"

"Nah. She hadn't come out by the time I went to bed."

"The night before the murder. Thank you, Mrs. Peterson." Brunton smiled grimly. "And now, just one more question. Has the accused ever spoken to you about her husband?"

"Yuss."

"When was the last time she spoke to you about him?"

"On the Sunday."

"What Sunday?"

"The Sunday"—Maggie Peterson's voice shrilled—"before she shot 'im."

"Please tell his lordship and the jury, to the best of your recollection, what she said to you."

The hard eyes of the woman in the witness-box turned to the woman in the dock. For a full second they looked at one another; and Ronnie, watching, saw that it was Maggie Peterson who first turned away.

"Tell his lordship and the jury," prompted Brunton.

"Well"—a fraction of its certainty had gone out of the shrill voice,—"it was like this. We meets in the passage, and she says to me: 'Bill ain't fit to be no woman's 'usband. I wish to Gawd 'e was dead. I shan't never know a moment's 'appiness till he is dead.'"

"And had the accused previously made, in your presence, similar statements?"

"Yuss. Time and again."

"Thank you. That will be all."

Hector Brunton sat down; but before Ronnie could rise to cross-examine, the judge had intervened.

"You say," said the judge, referring to his notes, "that on the night before the crime was committed, at about half-past nine o'clock, you saw the accused go into Robert Fielding's room. Was she—to your personal knowledge—in the habit of making such visits?"

"Yuss, m'lord."

"You're prepared to swear that?"

"Yuss, m'lord."

"Very well." Deliberately, Mr. Justice Heber wrote down the answer. "Now, on the night of July 4, you're prepared to swear that you actually saw the accused"—the legal voice was stern—"go into Robert Fielding's room; and you are also prepared to swear that by the time you went to bed, she had not come out."

"Yes, m'lord."

"Where were you at the time you saw all this?"

"I was standing in the passage—"

"What passage?"

"The passage between her room and mine."

Mr. Justice Heber relapsed into a meditative silence; and Ronnie, looking across the thirty feet of crowded space which separated him from the hard defiant eyes of Maggie Peterson, rose nervously to his feet.

"You told my learned friend"—the suave tone betrayed no hint of hostility—"that you are a married woman. Are we to understand from that that you and your husband live together?"

"No."

"I take it, then, that you are legally separated—"

"My lord, I protest." Instantly Brunton, too, was on his feet. "My learned friend is not entitled to cross-examine—"

"My lord, I submit," instantly, counsel for the defense took up the challenge, "that on the question of credibility I am entitled—"

The judge allowed the question, and Brunton, muttering, subsided.

Yes, admitted Maggie Peterson, she was separated from her husband.

"And you told his lordship"—his first victory over the enemy made Ronnie suaver than ever—"that you occupied the room opposite to that in which the accused lived with her husband. Can I take it, from that, that you were—and still are—on friendly terms with the accused?"

The witness faltered. "Well, she and me used to speak to one another when we met."

"Then you neither were nor are on particularly good terms with the accused. Now, were you on friendly terms with the accused's husband?"

Again the witness faltered, and Ronnie repeated his question. "I put it to you that you were not on friendly terms with Lucy Towers, but that you were very friendly with William Towers."

"Not very friendly. We were just neighbors."

"Just neighbors, eh?" For the first time since Maggie Peterson had entered the witness-box, Ronnie felt the atmosphere of the court favorable. The jury, and more especially the three women on the jury, had obviously taken his lucky point. He pressed it home: "You say the accused told you, some days before the crime, that she would never be happy until her husband was dead. Why should she tell you that if you and she were not on friendly terms?"

"I dunno," sulkily; "she just said it."

"Are you prepared to swear that those were the actual words she used?"

"Yuss," defiantly, "I am."

"Then if I put Mrs. Towers in the witness-box, if she denies on oath that she made any such statement to you, she will be guilty of perjury?"

"Well—"

"I want an answer to my question. If Mrs. Towers denies, on oath, that she made any such statement, will she or you be guilty of perjury?"

"Well," the red hands shifted on the rail of the witness-box, "I wouldn't care to say she used those actual words. But that was what she meant."

"You realize that what you are saying is of very grave importance?"

"Yuss."

"But you abide by what you have told us about the conversation between you and the accused?"

"Yuss."

Question and answer went on; till Maggie Peterson, gazing angrily at her interrogator, saw a black-coated figure move to his side.

"What the devil—" Ronnie, feeling a twitch at his gown, turned to see Bunce, all agog with excitement.

"Chap at the back of the court, sir, says you're to look at this before you ask any more questions."

The Love-Story of Aliette Brunton

Benjamin Bunce, having delivered himself of his message and a scrap of soiled paper, slipped away. Ronnie, taking no further notice of the interruption, continued his attempts to shake Maggie Peterson's evidence. But the witness had grown sullen. His suavity elicited only monosyllables. He felt the jury wearying, growing hostile once more—felt himself outwitted—felt it useless to continue the struggle.

Then, just as he was preparing to sit down, his left hand, fidgeting with his notes, touched the scrap of paper which Bunce had laid among them; and glancing down, he saw: "M. P. is a bloody liar. I can tell you something about what she was doing on the fourth of July."

Ronnie looked round for his clerk, but his clerk had disappeared. The ermined figure on the bench was growing bored.

"If you have no further questions to ask this witness—" began the ermined figure.

Maggie Peterson grinned. And suddenly Ronnie knew panic. Either he must close his cross-examination; or risk a shot in the dark. For a second he made as though to sit down; then, seeing some emotion almost akin to reproach flit across the pale face of his client, he took his risk.

"You told both my learned friend and his lordship that at half-past nine o'clock on the fourth of July—I want you to be very careful of the date, please—you saw the accused go into Robert Fielding's room. You are still prepared to swear, on your oath, that that statement is the truth, the whole truth, and nothing but the truth?"

"Yuss"—shrilly, but there was a trace of fear in the shrill.

"And supposing—mind you, I'm only supposing—that a witness were to come forward and say that, on the night in question, you could not possibly have seen any such thing, that witness would not be telling the truth?"

"What do yer mean?"

"I should have thought it was sufficiently obvious," said Ronnie gravely; and repeating his question knew, by the very look on the witness's face, that his shot in the dark had found its mark.

"I've told yer all I know," retorted Maggie Peterson stubbornly.

"Possibly more." Ronnie, warming to a subdued chuckle from Spillcroft, ventured one more question. "Tell me, please, what you did after you had—as you say—watched the accused woman go into her cousin's room?"

"Went to bed, of course."

"Then you were in bed by a quarter to ten?"

"I suppose so."

"Not later than ten o'clock, anyway?"

"No."

"Thank you." Ronnie turned to the judge. "That is all I have to ask this witness, m' lord."

To the woman in the box, it seemed that her ordeal was over; to the jury, that the bulk of her evidence remained unshaken. But Brunton—reëxamining at length—was obviously suspicious of a trap. He kept on glancing at Ronnie as though to find out what had prompted those last questions; and Ronnie, as though hiding some secret, kept on refusing to meet the glance.

"I shall adjourn till ten o'clock to-morrow," said his lord-ship—reëxamination concluded.

Sweeping his scornful way out of court, the "hanging prosecutor" deigned yet another glance at his enemy. But his enemy's eyes did not look up: they were still glued to that little scrap of paper which he had spread out on his brief.

Chapter XXXI

1

Walking back alone to the "ridiculous flat," Ronald Cavendish was oppressed with a sense of his own inefficiency. Even though his intuitive suspicions about Maggie Peterson's honesty had been to a very large extent confirmed by that piece of paper, the author of that piece of paper could not be found. Bunce, bullied to remember who had given him the document, thought it was "a common-looking kind of fellow." Cartwright, told, had said skeptically, "Those sort of things always happen in murder-trials. I'd forget it if I were you." But Ronnie could not forget.

Halting under the light of a street-lamp, he drew the paper from his pocketbook and reread it for the twentieth time. If only he could succeed in discrediting the Peterson woman. Yet, even if he did succeed in discrediting Maggie Peterson, in nullifying her evidence as to motive, Brunton—according to his opening—had other witnesses.

Walking on, he bought an evening paper. The paper reported Brunton's speech verbatim. Curse Brunton! What an orator the man was. Listening to him, one could hardly imagine Lucy Towers anything but the murderous adulteress.

2

Caroline Staley had prepared the usual faultless dinner; but her master ate hardly anything. In his mind, he went over Maggie Peterson's evidence, weighing it word by word. Obviously the woman hated Lucy Towers; obviously, almost obviously, she had had some sort of relations, probably immoral relations, with the dead man. But how the devil could one prove that? Even proved, how did it advance matters? If only Bunce hadn't been such an infernal fool. If only Brunton weren't such an infernally fine orator. Curse Brunton!

Half a bottle of claret and a cigar only added to Ronnie's depression. Alone in the drawing-room where he and Aliette had so often sat together, he felt as though, failing Lucy Towers, he would fail his own woman; as though the

364

fate of Lucy and the fate of Aliette were one fate; as though, by not saving the one from Brunton's hideous cleverness, he would never rescue the other from Brunton's hideous obduracy.

Brunton! The man's face traced itself, bewigged, implacable, relentless, in every up-curling puff of Ronnie's cigar-smoke. Behind that face hovered the faces of the jury. And the jury stood for public opinion; public opinion solid on Brunton's side. In his fight against Lucy Towers, as in his fight against his wife, Brunton had the world's judgment in his favor: yet both women—"*both*," repeated conviction—were innocent, at least in intent, of anti-social crime.

A hell of a lot "intent" mattered to Hector Brunton!

If only Hector Brunton were dead! If only for Aliette's sake, for Lucy's sake, he, Ronald Cavendish, could kill Brunton as William Towers had been killed! Surely that killing would be not murder, but justice. For more than a year Brunton, moved only by blind vanity, had been striving to compass the ruin of a woman against whom his only grudge was that she had denied herself to him. Now, moved by the same blind motive, he was striving to compass the ruin and the death of Lucy Towers. Between those two women and the tyrant who oppressed them stood but one man. Himself—Ronald Cavendish. Surely the killing of Brunton would be no murder!

The little mood of madness passed. Resolutely Ronnie put the personal issue out of mind. Resolutely he fetched his papers from his dressing-room and set himself to study the reports of the trial before the magistrate. If only he could discredit Brunton's evidence on the question of adultery, surely there was a chance, just the shadow of a chance, to secure the coveted verdict, justifiable homicide.

"But I'd need to be an orator for that," he thought; and all night, tossing sleepless, visions flickered across the taut screen-board of his brain. Alternately he saw Aliette, Lucy, his mother—sad faces, each oppressed, each pleading for deliverance.

Yet next morning, as he emerged from Temple Station and made his way along the Embankment to his chambers, Ronald Cavendish's self-confidence returned. And the self-confidence increased fourfold when Bunce, rather shamefaced, handed him yet another scrap of paper.

"Found this in our letter-box, sir," said Bunce.

Deciphered, the sprawly disguised handwriting read: "I seed her in the Red Lion, Hill Street, with Bill T. Time 10:15 pip emma. She's a bitch. I ought to know. I married her."

This time even John Cartwright thought the information of value. "Though I don't see how you can use it," he said dubiously. "Unless Standon's people can find this fellow Peterson for us."

"I sha'n't need Peterson," decided Ronnie, as their car swung them down Holborn. "He probably has his own reasons for keeping out of the way. A witness from the public-house will be enough. Will you send some one down at once? The fourth of July, luckily, is American Independence day. Some one's sure to remember if Towers was there on that particular night, and who was with him."

The solicitor, dropping his passenger at the Old Bailey, drove off hurriedly.

Public interest in the case had not diminished overnight. Already the early street crowd numbered hundreds. On the great staircase, on the wide landing, folks seethed and jostled. The packed court-room itself—as the dignified figures of Mr. Justice Heber and his accompanying big-wigs took their seats—was a lake of straining faces.

Immediately Brunton rose to examine his next witness; a tall black-mustached, black-haired type with flashy rings and a flashy tie-pin, who answered to the name of John Hodges.

He was a book-maker, John Hodges told the court. He had known Bill Towers for many years—long before he married. He had often heard the dead man speak of his wife. The dead man had been very fond of his wife; but the affection, according to Hodges, had not been reciprocated.

Question and answer flowed on. But to Ronnie, waiting anxiously for Cartwright's return, it seemed as though Brunton must be ill. Twice the harsh voice missed the sequence of its questions. Twice Henry Smith-Assher had need to prompt his leader. And twice, as the examination neared its ending, the gray eyes under the "hanging prosecutor's" gray horsehair deserted their witness to stare, fascinated, at the woman in the dock. Lucy Towers, it seemed to Brunton, stared back at him with his wife's own brown unfathomable pupils.

"You've known the accused ever since she married the deceased?" he asked his witness. "Has she ever spoken to you about her husband?"

"Only once."

"Can you remember what she said?"

"Yes. She said that she wished she'd never married him."

"When was that?"

"Some time in June."

"Can't you fix the exact date?"

"No, not the exact date. It was somewhere about the end of June, I think."

"Thank you." Heavily Hector Brunton sat down. All night the face of the woman in the dock had haunted him. And now, now the still, small voice of conscience was whispering again. "Cruel," whispered the voice; "cruel." But the sight of Cavendish, rising to cross-examine, silenced the voice of conscience, brought back the suspicion that Cavendish held some card, some trump-card, up his sleeve. And "Even if he gets the charge reduced to manslaughter," thought Brunton, "she'll do time. She won't be able to trouble me for years. Say seven years."

"Mr. Hodges"—Ronnie's voice recalled his enemy to the actualities,—"when the accused made this statement to you, were there any other people present?"

"Yes."

"Will you please tell his lordship and the jury who else was present."

"Bill Towers, of course."

"Why 'of course'?"

"Well, naturally he wouldn't leave another man alone with his wife."

"He was jealous of her, eh?"

"Jealous!" The rings flashed. "I should just about say he was jealous."

"Ah!"—Ronnie's coins jingled—"and did this jealous husband make any comment on his wife's remark?"

"No."

"Wasn't that rather curious? Now tell me, did you gather, from the way you allege the accused spoke, that she meant her statement seriously?"

"I thought she was serious."

"Oh, you did, did you? Please tell me something else. Are you prepared to inform his lordship and the jury that your impression at the time was that it was the accused's intention to kill her husband if ever she got the chance?"

"Well, I shouldn't like to go so far as, to say that."

"Naturally not. Now listen." Ronnie leaned forward; and his gaze traveled towards the jury. "I put it to you that the remark was meant as a joke."

"Well, not exactly a joke."

"Come, come, Mr. Hodges," said Ronnie, and his tone was a shade less suave than his words, "you're a man of the world. You must have realized at the time whether the accused was speaking seriously or not.'

"I thought she was serious." The book-maker, though obviously flustered, stuck to his guns.

"Very well. We'll leave it at that. The accused told you, in her husband's presence, that she wished she'd never married him. Her husband, apparently, didn't take any notice of the remark. But you thought it was serious. Not very convincing—but still—"

Ronnie's question trailed off into a sarcastic silence. Looking sideways at Brunton, he could see that Brunton was troubled; Brunton kept talking to Smith-Assher, kept fidgeting with his gown and tapes, with the pencils and paper in front of him. The sight gave Ronnie confidence. He continued his cross-examination.

"You told my learned friend that, although William Towers was very fond of his wife, his affection was not reciprocated. How did you know that? Did she tell you?"

"No."

"Did William Towers tell you?"

"No."

"Then who did tell you?"

"Well, it was common gossip."

"Gossip!" Ronnie jumped on the word. "Where?"

"Oh, all over the place."

"Ah!" Counsel for the defense jingled two thoughtful coins. "I'm afraid I don't know Brixton very well, Mr. Hodges. Tell me, please, when you say all over the place, do you include," more jingling in the trouser-pocket, "a certain public-house called—'The Red Lion'?"

"Well—" the witness hesitated.

"Let me put my point clearly. Do you know, in Brixton, a public-house called 'The Red Lion'?"

"Yes."

"How far is that public-house from 25 Laburnum Grove?"

"About half a mile."

"Shall we say about ten minutes' walk?"

"Yes. That's about it."

Obviously the judge was puzzled. "Mr. Cavendish," he intervened, "I'm afraid I don't quite follow."

"M' lord," every syllable of Ronnie's fell with its distinct emphasis, "the point is of vital importance in connection with the evidence of a previous witness." And he went on swiftly to ask the book-maker, "Do you know a woman called Maggie Peterson?"

"Oh, yes." The white teeth under the black mustache parted in a grin. "Oh, yes, I know her quite well."

"Mrs. Peterson told us in her evidence that she was a friend of the deceased. Is that true?"

"Oh, yes, they were quite friendly."

"Very friendly?"

"Yes."

"Ah!" Ronnie, glancing covertly at the jury, saw a little ripple of excitement pass over the stolid faces of the men. Behind him, among the barristers, he could hear excited breathing. "Now, just one more question, Mr. Hodges, and then I have finished with you. Have you ever seen Mrs. Peterson in company with William Towers at 'The Red Lion'?"

"M' lord"—Brunton, scruples and caution thrown to the winds, leaped upright,—"I protest at this attempt to cast aspersions—" But Mr. Justice Heber, who had now taken Ronnie's point, allowed the question; and John Hodges, reluctantly, answered it with a "Yes."

The K.C.'s attempt, in reëxamination, to prove the disinterestedness of the book-maker, added to Ronnie's elation. If only Cartwright succeeded in securing that evidence—

But Brunton's examination of the next witness pricked the bubble of his opponent's momentary elation. The "hanging prosecutor" was fighting again, fighting as he had never battled in his life, for a conviction. The gray eyes no longer dared look at the dock; the woman in the dock, thought Brunton, was the woman who had wronged him, the creature he must destroy.

"I swear to speak the truth, the whole truth, and nothing but the truth," said James Travers, a big blond seafaring man whose square-shouldered bulk almost filled the witness-box. And he spoke the truth according to his lights. A story deadly enough, even without Brunton's prompting. He and Bob Fielding had been shipmates during the war. Bob Fielding had often spoken to him about his cousin Lucy. Bob Fielding made no secret of the fact that he was in love with his cousin; "that he'd have cut off his right hand rather than that she should marry Bill Towers." Further, James Travers had visited Bob Fielding about three days before the commission of the crime.

"Did he, on that visit, speak to you about the deceased?" asked Brunton.

"Yes."

"What did he say?"

"He said that Bill Towers ought to be shot."

"Did he say anything about Mrs. Towers?"

"Yes, he said that she ought to have some one to look after her."

"Did he say she ought to have something to look after herself with?"

Despite Ronnie's protest at the leading question, his lordship allowed it; and James Travers answered, "Yes."

"And what happened then?"

"He showed me a pistol."

"A pistol!" Brunton signaled to the clerk of the court, and the clerk handed up a revolver to the witness. "Is that the pistol?"

"Yes."

"Was this weapon loaded when you last saw it?"

"It was."

"Did Fielding make any remark about it?"

"Yes. He said: 'That'll cook Bill's goose for him.'"

Once more the atmosphere of the court grew hostile. Watching the jury, Bonnie could see that his enemy had almost turned them. Impassivity settled like a mask on the faces of the nine men. The two spinsters gazed awe-struck at the big weapon in the seafarer's big hand. Even the red-hatted matron, whom he had decided a moment since definitely favorable, shook her head twice as though in new doubt. Then, turning from the jury-box to the dock, Ronnie was aware of his client's eyes. The eyes—Aliette's very own—looked pitiful. Imagination told him that they were afraid, that at last the woman realized her danger. He tried to signal to her; but she took no notice of his signal.

"That will be enough, I think," gloated Brunton; and, nervously, Ronnie started his task of cross-examination.

"You've known Robert Fielding for some time?"

"About seven years."

"Is he, in your opinion, a violent man? The kind of man who would commit a murder?"

"No."

"Or," Ronnie's nervous voice dropped two full tones, "the sort of man who would incite some one else to commit murder?"

"No."

"When Robert Fielding told you that he was in love with his cousin—that was a good many years ago, wasn't it?—did you understand that there was anything guilty in that love? That his cousin was his mistress?"

"No. I did not." The sailor's eyes—blue as the barrister's own—kindled.

"As far as you know, had misconduct taken place between Robert Fielding and his cousin?"

"I don't know anything about that."

"Was Lucy Towers in the room during any part of your conversation with Robert Fielding?"

"No."

"Has Robert Fielding ever suggested to you, since his cousin's marriage, that he would like to get her away from her husband?"

"No." The witness hesitated. "Not exactly."

"What do you mean by 'not exactly'?"

"Well, it didn't seem to me that Bob'd be exactly sorry if anything happened to Towers."

Brunton chuckled audibly. The chuckle enraged Ronnie. For a question or two he fenced aimlessly with his witness's honesty. Then suddenly he decided to try and turn that very honesty against his opponent.

"Tell me," he said suavely, "did you gather from the way in which Robert Fielding habitually spoke of him that the dead man, William Towers, was of a very violent disposition?"

"Well, more or less I suppose I did."

"And would it be too much if I suggested to you that it was solely because of her husband's violent disposition that Robert Fielding thought his cousin should have either some one to protect her, or some means of protecting herself? That he had that particular thought in his mind, and that thought only, when he showed you this revolver?"

The sailor seemed to find some difficulty in understanding the suggestions; and even after Ronnie had repeated them piecemeal, he refused, sailor-like, to commit himself.

Nervously, the cross-examination went on. "Now about this revolver: did you gather that Robert Fielding had only just bought it, or that he had had it in his possession for some considerable time? It's an old-fashioned navy revolver, isn't it?"

"Yes."

"He must have had it some time—ever since he left the service, probably?"

"Probably."

"He didn't, at any rate, tell you he'd just bought the weapon?"

"No."

"Coming back to the question of Towers, did Fielding tell you anything about his habits?"

"Not that I remember."

"He didn't by any chance mention," Ronnie referred to a note at the back of his brief, "that William Towers was addicted to drink?"

"No. He only said he ought to be shot."

Seating himself, Ronnie was conscious of partial failure. The sailor-man's innate distrust of lawyers had taken the edge off his questions. Brunton, infinitely experienced, limited his reëxamination to the main points: Robert Fielding had admitted himself in love with his cousin; Robert Fielding had said that William Towers ought to be shot.

Ronnie's hands, as he made his notes, trembled on the smooth foolscap. The mute figure in the dock was a reproach. Cartwright had failed him. Brunton's "That, members of the jury, is the case for the Crown," seemed to carry the unworded sting, "And let my learned enemy refute it if he can."

And then, just as Lucy Towers was being marched down to the cells, came Cartwright, his eyes twinkling behind his rimless eye-glasses. "I've got him outside," whispered Cartwright, "and I daren't leave him alone. It's too damned important. Here's your proof." He disappeared through the swing-doors with the crowd; and Ronnie, looking at the scribbled document, read:

"Bert Bishop will state: I am the licensee of the Red Lion Tavern, Hill Street, Brixton. I remember the fourth of July last year, because it was American Independence day, and I have some American customers. On the fourth of July I had difficulty in turning them out at closing-time. I have known Maggie Peterson for two years. I knew the dead man, William Towers. Maggie Peterson and William Towers were at the Red Lion that night. They came in about eight o'clock, and did not leave till a quarter past ten."

Chapter XXXII

1

Ronnie, shaking off Spillcroft, spent the luncheon adjournment alone. His bouts with the last witnesses, followed by the shock of Bert Bishop's proof, had rattled him. As he was leaving the court, the doorkeeper handed him another shock—a telegram. Opening it, he read, to his relief: "All love and all success. Julia." But the growing crowd in the street, the multiplying posters, the comments which reached his ears as he made his hasty way towards Holborn, rattled him still further.

His luck only added to his fears. Had it not been for the two anonymous notes, Maggie Peterson's evidence would have stood unchallenged. Now he could smash that evidence. But even now—even if the jury believed his side of the case sufficiently to discount Brunton's plea of premeditation—even if Bob Fielding and Lucy came well through the ordeal of Brunton's cross-questions—how, how the devil could he hope, unless some miracle gave his halting oratory genius, to secure a complete acquittal?

Lunching alone in the crowded grill-room of the South-Eastern & Chatham Hotel, Ronnie's thoughts went back to other days. He saw himself soldier again, and remembered the particular type of moral courage, of self-control, necessary for the winning of battles. That moral courage, that self-control must be his again if he would win this fight against Brunton. "This is my chance," he thought. "My one chance of downing the brute. I mustn't muff it."

Gradually solitude restored his balance. Gradually, his mind reconcentrated. Weeks of thought crystallized to short sentences. Lucy, Lucy Towers must be saved. Nothing but that mattered. The personal issue dwindled to unimportance.

Walking back to the court, he found that he could think, even of his enemy, logically.

2

But when, a few minutes later, Ronald Cavendish, rising to open the defense of Lucy Towers, saw Hector Brunton bowed over his brief, nothing of him visible except a patch of gray wig, the hump of a black back, and one gentlemanly hand clutched round the gold pencil-case—then, for a moment, logic failed; and only the fear-stricken eyes of the woman in the dock, only his personal enmity for the man keyed him to the struggle.

"M' lord, members of the jury," he began, and there was no attempt at oratory in his beginning, "it will be no part of my case to prove to you that Lucy Towers did not shoot her husband. She did shoot him. She shot him exactly as counsel for the Crown has proved to you. But when the Crown asks you to find my client guilty of wilful murder, when my learned friend brings what he is pleased to call evidence in support of malice and of premeditation; then I join issue with him. My submission to you is that there was, in what my client did, neither malice nor premeditation.

"Yet even if my learned friend fails—as it seems to me he must fail—to convince you of premeditation, that failure will not furnish me with sufficient grounds on which to ask you for my client's complete exoneration. Only on one ground can I ask you, as I intend to ask you, for your verdict of not guilty; and that ground, members of the jury, is justifiable or excusable homicide.

"Excusable homicide!" For a full ten minutes, the voice, grave, low, meditative, calm as the voice of the judge himself, dealt with the legal aspect of excusability; and all the while Hector Brunton listened, motionless. But suddenly, as Ronnie's tone changed to the tone of the pleader, the "hanging prosecutor" shifted on his seat; and savagely he stared at his enemy.

"Those, members of the jury, are some of the grounds on which our law excuses the killing of one human being by another. But there are other grounds, grounds which not only excuse but justify. It is such justification, the fullest possible justification, which I purpose to plead. My learned friend, you may have noticed, was very careful to avoid any reference to the character or disposition of my client's husband. I, on the contrary, intend to deal with that point rather fully."

Already the very quietness, the very certainty of that opening had impressed the court; and as, still quietly, yet with a hint of mounting passion behind it, the speech went on; as, point by point, counsel for the defense traversed the statements of counsel for the Crown, it seemed, even to the obtuse Spillcroft, as though the capital charge against Lucy Towers might fail.

"While as for the minor charge," continued Ronnie, "the charge of manslaughter—of which, as his lordship will tell you, even though it is not pleaded on the indictment, it will be open to you to find my client guilty—on that charge, too, I intend to ask you for the completest acquittal."

Brunton's stare relaxed. He hunched himself once more over his notes. And abruptly instinct, the instinct of the born advocate, warned Ronnie that he had spoken long enough. He glanced at the clock, at the jury. The jury—and especially the three women—were losing interest. Those women wanted neither argument nor oratory. They wanted drama. They were waiting, as spectators in a theater, for him to put Lucy Towers in the witness-box. So, abruptly, he regalvanized their interest.

"Members of the jury, my learned friend who leads for the Crown has been at great pains to convince you, out of the mouths of his witnesses, that Lucy Towers is both murderess and adulteress. I propose to afford him yet another opportunity of convincing you—by putting both my client and her cousin in the witness-box."

At that, the whole court stiffened to attention, and even the judge, who seemed to have been dozing throughout the speech, leaned forward. "Isn't he even going to deal with the evidence for the prosecution?" thought the judge.

But Ronnie purposely played his highest card last.

"Nevertheless, before you hear my client's story from her own lips, I must ask you to weigh very carefully certain evidence which the Crown has thought fit to call against her. With the testimony of John Hodges and of James Travers, honest testimony, let us hope, I shall deal at a later stage of these proceedings. But the evidence of Maggie Peterson calls for different treatment. Because Maggie Peterson has lied—and lied deliberately!

"Lied—and lied deliberately." Now, as passion mounted and mounted, kindling the quiet voice to rage, Brunton's head twitched from his brief, and his eyes, the cold gray eyes under the gray wig, glanced fearfully about the packed court-room.

"Because, on the night of July 4, the night when Maggie Peterson swears that she saw my client making her way to Robert Fielding's room, Maggie Peterson was not at 25 Laburnum Grove at all."

Ronnie paused, letting his every word sink home. Rain, pattering suddenly on the glass dome above, seemed to emphasize the silence below. Then passionately the speech ended. "My lord, members of the jury, I ask for no mercy. I ask only for justice. I ask you to remember, even while you are listening to my client's testimony, that the main evidence against her, the evidence of this woman Peterson is, from beginning to end, one tissue of deliberate lies, of the most wilful and corrupt perjury, as I shall prove to you out of the mouth of a competent witness, the landlord of the Red Lion Tavern, who will testify to you beyond the shadow of a doubt that from eight o'clock till after ten on the night of July 4, Maggie Peterson never left his establishment; who will testify, moreover, that Maggie Peterson's companion on the night in question was none other than my unfortunate client's husband, William Towers himself."

And on that, satisfied with the utter hush which followed, Ronald Cavendish put his client in the box.

3

There are seconds in every man's life when the conviction of his own wrong-doing shatters the edifice of conceit and flings illusion headlong.

Such a second came to Hector Brunton, K.C., as he watched Lucy Towers step down from the side of the dock and make her way past the packed benches to the witness-box. With her—he could feel—went a wave, a great wave of human sympathy, the wave against which he, Hector Brunton, had been swimming for more than a year.

Paralyzed he watched her—watched her take the oath, kiss the book. His mind was a torment, a torment of conscience. Conscience howled: "You knew! You knew all the time that your principal witness was lying. You knew! You knew all the time that this woman was no adulteress. She's innocent, innocent, Hector Brunton; as innocent in intention as that other woman you've been hounding."

Cavendish's voice, the voice of his enemy, broke the spell.

"Mrs. Towers, while the oath you have just sworn is still fresh in your mind, I want you to answer this question. Have you ever, at any time in your life, been guilty of immorality with your cousin, Robert Fielding?"

"Never." The answer, so diffident yet so definite, might have been Aliette's; and to Ronnie, his brain still throbbing from its own unaccustomed eloquence, it seemed, just for a fraction of a second, as though the woman he defended were indeed his own.

"Various witnesses for the Crown have stated that you were on bad terms with your husband. Are those statements true?"

"I did my best to get on with him." The brown eyes never flinched. "But he was a cruel man, especially when he was in drink."

"Nevertheless, you were faithful to him?"

"Yes. Always."

"You heard Mrs. Peterson's evidence? She said," Ronnie referred to his notes, "that at half-past nine o'clock on the night of July 4, she saw you go into Robert Fielding's room. Have you any comment to make on that evidence?"

"It's a lie. I never visited him at night. Only by day."

"At half-past nine on the night of July 4, where were you?"

"I was in my own room, washing up the supper things."

"Was your husband with you?"

"No."

"Where was he?"

"I don't know."

"One other point about Mrs. Peterson's evidence. She told us, if you remember, that you made a statement: that you said to her that you would never be happy till your husband was dead. What have you to say about that statement?"

"It's another lie." The lips pursed, stubbornly—it seemed to Brunton—as his wife's own. "An absolute lie."

"One moment, please!" Mr. Justice Heber—every syllable of his question audible as the tinkle of glass—intervened. "I should like to be clear on this point, Mrs. Towers. The witness to whom your counsel refers made the following statements: that at half-past nine o'clock on the night of July 4 she saw you enter Robert Fielding's room; that you were in the habit of making such visits, and that she was standing in the passage between your room and hers when she saw you. Do I understand you positively to deny all three of those statements?"

"Yes, m'lord."

"And the witness in question further stated that you said to her: 'Bill isn't fit to be any woman's husband. I wish to God he was dead.' What have you to say to that?"

The woman in the witness-box did not hesitate. Deliberately her eyes met the judge's. Deliberately she answered his question: "My lord, I may have said that Bill wasn't fit to be any woman's husband. But I never said," the shy voice rose, "either to Maggie Peterson or to any one else, that I wished he was dead."

"She never said"—word for word Mr. Justice Heber wrote down his answer—"that she wished her husband was dead."

But Hector Brunton—bent over his brief—could not write. For now, not only conscience, but all his years spent in separating truth from falsehood, all the experience of a legal lifetime, told him of Lucy's innocence.

Again his enemy's voice broke the spell: "You heard the evidence of John Hodges. He said that you told him somewhere about the end of last June that you wished you had never married your husband. Have you anything you would like to say in answer to that?"

"Bill was there at the time. I only meant it for a joke."

"And now, before I ask you to tell his lordship and the jury, in your own words, what happened on the afternoon of July 5, I want you, if you can, to give me some idea of the feelings you entertained, before that date, for your husband."

It was a daring, an unpremeditated, though not a leading question; and, even as he put it, Ronnie perceived its danger. Suppose the woman in the witness-box, the little dignified woman whose hands rested so quietly on the rail, whose whole attitude indicated nothing but the intensest desire to speak truth, should speak too much truth, should destroy—with one fatal word—the house of protection he was building about her? But neither the heart nor the truth in Lucy Towers failed.

"It wouldn't be right"—the hands on the rail did not move—"for me to pretend that I cared for Bill. He made my life an absolute hell. He drank and he used to knock me about. Many's the time I've wished he was dead. But I never thought of killing him."

"Ah." Ronnie paused in his examination—one of those long, indefinable pauses which have more value than speech. Now—feeling the jury with him—he was no longer haunted by thought of his own inefficiency, no longer afraid of Brunton. Not Brunton's self could shake such a witness. Already, the first faint foretaste of victory quickened his pulse. His questions grew more and more daring.

"You said, in your statement at the police-station: 'My husband didn't like me going to Bob's room. He was jealous of Bob.' Can you give us any further details about that?"

"Details!" Lucy, her eyes downcast, appeared to be considering the question. She shot a glance at Brunton. Then, quietly, she said, "Bill was always being jealous of some man or other—the same as Mr. Hodges said. But he hadn't got any reason to be jealous. I told him so, when he said I wasn't to go to Bob's room that afternoon. Me and Bob has always been pals—since we were kiddies. But if it hadn't been for Bob having no arms, I wouldn't have disobeyed Bill and gone to him.'"

"I see. And can you tell me, coming to the afternoon of July 5, what your husband said when you threatened to disobey him—when you told him," Ronnie referred to his brief, "'I must go and help Bob because he can't feed himself?"

"Bill said," the words were tremulous: "'If you don't stop here I'll come over and do in the pair of you.'"

"And what happened after that!"

"I just went to Bob's room."

"And did you say anything to your cousin about your husband's threats?"

"No."

"Can you tell me why you didn't?"

"Because"–unconsciously, the woman scored yet another point–"because I didn't want Bob to see I was frightened."

"And now"–Ronnie craned forward in his mounting excitement–"and now, Mrs. Towers, I want you to describe to his lordship and the jury, in your own words, exactly what happened in Robert Fielding's room on the afternoon of July 5."

"I made Bob his tea, and I was helping him eat it when Bill came in," began the woman.

No sounds save the scratch of reporters' pencils, the occasional tap of a boot-sole on the bare floor-boards, and the suppressed breathing of her tense audience interrupted the story Lucy Towers told her counsel and the court–a story so utterly resembling, yet so utterly differing from the toneless confession which the "hanging prosecutor" had read out the day before, a story so redolent of life and truth and certainty that, listening to it, it seemed as if one could actually see the dead man standing at the doorway of that bare tenement room, see the lifted stick in his hand, and hear his harsh, grim voice.

"Bill said, 'I'll do you in. I'll do you both in, damn you.' He had his stick in Ms hand. He lifted his stick. I was frightened. I thought he meant to kill Bob. I thought he meant to kill both of us. I remembered the pistol. I ran to the cupboard. I pulled out the pistol. I pointed it at him. Bob said, 'Look out, Bill. The gun's loaded.' Bill said, 'You can't frighten me.' I thought he was going to kill Bob, so I fired.

"So I fired." The little story ended to the indescribable, unbearable silence of men and women whose emotions are near to breaking-point. Through that unbearable silence, Ronnie's next question cut like a razor through taut string.

"You say that your husband carried a stick. Can you describe that stick?"

"It was a heavy stick."

"Can't you tell me any more about it?"

"Yes; it had a bit of lead in the handle."

"Was he holding the stick by the handle?"

"No. By the other end."

"And you thought he meant to kill your cousin with that loaded stick?"

"Yes. I felt sure of it. That was why I shot him."

Ronnie paused again, making sure that his point should sink home in the minds of the jury. Then, picking up his copy of the confession, he put his last questions: "I have here the statement which you made at the time of your arrest. You say, 'I'm not sorry I killed my husband.' Why did you say that?"

"Because I wasn't sorry—then."

"But you are sorry now?"

"Yes. I didn't mean to kill him. I don't know why I said that. I didn't quite know what I was saying."

"And there was one other thing you said. You said, 'I love Bob very much.' Is that true?"

"Yes." Lucy Towers answered fearlessly. "I do love him, but not in the way"—her eyes, which had scarcely left Ronnie's since the examination began, turned for a moment to Hector Brunton, huddled in his seat—"not in the way that he tried to make out."

"Thank you, Mrs. Towers. That's all I have to ask," finished Ronald Cavendish; and, seating himself, waited for Hector Brunton's onslaught.

But the onslaught tarried. Almost it seemed as if Hector Brunton were going to leave that cross-examination, on which the whole case hung, to his junior. For now Hector Brunton heard, louder than the whisper of conscience, the very whisper of God. "Thou art the man," whispered God; "thou art the murderer."

The "hanging prosecutor" looked at the woman in the dock, and his courage failed before the accusing glance of her. The "hanging prosecutor" looked at the judge, at the massed spectators; and his heart quailed before the doubting glances of them. Then the "hanging prosecutor" looked at his enemy; and rage, the rage of the lusting male, took him by the throat. God's whisper forgotten, man's duty forgotten, all save this one last chance of vengeance forgotten; he rose, heavy as the wounded bull, to his ungainly feet. His brain, the cold sure-functioning legal brain, had not yet failed. He still knew his strength. But a red mist blinded his eyes, and through that red mist he saw, not Lucy Towers but Aliette; Aliette, whom every cheated fiber of his body yearned to torture—and, torturing, possess.

"You admit that you shot your husband?" The words—grim, bitter, devil-prompted—grated in Brunton's throat.

"Yes."

"You admit that you said, just after you had shot him, that you were not sorry for the deed?"

"That's written down."

"Answer my question, please. Do you admit that you said, just after your husband's death at your hands, that you were not sorry you had killed him?"

"That's written down," repeated Lucy Towers stubbornly. And the stubbornness sent a chill through the red mist; a chill that pierced to Hector Brunton's very marrow. Thus—thus stubborn and unwrithing—thus clear-eyed and contemptuous, had this same woman outfaced him, long and long ago in the bright, miserable drawing-room at Lancaster Gate.

"You have admitted"—there was a singing in the K.C.'s ears; he could hardly hear his own voice—"that you love your cousin, Robert Fielding. I put it to you that you are Robert Fielding's mistress."

"No."

"I put it to you that you went to Robert Fielding's room nightly."

"It's a lie."

"I put it to you that ever since Robert Fielding came to live at 25 Laburnum

Grove you have been in the habit of misconducting yourself with him."

"It's a lie."

"I put it to you"—God! if only he could make her writhe; if only he could see one stab of pain twitch those cheeks—"that you love Robert Fielding."

"Not in the way you're trying to make out."

"I put it to you that it was because of your love for Robert Fielding that you shot your husband."

"No."

"Then why did you shoot him?"

"My lord,"—Cavendish's voice—"I protest. This is outrageous."

"I'm afraid, Mr. Cavendish,"—Heber's voice—"I must allow the question."

"Why did you shoot your husband?" Brunton heard his own voice, very faint through the buzz at his ears.

"I have already told you"—he heard Aliette's voice—"I killed him because I thought he was going to kill Bob."

"You meant to kill him, then?"

Again his enemy's protest. Again the judge's doubtful, "I feel I must allow the question." Again Aliette's stubborn reply:

"No. I never meant to kill him. I didn't think about that. I only wanted to save Bob."

Momentarily the red mist cleared from Brunton's sight. He knew this woman for Lucy Towers—Lucy Towers against whom, despite the flaws in the evidence, he had advised prosecution for wilful murder; knew himself doomed to failure with her—as he had always been doomed to failure with Aliette; knew that, against the sheer rock of truth in the one, as against the rock of sheer truth in the other, the spray of his lawless hate must beat in vain.

Then the red mist thickened, thickened and thickened, again before Brunton's smarting eyes. Rage kindled in his bowels, kindled from bowels to brain, burning away self-control. He was aware only of Cavendish—of Cavendish, utterly cold, utterly legal—of Cavendish protesting for his witness, protecting his witness—of Cavendish's will, thrusting bar after cold steel bar between himself and the woman.

The singing was still in Brunton's ears; and now it grew dark in court, so that the face of the woman faded from his sight; and now it grew light in court, so that the face of the woman showed itself to him as a white contemptuous sneer under the electrics; but still, blindly, he tortured her with his questions.

At last he heard his own voice clearly once again, "You deny, then, that you are an adulteress?"; heard her answer, "Yes. I deny that absolutely"; heard, as a murderer hearing his own sentence, Mr. Justice Heber's, "If that finishes your cross-examination, Mr. Brunton, I shall adjourn until ten o'clock tomorrow"; heard, as a murderer hears the tramp of feet outside his cell, Cavendish's quiet, "With your lordship's permission, there is one witness, one most important witness, whom I should like to call before the court adjourns"; listened, powerless to cross-examine, while the witness of Cartwright's finding tore Maggie Peterson's testimony in pieces.

4

As Ronnie, striding solitary home, saw on the posters "TOWERS CASE SENSATION; WITNESS ARRESTED FOR PERJURY." it seemed to him as though victory had been already in his grasp.

Chapter XXXIII

1

Hector Brunton tottered out of his car and up the steps into his chambers like a man in a palsy. Three clients were waiting in the outer office for consultations. He told Patterson: "Send them away. Get rid of them. Say I'm too ill to see anybody." Then heavily he sat down at his desk.

The shock of Maggie Peterson's arrest, climaxing emotion, was still on him. Definitely his experience knew himself defeated. "God!" he muttered, "another night—another night of the rack."

The previous night had been torment enough. Then he had thought: "I may fail. Cavendish may have something up his sleeve"; then he had seen only success in jeopardy; dreaded only the failure of his vengeance. But now—now he was beaten—worse than beaten—delivered up, body and soul, to the Furies.

The clerk came in to ask if he might go. "Yes," said Brunton; "go. Go as soon as you like." The clerk went out, leaving him alone; alone with his Furies.

The Furies showed him Aliette, infinitely fastidious, infinitely desirable; they showed him Reneé, Reneé who would even now be awaiting him; they showed Lucy, Lucy Towers, stubborn in her cell. "Don't let her go free from her cell," whispered the Furies. "You're not beaten yet. She did kill the man. Convict her, Hector Brunton. Convict her of manslaughter."

They showed him Cavendish, Cavendish gloating at the prospect of victory. "To be beaten," whispered the Furies, "to be beaten by Cavendish, by the adulterer who stole away your wife!"

But all the time Hector Brunton knew in his inmost soul that he had sought to compass the death of an innocent woman; that he had sinned against his own code, against the holy ghost of justice.

And gradually, terrifyingly, the reason of that sinning was brought home to him. He had sinned, not as a woman sins, lovingly, but for sheer hate. Out of his hatred for Cavendish he had plotted—as surely as any murderer—the death of Lucy Towers.

Gilbert Frankau

And suddenly, starkly, irresistibly, it was brought home to him that—even as he had plotted the death of Lucy Towers—so, and for the same hideous reason, he had plotted the social ruin of his own wife.

Till finally the ultimate pretext, the pretext of his love for Aliette, was stripped from him, and he saw that love in all its hideous nakedness, as lust—the savage sadic lust which had hounded him to crime.

*

David Patterson had long gone home; but Brunton sat on—alone in his chambers—alone with his conscience, naked before his God. His worldly house, the sure material legal house of his own making, had crashed, in that one second of time when he watched Lucy Towers step down from the dock, to ruin. The law, basis of work and life, lay—a tablet shattered to ten thousand fragments—at his feet. Ghosts—the palpable ghosts of those two women for the compassing of whose ruin he had invoked the law—sidled about the darkling room, terrifying him. He knew himself a prisoner—prisoner in the invisible house of God.

Was there no way out? No escape from God's house of conscience? Had he, abiding by the letter of man's law, forfeited—for all time—the merciful spirit of the law of God?

"Yes," said conscience, "there is one way out. One way, and one way only, of escape. Make reparation, Hector Brunton. Set both these women free."

Must he, then, give up everything—wife, vengeance, victory—because of this one damnable insistent whisper, this whisper of conscience that was driving him to madness?

And now, again, he saw the phantoms—phantom of Aliette and phantom of Lucy Towers. They were behind bars—bars—innocent women behind bars which he, Hector Brunton, had socketed home with his own hands.

*

At last, thought of those bars drove him into the night. King's Bench Walk lay deserted, chill-gleaming under autumnal trees. Leaves strewed it, swishing against his boots as he strode. "Autumn," thought Brunton. "Autumn! We've reached middle age, the year and I. And what have I garnered? Nothing."

Suddenly he realized whither his feet were carrying him; suddenly he found himself under the colonnade of Pump Court, at the door of his rival's chambers. The door was shut, the court deserted. Yet for a long time Brunton stood by the door; stood, as a man stands who waits for some sign, for an opening window or the gleam of a light. But no window opened, no light gleamed.

He came, hardly knowing how, out of the gloom of the Temple into the raw glare of empty Fleet Street. In front of him uprose the long façade of the high courts, the courts where he had won fame and money. What did fame and money matter to him—to Hector Brunton, who, gaining the whole legal world, had lost his own soul?

2

Counsel for the defense, as he watched counsel for the prosecution make his way into court next morning, could almost feel sorry for the man. Brunton, the overbearing, overconfident Brunton, looked the veriest wreck of his old self. He tottered rather than walked to his seat. His eyes were dull, bloodshot; his hands trembled; his jowl twitched and twitched.

The judge had not yet arrived; and Ronnie's eyes, switching here and there about the packed court, suddenly envisaged, below the judge's dais, the "exhibits" of the prosecution: among them the revolver which had killed its man. More than once, in the last year, he, Ronald Cavendish, had known the desire to kill his man. But now, looking on the wreck which had been Brunton, he knew the desire dead. No longer could he even hate Brunton. The man was beaten—beaten.

Bunce, approaching, handed up a telegram: "Congratulations. Masterly. Feel confident of your success. Bertram Standon."

Ronnie's heart glowed at the penciled words. Already he saw success, fame, victory; already the sentences he would speak throbbed in his brain. And then, abruptly, the sight of Lucy Towers entering the witness-box for reëxamination recalled the fact that Brunton was still undefeated. The alternative charge of manslaughter had yet to be fought out between them!

388

The judge took his seat. The short reëxamination of Lucy Towers began—ended. Quietly she went back to the dock; quietly she took her seat by the blue-uniformed wardress.

"Robert Fielding!" called the constables on guard outside the doors.

The armless sailor, unskilled in law, had taken small comfort from the morning's papers. His face, shaved clean, was gray with apprehension; his whole body drooped as he made his way into the box. Ronnie could see pity written clear on the faces of the jury. The fat matron—she still wore her red hat—made a convulsive movement as if to assist, when the crier of the court lifted the Bible to the kiss of that trembling mouth. Even the two dour spinsters seemed moved.

Robert Fielding's tale of the happenings at Laburnum Grove on the afternoon of July 5 corroborated his cousin's in almost every detail. Yet he told it haltingly; only when Ronnie asked, "Have you any knowledge of the relations between Mrs. Towers and her husband?" did any certainty come into the low voice.

"Nobody except me," said Robert Fielding, "knows all that Lucy had to put up with from that fellow. He was always a wrong 'un, was Bill Towers. I looked after her all I could, but a cripple like me hasn't got much chance."

"Did you ever make any secret of your affection for your cousin?"

"No, sir."

"When you told James Travers that your cousin's husband ought to be shot, what did you mean to imply?"

The sailor hesitated; and Ronnie, nervous of the one weakness left in his case, tried to prompt him. "When you told James Travers that Bill Towers ought to be shot, did you have any intention—"

But at that, the judge intervened—leading questions being barred in law; and Ronnie, a trifle annoyed with himself for the solecism, repeated his former query.

Again Fielding hesitated; then he said, self-excusingly: "When I made that remark, I made it as a good many of us who have been in the service do make it—in a general sort of way, meaning that Bill Towers was a bad lot, and that it wouldn't be any loss if somebody did shoot him."

"I see." Ronnie smiled; and a man on the jury, obviously an ex-service man, smiled with him. "Now, about the pistol—or rather the revolver. Can you tell us how long it had been in your possession?"

"Two years, I should say."

"Had it always been loaded?"

"Yes. Ever since I can remember."

"When did your cousin first know that you possessed this revolver?"

"Not until that afternoon."

"Which afternoon?"

"The afternoon she shot Bill Towers."

"One other point. James Travers told us that you said to him, 'I'd rather cut off my right hand than that Lucy should marry Bill Towers.' Did you ever make such a statement to James Travers?"

The sailor looked down, piteously, at his two empty sleeves. "I may have," he said. "But if I did, it must have been a long time ago."

"Before she married?"

"Yes, before she married."

"James Travers also told us that you said to him, when you showed him the revolver, 'This will cook Bill's goose for him.' Did you say that?"

"Yes." The answer was hardly audible. "He'd been knocking Lucy about—and I was mad with him."

"Was there any other reason why you were mad with him?"

"Yes, there was." And the sailor—fears momentarily forgotten—rapped out, so swiftly that even the judge could not stop him, "He drank, and he was carrying on with another woman. Everybody in the house knew about it."

On the hush which followed that statement—a statement confirmatory of the point which Ronnie, without specifically alleging it, had been trying to establish ever since his opening question to Maggie Peterson—fell the last question of Mr. Justice Heber: "Do you know, of your own knowledge, any woman other than his wife with whom the dead man was on terms of sexual intimacy?"

And Robert Fielding, looking squarely into those gleaming spectacles, answered, "Yes, my lord. With Maggie Peterson. Many's the time I've seen the blackguard a-sneaking into her room."

3

At two o'clock of the afternoon, in a court packed to suffocation point, Ronald Cavendish rose to begin his final speech for the defense of Lucy Towers.

Robert Fielding's testimony, unshaken in cross-examination, had been followed by more evidence, collected by Standon's assiduous reporters, as to the character of the dead man; and that evidence—Ronnie felt,—coupled with the arrest of Maggie Peterson, made the main issue, the issue of wilful murder, safe.

Nevertheless, the Wixton imagination in him was doubtful of the second issue, the issue of manslaughter. In England, the unwritten law did not run; and although, thanks to the press, the streets outside were black with people, with a mob hungry for news of the verdict, determined on his client's acquittal, Ronnie knew the difficulties of securing that acquittal too well for overconfidence.

Again he had spent the luncheon interval alone; praying—voicelessly—that his oratory might not fail; visualizing always those two dour-faced spinsters on the jury, and Mr. Justice Heber, having summed up in cold legal phraseology the bare facts of the case, awarding, on the jury's recommendation, the lenient sentence of a year's imprisonment.

In those few seconds of time before his speech began, Ronnie's imagination could almost hear the murmur of the mob without. The murmur flustered him. After all, Lucy had shot her husband. Between her, pale in the dock, and the dark cell of felony, stood only a dumb advocate, a fencer unskilled with the sword of the spoken word.

Till suddenly, standing there silent before Lucy's peers, it seemed to Ronnie as though all the emotions of the last year stirred in his heart, as though all that pity for womankind which Aliette had engendered in him

391

fought for utterance at his lips. For one fleeting moment, his keen gaze swept the court, envisaging judge, jury, the motionless figure of his client, the constable and the wardress either side of her, the spectators standing two-deep round the closed doors, Benjamin Bunce, David Patterson, John Cartwright, Brunton. For one fleeting moment he thought of Brunton, and of the wrong which Brunton had done to the woman he loved. Then, gravely, quietly, feeling the sword of the spoken word quiver like a live blade at his lips, he engaged his enemy.

Sentence by calm sentence, Julia Cavendish's son—making scarcely a gesture, referring hardly to a note—traversed the statements of his enemy and of the witnesses for his enemy; sentence by grave sentence, he demonstrated to those twelve watchful faces, to the nine men and the three women in the jury-box, that the crime—if crime it were—had been committed on a sudden impulse, without motive, without malice, without premeditation.

"Members of the jury, if we except the evidence of Maggie Peterson—evidence which we now know to be one tissue of lies,—what proof have we of motive or of malice aforethought? No proof, no proof whatsoever. When counsel for the Crown dared to call my client an adulteress, on what did he base his foul allegation? On the word of a proved liar. I venture to tell him that, if any one fact has emerged from the evidence which he has seen fit to put before you, it is the fact of my client's fidelity to the blackguard whom she had the misfortune to marry."

At that, fearfully, the "hanging prosecutor" craned forward in his seat; and fearfully—as though it were of himself and not of the dead that Ronnie spoke—his bloodshot eyes glanced up at the set, stern face of counsel for the defense. But counsel for the defense deigned him never a glance. Terribly, counsel for the defense went on:

"My lord, members of the jury, he, counsel for the Crown, is a distinguished, perhaps our most distinguished advocate. Behind him are all the resources of the public purse, of the public power. Yet I, the humblest of pleaders, should not be doing my duty to my client did I not tell him that this prosecution to which he has thought fit to add the weight of his advocacy is a prosecution founded on false witness, bolstered on perjury, a prosecution which no just advocate would have dared to support."

With those words, unprofessional, unpremeditated—for now the sword of oratory had out lunged Ronnie's self-control, so that he spoke from his heart, careless of etiquette,—a shiver of excitement rippled the gray-wigged heads behind. The wigged heads nodded toward one another, whispering, "I say! Why the deuce don't Brunton protest!" But Brunton did not protest. And counsel for the defense spoke on:

"Why he has so dared, is for my learned friend to explain. My learned friend spoke of mercy. The poet tells us that the quality of mercy is not strained. Did my learned friend ponder that saying when his hands drew up the indictment against my client? Did any spirit of mercy move him when his brain schemed the evidence which has been put before this court? Is he merciful or merciless, truthful or truthless, when he asks you to believe that this woman, this unfortunate Lucy Towers, is guilty not only of murder but of adultery?"

Still Brunton did not protest. His eyes, the bloodshot eyes under the wig awry, dared look no more upon his enemy. For now it seemed to Hector Brunton as though Ronnie pleaded with him—as he had pleaded long ago—not only for the freedom of the woman in the dock, but for the freedom of Aliette.

"Adultery!" pleaded Ronnie. "Has my learned friend brought any proof of that adultery? He has brought none. None. None. Has he brought any proof of murder? Any proof of that malice aforethought without which—as he himself has told you—there can be no murder? He has brought none. None. None. Yet deliberately he has sought to twine"—one hand shot out, pointing first at Brunton, then at the unmoving figure of Lucy Towers—"the hangman's rope round the neck of this innocent woman. For she is innocent! Innocent of murder as she is of adultery. Innocent—I declare it to you in all solemnity!—innocent before the sight of man as she is innocent before the sight of God—of any and of every charge that counsel for the Crown has thought fit to bring against her. Of no charge, not even of manslaughter, can she be found guilty! Is it manslaughter to defend the defenseless? Is it manslaughter when a weak woman protects the man she loves from the beast who makes her days and her nights a living hell?

"A living hell!" For a second the flood of oratory ceased; for a second, through the silence of bated breaths, it seemed to Ronald Cavendish as though once again he caught the murmurs of the crowd without. But now the crowd gave strength to his words.

"Members of the jury, I do not ask for mercy. I ask only for justice. I ask you, when you weigh your verdict, to remember what manner of man was this William Towers. I ask you to look upon my client. I ask you to think of this woman, faithful always, complaining never, enduring always—year after hellish year—the bestial defilements of the drunken reprobate into whose black heart, not of premeditation but in sheer and sudden defense of a fellow-creature, she fired her fatal shot. Oh, yes, Lucy Towers fired that shot. Lucy Towers and no other killed her husband. That is the one truth in the tissue of lies which has been put before you. But was that killing a crime? Is not the world well rid of men like William Towers? Members of the jury, you, who have heard from the lips of unbiased witnesses what were his cruelties, what his drinkings and what his lecheries, will you not say to yourselves—as I say to myself—when you come to consider your verdict: 'God save all women from such a man.'"

And then, for the first time, Ronnie deigned one scornful look upon his enemy.

"Yet, believe me, you men and you women on whose word depends life or death for this woman I am defending, it is not on the ground of her husband's cruelties that I ask you to let her go free. However degraded, however debauched, however cruel; this man, this William Towers still had the right to live. Neither by his lechery nor by his drunkenness did he forfeit his life. Yet his life was forfeit. Why? Let me tell you why. Let me tell you in one sentence. Because he sought to take the life of another.

"Remember that. Never forget that. William Towers sought to take the life of another!" Ronnie's voice slowed to emphasis. Subconsciously, he knew himself at the very core of his defense. But consciously he knew nothing. The faces of the judge, of the jury and the spectators—phantom symbols whose intelligences his own intelligence must now grapple—blurred to his sight. He swayed as he stood.

"Members of the jury, that is the issue; the whole simple issue before this court. Dismiss from your minds all prejudice. That my learned friend stooped to call false witnesses is for my learned friend's conscience to excuse. You have not been summoned to decide the guilt of Maggie Peterson. You are not here to weigh the sins of the dead. You have been summoned to decide whether or no my client is guilty of any crime. Judge—impartially yet compassionately—that single simple issue. And, judging, keep before your minds this picture, the picture my client herself painted for you in unshaken, unforgettable words, the picture of the poor clean room in the tenement-house where Lucy Towers sits with her cousin; with the armless man, whose arms (need I remind you?) were sacrificed for your sake and for mine.

"Day by day Lucy Towers has visited that room; day by day her hands and hers alone have ministered to its helpless, to its defenseless occupant. Day by day she has brought him, despite her husband's threats, a little money—food perhaps. Is that a crime? But to-day she has not even brought money. She has only helped him—the piteousness of it!—to drink his tea. They are cousins, these two. They are happy with one another; not, as my learned friend would have you believe, guiltily happy, but innocently happy. They love one another—as they themselves told you—in the best, in the highest way, even as brother and sister love one another.

"So, they are sitting. And then, without warning, comes the crash of a stick-handle on the door. Startled, they look up. Startled, they see, framed in the doorway, the cruel terrible face of a man, of this woman's legal owner, of William Towers. In his hand this reprobate, this cruel drunken reprobate, brandishes his stick. The stick is no ordinary walking-stick. It is a weapon—a deadly weapon—a loaded stick. William Towers grasps the loaded stick by the ferrule. He lifts it menacingly; he makes as though to brain Robert

Fielding—the armless, the helpless, the defenseless man, Robert Fielding. Robert Fielding's cousin is afraid; she fears this reprobate's violence, fears that he has been drinking, fears his ungovernable temper. There is a revolver in the cupboard. A revolver!

"A revolver!" Unconsciously, Ronnie's hand shot out, pointing at the weapon.

"My client runs to the cupboard. She opens the cupboard. She sees the revolver. Mad with fear, she grasps the revolver. She points it at William Towers. And William Towers jeers at her, jeers at them both. 'I'll do you in. I'll do you both in, damn you!' shouts this madman, this drunken madman who has made my client's life a living hell. And again he brandishes his stick, threatening a defenseless man.

"And then? Even then, does Robert Fielding call upon his cousin to fire? No. Remember that he knows himself in danger of his life; knows that one pressure of his cousin's finger on the trigger will save his life. Yet Robert Fielding does not call upon his cousin to fire. He warns the man—the reprobate who is seeking to slay him; he cries, 'Look out, Bill. The gun's loaded.' But William Towers only sneers. 'You can't frighten me,' sneers William Towers, and once more he brandishes his weapon, making as though to batter out Robert Fielding's life.

"To batter out Robert Fielding's life!" Now, irresistible, the sword of the spoken word plunges to its peroration. "My lord, members of the jury, was it murder, or a defense against murder, when my client, my innocent client, maddened by fear—driven to desperation by the thought of this foul crime which only she could prevent—pulled the trigger, sped the bullet which sent William Towers to his account with God? My lord, members of the jury, all you who listen to me in this court to-day, is there any one of you who—fearful as my client was fearful—provoked as my client was provoked—maddened as my client was maddened, by the sight of an armless man, of the one creature she loved in all the world, about to suffer death at the hands of a reprobate—would not have done what Lucy Towers did, would not have torn madly at the revolver trigger, would not have taken a life that a life might live?

"Men and women in whose hands lies the fate of my client, it is on that plea—on that plea alone—on the plea that the life she took was a life already forfeit—that I ask you to set her free. Were I in France, were I in America, I might plead the unwritten law. I do not plead it. By the written statutes of England; by every precedent of British justice; by the written law and by the written law alone; by that inalienable right which every citizen of this country possesses, the right to kill in another's defense, I ask you by your verdict to-day to manumit Lucy Towers of all and every penalty, to let her go free from this court, to acquit her at the hands of her fellow-men—as I, her advocate, am convinced that she stands acquitted at the hands of God."

4

To Ronald Cavendish, the actual world—the judge, the jury, the spectators, the motionless woman in the dock—were still blurred, a blur of many faces. He knew only that he had made his effort; that he was still on his feet; that he was tottering on his feet. His hands still gripped the lapels of his robe. He could feel the sweat of his hands as they gripped the black stuff; feel the sweat pouring down his body. He knew that his body was twitching; twitching in every nerve. But his brain was a gutted mechanism, unfunctioning, telling neither success nor failure. Of all the words his lips had spoken, no memory remained.

And then, sharply, the actual world came back. He saw the faces distinctly; Heber's face, the faces of the jury. Followed tumult. Men, men and women, were applauding; applauding him, Ronald Cavendish, who could remember no word of all the words he had spoken. Had he succeeded? Surely, he must have succeeded? Mr. Justice Heber was threatening to have the court cleared; but the men, the men and the women in the well of the court still applauded. Even Cartwright—"that old stick Cartwright" was applauding. . . .

At last the tumult quelled; and Ronnie was conscious of a silence, the silence of abashed English folk. Only one sound—the sound of a woman's sobs—intruded upon that silence. And Ronnie knew that the woman in the dock was crying; crying like a broken soul; crying to herself, faintly, feebly, careless of the judge, careless of the spectators, careless of the other woman, the woman in the blue prison-uniform, who bent over her, patting her shoulder, striving to comfort.

Then even that sound ceased; and Ronnie, leaning back exhausted against the oak, saw that his enemy had risen.

But no words came from Hector Brunton. Speechless, he eyed the jury. The jury turned from him; turned their heads this way and that in conference. The jury—men and women—shifted up and down on their benches, taking counsel with one another. Whispers carried across from the jury-box; tense shrill whispers: "It ought to stop." "I've heard enough." "Too much." "Don't let *him* say any more." And promptly, a bearded man rose among the jury and turned to the judge.

"My lord," the man's lips trembled, "we have heard all we want to hear. We are all of one opinion. We have made up our minds. We find the prisoner not guilty."

Once again, tumult—the tumult of men and women applauding—broke upon Ronnie's ears. Then he saw Mr. Justice Heber hold up his hand; heard the crier calling for silence; heard his lordship's quiet "Prisoner at the bar, the jury have found you not guilty. With that verdict I concur. You are discharged"; and saw Hector Brunton collapse, as a stricken boxer collapses to the knock-out.

5

There followed, on that amazing and unprecedented verdict, the craziest half-hour in Ronnie's life. Still stunned by the swiftness of his victory, he heard—as a man battle-mazed hears gunfire—the plaudits in the court, the plaudits on landing and staircase, the plaudits of the mob without.

The plaudits of the mob deepened to a roar, to a great sullen roar of cheers, till it seemed to Ronnie as though all England must have been waiting in the street below. And within, all about him, were men; mad excitable men. One of those men—Cartwright—was shouting in his ear, "Bravo, my boy! Bravo!" A second—Spillcroft—kept on smiting him between the shoulders. A third—the gigantic Henry Smith-Assher—had grasped both his hands, whispering, "By God, you deserved to beat us," as another robed figure, a figure whom Ronnie remembered to have been his one-time enemy, slunk off through the crowding people.

Then, for a second, the people parted; and his eyes—dazed as his brain—saw Aliette. Aliette stood, high above him, ringed by people, in the oak-paneled dock. A wardress, a blue-uniformed prison-wardress, was kissing her; kissing his Aliette on the cheeks. Damn it, he had freed Aliette, freed her from the dock! Why didn't the wardress release her? Damn it, he'd release her himself.

"Come on, old man," said a voice; Spillcroft's voice; and suddenly Ronnie felt himself impelled through the people, impelled toward the dock.

And Aliette came down to him from the dock! Only now his brain, clearing a little, knew that this was not Aliette, but Lucy, Lucy Towers whom he had saved from the hangman's rope and the felon's cell.

She came toward him through the ringing, crowding people. He was looking into her eyes; Aliette's eyes. The eyes were tear-stained; and he knew, thrilling, that her reserve—the reserve stubborn as Aliette's own—had been broken at last.

They had reached one another. Both her hands were outstretched. Her hands grasped his. He knew that she was trying to raise his hands to her lips. But people pressed on them. People—panting, emotional people—pressed them apart. He heard some one say, "Let's chair them. Let's chair them both." He felt himself lifted off his feet. He heard a constable's voice: "Easy on, gentlemen. Easy on. This ain't a bear-garden."

And suddenly he found himself in the street of Old Bailey. The street, from wall to wall, was a river of upturned faces, laughing faces, cheering faces, shouting faces.

For the London mob had gone mob-mad; and the police could not hold them, hardly tried to hold them. "Good old Cavendish," howled the mob. "Good old Cut Cavendish. Put that in yer pipe and smoke it!" And again: "Luc-ee Towers. We want ter see Luc-ee. Where's Luc-ee? We want to see Standon—Standon. Where's Bertram Standon?"

6

Hector Brunton, K.C., hearing, alone in the deserted robing-room, the hoarse cheering of the mob, seemed to hear in it his father's rumbling voice: "The man who lets his wife live with somebody else is a common or garden pimp."

Chapter XXXIV

1

"I think I'll be going now, if you'll permit me, sir," said Benjamin Bunce. "And, if I may be allowed to say so, sir, congratulations."

"Thanks, Bunce. Toddle off if you like."

It was past eight o'clock, and the Temple curiously quiet. Ronnie, kindling himself a pipe and leaning back in his battered armchair, heard his clerk's boot-soles hurrying through, the colonnade of Pump Court; and after that, never a footfall.

Despite Spillcroft's invitation and Cartwright's, despite an imploring wire from Bertram Standon to meet his entire staff at the Savoy, the barrister had dined early and alone. His work had played him out. Looking back, he could remember nothing of the case, except that last frenzied scene outside the court, whence—the police good-temperedly intervening—he and his client and the armless sailor had escaped in John Cartwright's car. Trying to recapture the events of the last three days, and more especially the words of his final speech, it seemed as though he had been some one other than himself, as though the hand of fate itself had steered him to victory. Perhaps that was why victory seemed so valueless!

To sit there in the old chambers where he had dreamed so many dreams; to watch the pipe-smoke curling round his head, and know Lucy Towers saved; to imagine Lucy Towers and Bob Fielding happily married; even to realize Brunton, his enemy Brunton, beaten—afforded no satisfaction. Curious, he thought, how little his public triumph over Aliette's husband, his public success, affected him! So often in the last fifteen months he had thrilled to the vision of himself successful: yet now—now that success had actually been accomplished—it held no joy.

Glooming, Ronnie's thoughts switched from the public issue to the personal. What did it avail that he, Ronald Cavendish, should have rolled the "hanging prosecutor" in the dust; that the press was already blazing his fame from one end of England to another—so long as Brunton remained, as Brunton would remain, the legal owner of Aliette? What did it profit him to have saved the woman in the dock if he could not save the woman in his own home?

The pipe went out, and his slack fingers could not be bothered to rekindle it. Depression, the terrible depression of overstrain, settled like a miasma-cloud on his brain. His triumph became a mockery, his fame a whited sepulcher. Saving others, he could save neither himself nor the woman he loved. Aliette was outcast, would remain outcast; and he with her. All the pleasant things his success might have won for them both—social position, companionship of friends, political possibilities—were beyond their reach. To them, success could only bring money.

Bitterly he fell to reproaching himself—as all the lovers of all the Aliettes do reproach themselves in those hours when love comes not to their aid—for ever having persuaded her to run away with him. What was the use of blaming Brunton, of hating Brunton? He himself and no other was responsible. He felt the flame of his old hatred against Brunton blow back, scorching his own head. Truly loving Aliette, he should have been satisfied—as Robert Fielding had been satisfied—with renunciation.

"I've been selfish," he thought, "selfish"; and, so thinking, remembered his mother.

Toward her, too, he had played the complete egoist; forgetful—in his self-concentration, in the absorption of his work and the battle against his enemy—of her need for him, of her illness.

And abruptly, luminous through the darkness which had settled on his mind, Ronnie saw a picture of Daffadillies. The great house stood foursquare under the moon. Trees spired sable from the gleam of its lawns. Its roof glittered under a glittering sky. From its gabled windows glowed the saffron welcome of lamp-light. Behind one of those gabled windows, his mother, who had loved him all her life, who had grudged him never a thought, never a sacrifice, lay ill; mortally ill perhaps.

And suddenly it seemed to Julia's son as though the darkness of his own mind came between the moon and Daffadillies. Black clouds, ragged and menacing, drifted down from the glitter of the skies, blurring the saffron window-gleams. Mists swirled about the spring trees, across the gleam of the lawns. Watching the menace of those ragged clouds, the cold swirl of the mists, he knew fear, the old battle-fear of death.

If only the clouds would break, the mists roll away from Daffadillies. But there came no break in the ragged clouds. Black they banked, and blacker, round the high moon; till the moon was no more, and only the ghost of a ghostly house trembled—as smoke seen through smoked glass—through the swirl of the mist.

Then even the ghost of Daffadillies vanished; and, sightless, he peered at the void.

Till, out of the void, sound issued—the sound of a woman's voice—of his mother's voice: "Ronnie! Ronnie! I am afraid. Come to me."

2

With a start, Ronald Cavendish awoke.

The green-shaded lamp still burned at his head, showing up every stain on the leather desk-top, every ink-spot on the pewter inkstand. There were his quill pens; his thumb-soiled brief. There, on the shelves, were his law-books. At his feet, its ashes spilled from cracked bowl to worn carpet, lay the pipe he had been smoking. "I must have been dreaming," he thought.

But the dream and the fear of the dream still haunted his mind. Vainly, rubbing his eyes, he strove for courage. Always, his imagination saw the darkness gathering about Daffadillies; always, out of the gathering darkness, he heard his mother's voice—calling—calling. Till, fear-haunted, he sprang to his feet.

His feet moved under him. They moved very slowly, as the feet of a sleep-walker. He said to his feet, "This is foolishness, foolishness." He said to his feet, "Be still."

He found himself in the corridor. He found himself at the telephone. He said to himself, "I might just make certain that she's all right."

Then, startlingly, the telephone-bell rang; and, startled, he picked the receiver from the clip. Ages seemed to pass before he heard the operator's:

"City double-four two eight? Don't go away. I want you."

Followed, very distinct at that hour of the night, "Horsham, you're through"; and after a pause, "Is that Mr. Cavendish? Mr. Ronald Cavendish? This is Mrs. Sanderson speaking. I rang up Embankment House, but the porter said you weren't back yet." Already Ronnie's ears, acute, apprehensive, knew the worst. "Can you get through to Dr. Baynet? Can you bring him down at once? Your mother has had another hemorrhage."

"A bad one?" Ronnie tried to smooth the fear from his voice.

"I'm afraid so. Your wife's upstairs with Dr. Thompson. Would you like to speak to her?"

"No. Tell her that I'll get on to Sir Heron at once. Tell her, please," the words snapped decision, "that I'll bring him down to Daffadillies to-night. Do you understand? To-night! Tell the lodge-keeper to wait up for us, to have the gates open. Is that quite clear?"

"Quite clear." The automaton's answer sounded irritatingly calm. "Quite clear, thank you."

"Then good night." With a click of decision, Ronnie replaced the receiver. Danger, ousting fear, galvanized him to action. He looked at the clock. The hands pointed to 9:15. The last train for West Water left at nine! He snatched up the telephone-book; found the doctor's number; called it.

A man-servant answered. "Sir Heron's engaged. Can I take any message?"

"No. I want to speak to him personally."

"Sir Heron is giving a dinner-party, sir."

"Tell him the matter is urgent ... Yes ... Cavendish ... Ronald Cavendish."

The man left the instrument. Waiting, Ronnie grew apprehensive. Suppose Sir Heron refused to come.... Then he heard, "Is that you, Cavendish? No bad news, I hope?"

"Very bad, I'm afraid. I've just spoken to Daffadillies on the telephone. My mother's had another hemorrhage. Can you come down to-night?"

"To-night?"

"Yes. With me. The last train's gone. I'm going down by taxi."

Silence ... and again Ronnie grew apprehensive. Sir Heron was a

404

specialist—a great man. Absurd to ask such a favor of him!

Interrupted Sir Heron's decisive, "Very well. No need for a taxi. You can come down in my car. Where are you telephoning from?"

"The Temple."

"Then be here in twenty minutes."

3

Snatching his hat and his coat, clicking off the light, and slamming his oak behind him, Ronnie darted downstairs into Pump Court, through Pump Court and up Middle Temple Lane toward the barred gate which gives on to Fleet Street. In seconds he was at the side door of the gate—through it—and into a taxi. In seconds he was whirling away from the deserted law courts, past the gleaming front of the Gaiety Theater, down the Strand.

He wanted speed—speed. Not till they were out of the Strand and through Trafalgar Square did thought oust action from his mind. And then thought was fearful—terrifying. Again, as on that night when he and Aliette had taxied from Embankment House to Bruton Street, he saw his mother dying. But now he saw himself guilty of her death.

Harley Street reached, a long blue car purred past his taxi and pulled up a hundred yards ahead. Reaching the car, the taxi stopped. Ronnie leaped out; flung a couple of half-crowns to his driver; leaped up the steps of the Georgian house; and rang. The door opened instantaneously; revealing—behind the portly form of the butler—a long tessellated hall. Down the staircase into the hall—his dinner-party abandoned—came the punctual specialist.

"That you, Cavendish? I sha'n't be a moment." Sir Heron, already in his fur coat, his slouch hat pulled on anyhow, disappeared round the newel post of the staircase toward his consulting room; and reëmerged, with a battered black medicine-case in his hand. "Come along. We can talk in the car. In you go—"

The butler closed the door of the limousine behind them; and the doctor's chauffeur, obviously preinstructed as to their destination, turned the long

Rolls-Royce bonnet south.

"Another hemorrhage, you say?" Sir Heron lit himself a cigarette; and in the red spurt of the match, Ronnie could see that his face was troubled. "I'm glad you telephoned."

"It's very good of you to come down at such short notice, Sir Heron."

"Only my duty."

The great car swept down Portland Place, down Regent Street. At the Circus, Heron Baynet picked up the speaking-tube, and called, "Take the Bromley road, please."

"Wonderful woman, your mother," he said suddenly. "I wish I could have done more for her."

"There's no chance, then?"

"None now, I'm afraid." The car purred on out of London, and after a long time the specialist said: "Not that there ever was more than the ghost of a chance."

"There was a chance then—once?" Ronnie's face, seen in the intermittent light of the passing street-lamps, showed white with misery. Again he was remembering that other night—the night when he had waited with Smithers outside Julia's door.

"Meaning?" prevaricated the specialist.

"This." Bonnie's teeth clenched on the Bullet. "Suppose that my mother had gone away to Switzerland or the south of France a year ago, she might have been saved?"

"I doubt it."

"But you advised Switzerland, didn't you?"

"Admitted." Sir Heron looked shrewdly at his cross-examiner. "Blaming yourself?" he asked bruskly.

"Yes."

"You needn't. Even if she had done what I told her, we couldn't have cured the diabetes." He plunged into medical details.

"Nobody's to blame then?" The voice of Julia Cavendish's son embodied a whole army of questions.

"No, nobody. Not even herself. If you blame any one, blame nature." And Sir Heron, who knew more of Ronnie's story than Ronnie guessed, added quietly: "Your wife has been a wonderful nurse, Cavendish."

"Thank you, Sir Heron." The men's thoughts, meeting, understood one another. "You've taken rather a weight off my mind. Tell me one thing more. This work she's been doing: has it been harmful?"

"Not as harmful as trying to prevent her from doing it."

"I see." Consoled, Ronnie fell silent.

But the consolation was short-lived. All said and done, what did it matter at whose hand—his own or nature's—his mother lay stricken? Remained always the bitter unescapable knowledge that the surest consultant in England spoke of her as one already doomed. In a little while there would be no Julia. Even now—impossible as it seemed, driving thus down the living breathing streets into the living breathing country—she might be already dead.

4

"We've done it in well under two hours." Sir Heron, who had been dozing, opened his eyes as the car-lights climbed West Water Hill and began to thread their illuminated path through the woods which surround Daffadillies.

The Rolls-Royce made the lodge-gates; found them swung back from their stone pillars; swept through; and, rounding the drive, pulled up noiselessly at the open door of the great house. In the glow of the doorway stood Aliette. Ronnie hardly saw, as she came down the steps to meet him, how lined and drawn was her face, how wide with anxiety her brown eyes.

"Sir Heron"—her voice sounded calm, controlled; the hand on her lover's arm did not tremble—"you'll go to her at once, won't you? I made the local doctor give her morphia. That was right, wasn't it?"

"Quite right."

Kate, appearing through the baize door at the end of the hall, led the doctor upstairs.

"I did what I could, dear," said Aliette hurriedly. "Nurse has been splendid. Dr. Thompson came at once. But I'm afraid it isn't much good. It was all so terribly sudden. She'd gone to bed quite comfortably. Neither nurse nor I had the least idea. She only just managed to ring her bell in time. Smithers said it was just the same that first time at Bruton Street. She asked for you—twice."

"Is she in any pain?"

"No, darling, not now."

"You're sure?"

"Quite sure."

"But—that's all we can do for her?"

"I—I'm afraid so. Unless Sir Heron—" They spoke in whispers, like people already in the presence of death. Kate, running downstairs, disturbed them. Kate's eyes were swollen. Tears choked her voice.

"The doctor says, will you please come up, Mr. Ronnie."

Swiftly Ronnie passed up that gloomy balustered staircase. He couldn't think. He couldn't feel. Pain numbed his limbs, numbed his brain. Just outside his mother's room stood Smithers. She, too—he could see—had been crying. He wanted to console her—but his lips found no word.

His mother's door was ajar. Pushing it open, he knew fear. In that room waited Death—an impalpable figure—a figure of mist—icy-cold.

Entering the room, he was just aware of the local doctor's tweeded figure stooped over his mother's bed, and of Sir Heron—hand on his arm—whispering, "It's the end, I'm afraid, Cavendish."

Dr. Thompson made way; and, still incapable of thought, Ronnie moved toward the bed. A light burned by the bed. In the ring of the light he saw a face. The face, he knew, had been in pain, in terror. But now both the terror and the pain were gone from it. Morphia—eons ago some one must have told him about the morphia—had driven the terror and the pain away.

Could this gray countenance—this mask of shrunken cheek-bones, of closed eyes, and open mouth—be Julia's? If Julia, surely Julia was already dead. Surely the last breath had already left that wasted body, motionless under its bedclothes.

He became aware that his mother was not yet dead. Every now and then, breath gurgled in her throat. The gurgle of her breath terrified him. She was still in pain—in pain.

But she could not be in pain. No agony twitched that wasted body. The fingers of that hand which lay, white and shrunken on the eiderdown, did not move.

Surely he had been standing by his mother's bedside since the dawn of time. Fatigue rocked his limbs. His eyelids smarted with unshed tears. He wanted to kneel down, to press his lips in homage on those shrunken fingers.

Surely, the fingers moved. Surely, even at the gates of death, his mother was aware of him. Her eyes opened. The gurgling of her breath ceased. And suddenly, desperately, he wanted to hear her voice, to hear one last word from those bluing lips.

Then, in fear, Ronnie knew that the soul was passing. Then, in fear, he saw the flutter of it at his mother's mouth; saw the hover of it—palest tenuous flame—above her head. Despairingly, his soul called to hers: "Mater! Mater!"

But the soul might not speak with him. The tenuous flame fled upwards; and he knew that the body which had born his body was dead.

5

Both doctors were gone. Already nurse busied herself in the death-chamber.

But to Ronnie and Aliette, sitting side by side in the empty drawing-room, it seemed as though Julia's spirit still haunted the house, as though at any moment they might hear her fine courageous voice and see her come in to them. Outside—weeping for her—rain fell. The drip of it among the shrubberies, heard through closed curtains, was like the patter of little unhappy feet. If only, like the voice of the rain, their voices could weep for her! If only, like the feet of the rain, their feet could busy themselves about some task in her service!

A faint diffident knocking startled them. Mrs. Sanderson came in.

The automaton's cheeks were swollen. The eyes under her tortoise-shell spectacles showed red and heavy-lidded. "I'm sorry to disturb you," said Mrs. Sanderson, "but it was her wish." She moved toward them across the carpet; and Ronnie saw that she carried under her arm a thick wad of papers.

"She told me"—they hardly recognized the woman's voice—"to give you this as soon as she died. She told me to telephone Mr. Wilberforce, Mr. James Wilberforce. There's a letter for him, you know. I'm going to telephone Mr. Wilberforce in the morning. But this—this is for you, Mr. Ronnie. She said I was to give it to you as soon as I possibly could. She said I was to tell you that you were not to show it to anybody else until you had spoken to Mr. Wilberforce, Mr. James Wilberforce."

"Man," Aliette had risen; "what can it be?"

"It's a book." Ronnie spoke in a whisper. "The manuscript of a book. I wonder if she finished it."

"Yes. She finished it." The automaton handed her burden, to Ronnie, and disappeared.

"She"—Aliette moved away from the sofa where they had been sitting—"she said you weren't to show it to any one else."

"But that couldn't have included you."

"I'd rather not see—not yet." She was at the door now; and Ronnie, looking up at her—the parcel still in his hands—saw that she had gone very pale.

"Darling," he asked, "you're not ill, are you?"

"Ill?" She laughed—unsteadily—her fingers on the door-handle. "Ill? No, I'm not ill—only ... only—"

"But you are ill." He put the parcel down on the sofa and came across the room toward her. "Why, you're shaking all over."

She laughed again, hysterically. "I'm not. I'm not. I'm only tired. Worn out. I'm going to bed. Don't come up, Ronnie. Don't come up." And, kissing him, she ran from the room.

"Poor Alie," thought the man, "it's been too much for her."

6

Alone in the drawing-room, Ronnie sat staring at the thick wad of papers, and at the envelope which topped them. "To my son," read the writing on the envelope; the well-known handwriting with the little loops at the top of the "o's" and the upright triangles of the "m's" and "n's."

He took up and opened the envelope. Inside of it, folded, lay a single sheet of note-paper: "Don't be unhappy, Ronnie. Don't blame yourself. This book is my last effort for you and Aliette. I feel it is your way to freedom. Use it as you and James Wilberforce think best. I have just had news of your great success. It makes me very proud. Your Mother."

Ronnie's eyes blurred, as Julia's eyes had blurred when her weak hands penciled the uneven lines. Puzzled and miserable—his heart choking in his mouth—he turned from the letter to the papers. The papers were in typescript; six pads, each holed and taped.

"'Man's Law,'" read the topmost paper of all; "'The Story of a Wrong,' By Julia Cavendish: and by her dedicated to all those of her own sex who have suffered and are suffering injustice."

Julia's son picked the top pad from the manuscript, turned over the title-page, and began to read his mother's preface.

For a few lines he read aimlessly, as folk obsessed by grief read, their thoughts wandering from the written word. Then, with one paragraph, the words gripped him, so that he forgot even his grief.

"All my life," read the paragraph, "I have believed in the sanctity of the Christian marriage tie. Believing that the oath taken by a man and a woman before their God—'so long as ye both shall live'—might only be set aside by death, I made the safeguarding of that oath a fetish and a shibboleth. The purpose of this book is to undo, so far as in me lies, the teachings of my former works on the marriage question; and I embrace this purpose the more firmly because it has been brought home to me by personal experience that there are and must always be many cases in which the application of a rigid doctrine leads to misery. Therefore I have felt it my duty—a duty not undertaken lightly—to combat that rigid doctrine; and to plead, in substitution for a code which I now believe un-Christian, the doctrine of 'The Right to Married Happiness.'"

Interested, Ronnie read on. Outside, rain fell and fell. Within was no sound save the rustle of turned paper. The first chapter of "Man's Law"—the second—the third raced through his brain, enthralling him, holding him spellbound. The words became symbols of speech—speech itself. It seemed to him as though Julia Cavendish were actually in the room, as though actually he heard her voice. And the voice told him a story similar to his own. The story of a Ronald Cavendish and an Aliette Brunton!

But so grandly did the story draw him on, that only gradually—gradually as a man sees dawn dissolving night—did Ronnie realize the personal application of it; realize that here, in words of sheer genius, an advocate not tonguetied—where he himself would always have been tonguetied, in Aliette's defense—pleaded not so much the cause of all the Aliettes in the world as, in sentences now so reasoned that they convinced the very intellect, now so passionate that they wrung the very heart, the cause of his own individual Aliette, the cause of Hector Brunton's wife against her legal owner.

And at that, a little, the lawyer in Ronnie's mind ousted, the lover.

*

Half-way through the book, he put it down for a moment. Sentences—certain sentences so venomous that he marveled his mother could have written them—comments, certain comments all leveled against one particular character, stuck like needles in his legal mind. His legal mind said to him: "Slander. Those sentences, those comments, are actionable."

Then he picked up the manuscript again, and read on—on and on,—unconscious of the clock-tick from the mantelpiece, of the rain ceasing without, of the day dawning wan across the Sussex Downs.

*

Till violently, with the ending of the tale, remembering his mother's letter, he saw her purpose plain.

"Man's Law" represented Julia's "flaunting policy" carried to its uttermost extreme! It wasn't fiction at all—it was his own story—his story, and Aliette's and Hector's—scarcely disguised! He recollected her interest in the Carrington case—recollected telling her how Belfield had broken Carrington, at long last, by the aid of the press.

Julia, obviously, had planned to break Aliette's husband in much the same way. This book once published, Hector Brunton would be compelled (Julia's photographic memory had etched the husband of her tale so accurately that no reader could mistake him for other than the "hanging prosecutor") to bring an action for divorce. Brunton, even as Carrington, could not permit the knowledge that his wife lived openly with another man to become the public property of Julia Cavendish's million readers.

"Yes!"—for a moment hope kindled in Ronnie's dazed mind—"'Man's Law' would bring Aliette's husband to his senses! Publish the book; and Brunton must file his petition! Unless—unless he brought suit for libel. But if he did that, surely he would have to admit that his wife was living unsued in open adultery. Could a man make that admission—and still wear silk?"

Ronnie's hope expired; violently reaction set in. His heart quaked. He saw, in a flash, the thousand consequences which the publication of "Man's Law"—if, indeed, any publisher would set his imprint on so libelous a story—must entail. This, his mother's last effort to set Aliette free, was a two-edged weapon. However wielded, it would have to be wielded publicly. And publicity—even if it injured his enemy—could help neither him nor Aliette.

Publish the book—and the whole world would know their story! Yes, but who, in all the world, knowing their story, would sympathize with them? Even sympathizing, who would take their side? It took more than a book to turn public opinion. As far as decent people were concerned, the very asking for sympathy would alienate it. Suppose Brunton risked the scandal—sued for libel but not for divorce? Brunton couldn't very well do that. Still—

Fearfully, clutching the letter and the manuscript, Ronnie stumbled up the fast-lightening staircase. "Man's Law" seemed like a ton-weight of social dynamite—of social dynamite he dared not use—in his arms.

7

A night-light still burned on the landing. Still clutching "Man's Law," Ronnie stole toward the door of his mother's room. If only he could speak with her, kneel by her bedside, ask her for counsel! But the door was locked and he might not go in. Julia Cavendish on whom, lifelong, he had relied for counsel, could counsel him no more. And fearfully, doubtfully, dreading lest the weapon she had forged for him should shiver in pieces if he dared draw it from its scabbard, Julia's son crept to his dressing-room, and locked the weapon away.

"I'll ask Alie," he thought, "I'll ask Alie what she thinks about it."

But Aliette, when he went in to her, was fast asleep. She lay averted from the window, her head on her right arm, the tumble of her hair vivid among the pillows. Every now and then a little tormented moan came from between her lips.

Listening to that moan, believing—in his ignorance—that Hector Brunton was the sole cause of it, Ronald Cavendish made oath with himself, whatever the personal consequences, to use the weapon of his mother's forging.

Chapter XXXV

1

They were burying that flesh which had been Julia Cavendish among the cypresses of the South London cemetery whither she brought back the flesh which had been Ronnie's father when Ronnie was still a lad.

To all save three of the mourners it appeared as though death had conquered scandal, as though their every personal enmity were being laid to rest. But to James Wilberforce, standing at the brink of the grave, it appeared that he stood on the brink of a scandal so tremendous that nothing except the combined brains of Wilberforce, Wilberforce & Cartwright could prevent a social catastrophe, a regular holocaust of public reputations; his own, possibly, and Mollie's of a certainty, included.

Covertly, James Wilberforce looked at the semicircle of facts gathered round the white-surpliced clergyman. All Julia's family—Benthams, Edwardses, Robinsons; all her literary friends—Paul Flower, Dot Fancourt, Jack Coole, Robert Backwell, the Binneys; most of her many acquaintances among the various circles with which she had been intimate, were there to do her the last honor.

A little aloof stood the reporters; and at them James Wilberforce looked, too. "God knows what the newspapers won't say if this thing isn't hushed up," thought Jimmy.

The letter of the dead, those four handwritten sheets in their bulky envelope which Mrs. Sanderson had handed to him immediately on his arrival at Daffadillies, burned the solicitor's pocket. He thought how cleverly, yet how unwisely "the old lady's" plans had been laid; how, by adding a certain codicil to her will, she had made it virtually impossible for her executors to save the situation.

The clergyman was reading. "Man that is born of woman," read the clergyman, "hath but a short time to live, and is full of misery." "O holy and most merciful Savior, deliver us not into the bitter pains of eternal death."

Jimmy's thoughts wandered. "I wonder if I ought to tell Mollie," he thought. "I wonder if we ought to get married at once. I wonder how the devil we're going to break things to Mollie's sister. I wonder Mollie's sister didn't come to the funeral. Better not, I suppose."

The coffin on its canvas slings sank from sight into the moss-lined grave. It touched the bottom of the grave; and the slings relaxed.

"Forasmuch as it hath pleased Almighty God of His great mercy," read the clergyman, as Ronnie sprinkled a handful of earth on the coffin-lid. "From henceforth blessed are the dead which die in the Lord; even so saith the Spirit; for they rest from their labors."

James Wilberforce's mind came back to the ceremony. He looked at his friend. "Poor Ronnie," he mused, "his labors are only just begun." And so musing, Jimmy's gaze fell on a bearded man with an old-fashioned top-hat in his hand, who held himself very erect and a little apart from the remainder of the mourners.

"Rather sporting of Rear-Admiral Billy B. to turn up," thought James Wilberforce.

2

The funeral service was over. The clergyman, his surplice crinkling in the October wind, had returned to the chapel. By twos and threes the mourners were deserting the graveside. Ahead of them, unrecognized except by Wilberforce, went Rear-Admiral Billy, his head high, his heart troubled. Soon—felt the admiral—a parson and mourners would gather for him, for an old man who would have to face his God with a promise unfulfilled, with a duty unaccomplished.

The last of the mourners disappeared through the cemetery fates to their conveyances, leaving only Ronnie, Sir Peter, James Wilberforce and the sexton by the grave.

"We'd better take him back to Bruton Street with us," whispered Sir Peter to his son. "The less we delay things, at the present juncture—"

"Ronald, old chap"—Jimmy put a hand on his friend's shoulder,—"pater says he'll drive you home in our car. We've got to get this matter settled, and the sooner we come to some decision—"

Gilbert Frankau

"Very well." Ronnie, his face a purposeful mask, turned away from the scarred earth. "The mater's dead," he thought. "Dead. It's my duty to do as she would have done had she lived."

And while the three of them made their way slowly to Sir Peter's Daimler, he fell to resenting that Aliette had effaced herself from Julia's funeral. His mother had wished that he and Aliette should face the world together. His mother's wishes must be carried out, carried out faithfully.

3

Arrived at Bruton Street, Ronnie led his self-invited guests into the little box of a work-room; and, facing the pair of them from across his mother's Empire desk, said provocatively: "Sir Peter, it's no use. I've made up my mind. As I told Jimmy when he showed me the will, my mother's wishes must be carried out."

"But what were your mother's wishes?" The white-haired, white-mustached old gentleman who had steered so many social ships clear of the rocks, smiled benignly. "What were your mother's real wishes? Naturally, both my son and I recognize her object. But, much as we appreciate the filial devotion which prompts you to carry out her exact wishes, we have to consider the spirit of those wishes. Now suppose, mind you I'm only supposing, that we publish this book. The publication, as you yourself must be the first to admit, may defeat the very object your mother had in mind when she wrote it. Moreover, quite apart from the expense to the estate—"

"But the expense is provided for, pater," interrupted Jimmy. "And in view of the testator's letter to me—"

"That letter leaves the ultimate decision with us." Sir Peter, who loathed interruptions, shot an irritated glance at his son. "If we decide that this book should not see the light of day—"

"I'll never consent to that." Ronnie's voice was the voice of a fanatic. "And besides, even if the book were not published, there's always the codicil."

"Admitted." Sir Peter frowned. "The codicil is the difficulty. I wonder if you'd mind reading it to me again, Jimmy."

417

The Love-Story of Aliette Brunton

Jimmy got up, fumbled in the pocket of his overcoat, drew out a bulky document, unfolded it, and began to read, very slowly, the paragraph appended in Julia Cavendish's own handwriting to the last page:

I empower and charge my executors, Ronald Cavendish and Sir Peter Wilberforce, to devote any sum they may think fit, up to ten thousand pounds, for the purpose of having published my book entitled, "Man's Law," and more particularly for indemnifying the publishers of the same against any libel action which may be brought against them by Hector Brunton, K.C. And I further instruct my executors to invest the sum of twenty thousand pounds for the benefit of Aliette, née Fullerford, at present the wife of Hector Brunton, K.C. The said sum to become the absolute property of Aliette Brunton so soon as her legal husband, either by his death or by the process of divorce, sets her free to marry my son, Ronald Cavendish.

"Rather vague," commented Sir Peter. "Is it properly witnessed?"

"Yes." James Wilberforce laid the will on the desk, and stared ruminatively at his father. His father stared back at Jimmy. Both knew how impossible it would be to contest that codicil without the publicity of the courts. Both knew how fatal any publicity would be to their client.

But their client only laughed. "You see, Sir Peter, there's no way out. Even if I consented not to publish the book, this will has to be proved."

"But that means *immediate* publicity."

"Exactly." Ronald's mouth shut like the teeth of a pike. His eyes, in their resolution, were his mother's own. "Exactly."

Sir Peter, hitherto blandness itself, grew irritable. "You don't appear to realize, Cavendish, that the proving of this will means a terrific scandal."

"I realize that perfectly, Sir Peter. But scandal—as I see it—is the only way to effect my mother's object."

"All the same, I should not be doing my duty, either as your mother's friend or as your co-trustee, if I did not ask you before we come to any decision, to consider, first, the effect such a scandal would have on your career, and secondly, the effect it would have"—purposely the baronet paused—"on the reputation of the lady in the case."

"As far as the lady in the case is concerned," Ronnie's fingers rapped the desk-top, "her freedom is the paramount consideration."

"Is that the lady's view, or your own?" Sir Peter, seeing an ivory paper-knife near at hand, drew it quietly toward him.

"My own."

At that, Jimmy, who had been watching his friend carefully, rose and began to stride slowly up and down the little room. Quite apart from the personal issue (if the worst came to the worst, he and Mollie would have to be married by special license before the crash came!), it seemed to Jimmy that his friend must be saved, somehow or other, from the consequences of his own obstinacy. But how—how in the name of the law—could that saving be accomplished?

"And if the lady disapproves?" said Sir Peter.

"She will *not* disapprove," countered Ronnie.

In the pause which followed, Jimmy drew out Julia Cavendish's letter, and read it for the tenth time.

If I have brought any happiness into your life by bringing you and the woman you are going to marry together, help me to bring happiness into my son's life and into the life of the woman whom he is not able to marry. I feel that I have taken the best, the only way to put things right for Ronnie; but if there is any other method by which my main object, the object of forcing Hector Brunton to set his wife free, is possible of achievement, by all means explore it.

"Don't you think"—James Wilberforce put the letter back in his pocket and turned to Ronnie, who was eying his father in positive hostility—"that it might be advisable to discuss this matter with—Hector Brunton?"

"I won't have that. I'll be damned if I'll have that."

Ronnie's answer was openly provocative; but Sir Peter apparently had recovered his temper. "We mustn't be hasty," purred Sir Peter. "We mustn't be overhasty. As Julia Cavendish's executors, we have to regard the spirit rather than the letter of her instructions. Believe me, the immediate publication of that codicil would be fatal to the plans which your dear mother obviously had in mind. Fatal!"

And the baronet, lighting himself a cigarette, relapsed into thought.

Privately he considered that his old friend must have been mentally deranged some time before her death. Yet he dared not say so to her son; and, moreover, to prove mental derangement would entail more publicity than to prove the will itself.

Various plans for the avoidance of publicity began to pass through Sir Peter's mind. Brunton, faced with the alternative of the book's being published, might consent to file his petition for divorce. Then, Julia's main object accomplished, the book might be—accidentally destroyed. Other methods, too—gentler methods—might be adopted with the book. But what in Hades was one to do about the will? Unfortunately, tampering with wills constituted a felony. Therefore, unless some one ("And whom could I get to do it!" mused Sir Peter) risked going to jail, that will, that deadly, damning, white-faced, blue-written testament on the desk would have to be filed in toto at Somerset House. Filed, every pressman in England would seize upon it for a column.

A knock, followed by a voice asking, "May I come in, Ronnie?" brought the three men to their feet; and, before any of them could answer, the door opened, revealing "the lady in the case."

Aliette, her face pale above the high black mourning frock, stood irresolute in the doorway.

"I'm so sorry if I'm interrupting," she said. "I thought you'd gone, Sir Peter. I'll go away if you're talking business."

"We *are* talking business, dear lady," purred the baronet, playing with his acquired paper-knife. "Business which affects you more than anybody." And he looked at Ronnie as though to say, "Surely you'll consent to my consulting the person most concerned."

Ronnie signaled acquiescence; Jimmy closed the door; Aliette sat down; and Sir Peter began to speak.

At first Aliette could not grasp what the baronet was talking about. For three days now, her mind, still numb from the shock of Julia's sudden passing, had been obsessed by its own problems. Ronnie, she knew, was keeping some secret from her—as she from him. *His* secret, she guessed vaguely, must be in connection with his mother's book. Hers—

Gradually Sir Peter's words became comprehensible. He was reading Julia Cavendish's will. In so far as Aliette could understand the peculiar legal phraseology, Julia Cavendish had left everything to Ronnie. It struck her as curious that Sir Peter should go to all that trouble. Curious, too, that both Ronnie and his friend should look so worried! Ronnie would be even more worried if he knew that—

"That is the will," Sir Peter's voice interrupted the disturbing thought, "as my firm drafted it some years ago. But that will has been altered. Perhaps, before I read the alteration, I'd better explain to you about the book."

Now Aliette grew conscious of a question in her lover's eyes. The eyes never left her face. James Wilberforce, too, was eying her in a way that she could not understand. And suddenly Ronnie laid a hand upon her shoulder.

Sir Peter went on; "As you probably know, Mrs. Cavendish finished a novel just before she died. I have not yet read the manuscript of that novel, but it appears, from what my son and your—er—husband, who have read it, tell me, that the book is a *roman à clef*. A *roman à clef*, as I need hardly explain to you, dealing, as it does, with living people, sometimes results in a libel action. It is, among other things, to provide against the possibility of such a libel action that Mrs. Cavendish, without my firm's knowledge, altered her will."

"A libel action, Sir Peter?" Aliette's question was automatic.

"Yes. A libel action." The baronet picked his every word with care. "A libel action which might be brought against Mrs. Cavendish's estate and against the publishers of her book by your—er—former husband."

"Brought by Hector!" The exclamation, low and immediately suppressed, barely escaped Aliette's lips. But her shoulder trembled under Ronnie's hand; for now, in one inspired moment, she had grasped the secret of the book. Memory, casting back, recalled and understood every personal question put to her by the dead.

Sir Peter had stopped speaking. His eyes under the gold-rimmed glasses were perturbed, yet kindly. Obviously he found the situation difficult. She waited for Ronnie or James to intervene; but they, too, remained dumb.

The Love-Story of Aliette Brunton

And, "Do I understand," asked Aliette, summoning up all her courage, "that this novel is a personal story—the story of my"—her whole body quivered—"matrimonial difficulties?"

Ronnie removed his hand from her shoulder. James nodded assent. Admiration and gratitude mingled in Sir Peter's: "You've defined the matter exactly. One of the questions on which I should like *your* views is," the careful words paused, "whether or no this book should be published."

Fleetingly, Aliette thought, "Shall I tell them ... about myself? Does it make any difference?" Her intuition, suddenly active, remembered two hints dropped—purposefully perhaps—by Ronnie's mother. "Public judgment is usually inaccurate because the public is not told the whole truth"; "My dear, if only the whole world realized, as I realize, your story, they would not misjudge you."

"My views—" she parried aloud, playing for time.

"Publicity," she thought. "The flaunting policy once more. Dear God, that too." And, revisualizing the ordeal at Patrick O'Riordan's first night, her nerve frayed. Why couldn't these three men leave her in peace—in peace? Looking at Ronnie, she saw his eyes very resolute. He said:

"My decision is that the book must be published."

"Please let *me* finish, Cavendish," broke in Sir Peter; and to Aliette: "There are other points besides the publication of this book to be decided." Then he read to her, always in the same soft purr, the codicil; and explained, in tense, reasoned sentences, the consequences of its publication in the press, ending: "It means, to use a rather old-fashioned phrase, social ruin."

For a long while Aliette sat silent, her eyes wide, her pale hands clutching the black folds of her dress. Womanlike, she tried to put herself into the mind of the dead. Why had Julia Cavendish done this thing? Why? Could Julia have guessed that— Womanlike, Aliette looked into the future, and her cheeks grew hot.

Ronnie said: "He can't bring an action for libel without bringing one for divorce"; Sir Peter, "Let's stick to our point; the publication of this codicil means disaster—for all three of you." "It means Aliette's freedom," retorted

Ronnie.

The words of the codicil stood out in fire on the screen of Aliette's mind. She saw those words published, saw the book published, saw scandal follow scandal. Sir Peter was right. This thing meant ruin, social ruin for herself, for Ronnie, for Hector. And yet, and yet—it meant freedom. But would freedom come in time?

She glanced at the three men: at Ronnie and James, on their feet, motionless; at Sir Peter, seated at the desk, his hand fidgeting the ivory paper-knife. Swiftly, as a shuttle through the warp, her mind threaded the skeins of the future. The future would hold more than Ronnie.

"Before you take any decision," Jimmy spoke, "read this." He laid a letter before her. She read the letter through twice, her mind fighting for self-control, before asking:

"And is there no other method by which Mrs. Cavendish's 'main object' can be achieved, Sir Peter?"

Sir Peter's hand ceased fidgeting at the knife. "There may be a way," he said doubtfully. "But whether we can take it or not depends on your—er—former husband."

Blazing, Ronnie intervened. "Once and for all, I'll have no favors from that—that blackguard. He's made his own bed. Let him lie in it. Who the devil cares about scandal nowadays? I don't. And if Brunton does, so much the worse for him."

But the baronet's next remark shattered heroics. "I think," said the baronet sarcastically, "that as my co-executor is getting so very excited, we had better adjourn our conference. Perhaps you'll let me know what you both decide."

4

Late that same evening, Aliette and her lover sat alone in the familiar drawing-room among the familiar things—the jade idols, the Toby mugs, the Spanish velvets, and the Venetian brocades which Julia Cavendish had collected for her delight. Ever since their hasty dinner—most of the staff were still at Daffadillies—Ronnie had been urging her decision. Ever since dinner, haggard, she had been playing for time.

"It was my mother's wish," he said. "Let's prove the will; publish the book; take the consequences. Anything's worth while—if only he'll divorce you."

"Is it?" Dully, the woman's mind was looking for a loophole. "Is it worth while to ruin three lives?"

"Three?"

"Yes, dear. Yours—and mine ... and—and Hector's,"

"Hector!" The rage in Ronnie's voice terrified her, as it had been terrifying her all the evening. "We needn't consider him. He hasn't considered us. There would have been no need for all this if he'd been reasonable; if he'd brought his action for divorce when I asked him to."

"There are others we ought to consider, too." Aliette's hand, as she fondled her lover's rigid arm, was tremulous. "Mollie, James, my parents. They'll all suffer if you—if we carry this thing through."

"They must look after themselves. They've done nothing to help us. Don't let's discuss the matter further. Believe me, it's the only way to get what we want."

"But Sir Peter said—"

"Sir Peter's only a solicitor. Even if that blackguard did file his petition, the will and the book would have to be published."

"Why are you so bitter, man?" Aliette's eyes suffused.

"I'm not bitter. Only just. He had no mercy on Lucy Towers. I'll have none on him."

Aliette's hands ceased their fondling. For a little while she sat silent, unmoving among the deep cushions. Her mind, busied so long, could function no longer. She felt her womanliness naked—flesh quivering under the lash. She wanted to say to him: 'Ronnie, there's something—something you don't know.' But suddenly her courage—the courage which had carried her, carried them both, through the hard-run months—broke. She began to sob. Like a broken soul she sobbed—sobbed to herself, faintly, feebly; careless—as Lucy Towers had been careless—of the man who strove to comfort her. Words came, feebly, through the sobs:

"Man, I meant to make you so happy. I meant to make everybody happy. But I've failed—failed. I'm not blaming you. I'm not blaming your mother. You and your mother have done everything. Everything. It's only I who have been useless—useless. And I meant, heaven only knows how much I meant, to be of use. Before I ran away with you I reasoned it all out. I thought that I was doing right. There didn't seem to be any one else to consider except you and me." She broke off. Then, almost fiercely, she asked him: "Tell me I've been a little bit of use? Tell me I've made you happy—just sometimes—"

"Of course you've made me happy." He tried to take her hands; but her hands shrank from him.

"I don't believe it You're only saying that to comfort me."

"I'm not."

"You are." Hysteria took her by the throat. "You hate me. If you don't hate me—you ought to. I killed your mother." She broke off again, sobbing.

"Alie"—the tone told her that he thought her crazy—"what's the matter with you? Nothing could have saved Julia. Sir Heron told me."

"Sir Heron wouldn't tell *you*. Nobody would tell you anything. You're only a man. All men are the same. You're only thinking about yourself. You're not thinking about me. You only want your revenge on—on Hector. Why shouldn't you have your revenge?"

Suddenly, her sobbing ceased; and she faced him—this Aliette he could not understand—dry-eyed and venomous.

"Have your revenge on him if you want to. But don't pretend you're being just. Don't pretend you're being heroic. Don't pretend you're any better than he is. You're not. He's a man, just the same as you are. You talk about my freedom. You say scandal doesn't matter. Perhaps it doesn't—to a man. Perhaps it oughtn't to matter to me, I've belonged to two—"

At that, for the first and last time in their lives, Aliette was physically afraid of her lover. His arms, which had been seeking to comfort, abandoned her. He sprang to his feet. Jealousy, a red and angry aura of jealousy, exuded from him.

"Christ!" he burst out, "Christ! You needn't remind me of that."

Speech died at his lips. Furiously he strode from her—strode up and down the familiar room, the room in which, months since, she had given her unspoken promise to Julia Cavendish. The scene came back to her now. She thought, "What have I been saying? Dear God, what have I been saying?" Hysteria went out of her, as fever goes out, leaving her weak, nerveless.

"Damn it!" he was muttering, "damn it! Do you think I ever forget that once—once—"

She wanted to cry out to him, "I didn't mean to hurt you. You're hurting me now, hurting me beyond all bearing." But she knew that, hurt, she dared not cry out; knew that this was the hardest of the path, the full price, the full torment exacted.

Sitting there, rigid, uncomplaining, teeth bit to the under lip lest the mouth should cry out its torture, she remembered the long years with Hector, the mornings and the evenings when, facing him over the breakfast-table or the dinner-table, listening after dinner to his voice in the library, tolerating—for the sake of the dream which this other man had made true—the ungentle fury of his caresses, she had learned to wear the mask which so many married women wear, the mask of compliance.

Must she, for Ronnie's sake, still wear the mask? Daren't she tell him—the truth? Wouldn't he—knowing the truth—flinch from his purpose? Wasn't it worth while, more than worth while, to keep silence till the die was cast? Couldn't she still play for time? Time! There might be some way—some other way to freedom. If only she weren't so afraid—so strangely and newly afraid! If only Ronnie were not so angry!

And suddenly she knew that Ronnie's anger had left him. His feet stopped in mid-stride. Slowly he came across the room toward her; and she could see a little of the old understanding tenderness in his blue eyes. "Alie," he said, "forgive me."

"What is there to forgive?" Her voice sounded listless, broken. "It was my fault. I oughtn't to have spoken as I did. I called up the past. I had no right to call up the past. The past's dead. There's only the future—"

"Our future." He was on his knees to her now; and dumbly she put out her hands to him; dumbly she fondled his temples. Once more she wanted to cry; but no tears came. Her tongue felt parched, as though by some bitter fruit. "It wasn't your fault, Alie. You're tired. And perhaps I'm not being just. Perhaps I do want my revenge. But it's only for your sake"—his hands sought her shoulders—"only for your sake that I hate him. I think, I know, that if he'd made you happy, if he'd been kind to you, I could bear the thought of him. But he made you miserable. He hurt you. He's hurting you now. When I think of that, I go mad; mad with hatred."

She leaned forward; and words came to her. "You mustn't hate him. We mustn't either of us hate him. We're as much to blame as he is. At least, I am. I'm a rotten woman. Rotten."

"You're not. You 're the best woman in the world." Still on his knees to her by the sofa, he pressed her to him—gently, with that gentleness which had first won her heart. And desperately her heart wanted to tell him everything. But tears, tears of sheer weakness, choked her once more.

"Don't cry, darling. Please don't cry." Conscience-wrung, Ronnie could find no other words. The sense of his responsibility, of that awful responsibility for another's happiness, which only illegal lovers know, coiled—tighter than her arms; tighter than any hempen rope—round his neck. Her tears on his cheeks were as warm rain conjuring up the seedlings of remembrance. He recollected all the miracle of their early love for one another, all their resistances and their yieldings, all the weeks and all the months through which they had faced the herd's hostility in mutual loyalty, setting love above the law, trusting in one another—he in her as she in him—for faith. Always they had kept faith with one another. Yet always she, the woman, had borne the heavier burden. And in his ignorance he thought: "That's why I must insist—insist on this thing going through."

Then a voice, as it were his mother's, whispered to the mind of Ronald Cavendish: "Comfort her, Ronnie, comfort her. Before you ask this last sacrifice, tell her that the past has not been in vain"; and then, leaning on her lover, her eyes tear-blinded, her hands slack, her limbs relaxed in misery, Aliette heard him whisper:

"Darling woman. Darling girl. You're not to think that I don't understand. I do understand—everything." Like waves, the deeps of his fondness poured from him, poured over her, healing her wounds; and for a moment she thought that he had guessed the truth.

But his next words dispelled illusion. "I know all that you've given up for my sake; all that I've made you give. The blame, if blame there be, is mine. You've sacrificed yourself for me."

"It's no sacrifice." Hardly, she stirred in his arms. "I've never regretted—"

"Nor I, dear. Nor I. I've never regretted for one single instant. I never shall regret. Ever since that first day I saw you, you've been all the world to me. All the world. That's why I want you to be strong, not to be afraid of scandal, to let me do as my mother wished."

"Ronnie"—her eyes, wet with tears, sought his,—"have you counted the cost?"

"Yes." He released her; and she saw, as he rose up, that he was still resolute. "I've counted the cost. And it'll be heavy—heavier than anything we've had to bear yet. But it'll be worth while, Alie. Anything's worth while—if only I can win you your freedom."

"But your career—"

"My career doesn't matter any more. I've had success. I know how little it's worth. Nothing matters to me now except your happiness."

"My happiness?" Wistfully she looked down at her pale hands.

"Yes, your happiness. Oh, my dear, don't think I haven't realized, all these months, that you'll never be happy—really and truly happy—while you belong, legally, to that man."

"Ronnie"—she was trying, trying to tell him—"I have been happy. Always. It isn't that—"

"Yes, it is." He was afraid lest, pleading again, she should weaken his decision. "It's only that. Once you're my wife, you'll forget all the unhappy times."

"Shall I?" she thought. "Will that little ceremony make me forget that once, once I was Hector's?"

"That's why I want you to make up your mind," went on Ronnie. "Now. To-night. That's why I didn't want you to listen to Sir Peter. Alie, it isn't for my revenge I'm asking you to let me do this. It's for your own sake. If you were a different sort of woman, a rotten woman, perhaps it wouldn't matter so much—our not being married. But you—you can't go on forever like this. Just think, darling, just think what it would mean if we were to have children."

"Children," she repeated dully, "children." And then, his very vehemence terrifying her again, "Oh, Ronnie, Ronnie—don't ask me to decide to-night."

Chapter XXXVI

1

Two more days, terrible days for them both, went by. To Aliette it seemed as though all her courage, all her clear-visioning mentality, had ebbed away. Everything terrified her; but most of all the thought of precipitating crisis by telling Ronnie the truth.

Vainly he argued with her, pleaded with her. Vainly he assured her that it was their duty to risk this last maddest hazard of the gamble; that to jeopardize his newly-won success mattered not at all; that "social ruin" existed only in Sir Peter's imagination; that not even "social ruin" should deter them from achieving his mother's main object; that there was only the one way of achieving that object; and that, matrimony once achieved, they would be free to enjoy the riches Julia Cavendish had left them—in some other country if scandal drove them from their own. To all his arguments, Aliette had but one reply: the same reply she had made to him long and long ago in his chambers in Jermyn Street: "Don't try to hurry me, Ronnie. You must give me time—"

She hardly knew why she was playing for time. She hardly knew which she could face best; suspense or certainty. She wanted, more than anything, to run away. Her terrors, vague at first, grew definite. She saw Ronnie's career smashed, Ronnie's child born out of wedlock. She saw them both hounded from England. She asked herself, terror-stricken, if it were better that the child should be born out of wedlock than born in scandal. She told herself that wedlock, won as her lover pleaded with her to win it, at the price of notoriety and exile, would be the blacker stigma.

"We can go abroad," he said. How would that help the unborn? Hide themselves wheresoever they might, their world would not forget. If she gave way to Ronnie, then—for at least a generation—men and women of their own class would remember, when they spoke of Julia Cavendish's grandchild, how Julia Cavendish's son had ruined his career for the sake of Hector Brunton's wife.

And yet, what else was there to do but yield to Ronnie's wishes? And yet, even yielding, what would be gained? The divorce, if divorce came, would come too late. Or would it be just in time? She didn't know. She couldn't think. She could only reproach herself bitterly for the pride which had so long prevented her from seeking out Hector.

But Julia, Aliette could not reproach. Even though Julia had carried her vendetta beyond the grave, it was—Aliette knew—no selfish vendetta. All that Ronnie's mother had tried to achieve had been planned selflessly, out of love for them, and not out of hate for Hector.

If only Julia were alive! If only *her* mother had been such as Julia! If only she could have taken train to Clyst Fullerford! If only she could lay the legal issue before the legal wisdom of Andrew! For there must be (did not intuition warn her?), there was (had not Sir Peter almost said so?) some way, legal or illegal, out of this coil, some method by which all four of them—she, Ronnie, Ronnie's child, Hector—could be saved.

Always, her distraught mind grew more lenient toward Hector. Ronnie, her love and loyalty could console even for his lost career. The child (that fear also she knew) might never be born. But Hector her love could not console. He (had not Sir Peter said so?) would suffer as much as they. He might have to leave the bar. Was that fair? Was anything fair?

2

Those two days, Bruton Street seemed to run on oiled wheels. The "ridiculous flat" was locked up. Once more, as she had maided her through that other period of indecision at Hector's house in Lancaster Gate, Caroline Staley maided her mistress. Now, as then, the routine of life went on. Yet routine's self—Aliette felt—demanded decision. Ronnie's mother had been a woman of possessions, of responsibilities. The proving of her will pressed. She had been a woman of genius, too. The publishing of her book was a duty one owed to the world.

The will and the book haunted Aliette. Ronnie had locked them both away in a drawer of Julia's desk; but it seemed to her that their presence pervaded all the house. She felt conscious of them, stalking her from room to room.

It was as though both demanded something of her; as though her mind alone could decide their destiny. The will and the book were children! Julia's brain-children! To destroy them would be murder. To jeopardize her own chances of motherhood (that impulse, also, she knew) would be murder.

What could one do? What could one do? Ronnie was adamant. Palpably the mantle of his mother's resolution had fallen on Ronnie's shoulders. Ronnie was no longer the boyish lover she remembered. Ronnie was a man; a man bent on self-destruction, willing, for her sake, to sacrifice his whole career.

What could one do? What could one do? If Ronnie knew about the child, Ronnie might kill Hector. Ronnie hated Hector. Ronnie wouldn't mind the consequences, so long as Hector suffered them equally.

What could one do? Only play for time! Time.

A third day went by. She must decide—decide! Ronnie said so: Sir Peter had said so.

She must act—act. Better certain ruin than this suspense! She would run away, renounce Ronnie forever, renounce her legacy. She would efface herself from London, take that little cottage of her dreams; live there, year in, year out, unknown and unknowing of the world, satisfied with a clandestine Ronnie. There she would bring up Ronnie's child, his manchild, her Dennis; bring him up in ignorance of the smirch on his name, until such time as he grew old enough to judge for himself whether she had done right or wrong. She would go to Hector for the last time, implore him—for Ronnie's sake—to take pity on her. She would go to Ronnie, implore him—for her own sake—to take pity on Hector.

Like a squirrel-cage, the future whirled under the crazed feet of Aliette's thoughts. Like a squirrel, her crazed thoughts spun the cage of the future. Was there no way, no way out of the cage? She *must* find the way, the way out.

3

"It was very kind of you to make an appointment so quickly, Sir Peter."

"Not at all, dear lady, not at all."

Inspecting his client benignantly across the leather-topped desk by the big window of his Norfolk Street office, Sir Peter Wilberforce could see that Aliette's mental tether was stretched to its tautest. In the low light of a waning autumn sun, the face under the black Russian hat showed pale as thinnest ivory. The vivid eyes were pools of fear. Lines of indecision penciled the temples. But the little black-gloved hand she gave him had not trembled; nor had there been any fear, any indecision in the shy, ladylike voice. And the baronet had thought, "Now, I wonder, I wonder if *she'd* have the nerve."

His eyes ceased their benignant inspection, and wandered—apparently aimless—from the sunlight outside to the closed door, round the pictureless walls, till finally they rested among the racks of black deed-boxes. There were many titled names gold-lettered on those japanned deed-boxes; but the two names which interested Sir Peter's eye bore no titles. "And how is my co-executor," prompted his voice; "still heroic?"

"Worse than that." Aliette managed a smile.

"And you?"

"I'm afraid I'm not a bit heroic. Sir Peter, tell me; were you serious when you said that the proving of this will, the publication of this book, would mean—social ruin for—all three of us?"

"Perfectly serious, dear lady."

"And is there"—her heart sank—"no other method by which we—Ronnie—can carry out his mother's wishes?"

"That"—Sir Peter's eyes left the deed-boxes, and resumed an inspection suddenly more purposeful than benignant—"is precisely what I have been considering for the last three days."

"You said there might be a way—"

"Did I?" The old gentleman took up his ivory paper-knife. "Did I, though?"

"Yes. You said it depended on my—my former husband."

"Then I made a mistake." The Wilberforce purr, was sheerest self-accusation. "It doesn't. As a matter of fact, the plan I had in mind depends more on"—the paper-knife tapped slow Morse—"the lady in the case than any one else. And even then—"

The paper-knife hung suspended. Although the founder of Wilberforce, Wilberforce & Cartwright was celebrated for his handling of delicate situations, he had never, in half a century of practice, encountered a social situation as delicate as this one.

"Does my co-executor know of this visit?" he proceeded after a pause which dropped Aliette's heart into the tips of her shoes.

"No. I—I wanted to consult you privately."

"And would you be bound to—er—tell him of any suggestion I might make?"

"Well—" Again Aliette managed a smile. "That would rather depend on the suggestion, wouldn't it?"

The baronet smiled confidentially in reply. "You see, the main point, as I view it, is whether we have any means at our disposal by which we can induce your—er—former husband to bring an action for divorce. My co-executor, I gathered, was—shall we say—a trifle biased on the subject. Now, in the first place, it appears to me that if your—er—former husband knew about this codicil, he would do—er—almost anything to avoid its publication. If, therefore, he were told that by bringing his action immediately—"

"That"—Aliette leaned forward in her chair—"that wouldn't be fair."

"My dear lady," Sir Peter's paper-knife emphasized his disapproval of the interruption, "this is a solicitor's office, not a court of morals."

"But"—a diffident tremor twitched the pallid features—"it would be blackmail."

"Let us call it justifiable blackmail, performed with kid gloves for the victim's benefit. The victim himself, remember, has hardly behaved chivalrously."

"That's no reason why we should behave"—the pallid features flamed—"caddishly."

A little taken aback—female clients with moral scruples being somewhat rare at Norfolk Street—the baronet changed his tactics.

"If I follow you," he said quietly, "your objection is not so much to the partial solution of our problem as to the method of attaining it. Very well.

Let us presume—mind you, it's only the merest presumption—that the divorce question is arranged without even justifiable—er—blackmail, and that the codicil to Mrs. Cavendish's will had—shall we say?—never been penned. That would still leave us faced with the question of the novel. My co-executor, I gather, still insists on its being published? He wouldn't approve, for instance, if I advised its total destruction?"

"Neither of us could bear that." Aliette's voice was unflinching. "Ronnie's mother sacrificed six months of her life to finish that book. To destroy it would be worse than blackmail, it would be—"

"Murder. Quite so." Once more, the purposeful eyes wandered from their client's face to the deed-boxes against the wall. "Mrs. Julia Cavendish," read the eyes among the deed-boxes; and, thereunder, "Mr. Paul Flower." "Of course the novel must be published. But need it be published exactly in its present form? Now presuming—recollect this is still only the merest presumption—that the—er—divorce were arranged, and the—er—codicil off our minds, don't you think we might—shall we say, alter the novel?"

"Alter it?" Aliette started. Here, at last, was a gleam of hope.

"You see," the purr grew pronounced, "this is not the first time, nor do I expect it will be the last, that the work of a talented author has required legal revision. As a matter of cold fact, most modern novels are more or less libelous. Publishers are constantly asking my advice on the point. In the case of Mrs. Cavendish's work, curiously enough, it was asked once before. I think I may say, without breaking confidence, that I suggested to Sir Frederick then, as I am suggesting to you now, that certain alterations should be made."

"And were they?" The gleam of hope brightened.

"After a great deal of protest, yes."

"But then"—the gleam flickered out—"Mrs. Cavendish was alive. She made the alterations herself."

"Your pardon." Sir Peter almost permitted himself a wink. "She did nothing of the sort. She told Sir Frederick and myself that we were vandals; and went off to Italy vowing she'd never set pen to paper again. However, she left the manuscript behind; and we—er—did what was necessary."

"You mean to say that Ronnie's mother let some one else tamper with her work?"

"Tamper!" This time the baronet actually did wink. "I wonder how my friend and client, Mr. Paul Flower, who—to tell you the truth—made the alterations on which I insisted, would like to hear himself described as a tamperer."

"And you think that Mr. Flower would—"

The house-telephone buzzed, interrupting them. Sir Peter answered it: "I told you I wasn't to be disturbed.... Oh, is that you James? Very important, eh?... Well, let's hear what it is."

Aliette, her distraught mind clutching at the baronet's suggestions as a drowning woman clutches her rescuer, hardly listened to the conversation. Yet she was aware, dimly, that a mask had come over Sir Peter's face; that his concentration had switched, as only the legal brain can switch its concentration, without effort from her to the instrument.

Woman-like, the switch irritated her. "Yes," she heard. "Yes. I'd better see him myself.... No, I don't think a meeting would be advisable.... Tell him that at present there are certain difficulties, certain very serious difficulties, in the way.... No. He'd better stop with you. I shall be able to see him in about ten minutes—a quarter of an hour at the outside."

Sir Peter hung up the house-telephone, and turned to Aliette. The legal mask still covered his face. Behind it, he thought, "Poor little woman. This will cheer her up. I wonder if I ought to let that particular cat out of the bag yet awhile? Better not. Much better not. It might upset the whole apple-cart."

"Let me see," the mask changed, "what were we talking about? Oh, yes, the book, of course. Now, what have you got to say to my suggestion?"

"I think it splendid." Aliette's irritation subsided. "But—even if Mr. Flower consents to alter the book—there's always the will. We couldn't"—hopefully—"we couldn't alter that, too, could we?"

"Hardly." Now, feeling himself at the very crux of their interview, Sir Peter took up his paper-knife again. "Hardly. Quite apart from its being a felony, it would be robbing you of twenty thousand pounds."

436

"But that wouldn't matter a bit."

"Seriously?"

"Quite seriously, Sir Peter." Strange that she had never even considered that point!

"Even then"—still more taken aback, for female clients who disdained fortunes were even rarer than moralists in Norfolk Street, the senior partner in Wilberforce, Wilberforce & Cartwright tapped a frantic SOS on the desk-top—"even then, I'm afraid, we couldn't alter the will."

"Couldn't we keep it out of the newspapers?"

"I'm afraid not. Mrs. Cavendish, you see, was a very important personage. The public will be interested, not only in the extent of her fortune, but in how she has disposed of it."

"But surely, with your influence—" Once more Aliette felt hopeless.

"Even my influence"—Sir Peter leaned forward, pointing the paper-knife at her—"even my influence cannot keep 'news' back. Therefore, I'm afraid that" ("this is the moment," he thought, "the absolute and only psychological moment") "unless some *accident* were to happen—unless the will were, shall we say, burnt—neither my first idea, which you will remember was that we should approach your—er—former husband with a view to his taking immediate action, nor my second suggestion, that we should alter the book, could be of the slightest assistance."

There intervened a long and peculiar silence; during which, as poker-players across a poker-table, the old man and the young woman tried to fathom one another's minds.

At last the woman asked:

"Tell me, suppose this—this accident of which you have spoken were to happen, what would be the consequences?"

"The consequences to whom?"

"To"—Aliette, her thoughts racing, fumbled at the phrase—"to the person who might burn—who might be responsible for the accident."

"That would depend." Sir Peter's words started pat from under his mustache. "If the person responsible for the accident were to benefit by the destruction of the will, the consequences to that person, if discovered, would be very serious. But if that person, instead of benefiting, stood to lose twenty thousand pounds—" He broke off; adding, rather gruffly, "You'll understand that if Mrs. Cavendish had died without making a will, her son, as next of kin, would inherit the entire estate?"

Ensued another momentous pause. Then quietly, Aliette said: "Sir Peter, tell me one thing more. How soon—after a divorce-case—can a woman re-marry?"

Startled—sensing, in one vivid flash, the reason of her question—the baronet rose from his chair; and Aliette—her mind, for all the quietness of her voice, in utter turmoil—rose with him.

"How soon?" she repeated.

"Not for six months," Sir Peter hesitated; "and we can't rely on less than three between the filing of the petition and the decree nisi."

At that, his client's face went dead white, so that, for a moment, Sir Peter thought she must faint. But she controlled herself. "And is there no—no exception to that rule?"

"It has been varied—once."

"Is that"—desperately, despairingly, Aliette flung all her cards on the table—"is that all the hope you can give me if—if I agree to every suggestion you have made this afternoon?"

"Dear lady,"—the man rather than the lawyer spoke—"I daren't say more than this: If my influence counts for anything, every ounce of it is on your side."

"Thank you, Sir Peter."

For a moment they faced one another in silence. Then, without another word, Aliette proffered her hand.

*

Hardly had the door closed behind her when Sir Peter rushed to the house-telephone. "James!" called Sir Peter. "James! Bring the admiral in here at once."

Chapter XXXVII

1

Dazed, hopeless, almost beaten, Aliette passed out of the offices of Wilberforce, Wilberforce & Cartwright.

The sun had already set. The Embankment showed steel-gray and violet; fantastic under a fantastic sky. Trams clanged by her. Taxis. Cars. She did not see them. She did not see London. She saw the country, the country under a March sunset. It seemed to her that she was riding; riding alone; riding for defeat in a desperate race.

Automatically her feet turned away from the sunset—eastward from Norfolk Street toward the Temple. Above her, the sky darkened. Lamps gleamed along the Embankment. But no lamp of hope gleamed in her mind. There was no way out of the cage. The book could be altered, the will destroyed. Hector, blackmailed, might bring his action. What did that matter? Freedom, even won, must come too late. Ronnie's child, the child soon to stir in her womb, would be a bastard. A bastard!

She must go to Ronnie. She must tell him the truth. The awful truth.

And suddenly, her brain clearing a little, she knew that she was standing at the gates of the Temple. Ronnie was in there—in there—barely a hundred yards away—behind those railings—across that misty lawn—among the lights and the pinnacles. Ronnie would help her. The law would help. Surely, surely man's law was not so cruel to man's women?

The gate of the Temple stood open. Slowly, she went toward the gate. Behind her she heard the vague ripple of the river, of London's river. The river called to her. "Come to me," rippled London's river, "I am the way out—the one way out of the cage."

Swiftly she passed through the gate. Swiftly, a blind thing seeking its mate, she passed up the lane. Figures hurried by her. She did not see them. She saw Ronnie—Ronnie in wig-and-gown; Ronnie pleading her cause before the law.

Swiftly she passed under the archway. Swiftly, unconscious of one hurrying behind her, she made the tiled passage which leads to Pump Court. Ronnie—Ronnie would not plead for her. Ronnie, knowing the truth, would know her for what she was. For a woman who had belonged to two men. On such, man's law had no mercy. She could go no further—no further. Better the river! Better the river than man's law!

Slowly, she turned away—away from the vision of Ronnie. It was all dark—dark. Darkness and the sound of feet. "Clop," went the feet, "clop clop, clop clop." The feet stopped; and a voice—a known voice—hailed her out of the darkness.

"Alie!" hailed the voice. "Alie! Is that you?"

Still dazed, she could not answer. The voice, close this time, hailed her again. "Alie! Is that you, Alie?"

"Yes. Who is it?"

"Your father-in-law."

The feet clopped again; and now—her mind all confusion—she recognized, within a yard of her, the trim, old-fashioned figure, the vast beard of Rear-Admiral Billy.

"Good God!" panted the admiral. "Good God—I've never run so fast in me life." And, without another word, he gripped her by the arm, steering her rapidly through the dark passage into Pump Court, out of Pump Court, past the Temple itself, and across King's Bench Walk.

"Billy!" she managed to gasp. "Billy, where are you taking me?"

"To my damn fool of a son."

She tried to free herself, but the grasp on her elbow tightened. For Rear-Admiral Billy, rushing hot-foot out of Sir Peter's offices and—directed by the commissionaire—down the Embankment in pursuit of his son's wife, had determined to take no more advice from lawyers.

"My damn fool of a son's been asking to see you for days," he panted. "Sir Peter—silly old codger—said it was not advisable."

It flashed through Aliette's distraught mind that she must be having a nightmare. A nightmare! Billy's beard meshed his words. Billy would go on walking, walking and talking and gripping her by the arm until she woke up. But it couldn't be a nightmare. Billy was real—real. Billy was dragging her away from Ronnie, dragging her back to Hector. They were within ten yards of Hector's chambers. She recognized the stone stairs, the lamp.

Stubbornly, then, she dug her heels into the gravel. Stubbornly—one thought only in her mind—she faced her panting captor.

"Billy, I'm not going in there."

"Why on earth not? Hector won't eat you."

"Ronnie wouldn't like it."

"Can't help that. Hector's game to divorce you. That's enough for you."

"It isn't." Other thoughts, terrible thoughts, harried her. "It isn't. Billy, you've just come from Sir Peter's. Did he tell you anything—anything about the codicil—anything about me?"

And Rear-Admiral Billy, for the good of his soul, committed the double perjury: "The only thing I know, me dear, is that my damn fool of a son made up his mind to divorce you nearly a fortnight ago, and that I've been trying to get Sir Peter to let the pair of you meet ever since. Come on, now, don't be obstinate."

Almost forced up the stone stairs by the renewed grip on her arm, Aliette was aware, dimly, of David Patterson's astonished countenance, of the admiral swinging past David Patterson, of a chair against which she leaned, of an opening door and a quick inaudible colloquy. Then the admiral came back and said to her: "In we go."

Automatically in she went.

Hector stood, motionless, behind his littered desk. She saw him through a glass, a glass of silence, not as the man she had feared and hated, but as a stranger whose eyes were gentle, whose shoulders were bowed, a complete stranger who proffered no hand. The glass of silence slid away; and the stranger spoke to her.

"Won't you sit down?"

Exhausted, she obeyed. The stranger turned to Hector's father, and said, pleadingly: "You'll leave us alone for five minutes, won't you, sir?"

The admiral went out without a word.

"I wanted to see you." The stranger, still on his feet, laughed—a pitiful little laugh, high in the throat. And suddenly she knew him for her legal owner.

"Why did you want to see me?" Could this be the man who had tortured her so long; this broken, stammering creature whose eyes seemed afraid to look into her eyes?

"I don't quite know. Shall we say that I just—just wanted to see you? You mustn't stay more than five minutes, you know. It might—it might invalidate the proceedings—the divorce proceedings. They're rather technical. You see, dear,"—the word came clumsily from between the thin lips—"as things have turned out, I'm afraid—I'm afraid that I shall have to divorce *you*. I've been trying to arrange things the other way. But it can't be done. Too many people know. There's the king's proctor, you see. But that wasn't why I wanted to talk to you."

Dumbly, realizing a little of the pain behind those gray unshifting pupils, Aliette listened. Speak she could not. What did the divorce matter? The divorce would come too late. Too late!

The man who had found his own soul went on: "What I wanted to tell you was that everything will be done quietly. As quietly as possible. If there's any publicity, you sha'n't suffer from it. I give you my word about that."

She managed to say: "You're being very kind to me, Hector. Too kind."

"It's you who are kind"—the voice of the "hanging prosecutor" was the voice of a schoolboy—"and I don't deserve kindness of you. I've behaved like a cad right through the piece. But you'll shake hands with me, won't you? You'll part friends? You'll say that you forgive?"

Automatically Aliette rose. "There's nothing to forgive," she said dully. "Nothing."

Automatically she took off her glove, and offered him her right hand.

Holding his wife's fingers for one last fugitive second, Hector Brunton was conscious that a shiver—the tiniest faintest shiver as of revulsion—ran through her body. And Hector Brunton thought: "This is my punishment, my supreme punishment. God, if there is a such a person, can do no more to me."

Then, releasing her hand, he said to himself: "But I can't let her go. I can't let her go out of my life like this. She's miserable, miserable."

His father's recent words flashed through his mind. Suppose—suppose Aliette were to die, as Lucy Towers had so nearly died? Suppose that Aliette, crazed and with child, were to kill herself. And he thought: "I've got to say something, something that will give her hope."

He asked, gently, looking into her eyes for the last time: "I'll do my best to get things through as quickly as possible, You'd like that, wouldn't you?"

She stared at him, blankly. "Can these things be done—quickly, Hector?"

"They shall be," promised Hector Brunton, K.C.

2

Somehow, she was in Julia's work-room. Somehow, she had reached home before Ronnie. To get home before Ronnie! That had been her one panic ever since leaving Hector.

Of her parting with Hector, with the admiral; of her scurry through the Temple; of her taxi chugging, chugging, chugging down the Embankment, chugging up Northumberland Avenue, chugging through Trafalgar Square, of her taxi blocked in the Haymarket, of herself calling frantically through the window, "Don't go up the Haymarket," of their sweep along Pall Mall, up St. James's Street and along Piccadilly, Aliette remembered nothing. She knew only that there was hope—a gleam of hope for them all, for Ronnie's child, for Ronnie, for herself, for Hector; knew only that she must act—act at once—before Ronnie came home.

Perhaps Ronnie was home already. Perhaps he had gone upstairs to dress. Perhaps he had heard her let herself in with her latch-key.

A key! If only there were a key, so that she might lock herself in Julia's work-room.

A key! If only there were a key, so that she might open Julia's desk. How the fire glowed on the red mahogany, on the yellow brass of the desk! How the fire crackled, crackled!

She must break open the desk. Break it open before Ronnie could stop her. She must save Ronnie—save Hector. They were only men. Men of the law—of man's law. Men only talked. She, the mother, must act—act!

The Love-Story of Aliette Brunton

Now, in the fraction of a second, Aliette was at the fireplace. Now she had seized the bright steel poker in both hands. Now she was at the desk. Now she had inserted the poker through the ormolu handle of the drawer in the pedestal of the desk. Now—gingerly—she levered her poker against the mahogany rim of the desk.

But the locked drawer would not open. Stubbornly its lock fought against her lever. Panic gripped her by the throat. She must be quick—quick. Suppose Ronnie were home, suppose Ronnie heard? Ronnie would hate her—hate her for damaging his mother's desk. Julia's beautiful desk. Never mind—never mind the desk.

Frantically, her hands dragged at the poker. The mahogany splintered and splintered. God! what a noise she was making. Would the lock never yield?

Her eyes blurred. Her breasts ached. Her wrists ached. She could feel sweat under her armpits, feel the breath whistling through her lips. She was beaten, beaten. She would not be beaten—she would conquer the stubbornness of that lock. Conquer it.

Teeth set, little hands steel on steel, Aliette propped both feet against the pedestal, and flung back her full weight from the lever.

*

The poker was bent in her hands, the mahogany desk-top splintered to white slivers. But the lock had yielded, the drawer stood out open from its pedestal. There—there lay the will, the will Sir Peter had told her she must burn. Quickly, she snatched at it. Quickly, she dashed to the fireplace, dashed it on the fire. Quickly, she snatched up the shovel, pressed the will down among the flames.

But the flames would not kindle. The thick parchment would not take fire. It would only curl—curl. The words on the curling parchment hypnotized her. "Twenty thousand pounds for the benefit of Aliette, née Fullerford, at present the wife of—"

Slowly, slowly, the parchment was kindling.

But even as Aliette's eyes saw the parchment blacken to the flames, her ears caught the sound of a key in the lock of the front door, of the door closing,

444

of feet—Ronnie's feet—coming swiftly down the passage.

"Alie, Alie! I say, darling, are you in the library?"

And a second afterward he stood in the doorway. She knew that he was eying the desk, eying her back as she stooped to hurry her work.

"What are you doing?"

Aliette neither looked up nor answered. Her thoughts were all for the flames—for the blessed consuming flames.

"What are you burning?"

He sprang across the room at her; and the shovel dropped with a clatter from her nerveless fingers.

Turning, she faced him. He put out an arm as though to fend her from the fire. She seized his arm with both hands, crying, "You're not to. You're not to."

He struggled with her; but she fought him, fought him away from the fire. Behind her, in the flames, the last shred of parchment charred to stiff black ashes.

"Alie"—the loved face was a blur before her eyes, the loved voice a far-away whisper in her ear—"Alie—what have you done? You haven't burnt it? You haven't burnt my mother's book?"

"No. Not the book. Sir Peter says we can alter the book. But we can't alter the will. I had to burn the will, because—because of Dennis."

"Dennis?"

"Yes. Dennis. Our boy, Dennis." Suddenly, the loved face went black, black as charred parchment before her eyes. "I only did it for the boy, Ronnie. Can't you understand?"

*

Holding her, fainted, in his arms, Ronald Cavendish understood a little of his own unworthiness.

Epilogue

1

Windmill House, a modest broad-eaved, slant-gabled Tudor building, stone below, brick and black oak above, the whole roofed with Colleyweston slate-slabs which time had lichened to dark-green velvet, surveys the Rutland hamlet of Little Overdine from the brow of Little Overdine Hill. Beyond its walled gates the white road switches down between two files of red cottages, past the Norman tower of Little Overdine Church, toward Screever Castle and the distant Screever Vale. Behind it and about it the shires sweep sheer fields of ridge-and-furrow to the far and the clear horizons whither—all winter—high-mettled riders and high-mettled horses pour at a gallop after the pouring hounds.

But now, all about Windmill House, the ridge-and-furrows stood knee-deep in hay; and hounds pattered mute at early morning exercise along the white road; and the high-mettled horses grazed leisurely in the shade of the hawthorn hedges; and, in every covert from Lomondham Ruffs to Highborough Gorse the red vixens suckled unmolested. For now, it was spring in Rutland—spring in the little county of the big-bosoming pastures and the big-bosomed women—spring, too, in the heart of Ronald Cavendish!

Yet, for him, spring held its fear. "Your wife will be all right," Dr. Hartley had assured. "Everything's going splendidly. Some time this evening, I expect. About six o'clock if we're lucky. Why don't you go out for a ride?"

And Aliette, smiling up at him through the increasing pangs, had said almost the same thing: "Go away, man. Please go away."

As he went from her, out of the high cretonne-bright room down the blue-carpeted stairs into a hall fragrant with white lilac, apprehension tightened its grip on Ronnie. Suppose Hartley had lied to him—suppose Hartley had made a mistake—suppose Aliette, his Aliette, were—were not to "get over things"?

"But that's ridiculous," he said to himself, "quite ridiculous. Alie's so strong. And besides, after all we've been through together, *that* just couldn't

446

happen."

He wandered into the low-ceiled library, picked a book at random, and sat down to read. But the words of the book conveyed no meaning to his brain. His brain was upstairs—with Alie. Kate came in to remind him of lunch. He said to her, speaking softly as though he were in a sick-room: "Oh, bring me something in here, will you?"

Kate brought some sandwiches, and a whisky-decanter. He ate a sandwich, and drank a stiff peg. Then he crept quietly up the wide staircase and listened outside Alie's door. But the closed mahogany let through no sound; and after a little while he tiptoed downstairs again.

"If only," he thought, "it were all over. Safely over!" His heart ached for the woman he loved, for the pangs which she must bear alone. Almost, he hated the unborn cause of her sufferings. What need had he and Alie of children? Was not their love for one another all-sufficing? Had they not won enough from life already? Why tempt Providence with yet another hazard?

Suppose—suppose Alie were to die?

Fretfully Ronnie wandered back to the library; fretfully he flung his long length into a big saddle-bag chair. But he could not rest in the chair. The Wixton imagination tore and tore at his brain. Windmill House, last of Julia Cavendish's Little Overdine properties; Windmill House, where his mother had honeymooned with his father; Windmill House, whither he had brought Aliette for sanctuary while the law was separating her from Hector—seemed sanctuary no longer. Death and life hovered about the place, each contentious for mastery.

He looked at the Chippendale clock on the dark oak mantelpiece. The clock-hands pointed two. "Another four hours," he thought. "Another four eternities!"

How the minutes dragged as one watched them! How cruel, how desperately cruel was time!

He looked out of the window, through the shining lattices to a shining garden. Yesterday's gale no longer blew. It had pelted all morning; and the tennis-lawn still glinted with raindrops. Thrushes hopped on it, and blackbirds. Through the open pane in the lattices, from under the eaves of the house, came faint eager twitterings. Out of doors, perhaps, one would feel more hopeful, less—less infernally jumpy.

Ronnie, closing the library door behind him, stole quietly across the square hall, and picked an old tweed cap from its peg in the cloakroom, an ashplant from its corner in the porch. The front door of Windmill House stood open. Through it he could see the flagstone path, bright either side with vari-colored primulas; and at the end of the flags, high-hung between brown stone walls, the wrought-iron gates that gave on to the highroad.

For a long time, hands in his pockets, the ashplant dangling by its crook from his forearm, Aliette Cavendish's husband stood ruminant under the sloped porch. For a long time his memory, apprehension-prompted, conjured up the past months.

He recollected how, by the sheerest luck, Windmill House had fallen tenantless just when they most needed a refuge from London; how, at first sight of the place, Alie, a white-cheeked pathetic Alie, nerve-wracked and listless, had brightened to interest; and how, as autumn deepened to winter, she had made the Tudor house a veritable home. He recollected himself, Friday after Friday, driving his new car down from London; finding her, week after week, braver, healthier, better and better equipped for the ordeal to be faced. He recollected their joyous Christmas together—and the black days which had followed Christmas—the days when "the case" loomed near and nearer, frightening her anew with the dread of "those awful newspapers."

Luckily, he had been able to keep most of "those awful newspapers" from her; so that she had seen only three reports of "The Hanging Prosecutor's Divorce-Suit."

Ronnie remembered, standing there motionless in the gabled doorway, how—each helping each through the difficult days—they had made light of that trouble, telling one another that it was "like having a tooth out; soon over!" Nevertheless, the memory still ached at times—as a broken bone aches to the cold long after the cure of the actual fracture.

And, "I wonder," thought Ronald Cavendish, lover, "whether the people who make their livings by it, the writing-folk, know how much the written word can hurt? I wonder if Julia knew, when she wrote 'Man's Law.'"

He began to think of Julia, tenderly, as the imaginative think of the dead. Julia would be glad to know that the purpose of her book had been accomplished before its publication; that, published, it would contain no hurt. Julia, chivalrous, would not wish to injure a man who—at the pinch of things—had behaved chivalrously.

For that in the end Hector Brunton had behaved well, even his enemy admitted. Had it not been for Brunton, Brunton with his tremendous influence, the six months between the granting of the divorce-decree and the making of that decree absolute would never have been shortened to three. Had it not been for Brunton, not even Sir Peter Wilberforce could have succeeded in setting Aliette free to marry her lover before her lover's child was born to her.

And on that, vividly, Ronnie's memory conjured up the scene of three days ago: he and she, Roberts the chauffeur for witness, being legally married in the dingy registrar's office of the near-by townlet. Driving back to Windmill House, they had laughed together—a little cynically—at the formality. Yet underneath their laughter had been tears, tears of gratitude to the kindly Fates.

"Man," Aliette had smiled, "it feels so—so funny not to be an outcast any more."

2

Ponto's sleek head nuzzling his knees disturbed Ronnie's musing. He took his hands out of his pockets and began fondling the dog's ears. But Ponto wanted his mistress; restlessly he tried to push his way into the house. His slitty eyes were a dumb miserable question; his great stern stood out, rigid as a pointer's, from his huge body.

"Down, will you?" whispered Ronnie. "Down—you panicky old devil."

The black-and-white hound, still protesting, squatted on his haunches; rose up again; and began to pad restlessly up and down the flagstones. Every now and then he came sniffing toward the porch.

"She's all right, Ponto," Ronnie kept on saying. "She's quite all right, old man." And somehow, soothing the animal, he succeeded in soothing himself. What a fool he was to worry! Children were born every day, every hour, every minute. And Alie was so strong. Besides, Alie wanted a child; she wanted a child more than anything else in the world.

After a while Ponto ceased his padding, and subsided—still dubious—at his master's feet. After a while Ronnie, consulting his watch, saw that it was nearly three o'clock.

"Three more hours," he thought; "three more hours of suspense." He wanted to go back into the house, to wait outside Alie's door. But instinct, and her last words, restrained him. One could do no good by one's presence; one could only hinder, flurry the nurse and the doctor at their work.

Slowly, the great dog at his heels, Ronnie wandered down the flagstones to the gate. Looking back, the house showed restful, a home of safety under blue spring skies. The laburnums made curtains of yellow for its latticed windows; the lilacs were cones of white and mauve to its sloping eaves. Surely not death but life hovered over that lichened roof, over those high stone chimney-stacks!

And life was good—good. Life had given to him, Ronald Cavendish, every fine thing of a man's wishing; love, victory over his one-time enemy, money, success in his profession. For him, life had been like some old story-book; a story-book that ended happily.

But with that thought apprehension gripped him again. Life, perhaps, had given him too much. Fate, perhaps—even now—meant to snatch the cup of happiness from his lips.

He looked up at Aliette's window. The silk curtains were drawn; and imagination shuddered at the task of visioning her behind them. She was in pain, his Aliette, the one being in the world who made life glorious to him. She was in pain. In danger. And he, her husband, could not help.

Slowly, unable longer to bear the sight of those drawn curtains, Ronnie—the unhappy dog in his wake—turned away; slowly, the pair began to wander about the gardens, round the house and round again, through the shrubberies, past the garage and the stables, across the tennis-lawn, up and down the rose-pergola. And, "I can't stand this," thought Ronald Cavendish; "I can't stand this another minute."

It seemed to him, in his agony, as though life must be planning revenge on him; as though the ultimate penalty were now to be exacted. Alie would die in child-birth; and all they had won together be lost eternally.

Vainly, he strove to curb his imagination. Vainly he said to himself: "It can't happen. It simply can't happen." Vainly he wished that Alie had accepted her mother's offer to join them for their wedding-day. One was so lonely, so infernally lonely. If only Mollie and James hadn't been on their honeymoon! If only Julia were alive! But Julia was dead, and James—selfish beast!—enjoying himself, and Aliette's parents waiting for a telegram.

He looked at his watch again. Barely half-past three yet! And Hartley had said, "Six o'clock." His hand, as he put the watch back in his pocket, shook like an apple-tree-spur in a spring gale. He could feel his brow damp with sweat under the cap-peak. Restlessly he resumed his tramp; restlessly the dog followed him; round the house and round again—till at last, to Ponto's delight, his master made his way out of the gardens, through the stables, to the gate of the paddock.

3

The paddock, a square two-acre of trampled grasses fenced with the high white of blossoming hawthorn, shimmered in the afternoon sunshine; and at far end of it, as he opened the gate, Ronnie saw Miracle. At the click of the gate-latch, the big thoroughbred, golden as a guinea to the rich light, lifted his head from the fragrant pasture; scrutinized his visitors; and with a whinny of delight came cantering toward them. Ten yards away, he stopped—his neck arched, his eyes wide in speculation. Then, pace by balancing pace, muzzle outstretched, he came on; snuffled down at the dog; snuffled up at the man.

Tactfully as Aliette's self Ronnie gentled the horse, caressing the smooth muzzle, the sleek skin under the branches of the jaws. Somehow, it seemed as though Miracle were aware of the fret in him, of the fret in Ponto; as though Miracle, following the pair of them up and down the paddock, were trying to say: "It's all right. It's quite all right."

And Ronnie thought, looking at Miracle's great shoulders, at the slope of his pasterns and the sinuous strength of his hocks: "You carried her over Parson's Brook, old boy. You'll carry her again, next winter, as you carried me this, across a stiller country than Mid-Oxfordshire, across the ridge-and-furrow and the cut-and-laids and the timber of the shires."

Miracle followed the pair of them back to the gate, and stood looking over it while they made their way to the stables. The big blue clock under the old-fashioned hunting wind-vane (a metal man on a metal horse capping on a metal hound) showed ten minutes to four. In the center of the deserted courtyard—ominous—stood Hartley's car. Toward it, through the archway, came the doctor himself.

Ronnie's heart sank at sight of the man. "Anything gone wrong?" he asked curtly.

"On the contrary." Hartley, a big-shouldered fellow who rode like a thruster and looked more like a vet. than a county practitioner, laughed under his large mustache. "On the contrary. Everything's going splendidly. If only we could get you husbands out of the way at these times—"

"How much longer?" interrupted Ronnie.

"Two hours at the least." The doctor abstracted a small package from the dickey of his car. "We can't rush our fences at this game, you know."

"Is my wife in pain?"

"Of course she's in pain."

"Bad pain?"

"Good Lord, no. Nothing out of the ordinary. She's a Trojan, is your missus, Cavendish." And Hartley, stuffing the package into a capacious pocket, added. "As a matter of fact, it seems to me that you're looking a jolly sight worse than she is. Why don't you take my advice, and get on a gee-gee for an hour or so? We don't want you kicking about the house, I can tell you."

The doctor hurried off through the archway toward the house, leaving Ronnie a little ashamed of himself. Hartley, for all his coarseness, knew his job. He began to wonder whether it wouldn't be a sound scheme to follow Hartley's advice, and go out for a ride. Driver, the groom, had asked for the Saturday afternoon off; but he could easily saddle up one of the hacks in the loose-boxes, either the old brown mare, Daisy, or the little bay horse which he had bought—a week since—as a surprise for Aliette on her convalescence.

Ronnie, Ponto still at his heels, made his way into the unlocked harness-room; picked a saddle from its rack, a snaffle bridle from its peg; and emerged again into the courtyard.

"Which shall it be?" he thought, "Daisy or the bay?" And hesitating in his choice, it came to him, quite suddenly, that if he really were going to ride—if, despite the apprehensions which had once more started nagging at his mind, he really meant to disregard the pull of that invisible halter which bound him to the house where Aliette lay in pain—then the only horse possible for him to ride was Miracle.

Why not? The thoroughbred had only been "lying out" a week. An hour's exercise wouldn't do him any harm. He'd enjoy, perhaps, a little canter across the grass to Spaxton's Covert.

Wonderingly, Ponto followed his master back to the paddock. Miracle still had his head across the gate; nor, when he saw the saddle over Ronnie's right arm, the bridle in his left hand, did he sulk away. The big golden-gleaming horse seemed rather pleased than sulky to feel the brow-band slipped up his forehead, the snaffle-bar slipped into his mouth, the throat-lash of the bridle buckled loose, and the saddle-girths gripping him. He tossed at his bit and hogged his back in the old playful way as Ronnie—the ashplant in his left hand—put an unhorsemanly-shod foot into the iron and swung an unhorsemanly-trousered leg over the cantle.

As the three of them, horse and dog and man, set off across the paddock, Ronnie knew the impulse to turn back, to off-saddle. It seemed heartless that he should ride out across green fields while Alie—had not Hartley himself admitted?—was in pain. But half-way across the two-acre the impulse weakened; and by the time they made the far gate it had altogether died away.

He unlatched the gate with his ashplant, and Miracle nipped through. Before them, up-and-down emerald between rolling grasses, lay the bridle-path to Spaxton's Covert. The horse, at a touch of the rein, broke from walk to trot, from trot to a springy canter that traversed the ridge-and-furrow without an effort. Southerly breezes blew across the sixty-acre pasture. Two hares, mating, scurried from their approach. The great horned beasts, white-faced Herefords and black Welsh steers, watched them incuriously till—catching sight of Ponto—they, too, moved lumbering away.

At the crest, Ronnie drew rein. Here, they were on the very spine of the county. Looking back, he could still see the high chimney-stacks and the stable-clock of Windmill House: but already Little Overdine had tucked itself away into a cup of the vale; so that only its church-tower and the motionless sails of the windmill betrayed it from the humpy fields through which Little Overdine Brook serpentined like a gigantic green caterpillar.

Mapwise, from that high eminence, the shires outspread their panorama, pasture on rolling pasture, with here a bright square of young green cornland, here a dark blob of covert, here a blue hill and there a vale, here a great house nestling among trees, there a red farm, there a church, and there a white railway-gate, but scarce a factory chimney from horizon to horizon.

Not for nothing do men hark back to the place of their father's birth! To Ronnie, ever since he had first set eyes on this panorama, it had been home. Already he knew its every landmark; already it had power over him, power to soothe, power to set him a-dream.

And to-day, more than ever before, the shires set their spell upon him, so that he imagined—sitting there motionless on the motionless horse—a son soon to be born, a son who would esteem the Tudor house on the brow of Little Overdine Hill, and all this wide champaign, these counties which were neither pretty-pretty as the garden South, nor rocked and sea-girt as the West, nor grandly cragged and forested as the North, but just—so Ronnie put it to himself that afternoon—just England, the old England of bold horses and bold hounds and bolder men.

4

The three, horse and dog and man, set off again. Down from the crest they came at a canter, through fields ridged yellow with buttercups, where the young lambs frisked bleating from their path, by blazing hawthorn-hedges a-chatter with startled finches, through the pasture-gates, to the little wooden bridge over the Brook. Now, on a slope above them, they saw the bright new green of Spaxton's Covert; five acres of blessed woodland whither, on some dark November afternoon, a dog-fox hard-pressed from Lomondham Ruffs or Highborough Gorse might, if only scent failed, perchance make safety from the beaten pack.

But to-day the dog-fox feared neither pack nor horseman. They saw him, a red shape at covert's edge; saw him grin at them from fifty yards' range, and lope disdainfully back through the wooden palings to his mate!

Ronnie, laughing at the incident, halted Miracle, dismounted, and called the rabbit-eager Ponto to heel. The half-hour or so of open air had steadied his nerves. Lighting a cigarette, looking at his watch, he saw that his hands no longer trembled. "Alie's all right," he said to himself. "Everything's all right."

He mounted again, and headed away from the covert toward Lomondham. From Lomondham to Little Overdine by the highroad is four good miles. "That'll get me home comfortably by five," thought Ronnie. But just before he made the Lomondham road, fear gripped him again. Suddenly some instinct, an instinct so strong that he dared not even fight against it, warned him that Alie was in danger.

And with fear came self-reproach. He had been away a whole hour, a whole hour of life or death for the woman he loved. He had been enjoying himself, enjoying himself, dreaming of a son when perhaps—perhaps—

Miracle, trotting at ease, felt himself abruptly gathered together, felt the ring of the snaffle hard against his off cheek, felt the grass at roadside under his hoofs, broke to a canter and from a canter to a gallop. Ponto, caught unawares fifty yards in rear, heard man and horse disappear round a bend in the hawthorn hedges; Ponto, quickening his lollop round the bend, saw the pair streak hell-for-leather up the hill; Ponto, laboring desperately not to be left behind, saw them halt for a moment at the gate of Lomondham Lane and knew that his master had taken the short cut home. "He can't have forgotten me," thought Ponto angrily.

But Ronnie, in that moment of fear, had forgotten everything except Aliette. The lane saved a mile and a half, and the lane was all soft turf—good going—the first five furlongs of it straight as a race-course.

Down those first five furlongs Miracle went like a steed possessed. The turf thudded under his hoofs. The hawthorn-hedges streaked past him like snowbanks alongside a train. "Hope to God we don't meet any one at the bend," thought Ronnie, his silk-socked ankles thrust home in the irons, his trousered knees gripping the saddle-flaps, his hands low and his body a little forward.

For now there was no controlling Miracle. The fear of the thoroughbred man on his back had communicated itself in some mysterious way to the thoroughbred horse. He, too, wanted to get home. Grandly he swept the ground from under him. Scarcely, with voice and rein, Ronnie succeeded in checking speed as they tore madly round the bend; scarcely, leaning hard over, he succeeded in keeping his seat.

And then, abruptly, he remembered the tree!

The tree, a great elm, overturned by the gale, was a bare four hundred yards on, just around the next bend, beyond the bridge that arched up like the back of a big red hog from the green of the lane.

"Steady, Miracle," called Ronnie, "steady, you old fool. This isn't the National." He was still terribly frightened about Alie; but for himself he had no fear. Even when his horse, head down, neck-muscles arched against the reins, took the red bridge as though it had been a water-jump, it never struck Ronnie that he wouldn't be able to stop him.

Two hundred yards from the tree, he still intended to pull up. Miracle, with no corn in him, couldn't hold that pace another furlong. Miracle, when he caught sight of those jagged branches blocking the path, would ease up of his own accord. Miracle had never bolted in his life. . . .

But Miracle came round that last bend as though it had been Tattenham Corner; and Miracle's rider, peering between his ears at the forbidding obstacle fifty yards ahead, knew that it would be fatal to try and stop him. As a matter of cold fact, he didn't want to stop the horse. The overturned tree, unlopped, five feet high and eight across, lay between him and Aliette: once over it, five minutes would see them home!

Ronnie took one pull at the reins, sat down in his saddle, grasped Miracle between his knees, sent up one voiceless prayer for safety, flicked once with his ashplant, felt the great horse steady himself hocks-under-body, felt his forehand lift, gave him his head—went up, down and over, his shoulders almost touching the croup—and landed like a steeple-chase jock to a crackle of twigs on the turf beyond.

Then, at long last, the tree fifty yards behind and the highroad half a mile ahead, Miracle answered to the rein. Gradually his pace checked from gallop to hand-canter; from hand-canter to a quick nervous trot that sent the loose stones scudding from his hoofs.

"Good lad," said Ronnie, easing as they emerged from lane to highroad. "Good lad," he repeated, as Miracle—scarcely sweating—clattered swiftly through the stable-gateway and stood for dismounting.

For somehow, even as he swung-from saddle, Ronnie knew that Alie's danger was over, so that it hardly needed the returned Driver's cheery grin and cheery words, "It's a boy, sir. Kate's just come out and told us," to reassure him.

5

"Sorry I spoofed you about the time," said Hartley, some hour and a half after. "But you were making such an ass of yourself that we all thought you'd be better out of the way. You can go up now, if you like. Only don't stay long."

Ronnie, one hand on the newel-post of the staircase, laughed as he answered, "I'm afraid I was a wee bit rattled"; and went up the blue-carpeted treads three at a time.

The door of Alie's room, as though expectant, stood a mite open. Through the chink of it shone a primrose gleam of light. Alie's husband knocked faintly; and nurse rustled to the doorway. "They're asleep," whispered nurse. "You may look at them if you like."

The uniformed woman let him in, closing the door of the room. The cretonne curtains were still drawn across the latticed windows. Candles glowed on the mantelpiece and the dressing-table. But the big bed, toward which Ronnie tiptoed, was in shadow; so that Aliette's hair, braided down either shoulder, showed dark against white pillows and whiter skin.

She slept—the child, his man-child, tiny in the crook of her arm—the ghost of a smile on her breathing lips. Ronnie stood for a long while, gazing down on the pair of them. His blue eyes were bright with thankfulness. His heart thudded, pleasurably, against his ribs.

"She wouldn't let me take the baby from her," whispered nurse. "You'll go away now, won't you? They mustn't be woken."

But at that, Aliette's eyes opened. Drowsily, she looked up at him; drowsily, smiling still, she murmured:

"Kiss me before you go, man. I'm so happy, so wonderfully and gloriously happy."

Bending, Ronald Cavendish kissed his wife's warm fluttering eyelids and the soft downy head in the crook of her arm.

www.ingramcontent.com/pod-product-compliance
Lightning Source LLC
Chambersburg PA
CBHW051933240626
47153CB00005B/1474